THE LAIR

THE LAIR

Emma Cave

Hodder & Stoughton

British Library Cataloguing in Publication Data
Cave, Emma
The lair
1. English fiction – 20th century
I. Title
823.9'14[F]

ISBN 0 340 63251 8

Typeset by Hewer Text Composition Services, Edinburgh
Printed and bound in Great Britain by
Mackays of Chatham PLC, Chatham, Kent

Hodder and Stoughton
A division of Hodder Headline PLC
338 Euston Road
London NW1 3BH

For Camilla
and for Wendy
with love

ACKNOWLEDGEMENTS

There are those whom I can never thank enough:

Ward and Pat,
Tedina and Michael,
also Prue, Beti, Rebecca, Ruth
. . . and Demetris

Gratitude for research to C de C and S.F.

This book, set in 1991, is
Volume Two of the *Rooms* Chronicle

Lair: . . . the resting place of a corpse; a grave, tomb . . . A place for animals to lie down in; esp. for beasts of chase or of prey
Shorter Oxford English Dictionary

PROLOGUE

Slow steady rain was falling in North London: on Hampstead, on Willesden, on Hackney, on Islington. Everywhere, under a dense grey sky, the air was damp and cold. This dank chill seemed especially insidious in the gloom of Tolland Road, Finsbury Park.

Beyond the scabbed, blackened columns of a ponderous stone church, beyond a builder's yard, its high walls topped by barbed wire and bearing a metal plaque of an Alsatian's head with the words 'Beware of the Dog', the house stood on a corner.

Although set well back from the road, it had no garden. The large space around it was all cemented: from the builder's wall to the pavement in front and on the corner. This bleak setting intensified the atmosphere of desolation created by the house itself.

Three-storeyed, built of dingy yellow brick, it was meanly narrow. Steep unrailed steps, with uneven, awkwardly high treads, led to a brown-varnished front door numbered 63 in slanting metal characters. At the top, two urns of geraniums, meagre and straggling, only emphasized the surrounding drabness.

Evidently the upper floors of the house were occupied. There were names by their doorbells. Their windows were clean and curtained. On one top-floor windowsill stood a bowl of hyacinths, and on the other a smirking china cat. The sound of a scale played on a flute came from the middle floor.

The ground-floor bell was unlabelled. The big ground-floor bay window was thick with dust, smeared and clotted by rain. No curtains had replaced the pink satin festoon-blind that had hung there eighteen months before.

The crime committed there remained unsolved. No heir or family had been traced. After the police had discontinued their investigation, the murdered woman's possessions had become Crown property. The State had been dowered with the festoon-blind, the ugly furniture and the sentimental pictures: kittens among roses, a small tear-stained boy, an orchid discarded on a flight of steps. The State had inherited the huge wardrobe with its two-way mirror, the whips and other instruments, the range of titillating disguises. (Had the State dismantled the metal stanchions attached to the bedroom wall behind the embowered kittens?)

After the forensic examinations, the woman's body had been buried by the local authority. However, on this day of seeping damp and creeping chill, it would have been easy to imagine that her unquiet spirit – dark, vengeful, malignant – still lingered in the house where she had lived and died.

PART ONE

ONE

Three people sat at the table with the best view over the harbour of this small Aegean port.

The man with the ponytail and stubbled chin, the eyebrows that merged over close-set eyes, was decked with as much gold jewellery as he could accommodate. The teenage girl – her shiny green dress and orange hair in fearsome contrast to her grey complexion – was orphan thin, with dilated pupils and a dazed stare.

Only the woman between them looked at home in this informal but expensive restaurant, and she was obviously the hostess. The wine waiter had just brought a fresh bottle of wine; it was she who tasted it before he filled their glasses.

She was sleek. Her matt skin and her smooth hair were the same equable beige. Her eyes were darker: the clouded colour of a river in spate. They dominated her face, though her nose was strong, her jaw square, her mouth forced slightly open by an arc of perfect teeth.

The party drew attention from people at other tables: disparaging glances at the man and girl, so blatantly pimp and whore, and longer study, puzzled and intrigued, of the woman.

A man who was dining alone, and reading a book, also attracted notice. He was not young, but he was exceptionally handsome and the effect he created was weary rather than old. His hair could have been white or blond. His eyes, of an unusual blue tinged with slate, were also startlingly bright. He wore dark trousers and a blue silk polo-necked sweater.

He had finished eating and was drinking an espresso. A large party near him rose to leave; glancing up from his book, he had an uninterrupted view of the threesome. He raised his eyebrows

5

and smiled; when the smile faded, he stared.

The man of the party, who sat facing him, saw the stare and scowled; this made the woman turn her head. Turbid brown eyes met sparkling blue.

A minute can seem long: a minute passed. Without shifting her gaze, the woman, elbow on the table, raised her right hand. She did not look at the waiter – who came at once – but she spoke, and her hand drooped from the wrist to point directly at the blue-eyed man: the waiter crossed the room and murmured to him; he glanced up and nodded. Then, smiling, he looked back at the woman.

Now the waiter hurried to put a fourth chair opposite her. At once she gestured the girl towards it. When the only response was a blank look, the man – he was still scowling – leant across and pinched the girl's arm. She winced, gaped, then shifted with what seemed – she clung to the edge of the table – an enormous effort.

The blue-eyed man, picking up his book, came over. The waiter pulled out the chair on the woman's left, and he sat down.

'You looked lonely,' she said.

'Lonely?' he said. 'I was alone. That's different.' Then he smiled. 'They say one's never alone with a book.'

She laughed: two notes, both low, but the second lower and more stressed. 'Depends what you're reading, I guess.'

He held out the book. She read aloud, 'Suetonius – *The Twelve Caesars*. And who's Suetonius?'

'An Ancient Roman historian.'

'That does sound boring.'

He laughed. 'You'd be surprised.'

She said, 'It takes a lot to surprise me.'

'I can imagine.' Until now, they had both ignored her companions. Now he glanced at them: the girl again lost in her trance, the man scowling from one speaker to the other.

'So what's your name?' she asked.

'Rupert. Rupert Deyntree. And yours?'

'Disa Trapani.'

'Disa!' he said. 'I've never known a Disa before.'

'My mother said she'd invented the name. That woman was

always trying to be different – less dull, you know – and she never succeeded. Someone once told me there's a flower called Disa. But I don't mind the name – I've made it mine.' She smiled.

He smiled too. He said, 'I thought it might have come from Dis.'

'Dis?'

'A Roman god. God of the underworld. Of death and funerals. Ruler of hell. Whoever enters Dis's kingdom is never permitted to return. Everything ominous is sacred to him – especially two, the number of ill-omen.'

'Two's unlucky?'

'The Romans certainly thought so.'

'Keen on Romans, aren't you? Of course my surname's Italian. But my father's family weren't from Rome. They were from the south. And I'm sure neither of my parents ever heard of Dis. You know a lot of stuff, don't you?'

'Stuff!' He laughed. 'Oh yes, I know a lot of "stuff".'

'I suppose you picked it up at that English public school you must have gone to?'

'Must have?'

'It's obvious from the way you talk.' She laughed.

'Whereas your accent is fashionably mid-Atlantic. No, more American than that, really.'

'Yeah. I'm American. But I've lived in Europe for years. Citizen of the world – that's me. Are you gay?'

'Gay?' He raised his eyebrows. 'No. Do I look it?'

'No, I guess not – it's just that you're still so beautiful.'

He laughed. 'Still?'

'Well, let's face it, you're no spring chicken.'

He laughed. 'I'm forty-nine. And I'm not gay. Satisfied?' He smiled, widening his startling eyes.

She blinked, then laughed. 'I suppose that'll do for now. But I've got nothing against gays. Lots of my pals are gay.'

He said, 'My best friend is.'

'Oh yes? Anyway, I guess I'm kind of bi myself – I've had lots of women. I like it with women. And with a woman and a man – that's good too.'

He laughed. He said, 'Oh, a man and two women – that's a

7

delightful arrangement.' He paused, then said, 'One of my best experiences ever was with two women.' He was studying her. Now he said, 'You've got what someone once described as "sex without gender".'

'Sounds like a hermaphrodite.'

'That's not what I meant.'

She laughed. 'I had a hermaphrodite once.'

'You've outdone me there, Miss Dis!' Then he said, 'You're really very Roman. Ancient Roman!'

'Not as ancient as you. Only thirty-six.'

He laughed. Then he said, 'Your eyes are remarkable. So opaque and that strange muddy colour.'

'Muddy!'

'Perhaps "rusty" would be better.'

'I don't think I care for that either.'

'It's very unusual.' He added softly, 'And very attractive.'

'Hmm.' Then she glanced at the other two at the table. She said, 'I wonder if we really want company . . . tonight.'

Eyebrows raised, he surveyed the pair. 'I must say *I* wouldn't have thought so.'

She laughed. 'Nor me. Not tonight.' She reached for the huge pale Florentine handbag that dangled from the back of her chair, opened it, and took out a wad of money. Carelessly she peeled off a chunk and held it out to the man on her right, speaking to him in a low voice. He looked too coarse for shame, but now he flushed, then glared. A moment passed. Then he snatched the money and stood up. Waiters and diners at neighbouring tables watched as angrily he gestured the girl to stand. When she gaped, he seized her skimpy sleeve – there was a glimpse of needle-tracks on her arm – and pulled her to her feet. Almost dragging her, he set off towards the door, with a doomed attempt at swagger.

Disa did not even glance after them. She said, 'Where are you staying?'

'At an extremely dull little hotel. I've only been there one night.'

'What brings you here? To this crummy little port?'

Rupert smiled. 'Oh . . .' he said, and then, '"He travelled."'

'*He* travelled?'

8

'"He travelled. He came to know the melancholy of the steamboat, the cold awakening in the tent, the tedium of landscapes and ruins, the bitterness of interrupted friendships." That's a quotation – from Flaubert.' He smiled again.

'More "stuff"!' she said, then, 'I guess what you're saying is that *you've* travelled.' She laughed. 'You don't look as if you've been sleeping in a tent. Where have you been?'

'Oh, all over Europe. I stopped here and there. I looked at art – I've always wanted to do that at leisure. I read books I'd been meaning to read for years. I thought a lot, too.'

'Thought? What about?'

'All sorts of things.'

'And how long have you been travelling?'

'Oh, about eighteen months.'

She said, 'Have you got a lot of baggage?'

'No. I travel light. One suitcase and a picture.'

'A picture?'

'Yes, a Blake.'

'I don't know anything about art.'

He laughed. 'But you know what you like?'

'I don't go for any of it.'

He smiled. 'Just like my third wife, Chris – but she would never admit it.'

'How often have you been married?'

'Three times. Sarah was a drunk, Barbara was a dyke, and Chris was a frigid workaholic.'

She laughed. 'What a lousy picker. Me too, but I learnt faster. I only did it once. A hundred years ago. What a drag!'

'Any children?'

She paused. Then she said, 'No. Have you?'

'A dreadful son by the drunk – I think he's tied up with the worst bitch in the world – and a dreary daughter by the dyke.'

'God!' she exclaimed.

He laughed. Then he said, 'Do you believe in him?'

'Believe in who?'

'God.'

'Sometimes. Then I hate him. Have you ever tried the Satan thing? It used to turn me on at one time.'

'No. You have to believe in God for that. I never have. Though I nearly became a Roman Catholic.'

She laughed. 'You're so funny. My father's family was Catholic – but I was brought up Episcopalian, like my boring mother. I'd rather have been Catholic. Sort of meatier. The Black Mass is based on the Catholic one, you know.'

He nodded, but now he had an abstracted look. He said, 'Actually, by now, I think I've got another child. It must be about six months old. I don't know if it's a boy or girl.'

She said, 'Perhaps it's a hermaphrodite.' She laughed. When he didn't, she said, 'Why don't we fetch your things from that dull little hotel in a taxi, and take them to my boat?'

'Boat?' he said.

'Yes. I have this yacht. It's in the harbour. Tomorrow I'm going to my island.'

'Your island?'

'Yes, I own a little island off the Greek coast. It's called Kameni. It's my private place.'

He laughed. 'Your lair, perhaps? You rather remind me of a tiger.'

'My lair . . . I quite like that.'

'I thought you might. You run the yacht yourself?'

'No. Oh, I *can*. But there's this Greek who works for me. Shall we fetch your gear?'

He said, 'So I'm being kidnapped? How exciting!'

She said, 'Oh, I know a lot about kidnapping.'

'Even more exciting!'

'This certainly does look dull,' she said, when they reached the quiet hotel. 'Will it take you long to pack?'

'Only a few minutes.'

'Then I'll wait in the taxi.'

'All right.' He went inside, asked at the desk for his bill to be made up, went to his room.

When he had unlocked the door, he stood in the doorway for a moment. The curtains were open, and a street lamp outside shone straight onto the picture. Propped on a table against the wall, Blake's *The Good and Evil Angels* rose from folded-back wrappings as if from a shroud on Judgement Day.

10

Shocked, reproachful, the Good Angel held a shrinking child. It was just beyond the Evil Angel's reach. But despite this, despite blindness – his eyes were mere fleshy marbles – and despite a heavy fetter on his foot, the Evil Angel ruled the picture. Hovering, brooding, shadowed by dusky flames, he was dreadful; the Good Angel seemed diminished by his hideous glow.

Rupert switched on the light. He quickly wrapped up the picture, and packed the suitcase that stood on a stool at the foot of the bed. Then he felt under the pillow. His hand emerged, holding a long plait of hair. It was frayed. It must once have been golden; now it had faded and lost its lustre, like a snake's dry, discarded skin. But he raised it to his lips before he coiled it under a shirt, and then closed his suitcase. Rupert was ready to travel again.

TWO

It was eleven in the morning on the last Wednesday in March. Vee Westwood, assistant tour manager of a rock band, had been travelling through Britain for the past two weeks. This morning James Deyntree had driven to London to pick her up at the Mayfair Hotel and drive her down to the cottage in Suffolk where he lived with his mother. Vee was to stay there until Friday, when she would return to London: the band's last English concert was at Wembley on Saturday.

She came from the lift to the reception desk, eager, quick and light, swinging a small travelling bag, and carrying her mobile phone. They embraced. Then, 'A mobile phone!' he exclaimed. 'How fashionable!'

'Wow, a mobile phone! The miracles of modern technology come to Suffolk!' They both laughed, but then she said, 'Actually, it's not "fashionable" – it's essential. I'm sure to get quite a few calls in the next two days. You see, all sorts of things could need my attention.'

'Apart from me,' he said.

'Yes, I'm afraid so.' They laughed again. Then he said, 'You're amazing. I thought you'd be exhausted, and you look so fresh and lovely.'

'Well, I've had some sleep. We got down from Birmingham at two, and I flaked out as soon as I hit the bed. I didn't wake till half after nine and then I had a big English breakfast in my room.'

He said, 'Is that all your luggage? That little bag – and of course your telephone? Didn't you bring your glamorous silver suitcase?'

'My Haliburton? I'm leaving it here. I'll be staying Friday and Saturday nights. I'd wondered if you'd like to stay too.'

13

'What? Here at the Mayfair?'

'Yes. Here at the Mayfair. And come to the show on Saturday night.'

'I've never been to a rock concert.'

'Well, it's about time you checked out my lifestyle.'

'Mmm. But I couldn't stay here.'

'Why not? You mean the money? Don't even think about that – the tour pays for me, and no one cares who's in my room. But I'm seeing Lucy and my honorary godson on Friday. And perhaps you'd really hate the show. Anyhow, I'll have to stay on at Wembley till late – I mightn't get back till about two on Sunday morning. And we're off to Paris on Sunday afternoon. So I think you can be spared those unfamiliar experiences this time.' Her laugh was slightly brittle.

'Oh, Vee,' he said. 'Let's go to the car.'

In the car, he said, 'Alone at last.' They kissed fervently. When they drew apart, he said, 'My sweet lovely Vee.'

'Ah, James!' She breathed in, let the breath out in a deep soft sigh. Then she said, 'And how's Sarah?'

'She's fine.' He started the engine. He said, 'You changed everything for her – and for me as well, of course – when you got her to AA.'

'I'm so glad about that. And how's Mansfield? Still trying to bite the postman?'

'Frustrated! We've finally installed a letterbox by the front gate.'

'I wonder if he'll recognize me.'

'How could he fail to? Darling Vee, you look so much happier than last time I saw you. You sound it, too.'

'Yes. You're right. You know, I think I've worked through all that stuff I was so disturbed about last time I was here. I've been seeing my therapist again.'

'You *told* her?'

'Oh, not the facts. I told her I couldn't do that. But I said I was anxious about something I'd done. She asked me if I could do anything about it, and I said no. So we decided I should put the whole thing behind me and start to live my life again. I've been working on it.' She paused. Then she said, 'I say the serenity prayer a lot.'

14

'Serenity prayer – the thing Mum talks about? This prayer thing they say in AA.'

'That's it. "God grant me the serenity to accept the things I cannot change, the courage to change the things I can, and the wisdom to know the difference." Well, I can't change *that* – so I'm trying to be wise and calm about accepting the situation. I say that prayer every day.'

'You pray?' His tone was startled.

'I say that prayer.'

'Whom do you say it to?'

'There's that famous "whom" of yours again – I love it. Like your mother does, I say it to a Higher Power. Oh, I don't know exactly what that Power is. And don't worry – I'm not into organized religion.'

He smiled. 'I thought you might be going to announce your conversion to Catholicism – joining your friend Lucy.'

'Catholicism! Apart from being half Jewish – even though I know nothing about Judaism – and all sorts of other objections, my stepmother and Lucy's mother certainly put paid to that!'

'I'm relieved.' He laughed.

She said, 'You mind my praying?'

'No. No, of course not. It's just a bit strange to me. Being an agnostic. But what you say about accepting there's nothing we can do about what happened, and feeling calm about it – that's absolutely splendid. I'm really glad . . . oh, and so glad you've stopped being so anxious.'

'Yes, I believe I have.' Then she said, 'You've got it safe, haven't you? Really safe . . . from him.'

'Of course I have.' Then he said, 'Anyway, all that's over and done with. I thought you said you'd accepted that?'

'I have. I have. It's just that sometimes . . . I feel a shadow.'

'Vee – there are no shadows.' He laughed. 'Look, the sun's shining.'

She smiled. 'All right – no shadows! Just the ones the clouds make. Forget it. I'm happy – really I am. So happy to be with you.' At that moment her phone rang, sounding loud and shrill.

After she had rung off, he said, 'You're quite different when you're working. So pithy.'

'Sounds like a nasty orange.'

15

'But you're more like a perfect peach.'

She exclaimed, 'Oh James! I've missed you *so* much.'

'And I've missed you. In fact, I miss you every day of my life.'

It was when they had turned off the main road, and were in the narrow, winding Suffolk lanes, interrupted by small villages with pink-washed cottages and square-towered churches, that he said, 'Oh Vee, do you think we'll ever be together?'

'We're together now.'

He took his hand off the steering wheel, and squeezed hers. 'I know. And it's wonderful. But I mean . . . always.'

She was silent for a moment. Then she said, 'You know, I'm beginning to get tired of touring. It's such a restless life. And I don't think I'm the restless person I used to be. Back in LA, I seem to spend weeks just getting myself together again. Oh, I've got my lovely apartment, and music and movies, and I go to the gym. And I've got friends, of course. But there's such tension. All the crime and the racial hatred. England seems so peaceful.'

He gestured to the wide fields beyond the hedges, and then to the great, cloud-scattered Suffolk sky. 'Peaceful – here, yes. But in the cities?'

'They're better than they are in the States.'

'Perhaps they are. All the same, they're where you can really see the wreckage of ten years of callousness and greed: of people being indoctrinated not to care. Told that making money efficiently is all that matters, and damn the unemployed. Margaret Thatcher! Oh, what an evil woman!'

Vee said, 'I thought you didn't believe in evil.'

'When I think about her, I almost do. You know, England used to be a kind, decent country. Until the eighties. Now that's all changed. Now it's the penny-pinching managers that matter in the hospitals, not the doctors and nurses or what the patients need. Now people sleep in cardboard boxes on the streets of London. And all the vital things that used to belong to everybody – transport, communications, light and heat and water – are being sold off to line the pockets of the money men. Privatization! They'll privatize the air next – we'll have to pay to breathe. And what vision of the future do they offer? Nothing but the lure of lower taxes. It's so mean. It's so squalid.'

16

'Wow – what a speech!' she said. 'You should go into politics.'

'Politics!' he said. 'No chance of that!'

'Well, anyhow, Lucy feels just the same as you do about how things are here. But, like I said, it's worse in the States. And there's the rage! This country isn't so angry. Anyhow, I want to feel it isn't. You know, I always said I'd never live in England. But now . . . Well, the two people I care about most in the world – you and Lucy – are here. I suppose that's the real reason why I'm thinking of moving.'

Briefly, the car swerved. 'Moving!' he exclaimed. 'You mean you're thinking of coming to live here? Oh, Vee!' He sounded breathless, joyful.

'Well,' she said, 'Greg, the guy I'm working for – the guy who manages this band – has an office in London and he's not happy with the way it's being run. I can see why. It's a mess. And he might give me the job. Though I could have a problem getting a work permit.'

He said, 'You wouldn't need one if you married me.'

'Married? Oh James, it's too soon for that.'

'Is it?'

But they were in the village. A minute later, they had reached the cottage, and, at the sound of the familiar old Fiat, the dog Mansfield – named after the writer, Katherine Mansfield because of his similar fringe, or, as Vee said, 'bangs' – came, woofing joyously down the path between the flower beds. A moment after James opened the gate, Mansfield's front paws were on Vee's legs, and his feathery tail was wagging in frantic welcome.

'Oh, Mansfield! You amazing dog! After all this time, too!' She stroked his head. His eyes peered up at her appealingly between the strands of his fringe.

'I knew he'd recognize you!' James said triumphantly.

'Vee!' Now Sarah, beaming, was hurrying down the path.

Vee said, 'What a welcome! It's like coming home.'

The interior of the cottage had changed in the twenty months of Sarah's sobriety. She and James had repainted it. There were new curtains and cushion covers. In the kitchen, its floor retiled, were a new and efficient cooker, a new self-defrosting refrigerator, a freezer, a dishwasher and a row of new cookery books, all evidence of Sarah's new hobby: food. In the sitting room, recent paperback novels and biographies had been added to the faded hardcover volumes, mostly dating from Sarah's Oxford days, which had formerly given a disused look to these bookshelves: James's were upstairs in his room. A new video recorder stood under the old television set. Sarah had bought it to follow a cookery course, but had now rediscovered a youthful taste for films, though she preferred old ones: 'All these new ones have so much sex and violence in them.'

Sarah herself, in pursuit of her interest in cookery, had put on a few kilos; it suited her, particularly as her stomach no longer sagged with alcoholic bloat. Cheerful casual clothes had replaced dim dresses and dull skirts and blouses. Most noticeably, her face had lost its mauve tinge, her eyes were clear, and what had been patchy grey hair was now enlivened by a chestnut rinse. 'Oh, Sarah, how great you look!' Vee exclaimed with obvious sincerity when they hugged each other by the gate. Vee's enormous, long-lashed brown eyes – disparagingly compared by her friend Lucy's mother to Bambi's – and Sarah's faded blue-grey ones suddenly and simultaneously filled with tears.

A woman, a man, and his mother – or, indeed, a man, a woman and hers – constitute a recipe notoriously difficult to follow. Today, however, the outcome was as successful as the airy cheese soufflé that Sarah produced for their lunch.

'You're such an amazing cook!' Vee said when a pear and almond tart had followed the soufflé and salad.

'I never used to be. It was always an enormous effort,' Sarah said. After a moment she added, 'When I was drinking, everything was an effort. Doing something quite ordinary seemed like having to climb a mountain. Do you remember, James, when I persuaded you to have those four friends and that dreadful Sue to dinner? I thought I'd be able to manage perfectly, but when the time came it seemed like Everest looming in front of me. So I got drunk. I don't remember much about the evening but I know the food was terrible and I passed out at the dinner table.'

There was a look of remembered pain on James's face. Vee said quickly, 'Who's the dreadful Sue?'

'Sue's not dreadful,' James said. Now he smiled. 'She and I used to go out together. We're still friends. We're colleagues at the university – you must meet her.'

Sarah said, 'Well, *I* always thought she was dreadful. She wore a woolly hat with a bobble on top.'

Vee laughed. 'I've got one of those – I wear it when I go skiing.'

'*Skiing?*' James said.

'Yes, I love to ski.'

Sarah said, 'I'm sure you look *quite* different in *your* hat. No, Sue was impossible. I'm reconciled to James not eating meat, but she was a *vegan* – so inconsiderate! And she was so disapproving. Always wanting people to stop doing things – hunting and smoking, and so on.' Now Sarah took a cigarette from the packet by her plate, lit it and inhaled more deeply than usual. Both Vee and James burst out laughing, and after a moment Sarah laughed too. 'Not that I ever liked hunting,' she said. 'I was terrified – quite apart from the poor old fox. My sister loved it, though.' She turned to Vee. 'Does your friend Lucy hunt?'

'*Lucy!*' Vee's laugh was startled. 'She doesn't even like people shooting – the shooting's let at Rivendale, and she hates it when the guns are firing.'

'I just thought – being a country girl and so grand, too.'

'Grand? Lucy's not grand.'

'Well, such an old family . . .'

'Oh, I don't think the Rivens have ever been *grand*. Lucy's mother's family perhaps – the de Rawleys – but she doesn't like them much. And, yes, she's a country girl, but not the hunting kind. She loves animals. She's got this wonderful dog called Rufus up at Rivendale. She doesn't think he'd like London – not even Hampstead, with the Heath. Anyhow, she feels he's too old to change his ways, but she really misses him.'

'That's nice – isn't it, Mansfield?' Sarah leant down to pat the head of Mansfield, who was lying beside her chair, occasionally glancing up at the table, though the meatless delights on offer held no attraction for him. Then she said, 'It's wonderful having a dog.' She paused before she went on: 'Rupert really hated them.' She added, 'They never liked him either.'

A shadow crossed Vee's face. 'I know.' Then she added quickly, 'Lucy told me that Rufus didn't like him.' Then she said, 'Lucy'd really fall for Mansfield.'

'Well, she must meet him. When are you going to bring her to see us?'

Again Vee's face was briefly clouded, but then she smiled. 'Soon,' she said. 'Very soon indeed.' She turned to James: 'How about that walk we planned? Are you coming, Sarah?'

'No, I think I'll have a little rest. Easy does it, as we say in AA.'

'Yes, you take it easy – you deserve to after cooking that meal. James and I will load the dishwasher, and then we and Mansfield will take off.'

'Oh, please don't bother with the dishes,' Sarah said. But Vee and James were already clearing the table, and she added, 'Well, thanks very much.' Then she said, 'Buying that dish-washer was really a big step for me. I'd always thought they were self-indulgent, but actually I think I was just being masochistic. I bought it as a present to myself on my first AA birthday, after I got my one-year chip – that's a sort of medal.'

'I know,' Vee said, and then, 'When I went through my mother's things after she died, I found five chips: thirty days, sixty days, ninety days, six months and nine months: she must have got the nine months very soon before she died. Those ones are plastic, but the birthday chips are bronze. I wish she'd got one of those.' Vee's face clouded: perhaps at the memory of her mother's suicide. It had followed a quarrel between them. They had met after many years' separation, and a sense of having been abandoned had filled Vee with resentment.

'Yes – like medals, as I said.' James was in the kitchen. Sarah went on, speaking in a low voice, 'My grandfather was killed in the 1914–18 War. He won two medals. They were in a box with a scrap of paper with "My battle honours" scribbled on it in his handwriting. I know war and battles are considered beyond the pale nowadays – that's how James feels – but I still find that . . . well, sort of moving.'

'My battle honours,' Vee repeated. She said, 'Lucy would really like that. Lucy's very patriotic.' Then she said, 'So you feel your AA medal's kind of the same? Your battle honour.'

'Well, yes. Something like that. I know it's silly.'

'No it isn't.'

At that moment James came back into the room, and Sarah said in a louder tone, 'Yes, I'm really looking forward to meeting Lucy.'

'And so am I,' said James. 'Ready, Vee?'

'It may rain,' Sarah said. 'There's an anorak of mine in the hall you could borrow, Vee.'

'No, it won't rain,' Vee said. 'Look, the sun's quite bright. All I need is my phone. Come on, Mansfield.'

But they had only walked the two kilometers to the next village, when a sudden shower came down, and they took shelter in the church porch where Mansfield vigorously shook rain from his coat over their legs.

'I might have known!' Vee said, putting down her phone. 'After all those years I spent here, at the convent. You can never trust the English weather. Do I really want to move back?' They stood, watching the rain fall on ancient, mossy gravestones. Vee sighed, but then she said, 'Come to think of it, the California climate can get a bit monotonous. A touch of unpredictability might be welcome.'

James laughed. 'I must try to develop some.'

'Oh, I don't want *people* to be unpredictable – especially you. I want to be able to trust them absolutely.'

He said, 'I think you can trust me.'

'I think that too. I almost feel I can trust you the way I trust Lucy.'

'Almost?'

'Well, I've known her for so long. And it's hard for me to trust a man that much. My past experiences with them haven't been so great.' Then she said, 'And look where trusting a man got Lucy.'

James's face wore its withdrawn look. After a moment, he said, 'Surely you aren't comparing me to *him*!'

'No. No, of course I'm not. Don't look that way, please.'

21

James said, 'It's so difficult for me to accept that he's my father. It makes me feel so . . . tainted.'

'Oh dearest James, you aren't tainted. You're yourself. Kind and good. Much more like your mother.'

'An alcoholic!' There was slight bitterness in his tone.

'But she's recovering.'

'Yes. Yes, I know. But I keep feeling she may relapse. It's hard to trust her after all those years of hell.'

'But you must try.'

'Yes. And you must try to trust me.'

'Oh, I do. Really I do. I wouldn't be thinking of moving to England if I didn't.'

'But you don't trust me enough to marry me.'

'Perhaps I do. Oh, just let me get this job thing sorted out.'

He said, 'And what if you can't get a work permit?'

'Perhaps I can. Anyhow, surely you wouldn't want me to marry you just to get a work permit?'

He smiled. 'No. Or perhaps yes. You might come to love me after marriage, as the Victorians used to say.'

She said, 'I love you now.' But she hurried on: 'We'll finish the European tour next month. Then, when I'm back in LA, I'll work out everything: the job, the permit, the Lucy situation.'

'The Lucy situation?'

'You don't realize how difficult that is for me. It's trust again, you see. Lucy's always trusted me the way I've trusted her – completely. I told you before – the only cloud there's ever been between us was when she felt I didn't like your father. I hope she's got over that by now – I'll find out on Friday. But I lied to her about you – really lied to her. All that time I was seeing you, and pretending I was seeing some guy called Jim.'

'Well,' he said, 'Jim is short for James.'

Reluctantly she smiled. 'But nobody calls you Jim. Anyway, I said he was a musician, and she still believes I only met you that once, in the pub, when I went, in her place, to find out if your mother could be responsible for those awful things that were happening. Lucy didn't want to meet you then because she knew you were hostile to *him*, so can you imagine how she'd feel if she knew we'd been involved ever since and I'd never said a word about it?'

22

'But now he's been gone so long – it must be eighteen months.'

'You don't know Lucy!'

'No, I don't – but I want to.'

'And you will. Anyhow, I'll see how things are on Friday.'

'You may tell her then? On Friday?'

'I'll see how things are.' Vee's voice had risen a little. Now she turned to the church door, and twisted its iron handle. 'Locked,' she said.

'Yes. Because of thieves. But we could get the key from the vicar. It's a nice church. Lovely carved pews.'

'Next time,' Vee said. 'Let's not get involved with the vicar now. It's stopped raining. Let's just walk some more. Mansfield's dying to get moving. And then – home to English tea.'

'Yes. Mum's been baking. Scones and a cake.'

Tea was in the sitting room; Sarah had lit the log fire while they were out. Gradually, visibly, and in spite of three sessions on the mobile phone, tension eased from Vee's face and body. After supper – vegetable soup and homemade bread – they went early to bed.

'I never felt so peaceful after sex till I met you,' Vee said to James. Then she murmured, 'That must be because it's real love, I suppose.'

'Yes. Oh I really, really love you, Vee.'

'And I really love you.' Then she said, 'I'm sure everything's going to be all right. Yes, I feel . . . serene.' She gave a huge yawn. 'Really serene,' she murmured, and fell instantly asleep. James, however, stayed awake for some time, leaning on one elbow and looking down into her face.

'You look lovely when you're asleep,' he said next morning.

'You were watching me?' Her laugh was happy. 'It's the guy who's supposed to fall asleep right away, while the woman kind of broods over him.'

Now he laughed too. 'Kind of broods! I wasn't exactly doing that. Just thinking how beautiful and sweet you are.'

'It's wonderful you think that, even though it isn't true. And even more wonderful that you say it. Till I met you I didn't believe men ever said things like that.'

'What awful men you must have known.'

'I suppose they were just trying to be tough guys. Macho, you know.'

'The Hemingway style. It's not for me.'

'Well, thank goodness for that.'

He said, 'I was so glad last night when you said you were sure everything was going to be all right. I believe that too. Suddenly my old Suffolk poet is being rediscovered. There was a programme on the radio about him the other day. Did I tell you a publisher's interested in my turning my thesis into a book?'

'You *know* you didn't tell me. And why not? Couldn't you have guessed how thrilled I'd be?'

'Well . . . obscure poets aren't really your thing, are they?'

She said, 'Poetry usedn't to be a thing of mine – I really hated the nun who taught us English at the convent. But I've changed a lot since then. It could be different now. Anyhow, I'm interested in *you* – and that includes the things you do. I want us to share more – and that applies to you, too, James. I'd like you to loosen up about my staying at the Mayfair and about rock concerts – why, I even felt you disapproved of my mobile phone, though I hope, by now, you can see I need it. All these things are part of my work. They're the things I *do*.'

'Yes, I'm sorry. I'm a prig and a puritan.'

'No you aren't. Well perhaps a little. Why, when I talked about skiing yesterday, you looked as shocked as if I'd said I played polo.'

'*Did* I? Perhaps I did. It always makes me think of rich people swanning off to Switzerland with a lot of expensive equipment.'

'Yes, you're a puritan all right. Why shouldn't rich people enjoy some healthy exercise? Anyhow, in the States it's not like that. All sorts of people ski.'

He said, 'I'm sorry.'

'Don't be. You just have to lighten up a little – and I have to get a bit heavier.'

'Heavier!' He laughed. 'I like you just as you are. Don't put on a single kilo.'

She laughed too, but then she said, 'No, I mean it. More serious. Anyhow, I'm dying to read your book.'

'Well, you shall. Just as soon as it's finished.'

'You promise?'

'I promise.' He paused. 'I might even dedicate it to you.'

'Oh, wow!' But then she said, 'No, you should dedicate it to Sarah.'

'I'll dedicate it to both of you.'

'Perfect. But what about Mansfield? Won't he feel left out?'

'Mansfield will have to wait for my next book.'

They laughed. She said, 'Oh James, I'm so happy.'

THREE

It had been in February 1990, three months before her baby was due, that Lucy Riven went back to Rivendale.

Although she loved her Yorkshire home, she told Vee, who telephoned from Los Angeles every week – 'Such ridiculous extravagance!' Lucy's mother would exclaim each time – that this winter seemed unusually bleak. On their walks, Lucy and Rufus – she so pregnant, the dog so old – were slower and winced from the relentless wind. Soon they seldom went farther than the barn where the tomb of the Riven crusader had been taken after Puritans burnt down the medieval chapel. Here Lucy's parents, Edward and Teresa, had argued about chivalry, as they had argued about everything, especially the religion in which they both believed.

As a very modern Catholic, Lucy's father had disapproved of the crusades, but Lucy knew that he had felt affection for the stone crusader: for his stern, calm face, his legs crossed at the ankle, his little dog lying at his feet. The sides of his tomb were darkened by the flames that had destroyed the chapel. Exiled to the barn, he – like so many other Rivens – had been a victim of religious persecution. When Lucy and her father had paused at the barn on one of their long walks, her father had stroked the crusader's mailed head with a gentle hand. Now Lucy – Rufus panting at her feet – always made the same caressing gesture.

Indoors, Lucy sat in the library.

'I can't think why you want to sit in that cold, gloomy room,' Teresa said one evening. She, Eva – the upper-class Hungarian refugee who was her worshipper, housekeeper and, nowadays, cook – and Lucy were having dinner in the breakfast room. At Rivendale, the former morning room and breakfast room, though always still referred to by these names, had replaced the large drawing room and dining room, which were now closed, with their furniture shrouded in dust sheets.

Lucy said, 'I always light the fire – there's plenty of fire-wood.'

'That's not the point. Mrs Ashe keeps a good fire going in the morning room.' Mrs Ashe, who lived in the nearby village, was the daily cleaner. Teresa added, 'And you shouldn't be heaving logs about in your condition.' Invariably, Teresa made Lucy's pregnancy sound like an unpleasant disease.

'I can easily cope with the library fire, and I like sitting there.'

'It's not as if you were a *reader*.' Teresa read a lot – old novels, new biographies, devotional works – and the tone in which she said this was disparaging.

'The library reminds me of Daddy.' Lucy's eyes clashed with Teresa's. It was Teresa who looked away.

In the library – Lucy's father's refuge – on the night of his death, Teresa and Eva had gathered up his mass of notes on religious history, his letters from fellow ecumenists, and various books, including his favourite, *On Being a Christian*, by the progressive theologian, Hans Kung, whom Teresa always referred to – he had been rejected by her hero, the Polish pope – as 'that heretic'.

Lucy had been away at school, but, when she came home for the funeral, her old nanny had described the bonfire in the stable yard: Teresa's and Eva's faces in the firelight, as they burned the books and papers, had reminded Nanny of old tales of witches. Back at school, Vee compared the episode to an *auto-da-fé*, and started to refer to Teresa as 'Mrs T': T for Torquemada.

Ever since, Lucy at the end of her evening prayers – kneeling by her bed, speaking the words aloud, as she always did – had asked to be able to love her mother. She made this request every night of her life, so presumably it had not yet been granted.

Certainly, mutual affection between mother and daughter was not evident at the dinner table this evening. Although Teresa looked away, her recovery was rapid. She shook her head. 'Your father! I'm surprised you can bear to think of him. He would have been shattered by this disgrace – absolutely shattered!'

Lucy – she had been picking at her food: overpoweringly flavoured with paprika, like most of Eva's cooking – put down her fork. Her hands were trembling, and she clasped them on her swollen stomach. 'No! You're the only person who's shattered. Sometimes I think you're the only Catholic I know who would have liked me to have an *abortion*.'

'Lucy!' Teresa exclaimed. Her tone was outraged, but again she glanced away.

'Well anyway, even if that isn't true, you're the only person who said I ought to have my baby adopted. I think you still feel that, but I know Daddy wouldn't have. Oh, he might have been a bit shocked at first, but he wouldn't have been "shattered". He loved me. He might even have been pleased.'

'Pleased?' Teresa's voice had regained its normal quiet chill; this contrasted with her words. 'Pleased by your having the illegitimate child of a cad, a bounder, an ageing, thrice-married Lothario, a seducer who deserted you as soon as he learnt your sin was going to bear fruit—'

Lucy interrupted with a harsh, humourless croak, completely different from her normal laugh. 'Cad! Bounder! Lothario – whatever that is! How can you use such ridiculous words? Like in some old melodrama . . . Anyway, none of it's true. You know the Church authorities agreed that those civil marriages didn't count.'

'Perhaps my words *were* ill-chosen. Not strong enough to describe him. He's more like some "wicked spirit who wanders through the world for the ruin of souls".'

After this quotation from an old prayer, Lucy's voice rose in pitch: 'You're not to say that. You're not to. It's horrible.'

Teresa said, 'Please don't become hysterical. It's not good for you – in your *condition*.'

'No, I dare say not.' Lucy spoke normally now. She stood up.

'Where are you going? We haven't finished dinner.'

'I've lost my appetite.'

'It's ridiculous for you to sound like a martyr. What you *can't* deny, Lucy, is your sin.'

Lucy, on her way to the door, did not turn or answer. In the library, she revived the fire; huddled in an armchair, close to it, she dozed off, and was woken by the telephone.

29

She and her mother, who was now in the morning room, answered simultaneously. 'Lucy?' said Vee, in Los Angeles.

'Vee!' exclaimed Lucy. There was a click as her mother put down the receiver. In Teresa's code, Catholicism and snobbery – often allies – were united; eavesdropping, dishonest and vulgar, would have transgressed both.

To Vee – as to no one else – Lucy could relate that evening's events. At first her tone – like that of Vee's interpolations – was indignant, but gradually it saddened until, at the end of her account, she said, 'Of course she's right.'

'Right? What can you mean?'

'Oh, not about my father . . . or about Rupert. But I did sin.'

'Oh, Lucy – that's such nonsense. I mean, you know how I feel about all that. But, even from your point of view . . . well, after all, you were engaged to the guy, and it was only *once*—'

'No, after I knew I was pregnant, that weekend when I stayed with him—'

'Lucy, you were arranging to get married then. Anyway, you've confessed it all. You've had absolution. Why, that's one of the things I like about your Church – being able to make a fresh start. And now suddenly you're crawling with guilt, like some screwed-up Calvinist.' At this, Lucy laughed, and Vee said, 'That's better!'

'Yes. I'm sorry. I just feel a bit down.'

'Mrs T could get anyone down. And that awful Eva – Torquemada's handmaid.'

'Oh Vee, you're dreadful.' But Lucy laughed again. Then she said, 'I suppose I just feel a bit . . . isolated. Everyone disapproves. Even Nanny, when I went to see her in the village. But I've stopped going there – she said . . . horrible things. Oh, not about me, but about Rupert. How she knew he was a right wrong un the first moment she saw him.'

'A what?'

'Oh, it's a Yorkshire expression. Means a rotten person. Well, I get enough of that from Mummy.'

Vee was silent: Lucy had once told her that criticism of Rupert was the only thing that could spoil their friendship. Now she said, 'It's not long till you have the baby. After that, you'll be able to escape.'

Lucy said, 'We'll see. Anyway – as usual – you've cheered me up.' But her tone was wistful when she added, 'I never thought I'd ever want to escape from Rivers. It's my *home*.'

'Well, you're a big girl now.'

The laugh with which Lucy responded to this was whole-hearted. 'That's certainly true. I'm *enormous*. I look awful.' Then she sighed. 'Oh Vee, I do miss my hair so much.'

'It's growing again, isn't it?'

'Yes, but so slowly. It hasn't even reached my shoulders. It'll never be like it was before that hateful person chopped it off in the underground. I still wonder who could have done such a thing. *Who? Why?* And Rupert loved my hair—' She broke off. Then she said, 'Vee, this telephone call must be costing you a fortune.'

'I've told you, calls are much cheaper here than they are in that backward country you inhabit.'

They both laughed. Lucy said, 'But still . . .'

'Well, I'll call again next week. Keep on trucking, as they used to say.'

'I've never known what that meant.'

'Oh, kind of "battle on", I guess.'

'Mmm. Vee . . .' Lucy hesitated.

'Yes?'

'Well – who knows? – perhaps when the baby's born, Mummy will . . . soften.'

'Like you say, who knows? Perhaps pigs will grow wings. But I doubt it.'

'Oh, Vee, you're such a cynic,' Lucy said.

However, Vee's cynicism was justified. After the birth of the beautiful blue-eyed child, Teresa remained cold and sarcastic. The baby was born on May Day, immediately stigmatized by Teresa as 'that dreadful communist holiday'. But, as Lucy told Vee when Vee came for the christening, 'The moment I saw him . . . well, it was like falling in love.'

'Really?'

'Yes. That's the only way I can describe it. Overwhelming. An overwhelming love.'

'Wow! That's great. He's beautiful.'

'Yes. He's got Rupert's wonderful blue eyes.' There was an

instant's pause. Then Lucy went on, 'The doctor says I'm made for motherhood. Breast-feeding being so easy, and the birth being so quick.' She paused. 'Just like a peasant, Mummy said. And Eva started talking about women on their estates in Hungary who'd be back working in the fields three hours after their babies were born. I said, "You must have been terrible employers."'

Vee burst out laughing. 'What did she say to that?'

'She and Mummy were both furious.' Lucy laughed too. But then she sighed. She said, 'I'm glad to be like a peasant, healthy and natural, and so on. But Mummy meant it as an insult. That's what upsets me – that she should want to insult me.'

Vee said, lightly, 'Oh, you know Mrs T!'

'Do I? I sometimes wonder. She isn't even pleased that the baby's a boy. You remember how she was always telling me she wished I'd been one?'

'Oh, yes. Last of the Rivens, and all that.'

'Exactly! So I said to her, "Well, at least there's a boy in the family now." I wasn't being sarcastic. I said it nicely. But she said, "*In* the family? You're joking, Lucy. A *by-blow*!"'

'A what?'

'Yes, I had to look it up in the dictionary, myself. It means "a bastard child".'

'Oh, how obnoxious that woman is. I really hate her.'

For once, Lucy did not protest at the strength of Vee's antipathy towards Teresa. After a moment she said, 'You've no idea how wonderful it is to see you and how glad I am that you could come.'

'Me too. But obviously Mrs T doesn't feel the same. She – plus Eva for back-up – can certainly produce a big chill.'

Lucy said, 'I'm sorry.'

'For heaven's sake! It's not your fault. Anyhow, you and old Rufo love me. And I'm used to her little ways. Ever since my first visit here, when your father was so sweet and she wasn't, and you told me afterwards that she said I looked like one of *Walter* Disney's animals.'

They both laughed. Lucy said, 'Well, you do look like Bambi. So pretty. With those huge trusting eyes.' Then she said, 'I'm so sad that you can't be a godmother, not having been confirmed as a Christian.'

'Confirmed! I'm not a Christian at all. Oh, I believe in a sort of God – well, in a Higher Power – but I suppose Mrs T would call me a heathen with a Jewish mother.'

Lucy said, 'I want to think of you as an honorary godmother. Will you be that?'

'Dear Lucy, of course I will. For everything but religion, I'll think of myself as Edward's godmother from now on. Birthdays and Christmas, hugs and kisses – the whole package! And with such devout Catholics as Mag *and* Bernard Dumble as the official godparents, little Edward's soul will be in safe hands.'

'Little Edward.' Lucy smiled. 'Edward Hugh.' Then she said, 'I was going to give him Rupert as a first name, but I couldn't face the tussle with Mummy. One can't fight *all* the time.' She sighed.

'So it's Edward after your father, and Hugh after the family martyr – he'll be Catholic through and through!'

'Of course,' Lucy said quietly. 'Like me.'

'Sorry,' Vee said, and then, 'You'll never stop me being flippant about sacred things. Anyhow, a little flippancy will probably be good for Edward, with his Riven ancestors – and his mother and his other godparents so earnest.'

Lucy laughed. 'You're right.' Then she said, 'Mummy suggested Eva might condescend to be a godmother. But I put my foot down. Eva didn't like Daddy, and she doesn't like me. Anyway, at least I've been spared Mummy's snobbish family and grand friends at the christening. Since he's a *by-blow*.'

'Lucy! When you said that word, you almost sounded bitter.'

Lucy sighed. 'I almost felt it.'

The christening was held in the neighbouring town, at St Cuthbert's: Teresa disliked this ugly little redbrick church, but Lucy's father had felt affection for it, and so did she. The ceremony was attended only by the Riven household, including Vee and the Dumbles, and by a few local Catholics whom Lucy had insisted on inviting; there was no party afterwards. But back at Rivendale the atmosphere of gloom was lightened by Vee's vivacity and Mag's good-humoured chatter.

However, after the visitors had gone, there was no one to dissipate Lucy's sense of isolation. 'Except darling Edward, of course,' she told Vee on the telephone. 'He should be enough. Especially as I love him so much. But Mummy does make things difficult. Edward does cry quite a lot – he is rather restless – but why should she complain about that? Her bedroom's on the other side of the house – she can't possibly hear him at night. The other day she said he was a very bad baby. A *bad baby* indeed – what nonsense! She doesn't love him the least bit – she never picks him up or kisses him. And she never stops criticizing me.'

'You've got to get away.'

Lucy sighed. 'Yet I love this place. I take Edward up on the moors, in his sling. That's another thing Mummy criticizes. "Just like some black savage with its piccaninny," she says.'

'Oh, shit!'

'I agree,' said Lucy, though she herself never used four-letter words. Then she said, 'It's lovely here, now summer's come.'

But when Vee came to Rivendale again, it was in November. Icy winds were blowing; Teresa's welcome, punctiliously polite, was equally chilly. Lucy looked pale and exhausted. 'Mrs T's really getting you down,' Vee said when they were alone. Lucy said nothing, but she gave a little nod. However, next day, a letter arrived.

Before her pregnancy, Lucy had spent nearly four years as a fundraiser with the charity called Feed the Children. Her successor viewed the job as a stepping-stone to one with higher pay and – as he put it when, after ten months, he gave notice – 'higher visibility'. Although competent, he had not been as exceptional a fundraiser as Lucy. When he resigned, the committee wrote to ask if there was any chance that she might return.

'Accept,' Vee urged her.

'How can I?'

'They obviously need you.'

'Edward needs me. It's Edward I have to put first.'

'Of course you'd take him with you.'

'But who would take care of him? Where would we live?'

'You'd live with the Dumbles again, of course. I'm sure Mag

would be thrilled. She'd find someone to look after him while you're at work.'

'One of Mag's lame ducks.' Lucy shook her head. But, at Vee's insistence, she telephoned. Mag, overflowing with warmth, expressed delight: 'I miss you *so* much, Lucy.' Eagerly she volunteered to look after Edward herself. As the mother of six grown-up children – her four beloved grandchildren all far from London – her enthusiasm was unmistakable, her reliability unquestionable. By the first of January, 1991, Lucy was again working for Feed the Children, and she and Edward were established at the Dumbles' house in Hampstead. In March – on the day Vee returned from Suffolk to London – Lucy and Francis Larch had arranged to meet for lunch.

'So you're happily settled in London,' Francis said, when the waiter had taken their order.

They had first lunched at this small Italian restaurant near Lucy's office soon after Lucy's engagement to Rupert. Since then they had grown to like each other; nonetheless, Rupert was the bond between them: their shared feeling for him was the most important reason why they met.

'Settled – oh yes. Happily?' Lucy's smile was wistful. She leant her right elbow on the table, resting her chin on her hand. She sighed. Then she said, 'You know, I often feel you're the only person who really understands how much I miss Rupert.'

Francis sighed too. 'Oh yes, I'm sure *I* understand. Hardly a day passes when I don't think of him.'

'I think of him every day,' Lucy said. 'And miss him. And pray for him.' She added, 'I hope I'm not embarrassing you.'

'Of course not.' Then he said, with a little laugh, but also a hint of sharpness, 'You Papists don't have a monopoly of prayer, you know. We Anglicans also engage in it.'

'Oh, I didn't mean *that* – nothing like *that*.' She sounded horrified. 'I'm so sorry. It's just that Catholics – Roman Catholics – tend to talk about religion more . . . and I've noticed that other people find it a bit—'

'My dear Lucy,' he broke in. 'I didn't intend to upset you. And of course I know what you mean. Many members of my church feel that talking about religion is tremendously *infra dig*.'

'Mmm. I sometimes felt that about Rupert.' She frowned. Then, leaning forward and fiddling with a strand of hair – now shoulder-length – as in the past she had tugged at her long golden plait, she said, 'Francis . . . you don't feel I was pushing Rupert to become a Catholic, do you? Honestly I wasn't. He suggested it . . . really he did. And Father Jessop said he was so receptive, when he went for instruction.'

Francis said, 'Lucy, I'm sure Rupe didn't feel you were putting pressure on him.' He added, 'And he told me he thought Jessop the Jesuit was a very intelligent man.'

'Jessop the Jesuit!' She smiled, but did not sound happy when she added, 'Is that what Rupert called him?'

'No, no – that's *my* name for him. He's quite famous for his converts, you know. So many eminent people.'

Obviously, she did not care for this, either. She said. 'Rupert wasn't eminent.'

'No, no, of course he wasn't.' Francis put out a hand and rested it on hers for an instant. 'Lucy,' he said, 'you're awfully touchy today.'

'You're right, and, oh, I'm really sorry. But Francis . . . do tell me what he actually said about . . . his feelings about going to be converted. Obviously you talked about it.'

Francis ran a hand through his wispy grey hair. 'Not a great deal. As you said just now, most people don't talk about religion all that much . . . and I'm afraid Rupert and I were no exception. Oh, I'm sure he was pleased about . . . joining you. But our conversations tended to be more frivolous.'

'Frivolous?'

'Well . . . joky.' Francis went on, 'You know how Rupe loved jokes.'

'Oh yes, he did didn't he?' For the first time Lucy looked and sounded happy and carefree. 'He made such wonderful jokes.' But then her expression changed completely; it was in a voice of extreme dejection that she said, 'We're talking about him as if he were dead.'

'Oh, Lucy – no! No, I'm sure that's not so. Quite, quite sure.' Then he said, 'Just the other day, my mother was saying she was certain he'd turn up.' Francis did not add the phrase that had followed: 'like a bad penny'.

'Turn up!' Lucy exclaimed. 'But that sounds so trivial. As if he'd just been *wandering*, like those old hippies used to.'

'Melmoth the Wanderer,' Francis murmured.

'What?'

'There was a book called that. And when poor Oscar came out of prison, and had to leave the country and wander about the Continent in such dire poverty and misery, he called himself Sebastian Melmoth.'

'Oscar?'

'Oscar Wilde.' But then, seeing Lucy's distracted look, he said, 'I'm sorry. That's quite irrelevant. I can never resist a quote – just like Rupe. But, Lucy, I feel quite sure he isn't dead.'

'It's been so long,' she said. 'Twenty months. This . . . mission of his. Oh, surely it must be completed now? The alternative seems to be that he's dead.' She paused, then hurried on. 'Or he could be a prisoner in some terrible Middle Eastern jail? Tortured, even. When I was a child I used to have nightmares about Topcliffe, the persecutor of Catholics in Queen Elizabeth's day, who broke my ancestor Hugh Riven's bones on the rack, and had him cut down at Tyburn from the scaffold, and his bowels torn out before he was dead. I used to dream Topcliffe was coming towards me along one of the dark corridors at Rivers. In the dream, I couldn't move. He came nearer and nearer until I knew I'd have to look into his pale twisted face, into his eyes, and that then I would experience evil. That was always when I woke. I know it sounds silly saying I knew I was going to experience evil, as I was only a child, but it's true. Because lately I've been having that dream again – exactly the same – and my feelings are exactly the same, too. Oh Francis, often I dread going to sleep, in case I have that nightmare. I have it so often – and I have this feeling that it's something to do with Rupert. I don't know what.' She paused. 'Sometimes I wonder whether he might be the victim of some modern Topcliffe. There are so many of them. You only have to read the newspapers. Oh Francis, say Rupert's in prison in one of those terrible countries.'

Francis gazed at her as the words poured out, and for several moments in the silence that followed. At last he said, 'My dear Lucy, you're overwrought. Your imagination's running away with you. If Rupert were in any such situation, working for our government, they'd be doing something about it.'

'*Would* they . . . if *trade* was at stake?' Old Catholic revulsion from moneymaking – values surviving from ancient struggles with industrious Protestantism, values that had been held by her own father – were the fuel for Lucy's fire. She went on, 'Ever since the invasion of Kuwait last summer, all through that dreadful Gulf War this year, I worried about Rupert. I said something about it to my American friend, Vee . . . but she doesn't understand.'

'Did she call it Desert Storm?' Francis asked, adding, 'Only the Yanks could make a horrible war sound like a cheap film.'

'You're like my mother. She's always saying how vulgar Americans are – *she* does it to get at me about Vee, who's my best friend. You know, I love Vee more than anyone in the world – except Edward and Rupert. But she never liked Rupert – that's the one shadow between us. When I told her I thought he might be involved in the war, she said I was crazy.'

'Lucy, I honestly think it's most unlikely, myself. Whatever secret work Rupe may have done in the past, I'm sure it's just been in the field of gathering information.'

'So? In a war, that's needed more than ever. It's just even more dangerous than in peacetime.'

'My dear girl, don't you think Rupert's rather too old for the sort of thing you're imagining? After all, he's fifty-one, now – only a year younger than I am. Can you imagine *me* spinning around behind enemy lines?'

Lucy surveyed Francis: small, plump, wispy-haired. Her lips twitched, but all she said was, 'That's different. You've never done that sort of work.'

'I don't think Rupe—' But he broke off, for now on Lucy's face was the look of faith, her heritage – something that no argument could counter – and he changed the subject with an unaccustomed crudeness that could only have come from an acute sense of impasse: 'I really do want to see little Edward. Perhaps you could bring him down to Oxford sometime?'

Lucy said, 'I'd like to.' After a moment she added, 'I do hope you understand my not asking you to the christening . . . or to be godfather. I would have liked that – Rupert's best friend. But my mother would have been like an iceberg to any friend of Rupert's. She was being so very difficult about everything. Of course I couldn't have Vee for a godmother, as she isn't a Christian. The Church doesn't allow it. But she and I have decided that she's a sort of honorary godparent. Perhaps, as Rupert's best friend, you could feel the same?'

'That's sweet of you Lucy, and I shall. I've only once been a godfather.' He paused. 'I'd almost forgotten. To Rupert's son, James.'

'Oh?'

'Yes, But I haven't seen him since the christening. When Rupert and Sarah split up, I lost touch completely.'

'I can understand that – you and Rupert being so close.'

'Yes.' Francis sighed. Then he smiled. 'I'll try to be a better godfather this time. In fact you can count on it.' Then he said, 'You've had a hard time, Lucy, and I think you're very brave.'

She pushed at her hair: the gesture that in the past had made her long golden plait swing back. 'Oh no, not really,' she said, and then, 'Anyway, I've got darling Edward. He makes me very happy. It's just . . . not knowing about Rupert that's . . . a strain.' Then she said, 'But of course, if he's alive, I know he'll come back as soon as he can.' She stroked the ring on the third finger of her left hand: the ring with two sapphire hearts, with flowers made of seed pearls and garnet chips, and little sprays of tiny diamonds. Seeing that Francis observed the gesture, she said, 'Rupert's ring. It belonged to his mother, you know.'

'Yes,' Francis said, and added, 'It's charming.' He did not add that it had belonged, as well, to Rupert's three former wives: Sarah had loved it and been upset when he took it back from her; Barbara had thought it old-fashioned; and it had not been costly enough for Chris.

Now, glancing at her watch, Lucy said quickly, as if to preclude further discussion, 'I must get back to work. I have to leave punctually this afternoon. Vee's coming round – she's over here on tour with a rock band, and it's our only chance to meet. Are you going back to Oxford now?'

'Not till tomorrow. I have . . . a few things to do in London.'

Lucy's blink, as she stood up, could have been caused by a memory of Rupert's allusions to Francis's 'bolt-hole' off the

Euston Road – always referred to by Francis himself as 'my little *pied-à-terre* in Bloomsbury' – where, on visits to London, he indulged his sexual proclivities.

'We must meet again soon,' she said.

'Yes indeed. And do try to bring Edward down to Oxford. For a weekend perhaps? My mother would be so pleased. You know how fond of Rupe she is.'

'Yes. Yes, it would be lovely.' They were on the pavement under the restaurant's striped awning. Neither perhaps had a firm intention of making the proposed weekend an actuality. Their mutual liking, as always, was tempered by a certain awkwardness evident in hesitation whether to kiss or touch hands or just – as happened – step back from each other with a little, friendly prolonged wave, reminiscent of the hand movements of the Charleston, a dance Lucy had certainly never attempted, though, thirty years ago, Francis might have incorporated it in an undergraduate revue.

FOUR

'Belinda never seems to want to come here.' Barbara Korn, who – unlike her ex-husband's first and third wives – had reverted to her maiden name after her divorce, put down the receiver with a sigh. 'She doesn't even like to chat on the telephone. She always says she's in a hurry, and rings off as soon as she can.' Barbara sighed again. 'That awful job of hers! Advertising is so parasitic – I sometimes think it's starting to corrupt her.'

'Starting!' Michel Porter, Barbara's lover, laughed. Sprawled in a macho attitude in a battered armchair in their Willesden living room – littered with left-wing books and pamphlets, and rather dusty – Michel went on, 'Advertising suits her down to the ground. I've always said she was a born yuppie.'

'Oh no, not really. Not at heart.' Barbara's tone was forlorn.

'Has she got one?' Michel laughed again, but, seeing a look of dismay on Barbara's face, added quickly, 'I didn't mean that. I was only joking. Oh love, will you never understand that I'm the reason Belinda doesn't come here? She can't stand my relationship with you.'

'And how often must I tell you that's complete nonsense. Belinda's a modern woman.'

Now it was Michel who sighed. Then she shrugged, and said, 'Well, anyway she can't stand *me*.'

'Oh that's not true. Why, she borrowed the deposit on her flat from you.'

'And still resents it. But she couldn't think of any other way to get out of here. To Hackney . . . though of course she calls it Islington.'

'It's on the border,' Barbara said defensively.

'On the border! The border of the heartland of that dreaded Chris and all her kind.'

'Chris!' Barbara exclaimed. 'I always felt she was such a bad influence on Belinda. Anyway at least *that's* over now.'

Michel laughed. 'I think she and Belinda are two of a kind.'

'Oh, how can you say that?'

Rupert had met Chris long after he and Barbara had parted, and Barbara might have regarded her marriage to Rupert only as cause for commiseration. However, everything she had read or heard about Chris's commercial orientation, about the books she published, about her extravagantly chic appearance – Barbara's rejection of her own youthful modelling career made her particularly averse to fashion – was abhorrent to her. During Chris and Rupert's marriage she had also reacted with irritation to Belinda's frequently expressed admiration for Chris's glamour.

Now a large cat – one of three – jumped into Barbara's ample lap, and started to knead the skirt of her Indian kaftan. Detaching its claws, and starting to stroke it absentmindedly, Barbara said, 'My poor daughter! I'm sure she must be unhappy. That pointless job! And she's probably lonely, too. There never seems to be any man in her life, and I don't think she's got many friends. There's that Debbie she sometimes mentions. I've often asked her to bring her here for a meal, but she never does. Oh dear!'

Michel said, 'She's secretive.'

Ignoring this, Barbara said, 'I only wish she was in love with some nice young man. But I doubt it. Her neglectful father's probably put her off men.' Now Barbara paused. 'But I'm sure she's not gay.'

'No indeed! In any case, it's good that her father *is* neglectful. Rupert the wrecker!'

'You're right! Imagine deserting that Lucy he was engaged to, when she was pregnant!'

Michel said, 'The woman's far better off without such a swine . . . just as Belinda is.'

'It's strange – you hardly know him and yet I think you really hate him.'

'Mmm.'

Barbara, stroking the cat, did not notice Michel's sombre, preoccupied expression. 'My poor Belinda!' she murmured.

'*Poor Belinda*!' How much Rupert and Barbara's twenty-four-year-old daughter would have disliked this description. She would have been horrified by how many people used it.

She was now a full account executive at the advertising agency where she worked. She was respected there for her energy and dedication; almost always civil and pleasant, she was not disliked. Yet colleagues and secretaries would, when she had left a room, often remark, 'Poor old Belinda!' – especially after Keith, a fellow executive, had been fired and had moved to another agency; during her romance with him, her unaccustomed glow had briefly made the description inapplicable.

'Poor old Belinda!' Her best friend Debbie murmured the words to herself on her way home after – having abruptly terminated her mother's telephone call – Belinda, in an uncontrollable burst of sobbing, had told her she had ended her love affair.

'*You* did?' Belinda had been too distressed to notice the unflattering emphasis – caused by Debbie's astonishment that Belinda had been the one to break off the relationship – and Debbie had hurried on, 'But why? You said you really liked him. I thought it was going so well. You seemed so great together.'

'It didn't work out,' was Belinda's answer, between sobs, and, when Debbie suggested that it was just a lovers' tiff and that they might 'make it up', Belinda said, 'No . . . no. It's over.' And then, 'But, oh Debbie, I'm so unhappy.'

'But what went wrong?' Then Debbie added, 'Was it . . . sex?' The question was tentative. Although Belinda had implied that this aspect of earlier – very brief – encounters had been unsatisfactory, it was a subject on which she was always reticent; in fact, in the past, Debbie – herself cheerfully communicative about a series of sexual partners – had teased her about this 'hang-up'.

'No . . . no.' Then Belinda muttered, 'That was . . . really nice.'

'Then . . . *why*?'

'Oh, forget it.' Dabbing at her eyes with a wad of tissues, Belinda made an effort at a smile and added, '*Please*!'

'Okay, if that's what you want.' Debbie shrugged but she looked hurt, even a little offended.

'I'm really sorry. Please don't be cross with me.'

Belinda's look was so pathetic that Debbie at once responded with a quick squeeze of her friend's shoulder, and now, in her turn, said, 'Forget it.'

'Poor old Belinda,' Chris Deyntree, that same evening, said to her father, Jack Puttock, during his telephone call from Yorkshire. 'She seems really down these days. She'd been so happy. There was this man from her office she was seeing. I told you they came round for dinner here. Very ordinary, I thought, and not a bit good-looking. Of course that was to be expected – she's certainly no beauty herself. Though she was looking almost pretty that evening . . . really I was quite surprised. Anyway, they seemed to get on like a house on fire. Little jokes and so on. But now she says it's over. That's all she'll say so far, but I suppose he ditched her. Another bastard!' Chris gave her hard little laugh.

'That bastard' was the term by which her father always referred to Rupert, her ex-husband. Now he said, 'Funny the girl should be plain. Even I'd have to agree that that bastard was a good-looker. And the mother – the Jewess – was a model, wasn't she?'

'Barbara – yes. A hundred years ago. But now she's really overweight, Belinda says.' Chris spoke with the shocked disapproval that a Victorian woman would have reserved for a sexual misdemeanour.

Jack Puttock laughed. 'Well, Chrissie, you could do with a few pounds extra yourself. I've said it before and I'll say it again.'

'I'm sure you will, Dad. Don't fuss.' But Chris's tone was good-humoured.

'You're much too thin, my girl.'

'*I* don't think one can be.' Chris laughed, then went on, 'Anyway, apparently Barbara's let herself go completely.'

'So that's why she's not married again. Shares a flat with another woman, doesn't she?'

'That's right.' Chris could never have told her father that Michel Porter was Barbara's lover. Chris could never have discussed sex with her father at all; she could certainly never have told him about what had happened to her three years before. Now she said, 'I suppose I really ought to find out exactly what went wrong.'

Jack Puttock said, 'Well, I think it's really good-hearted of you to be so kind to the girl, after all you went through with that bastard.'

Chris said, 'That wasn't Belinda's fault. Anyway, it's years now since they've been in touch. As I told you, I heard he'd vanished off the face of the earth.'

'What a terrible parent he's been, too – the bastard! And the way he treated that Riven girl – a decent girl from a respected family! To hell with him!'

'I'll drink to that, Dad. *To hell with him*!' Before she uttered the curse, Chris had drawn in her breath, but she spoke it in her usual brittle drawl.

When their conversation had ended, and they had rung off, Chris lay back on her spotless white pillows for a moment. Then she picked up the manuscript she had laid aside when her father telephoned, and started to read.

Downstairs, the front door was double-locked and the chain fastened. When she came upstairs to bed, Chris had closed all the metal blinds on the back windows and set the ground-floor and basement alarms. However, these were precautions that any woman living alone in London might have taken.

In the daytime, she still kept the ground-floor and basement doors to the garden locked. Chris was still careful, but in the past eighteen months she had undergone a change.

Her frequent fits of trembling had stopped; perhaps they had been caused not only by what she had experienced three years before, but by a terror of the unknown. Now she knew the truth, and her only tremors were of rage.

Sometimes she seethed, muttering to herself like some crazed vagrant – she would have been outraged if this resemblance had been pointed out to her – as she moved about her house.

Sometimes she swore and shook her clenched fists. But after only a few moments she would be calm again. Perhaps such outbursts were now merely indulgences: in part, perhaps, substitutes for orgasms she had never experienced. Perhaps Chris had now discovered, beyond fear and rage, her own way to triumph over the past: to become – as she was reflected in the adoring eyes of her protégée, Belinda – a glittering, gracious Snow Queen, cool, controlled, immune.

FIVE

The voyage to Kameni took three days. Down in the cabin of the yacht, Rupert often showed astonishment. At other times – Marios, the impassive Greek, at the helm – he and Disa paced the deck. Once, when they paused to lean on the rail above the restless sea, he asked, 'Would you call yourself an amateur or a professional?'

Disa laughed. 'Depends what you mean. Doesn't professional mean doing it for money? I don't need money. Though once I pretended I was a prostitute.' She laughed again. 'The guy was crazy about me.'

'Did you take his money?'

'Oh – you bet! I wasn't going to give him something for nothing. But then I burnt the money in front of him. At first he was shocked. Then he was flattered. He thought I'd done it because he was so great in bed.' She laughed again. 'But then I told him he was a boring creep. I told him to get lost.'

'That could have been dangerous.'

'Yes. But I controlled him.' Then she said, 'I go for danger. For living on the edge.'

'Mmm. On the edge.' He paused. 'So you'd call yourself an amateur?'

'Amateur?' Her tone was affronted. 'That's a pissy sort of word. Sounds like the way my mother played the piano.'

Now he laughed. 'I mean – you do it for love.'

'*Love*? Come on! What's *love* got to do with it?'

'Don't sound so indignant. I didn't mean love in that sense. I meant love of the thing itself. All those skills of yours. Like an artist's.'

'*Artist* – you're really keen on art, aren't you? That weird picture of yours – those *angels*! Art and angels!'

47

He said, 'There's a poem called "Air and Angels".

> *'Twice or thrice had I loved thee,*
> *Before I knew thy face or name,*
> *So in a voice, so in a shapeless flame,*
> *Angels affect us oft, and worship'd be;*
> *Still when, to where thou wert, I came,*
> *Some lovely glorious nothing I did see.'*

'You've lost me. What's all that love stuff? And are you saying I'm nothing? Thanks a lot!'

'It would have been a sort of compliment, actually. But I wasn't thinking about you.' Then he said, 'Oh, it just came into my head. Quoting, you know.'

'Quoting!' She laughed again. 'Stuff! You quote that stuff a lot.'

'I know. It's old-fashioned – but I can't get rid of the habit.' He laughed. 'I've only one friend who can match me at quoting. He's a don.'

'Spanish, is he? I love the bullfights.'

Rupert laughed again. 'No, he's not Spanish. He's a don at Oxford – he teaches Latin.'

'Oh.' Then she said, 'Being with you's like being back at school.'

'Dull, do you mean? But this friend of mine is very amusing. I remember the first time I saw him. We were undergraduates. He was singing in a revue. He was wearing a turban, a Marlene Dietrich make-up and a wraparound skirt, and holding a cigar.' Now, in a German accent, Rupert sang:

> *'I'm Cosmopolitan Clara,*
> *Famous for my walk and my cheroot.*
> *I wander on my own, a lone wayfarer,*
> *Following the old trade route.'*

She said, 'He's the gay pal you mentioned when we we first met?'

'That's right. What a good memory you've got. Nowadays

he's got this little bolt-hole in London he escapes to from his mother. He has a taste for rough trade.'

'So he's like me – enjoys danger. Did you fancy him – at Oxford?'

Rupert laughed. 'No. Not at all.'

'Did he fancy you?'

'Perhaps. Sometimes I thought so – just a bit. But I wasn't really his type. Too well-educated. Anyway, now it's just friendship. On his side, too.'

'Friendship!' Then something flickered in her turbid eyes. She said, 'So I'm an *artist* in the love game, am I?'

'All those tricks of yours. You must have worked at them.'

'Oh yes. If that's what you've been talking about. Yes, I've studied. I even took lessons at one time. From a Chinese woman. And, of course, practice makes perfect.' She laughed.

'And you want to be perfect? But why? To please men? Or so that they'll please you?'

'Come on! I please myself. Men aren't so great at sex. They don't *work* at it. Except a few gigolos, I guess. But most men – no! They just want to do it. They want that all the time – till the day they die.'

He laughed. 'That's a bit of an exaggeration, isn't it?'

'Is it? They simmer all the time. Like stew. Of course they can't always come to the boil. I'm sure you find that yourself sometimes, don't you? Now you're older? Don't get angry – I like to hear the truth.'

'You do? Now *that* can be really dangerous.'

'I told you – I go for danger. Anyway, of course it's easy for you now – with me. But that could be my *art* . . . and the novelty. The more a man's into sex, and the older he gets, the more novelty he needs. You must have found that. Somehow I'm sure you've done the weirdest things. Much weirder than just having two women, like you said. Haven't you? Be honest now.'

'Perhaps I'm not so honest as you are.' He laughed.

'But you could be . . . with me. You *will* be. I'm sure of it. I knew it from the moment we met.'

'A sort of rapport?' he said.

She said, 'Yeah. That's it.' She laughed. 'Let's test it all over again. Come on down to the cabin. Now!'

Kameni was an island of volcanic rock: dark brown with a rusty look. There were a few ancient olive trees, huge, knobbed and twisted, but the pines predominated. They crowded up the steep hillside to the plateau where Disa had built her villa; they grew close to the walls of the house, massing so densely below the terrace in front that they hid its concrete and metal supports. Looked at from below, the villa seemed borne up on them. Their seedlings clung to the walls of the road – blasted from the rock after Disa bought the island – that wound up to the villa from the landing place. Only the stony beach and the nearby enclosure round the small house where Marios and his wife lived were free of them.

When they arrived, Rupert said, 'The Emperor Tiberius would have appreciated this place. It would have reminded him of Capri. Sheer cliffs surrounded by deep water, and just one landing place – Tiberius felt safe on Capri. That was one reason why he loved it. Of course there were others.' Rupert laughed.

'What were they?'

'Oh, it was the perfect place to cultivate his vices. On Capri, he set up his own private brothel. He imported troops of girls and young men from all over the Roman Empire. Suetonius says they had to be experts at what he calls "unnatural practices" and used to perform for Tiberius in groups of three to "excite his waning passions".'

Disa laughed.

'His villa had rooms full of pornographic pictures and statues – and Egyptian sex manuals to teach the inmates exactly what was expected of them. There were picturesque mini-brothels dotted about in the woods and glades of the island. Boys and girls dressed up as Pans and nymphs were posted in front of grottos with orders to get active whenever the Emperor was sighted. Never a dull moment!'

'Mmm – it sounds fun, but it must have taken a lot of organization,' Disa said.

'Yes. After a certain point, debauchery does.' He sighed. 'But being Caesar meant having absolute power. You were a god. Officially a god. And, if you're a god, you can do whatever you want. But you're bound to become jaded. So you behave more and more extremely. Nothing is enough. Your pleasures become more and more exotic, more and more calculated. The slaves who cater to your desires are rehearsed like actors. Homosexual . . . heterosexual . . . paedophile – terms like that cease to apply. Men, women, girls, boys, little children – Tiberius used them all. Such elaborate scenarios! Yet some-times he got carried away – departed from the script, you could say. Once, sacrificing in the temple, he took a fancy to the acolyte with the incense casket and could hardly wait for the ceremony to end before hurrying him and his brother out and assaulting them. I suppose it was the sacrilegious aspect that suddenly took possession of him. When the boys protested, he had their legs broken. He was very cruel. On Capri, they still show the cliff top where he used to watch his victims being thrown into the sea after long terrible tortures. Cruelty always gets mixed up with sex, if you're jaded. Especially if you're Caesar. Most especially if you're Tiberius.'

She gave her two-note laugh. 'Would *you* like to have been Tiberius?'

He frowned. His startling eyes narrowed slightly. Then he smiled. 'Yes,' he said. 'I think it would have been absolutely fascinating.'

She smiled back. 'Well,' she said, 'we've got our own little Capri. Though not up to your old Tiberius's standard, I guess.'

'No brothels.'

'True. But I know all sorts of people who can come to stay, when we get bored.'

' "If" ' would be more romantic than "when",' he said.

'But we aren't romantic, are we?'

He laughed. He said, 'So it's appropriate that we've got no glades or grottos. Only these sombre pines.'

'There are the olives, too,' she said. 'But I prefer the pines.'

'Then you must like it here. In your lair.'

'Oh, I do,' she said. 'And you will too.'

'Mmm,' he said. 'But I must say I could do without that big black Doberman.'

She laughed. 'Yes, Karl certainly took against you. I've never seen him quite like that before. Lunging and straining at his chain, and barking so ferociously. But he'd never attack you with me there. I have him completely under control. He does exactly what I tell him. So don't worry about dear old Karl!'

'"Dear old Karl", indeed! I suppose you call him that because he's German. I think Cerberus would suit him better.'

'Cerberus?'

'Yes. A dreadful dog in the ancient world. He was stationed at the entrance of hell to prevent the dead from escaping and the living from entering the infernal regions.'

'The infernal regions . . . you're not very polite about my island!'

'I'm only talking about your canine chum.' Rupert grimaced. 'He certainly seemed pleased to see *you* – licking and fawning like that.'

'He's really a one-person dog. Though he tolerates Marios and Sophia.'

'Sophia! What a pretty name for such a hideous woman.'

'Mmm, she's no beauty. And she's supposed to have the evil eye – that's why people from other islands never come here. Anyhow, they're afraid of Marios. He killed a man once, though I got the charge dropped; that certainly cost a lot! But they're useful; apart from looking after the boat, he's tough and strong and good with electricity; he keeps the generator working, as well as doing all sorts of odd jobs. Sophia cleans the villa. And she's quiet. Most Greek women never stop talking.'

'You keep Cerberus chained?'

'Yeah.' Disa laughed. 'In the daytime, when I have guests. But Marios lets him roam loose at night.'

'That puts paid to moonlight walks, as far as I'm concerned.'

'Not if you're with me. But the terrain's a bit rough for moonlight walking. I'm afraid we'll just have to amuse ourselves indoors.'

He laughed. 'Perhaps that won't be too difficult.'

SIX

James had dropped Vee outside the Mayfair at ten that morning. She was crying and smiling. 'Bye,' she said. 'Bye, sweetheart. I'll call you. And I'll see you in the summer.'

'Goodbye, darling Vee. Yes, summer!' And he repeated, 'Summer!' as, with bag and phone, she hurried into the hotel, whirling, before she disappeared, for one swift wave. He waved back, then started the car, and, with a gulp and a violent shake of his head, drove off: back to Suffolk, to the college where he lectured, to his book, while Vee was at once immersed in her very different world.

At half past six, the minicab she had ordered picked her up, and took her to the Dumbles' house in Hampstead. As she got out, Lucy opened the oak front door and came bounding down the steps from the rustic porch. They met on the path, Vee loaded with packages and with a giant teddy bear wearing a spotted bow-tie.

'Lucy!'

'Vee, how wonderful – and oh, what a gorgeous teddy bear! Let me carry some of those parcels – what *are* they?'

'Gear for my godson, of course – we can drop the "honorary", can't we? It's such a mouthful.'

'Of course we can. Oh, Vee, you spoil him.'

'No I don't – and it's such fun.' Laughing, they moved towards the porch.

'What about that cab?' Lucy asked.

'It's going to wait for us. In half an hour or so, when I've got acquainted with Edward again, it'll take us back to my hotel. You said Mag would babysit.'

'You're as extravagant as ever. Yes, it's all arranged. But Mag's sorry you aren't going to have supper here.'

53

They were standing in the porch. 'She's very kind – but you know my Dumble block. Mag always makes me feel so "worldly" – she's the only person I've met since we left school who uses that word.'

'Mmm,' Lucy said. 'Rupert felt that a bit, too.' Then she said, 'I think Mag thought Rupert was rather worldly.'

'Anyhow,' Vee said, 'it'll be nice to be alone, so we can talk.'

'Yes, that'll be wonderful.'

Vee said, 'I feel sad to break our great curry tradition, but I may have to make some calls, and I hate taking my phone to restaurants, so I thought we'd have room service.'

'Room service!'

'Don't *you* turn puritan on me – I seem to meet nothing but puritans these days.'

'Really? Anyway, I'm no puritan – remember how they burned down our chapel at Rivers?'

'I was joking.'

'So was I.'

Mag had appeared in the doorway: earnest, untidy, grey-haired, yet retaining an oddly youthful look. Lucy had once said to Vee, 'It's odd when Mummy's so elegant and beautiful, that Mag looks younger,' and Vee had replied, 'Mag's kind of innocent, like a child – I think that's the reason.'

'Vee!' Mag exclaimed now. 'How nice to see you again. Come in.' Then she said, 'Goodness, what a lot of shopping you've been doing!'

Vee said, 'Hi, Mag. I haven't had much time to shop here – I brought these things for Edward from LA.'

'The teddy bear, too?'

'No, I rushed into Hamley's this afternoon. I thought just clothes would be so tedious for him.'

They were in the living room now: heart of Dumbledom, with its shabby furnishings, its Sistine Madonna over the chimney-piece, and Bernard Dumble on the window seat in earnest conversation with a young priest. Edward, surrounded by toys – he was banging a battered rabbit against the sofa – sat on a blanket on the carpet, and Vee, dropping her parcels on a chair but retaining the teddy bear, rushed over and crouched down beside him. 'Edward!' She sat the teddy bear down, facing him – it was considerably taller than he – and said to Lucy, 'Will he mind if I kiss him?'

Lucy laughed. 'No, I don't think so,' and, indeed, Edward did not mind the kiss; he disregarded it; his large blue eyes – larger than ever because open so wide – were fixed on the teddy bear.

'I wonder if he'll like it. Perhaps it's too big.' Vee's tone was anxious, but now Edward stretched out a hand. He prodded the teddy bear's chest, and it subsided, on its back, hind paws in the air. Edward gave a triumphant crow of laughter.

Everyone else laughed too. Bernard had risen, greeting Vee and introducing the priest. Now he said, 'Would you care to partake of a glass of wine? We were just broaching a bottle – not a cask, I fear – of honest red *ordinaire*.'

'I'd love some,' Vee said, and then, to Lucy, 'Oh, Edward really is beautiful. Such wonderful blond hair! Just like yours!' She stroked it with an eager hand, but stopped when he shook his head restlessly. 'So soft – and those eyes!'

'Yes, his eyes are nice . . . Rupert's eyes.'

'No,' Mag said, 'I think they're your eyes, Lucy.'

'Nonsense, Mag. They're just like Rupert's – much darker than mine . . . and brighter, too.'

There was a moment's silence. Then Vee said, 'Anyhow, they're simply great.' Bernard handed her her glass of wine, and she raised it. 'To Edward,' she said.

'My godson,' said Bernard.

'And mine,' echoed Mag.

'My son,' said Lucy, and they all drank.

An hour later, Lucy and Vee were in Vee's room at the Mayfair; she had just ordered champagne and smoked-salmon sandwiches from room service.

'Oh Vee, how wicked, but what bliss!' Lucy had taken off her shoes and was stretched on the sofa, while Vee was curled in an armchair. Then Lucy said, 'Rupert used to call me "blissy Lucy"! I thought that was so sweet and funny.'

'At least it's warm here,' Vee said. 'That house of the Dumbles is always freezing.'

'I don't notice. You forget I'm a hardy Yorkshire lass.'

'Well, I'm not. I'm a decadent Californian. But I suppose I'll have to get used to the cold if I move here.'

'Move here? Oh, Vee!' Lucy sounded almost as surprised and delighted as James had. 'Are you going to?'

'Well, it's a possibility. There's a job I just might get here in London.'

'That would be wonderful. But you've always said you'd never live in England.'

'I know, but people change.'

'I thought you loved LA?'

'LA's changing too. Sleazier . . . more dangerous.'

'That's true of London as well.'

'Are you trying to put me off coming here?'

'Good heavens, no. I'd simply love it. You've no idea what it would mean to me.' Lucy paused. Then she said, 'In spite of darling Edward, and though Mag's so sweet, I do get lonely sometimes.' She paused again, then she said, 'I miss Rupert so terribly.'

'You still miss him?'

'Yes, of course. I love him. He's the only man I've ever loved – goodness, that does sound mushy, but it's true. Of course I miss him!' There was a note of impatience in Lucy's voice, and now she added, 'Oh Vee, can't you understand that?'

Vee was silent for a moment. Then she said, 'It's still hard for me. After he . . . disappeared like that, without a word. Oh, I know how *loyal* you are—'

'Loyal!' Lucy broke in. 'Loyalty means sticking to what one believes is true, whatever happens. You make it sound as if it's something blind, something against reason. It isn't.' Then she said, 'I wonder if you feel that about my religion, too.'

Lucy had never spoken to Vee in this cool tone before, and she exclaimed, 'Oh Lucy, I don't feel that at all! I never have! Just that *I* couldn't become a Catholic doesn't imply that I don't respect your faith and what it means to you. I do. And I think the way you live it, in every way, is . . . well, quite amazing. It really impresses me.'

'Oh Vee, you make me feel ashamed. I'm not half so . . . good as you say. And I'm really sorry I sounded so bitter and twisted.' Lucy sighed. There was a knock on the door: room service had arrived.

When the waiter had gone, Lucy went on: 'Vee, you've been
. . . well, involved with more than one man in your life. I mean
. . . you were married . . . and there've been all those musi-
cians. You're bound to feel differently from poor stick-in-the-
mud old me with my one true love. In fact, you must think the
whole idea's really silly.'

'Silly?' Vee said. 'I don't think that's silly – I think it's
wonderful. A one true love!' She lingered on the words.

'But you don't think it's possible?'

'No, I think it may be. I really do.'

'You just haven't found it yourself?' But at Vee's instant of
hesitation before she shrugged, Lucy's eyes widened. Joyfully,
she pounced: 'You have?'

Vee hesitated again. Then she said, 'Maybe.'

'Maybe?' Lucy said. 'Oh, but if you had – you'd *know*!'

'Well . . . perhaps I do.'

'Oh, Vee – that's wonderful. Who is he? And *where* is he? He
can't be in LA, or you wouldn't be thinking of moving here. Vee
– is *he* here? Is he English?'

'Hey there!' Vee gave a small nervous laugh. 'You sound like
the Grand Inquisitor.'

Lucy's laugh was uninhibited. 'I suppose I do. But I'm so
thrilled. Do you know, Vee, even after all that's happened, I feel
that loving Rupert was worthwhile. *Is* worthwhile, I should say,
because I still believe he'll come back to me and Edward.' Her
tone changed suddenly: 'Unless, of course, he's dead. Today I
saw Francis Larch, his old friend who's so fond of him, and I
told him I thought Rupert might be dead.'

'And what did he say?'

'Oh, he doesn't think so. But, oh my poor darling Rupert –
sometimes I think of him dead, buried in an unmarked grave in
some awful country. Sometimes I've thought of trying to find
out from someone in the government – my mother's family
know all sorts of so-called important people. But I don't want
her involved – and they'd be sure to tell her. Anyway, I don't
believe Rupert would have wanted me to do that.' Again she
exclaimed, 'Oh, my poor darling Rupert! I feel he had such a
dreadful life until he met me. Those awful wives . . . and those
cruel children who wouldn't have anything to do with him. Oh,

I know their minds were poisoned against him by their mothers, but after all they're grown up now, and I can't help feeling they're cruel. That dreadful son, James, who was so hateful about his father on the telephone – I'm really glad you went to meet him instead of me. I'm sure he would have told me horrible lies about poor Rupert. But I mustn't call him "poor" – even if he's dead. Brave people aren't "poor" – I never think of the Blessed Hugh as "poor" – even though he was tortured on the rack and died in such agony.'

The silence that followed this speech was broken by the telephone ringing. Vee, as if released from prison, leapt to answer it. 'Yes,' she said, and then, 'Yes, I'll be there as soon as possible. Right.' She rang off, and said to Lucy, 'I'm afraid I'll have to go to Wembley in a few minutes. I'm so sorry, but it's unavoidable.'

'I'm sorry too. And, oh Vee, I'm sorry I've been so selfish. Talking about myself when you were just going to tell me about your own life.'

Vee said, 'Well, there's no time now. I'll tell you all about everything in the summer.'

Lucy said, 'Perhaps Rupert will be back by then – and you can really get to know him. And we can all have lovely times together – I and my one true love and you . . . and perhaps yours, too.'

'Sounds great,' Vee said. 'I must get a car now.' She picked up the telephone and booked two cars. 'Yes,' she said. 'One to Wembley and one to Hampstead. Right away.'

She rang off, and Lucy said, 'Oh Vee, I could easily have taken the tube. Green Park station's just round the corner.'

'I dare say. But humour me tonight. It all goes on expenses, anyway. Okay?'

'Well, all right then.'

In the lift, Vee said, 'Lots of kisses to Edward.'

'Oh yes, and thanks again for all his presents. Especially that wonderful teddy bear.'

'Which reminds me.' Vee took a little wrapped packet from her bag. 'This is for you.'

'What is it?'

'Just a tiny bottle of Fleurs d'Orlane – hope it's still your favourite perfume.'

'Oh how sweet you are – but how extravagant.'

'Duty free.'

'I'd run out of it. Rupert used to give it to me. It'll remind me of him – not that I need reminding, of course.'

From the car, Vee telephoned Suffolk. She thanked Sarah for her stay, then spoke to James.

'How did it go?' he asked.

'Oh, I saw Edward. He's beautiful – and very active, banging his toys about! But he didn't take much notice of me. And afterwards Lucy and I went to the hotel.'

'Did you tell her about me?'

'I sort of started. I said I was seeing someone, but then – well, the phone rang and I had to rush off to Wembley. I'll tell her in the summer.'

'Summer!' he exclaimed, as he had when they parted. Then he said, 'How I long for it!'

'Me, too, sweetheart!'

SEVEN

Next day when Francis returned to Oxford his mother commented that he looked tired. However, when he replied, 'London always exhausts me,' she said no more. What took place on his visits to his 'little *pied-à-terre*' was one subject they never discussed.

In his study that evening, Francis wrote a note to Lucy, saying how pleased he had been to see her the day before. He paused for a moment, then added, 'If there's anything I can ever do for you – or for little Edward – please don't hesitate to let me know. By the way, I enclose a small cheque. Do buy my "honorary godson" – I was so touched by that charming thought of yours – some little thing he needs.'

He had just put this letter and a – by no means small – cheque in an envelope, when he heard his mother's footsteps in the passage, and he shoved the envelope under some papers before she appeared in the doorway: it was time for the evening nightcap, always the most intimate moment of their day.

Age hardens women, mutating them towards maleness, and feminizes men. Mrs Larch, solid in her armchair, whiskery and waistless, feet planted apart, Scotch and soda in strong, veined hand, seemed more masculine in her mid-seventies than her son – pale and plump, sipping his glass of port – did in his early fifties.

'Really absolutely baffling – what on earth Rupe can be doing all this time,' Francis said. 'Of course Lucy still believes he's on some secret, noble patriotic mission – quite ridiculous, of course.'

'Absolutely ridiculous. As I've always said, it's a case of "*Cherchez la femme*".' Mrs Larch often resorted to French phrases, though she pronounced them in a very English accent.

61

'Especially where Rupert's concerned. As I've often told you,
I'm sure he's gone off with some woman.'

'But *what* woman? He never breathed a word to me.'

'I still believe it must be the fascinating Jeanne Duval.'

'Jeanne Duval' – the name of the poet Baudelaire's mixed-
race mistress – was the sobriquet by which the Larches knew
and spoke of the Cape Coloured woman with whom Rupert
had been involved for nearly twenty years. They had never seen
her; they did not know her real name.

'I thought that to begin with, but now I don't think so. I've
changed my mind.' Francis was silent for a moment. Then he
said, 'At first the real Jeanne Duval – "strange goddess, dark as
night" – inspired Baudelaire. But later she came to weigh him
down. He described her as a carcass, as a vampire. I'd begun to
wonder if Rupe was starting to feel something similar about *his*
Jeanne when he fell in love with Lucy. And, of course, if it *was*
she who persecuted Lucy, if she cut off Lucy's hair in the
Underground – Rupe was mad about Lucy's hair – I think he
would have come to hate her.'

'And you really believe *she* did that? I must admit it's possible
in the light of the way she persecuted his last wife – that
dreadful Chris who was so rude to me.'

'Yes – trying to push her under a bus. But in Chris's case
Rupe didn't mind – you remember me saying he laughed when
he told me about it.'

Nodding, Mrs Larch clicked her tongue against the roof of
her mouth as she always did when Francis referred to this
reaction of Rupert's. Her expression, however, was one of
relish. 'Such a scamp!' she exclaimed

Francis went on, 'But he'd come to detest Chris. With Lucy it
was another matter altogether. Rupe was really *in love* with
Lucy.'

'*In love!*' Mrs Larch's laugh was cynical and held the distaste
she invariably showed for an emotion she associated with
sexual passion. She said, 'Rupert has been "in love" so often.'

'No, I don't think so. With Lucy it was something different.'
When his mother smiled, he said, 'No, I'm quite serious,
Mother. I believe it really was different. He loved her good-
ness.'

Mrs Larch's smile was chilly now. She said, 'I must admit I find it a trifle difficult to think of a girl who has an illegitimate baby as personifying goodness. But perhaps I'm old-fashioned.'

'Yes, I must say, I think, in this case, you are.'

'And I must say I didn't see anything so very remarkable about the girl when Rupert brought her down here. Though of course she'd lost the famous hair by then. Perhaps the hair was the best thing about her.'

'No, Mother, you're wrong there. Her goodness, her sweetness, her loyalty – those have always been the best things about her.'

'Why, Francis dear, from the way you talk, anyone would suspect *you* were in love with her.'

Francis's sigh was one of exasperation. 'Oh, really, Mother! How ridiculous! It's just that, as I've said before, I feel that, this time, Rupe has gone too far.' The sigh that followed this was a melancholy one.

'You miss him, don't you?' Now his mother's tone was affectionate and concerned.

'Oh yes, I miss him.'

'Of course you do. Your oldest friend. Those weekly chats you always had on the telephone. Well, I'm sure, one day sooner or later, there'll be a ring' – here, sounding foolish, as if addressing a small child, she imitated ('Brr, Brr') the ring of a telephone – 'and it will be Rupert, back again.'

Francis sighed. 'Mmm.' Then he stood up. 'Mother, I'm really exhausted tonight. I must go to bed now. I'll just make sure everything's locked up.'

When they had exchanged goodnights, and she had gone upstairs, he stood by the study window for a minute or two, peering out into the dark garden. As well as tired, he looked deeply depressed. When he turned away from the window, he shook his head, murmuring aloud, 'Oh Rupe, my old friend, this time you've really gone too far.'

INTERLUDE

In the villa, Disa had her own library. 'Rather crude,' Rupert said, after looking through the books. 'I think Tiberius probably had a better collection.'

Disa laughed. 'But Tiberius didn't have videos.'

'Very true. And what a lot – a whole wall of them! Many more videos than books.'

'I prefer them.'

In the kitchen, Rupert exclaimed, 'Goodness – how opulent!' when he opened a refrigerator wholly devoted to caviar.

Disa smiled. 'You like it – the fish jam?'

'Very much indeed!'

'Yes, a lot of people seem to. I can take it or leave it.'

There were also three giant freezers packed with meals to which a famous chef had given his imprimatur: each day Disa heated their choice in the microwave.

Sometimes, in the evening, after they had eaten, they watched videos in the living room, but usually they preferred to watch them on the bigger screen at the foot of Disa's bed. Although he always went back to his room to sleep – Disa insisted she could only sleep alone – they spent a lot of time there.

'It's odd,' Rupert said. 'Everyone talks about Greek light – it's a cliché. When I was in Greece, I was conscious of it myself. But here, it's different somehow. Outside, even when the sun shines, all those pines seem to drain the light away – and of course these heavy metal blinds keep the house dark. Where I stayed in Greece, there were wooden shutters. Even when they were closed, light came in.'

'I like the dark,' Disa said. 'Just a spotlight or two. Like this one that shines onto the bed so one can see what one's doing.'

'Yes, very practical! And spotlights make the dark look

darker. You like the cold, too, don't you? I know it's getting hotter every day – but I wouldn't have thought you'd need the air-conditioning quite so high.'

'I like to be cool,' she said.

He laughed. 'You're the coolest person I've ever met.' Then he said, 'My third wife, Chris, was cool, too. She was like you in some ways. As I said before, she didn't care for art. And she didn't like my picture – though she wouldn't have dared to say it was *silly* as you did. After all, Blake's a famous painter – and, if there was one thing Chris respected, it was fame.'

Disa said, 'I didn't say the whole picture was silly. I quite go for that bad angel with those crazy eyeballs with no pupils, like something in a horror movie. It's the good angel that's silly, with that shocked expression, and the stupid child doesn't even look like a child – it's a mini-adult.'

'That's Blake's style.' But, seeing her blank look, he shrugged. He laughed and said, 'Chris was a great one for what she called style.' Then he said, looking round the room, 'Though I suppose she had taste of a kind.'

'And I don't have?' Disa said. She did not sound offended, only mildly surprised. 'Everyone says I dress well.'

'Oh, you do. But *decor* isn't one of your things, is it?'

'Decor?' She shrugged. 'The stuff here's all right, isn't it? It cost a lot. I gave a list of everything I needed to the best shop in Athens, and they shipped it out.'

'And that's exactly how it looks,' he said, but his smile was amiable. He added, raising a hand and running it over the bedhead, 'This bed is really the only individual piece of furniture in the house.'

'Yes, I saw this woodworker guy's stuff and I kind of liked it. All twining, like snakes. Or like thin people's legs and arms, sort of mixed up together.' She laughed.

'It's a remarkable bed. And these dark-red sheets suit it. I've never seen dark-red sheets before.'

'They're okay,' she said. 'Black's so ordinary, and I can't stand white or those insipid pastels. Anyhow, I really don't care a fuck about all that. I think fussing about furniture's just showing off.' She added, calmly, 'I don't need to do that.'

He said, 'You know, Miss Dis, I simply adore your arrogance. It's so total.'

Often, lying in her bed, they drank wine.

Next to the kitchen was a huge windowless room filled with rows of racks of French, German and Italian vintages. 'Opulent indeed! You've certainly got good taste in wine,' Rupert said.

She shrugged. 'Oh, I don't know that much about it. This lot certainly cost a bit. I had some old guy who runs a wine society order it and stack it, and set the thermostat to the right temperature and all that stuff. People say he's an expert.'

'People are right.'

Disa drank white wines, usually champagne. 'I like it too,' Rupert said. 'But not every night. Especially when there's such a range of amazing reds.'

She gave her customary shrug. 'Open two bottles, then. Choose a bottle of whatever you feel like. You don't have to finish it. There's plenty more.'

'It's a shame you've got no halves.'

'There's something petty about half bottles.'

He laughed. 'If you're not careful, I'll turn into a drunk, like Sarah, my first wife.'

Disa surveyed him. 'I've known a lot of alkies. You're not the type.'

'How are you so certain?'

'Oh, they're all kind of shy – even the noisy ones. There's nothing shy about you.' She laughed. 'And alkies really don't care what they drink – although they sometimes pretend to. No alky would be so serious about which bottle to open – or keep it waiting till it's just the right heat. Anyhow, you're too cautious to be a drunk.'

'Cautious?' His tone expressed distaste for the word.

'Oh, yes. Cautious, cagey, careful.'

After a moment he said, 'Well, it's nice to be able to be so careful about what I drink.'

He took the wines more seriously than she did, but was more flippant about some of the videos she put on. Ludicrous scenarios and inept, though usually minimal, dialogue made him laugh.

'You don't need to bother about that stuff,' she once said irritably. 'It's what they *do* that counts.'

'But that "stuff" makes it so unconvincing.'

When a film was particularly crass, he pressed the fast-forward button. Once, he played a tape in reverse; Disa's laugh was reluctant. She said, 'You should take sex more seriously.'

'I do take it seriously. That's why I have to joke when it's made ridiculous. Otherwise, I'd get quite angry. Oh, I certainly take sex seriously. Don't I?'

'Oh, I guess so.' Then she said, 'You really only like the heavy videos, don't you?'

'Heavy?' He smiled.

'Yeah, heavy . . . dark, you know. I don't think I could find anything too dark for you.'

'Try me and see.'

She became more selective, but he switched off one of her first choices: 'I draw the line at dogs.'

'What's wrong with dogs? Why, once when I was partying—'

He cut her off: 'I don't want to hear.'

But during other videos, sometimes made in black and white – and sometimes seeming to be so, even when filmed in colour – she saw how his glass, from which he usually sipped as he watched, would stand, ignored, on the bedside table, and his brilliant cyanotic eyes under half-lowered lids would blur while his lips – Lucy's mother had described his mouth as 'petulant', though Lucy's word for it was 'sensitive' – would seem to swell.

The word 'opulent', uttered with an approving smile, was often on his lips. Yet there came an evening when he asked, 'Got any spaghetti?'

'Spaghetti? I don't think so. It doesn't freeze well.'

He laughed. 'I meant in a packet. I could cook it.'

'You can cook?'

'Well, I can cook spaghetti. With a simple tomato sauce. Or just with salt and freshly ground black pepper and plenty of butter and grated cheese?'

'Wow! You're a real cholesterol freak!'

Ignoring this, he said, 'I'm in the mood for Colonel Al Dente tonight.'

'Colonel Al Dente – who the fuck's he?'

'He likes to be called "Colonel" but actually he's a mafioso.'

'One of the mob? I know plenty of them – but not him. Al Dente – what a weird name! That's the way to cook pasta . . . just firm enough to bite.' She snapped her white teeth together.

'That's right. That's the joke. He's not a real person – just a character I invented.' But, seeing that blank look of hers, he said, 'Forget it!' Then, 'And with the spaghetti a rather rough Chianti.'

She said, 'I don't think I've got any like that.'

'What do *they* eat – Marios and Sophia?'

She shrugged. 'Oh . . . Greek stuff. He stocks up on the mainland – they've got their own freezer for those great chunks of lamb they like to barbecue, and they keep chickens and she grows veggies. I think they drink that awful retsina. I suppose they might have some macaroni. They eat it on Sundays before the meat. They make it into a sort of solid cake.'

'Sounds disgusting.'

'You could go down and ask them.' She laughed. 'But Karl may be on the loose by now.'

'Forget it!' he said again.

There was a silence. When she broke it, her tone was bright. 'There's some cannelloni – that freezes okay. It's good. And lots of Iti wine of course – even Chianti, I think. Though I'm not sure if there's a really *rough* one.'

At this, they both laughed. He said, 'It was just a whim. We all have them.'

'Oh, don't we just!'

They ate cannelloni. She had a glass of dry, sparkling Bianchetto Frizzante and he opened a bottle of 1937 Brolio Chianti. Afterwards she drank espresso from her big hissing machine, and he finished the Chianti. He was drinking faster than usual.

'An excellent meal,' he said.

'Yeah – it was okay. Sure you don't want a coffee?'

'Quite sure. But I might have a glass of that Bianchetto of yours.'

'Sure. I don't want any more myself.' She laughed. 'Perhaps you *are* becoming an alky.'

'No, I'm just in a drinking mood this evening. Another whim, you know!'

'Indulge it! And how about a video?'

He said, 'Have you got any *other* films?' Then, 'Suddenly I long for *Elvira Madigan*.'

'Who the hell's she? Some old movie star?'

'No, it's a film. But it's quite an old one. I first saw it in my twenties – don't say it!'

'Say what?'

'"It must be old."'

She laughed. 'I wasn't going to.'

'I saw it again in London, at the Hampstead Everyman, a couple of years ago. I took a girl to it. She loved it too. She cried. It's Swedish. It's about this army officer who runs away with a circus girl. She was tremendously beautiful, with wonderful hair. They go to live in the forest. It's very romantic – lovely photography . . . I remember some butterflies. In the end they commit suicide.'

'And this girl of yours cried? Sounds like a great evening's entertainment. No, I'm afraid Elvira Whatzit isn't in stock here. But I've got a film I've been saving. You'll really enjoy it. It's quite a collector's item. Come into my room. We'll be more comfortable there.'

He brought the bottle of Bianchetto with him. While she took a shower, he drank another glassful, reclining against the dark-red pillows and staring up at the low ceiling which, though the walls were matt white and the floor white marble, was painted shiny black. When she returned, in a heavy satin robe of her favourite beige, she had the video cassette in her hand.

'So – entertain me,' he said, refilling his glass.

Raising her eyebrows, she said, 'I'll do my best.' Then she said, 'It's a real genuine snuff movie. You've heard of a snuff movie?'

He paused. Then, 'Oh yes,' he said. 'One where the victim actually dies. People used to talk about them a lot back in the sixties, but I never met anyone who'd actually seen or owned one. Anyway, I believe they were mostly fakes.'

'Well, this one isn't.' She added, 'It was expensive. There were only three copies made, and this is the original. It's the real thing all right. You can tell.' She put it on, and came to lie beside him.

During the film – it lasted about forty minutes – he was silent, but when it ended, he said, 'Yes – you can tell. Oh yes. At first she was just a zombie, going through the motions – she was rather like that girl at your table the first time we met. She was so drugged that she hardly seemed aware of what was happening – but then it started to get through to her. You could see it. But she still didn't know what was coming. She still thought it was just a nasty day's work, even when that man in the mask and the leather gauntlets put his hands round her throat. But then, when the other one touched her with the knife – then she knew. There was that look of shock. Before that, she had no idea.'

Disa laughed. 'Well, of course not. She'd never have taken the job, would she, if she'd known she was going to die? I'm sure she wasn't planning to commit *suicide* – like your dumb Swedes in the wood with the *butterflies*.' Then she said, 'Well, I've opened up your little world a bit, haven't I? I bet you've never seen anything like *that* before.'

'Not exactly.' He poured himself another glass of wine.

'Not exactly.' She mimicked his tone. Then she said, 'You're really hitting that bottle, aren't you? You know . . . I think seeing the real thing *unnerved* you.'

'*Unnerved* me?' He sat up. He drained his glass in one swallow, and put it down.

He snatched one of the red pillows that were heaped against the serpentine entanglements of the bedhead. Swinging across, in a sudden violent movement, he pressed the pillow over Disa's face, pushed down with fingers spread, and then – she had not even time to struggle – let go, thrust away the pillow, was on top of her, then inside her: savage, urgent, staring down all the time into her clouded, rusty eyes.

Afterwards, they lay side by side, not touching. His eyes were closed, though there was a little pulse in the lids; hers were open, but for once their restless movement was allayed.

It was she who moved first. Raising herself on her right elbow, she ran the forefinger of her left hand down from his forehead to his chin. Then she said, in a soft, reflective tone, 'Sometimes the simple things are still the best.' Leaning over, she licked his cheek once, with the tip of her tongue. He opened his eyes. He smiled, and then so did she, as she lay back against the pillows.

They were silent again till he said, 'I seldom feel so peaceful.'

'Peaceful . . .' She said the word as if examining an unfamiliar object. 'Peaceful. Yes, it's strange. I guess I kind of feel that too.'

He said, 'Weren't you just a bit afraid.'

'Afraid?' She laughed. 'I've often told you I like living on the edge.'

He stretched and smiled. He said, 'You know, you really are the coolest person I've ever met.'

She smiled. 'Cooler than that Chris you were married to?'

He laughed. 'Well, actually not in one way. Chris was frigid.'

She said, with another smile – her white arc of teeth was very prominent – 'You mean you couldn't turn her on?'

'No one could have.'

She slightly raised her eyebrows. Something stirred in her eyes. She said, 'I bet I could have.'

'I don't think so.' A moment passed. Then he said, 'I once made a video cassette of her that would have amused you.'

'Amused me? I thought you said she was frigid.'

He smiled. 'That was rather the point.'

'Oh?' Then she said, 'It's a pity you haven't got it here.' This was a statement not a question.

He said, 'How do you know I haven't?' and then, 'So you've been through my things.'

'Once a guy brought a gun here – there was a bit of trouble. Since then I always look at people's stuff.'

'I see.'

'You didn't have anything interesting – except that long blonde braid. Are you kinky for hair? Would you like me to wear it? I could fasten it on.'

'No.' He stiffened. 'Absolutely not.'

She raised her eyebrows again. 'Come on!' she said. 'Why are you so uptight all of a sudden? Loosen up!' and then, 'Well, tell me about that cassette of Chris. Can't you get hold of it?'

There was a moment's pause. Then he said, 'It was stolen.'

'Stolen? Who by?'

'A bitch,' he said. 'A bloody American bitch! Excuse me! But she was a Yank of the worst kind. A self-righteous women's libber.'

'I know the type. Anyway I'm not patriotic – what a load of crap! But why would she have wanted it?'

He said, 'To blackmail me.'

'Blackmail you? Come on – do tell me.' Her eyes were moving. She was smiling. She ran her hand up from his knees to his waist in a rippling movement.

'Ah!'

She took her hand away. 'Now come on – do!'

He sighed. Then he said, 'Vee, this American woman—'

She broke in, 'What an odd name!'

'She'd changed it from Veronica, but let's not go into that.'

'No don't let's. It sounds dull. I'm sorry I interrupted. Go on.'

'Vee was best friends with this Roman Catholic girl I was going to marry. I told you I nearly became a Catholic.'

'Even though you don't believe in God.'

'That's right. This Catholic girl—'

'What was *her* name?'

He paused. Then he said, 'Her name is Lucy.'

A moment passed. Then Disa said, 'Well? Go on.'

'She – Lucy – was pregnant. I told you that I've probably got a third child by now.'

'And that's why you were going to marry her? What a gallant English gentleman!' Disa's laugh was mocking. 'A fourth marriage! Some people never learn.'

He made no comment on this. He said, 'Vee hated me on sight. It was mutual. So she started digging, and she found the cassette.'

'You'd *buried* it?'

Now he laughed. 'Not literally. It was in a cupboard in my flat, and she stole it.'

'You must have been very careless to let her do that.'

'I was away. Vee told me she broke in. But I don't believe that. There was this woman who lived upstairs and kept a spare key for me. When I packed up and left the place, she told me that a girl had come there with a young man who said he was my son.'

'Your son?' Disa said.

'Yes. He told her I'd asked him to borrow the spare key and fetch something from my flat. She said she believed him, and gave him the key because he looked so like me.'

'Another dazzling Deyntree?'

Rupert shrugged. 'I haven't seen him since he was a child. Vee told me she'd left the tape with a friend, and I believed her. If she'd hung onto it herself, she would have been afraid I'd track her down, and take it back. Perhaps the "friend" *was* my son. Probably, if she was investigating my past, Vee could have found him. He lives with his mother – the drunk – in Suffolk. And I'm sure he detests me.'

Disa said, 'But why was this Vee investigating your past?'

After a moment he said, 'So that she could stop my marriage. She told me that if I didn't break off the engagement she'd show the tape to Lucy.'

'And you didn't think this Lucy would approve of it?'

'Approve of it! It would have shattered her. I could never have let her see it. Lucy's good. She's innocent—'

Disa interrupted him with a particularly raucous version of her laugh: a double caw. 'Oh – bring on the violins! You'll be telling me next that you *lurved* her! So you broke off the engagement – that must have been quite a touching scene.'

'There was no scene,' he said coldly. 'Touching or otherwise.' Rupert paused. 'Then he said, "*He travelled.*"'

'Oh, don't give me that Frog crap about tents and friends again.' But she was smiling. She said, 'So what you did was run away without saying a word to that sweet innocent little Lucy?' Disa laughed again. 'I'd never have guessed you were such a coward.'

'You should be more careful what you say.' Rupert spoke softly, but his eyes glittered and his face was pale.

'Okay, okay. Perhaps you're not cowardly after all, just ruthless – that's much more attractive, of course.' Then she said, 'Why was this Vee so keen to stop you marrying Lucy?'

'Oh, I think the answer to that's quite simple. The bitch loves her. Actually, they love each other.'

'They're dykes?'

'Absolutely *not*!'

'Okay, okay. Sorry – I forgot about Lucy being so *innocent*.'

She laughed. 'Innocent indeed!' she said, then, 'They say children are *innocent*.' She laughed again. Then she said, 'I was a child. An only child. Only children are meant to be spoilt, aren't they? I guess you could say my father spoilt me, when he had the time . . . when he wasn't busy making money. I must have been six or seven when he started. Child abuse, they call it. I don't.'

'You liked it?' He raised his eyebrows.

'*Liked* it? I don't know about *that*.' She laughed.

'You were afraid to tell anyone.'

'Afraid? No, I wasn't afraid. And who would I have told? The servants?'

'Your mother?'

'*Her*? No way! Anyway, I always felt she knew. Once – I'm almost sure, but I was so young . . . it's hard to remember – I saw her standing in a doorway, when he was at me. Over his shoulder – I'm sure I saw her there. But then – a moment later – she was gone. Back to the piano, I suppose – to her Chopin. Or to talk about culture – she was a so-called patron of the arts. Opera and all that shit.'

'I'm rather fond of opera.'

'Well, don't expect me to tag along with you. To *Cosi fan fucking tutte*.'

He laughed. 'I prefer Wagner.'

'Wagner! I don't remember her liking him. Too heavy. She liked things to be pretty. So you can see why she didn't want to know about me and him. Any more than she wanted to know about some of his business connections. She had this pretty life . . . and his money to spend – she wouldn't have wanted anything to upset that.'

'Poor old Disa!' He put his hand on her arm.

She shook it off. 'Don't call me "poor old Disa". It sounds like some dog, some old bitch that's got to be put down.'

'I'm sorry. I didn't mean it to sound like that. Especially as I loathe dogs.'

She laughed. 'I guessed that already – from your reaction to Karl. Anyhow, I'm not *poor*. I never was. I had power. We had this secret and I knew it made me powerful. He gave me anything I wanted – always. I was the one in control.'

'So what happened?'

'Happened? I grew up.' This time her laugh grated. 'My father died when I was thirteen. He was killed in a car accident – though perhaps it wasn't an accident; it could have been fixed by one of his enemies – and my mother started sending me to all these schools. They couldn't control me. Nor could she. I was due to get my money when I was eighteen. But when I was sixteen my mother wanted to put some kind of restraining order on me. I was doing a lot of drugs then and I mixed with a lot of "undesirables", as she called them. So I got married.'

'Didn't she try to stop you?'

'Not a chance! I picked out a really respectable guy. Jack was rich, though not as rich as me, of course – he ran a big company of my father's: one of the respectable ones started with laundered money. I don't think Jack knew where the money came from – my father probably wanted it that way. Oh, perhaps old Jack guessed . . . but I'm sure he never admitted it, even to himself. That figures. A Harvard hypocrite! He was forty and a widower. A widower! Doesn't that sound boring? Well, he *was* boring! But my mother was thrilled. She thought I'd settle down at last – and, better still, I was off her hands. When I was seventeen I had this *baby*. I didn't want it, of course, but Jack was thrilled, and I played along. Biding my time, as they say. It was six months old on my eighteenth birthday. A week after that, I was gone. I've never seen Jack since. Or my mother. The lawyers handled the divorce and custody stuff.

'You said you hadn't got a child.'

'I haven't now . . . She died.'

'Died?

'Yeah, well, I tried to kidnap her. Those mob connections of my father's were my pals: still are. Sort of family. I can always count on them.'

'I see. Go on.'

'Well . . .' She broke off. 'Little Louise! What a corny name! She was called after Jack's mother. He wanted to give her Mary as a second name – after my mother – but I drew the line there. I wasn't giving *her* the satisfaction of calling the brat after her. After I took off, I didn't think about Louise for years. Anyhow I couldn't go back to the States.'

'You couldn't? Why?'

'Oh, there was some charge . . . corrupting a minor, they called it. A guy I was with went to jail – he was killed there by another prisoner a few years ago. But my lawyers still haven't sorted it out for me.'

'Corrupting a minor? A hereditory predilection?'

'What?'

'I mean – you take after your father?'

She blinked. Then she said, 'Actually you could be right.' She laughed, then frowned.

'Go on about your daughter. I'm fascinated.'

'Oh well, time passed, you know. Then, when she was fifteen, someone told me how they were all so *close*: Jack and Granny and Louise. Such a smug little family. It made me angry. I wanted to tell her a few things about her beloved Granny. How *caring* she really was. *Caring* – yuk!'

'Yes, I've always thought it was an awful word. It conjures up interfering little social workers with spots and spectacles.'

Disa ignored this, and went on: 'I thought it would be fun to tell Louise the truth. Anyhow, I felt it was about time she learnt about real life. I thought I'd get her brought here by those friends of mine. But they were careless – she threw herself overboard from the boat. I've often wondered if those guys got carried away and broke her in. That would have made me so angry. I wanted her "innocent", as you call it, when she got here. But they swore there'd been nothing like that.' She shrugged. 'Anyway, I wasn't going to quarrel with them about it – spilt milk, you know, and I'm sure to want other favours from those guys sooner or later.'

Rupert was silent for a moment. Then he said, 'What happened?'

'She drowned.'

'I gathered that. I mean back in the States. About the kidnapping.'

'Oh – an unsolved mystery right up to this moment in time. According to the press, the police decided it was a ransom kidnapping that had gone wrong'.

'Quite a story.'

'Yeah.' Then she said, 'So, Mr Cagey, now it's your turn to talk. What about *your* parents? Tell me about *them*.'

'Tell you what?'

'I talked – now it's your turn, like I said. Tell me about them. Unless they were too dull. Was your mother a stupid bitch like mine?'

His tone was chill: 'She most certainly was not. She was very beautiful and very good.' He added, 'She had this wonderful long blonde hair. I used to brush it for her.'

'And you cut it off when she died?'

He looked horrified. 'Good heavens, no.'

'Oh, I just thought that braid might have been hers.' She laughed. 'The shrinks call it an Oedipus complex, don't they?'

He said, 'I attach no credence whatsoever to Freud's theories.'

'Wow! There goes Mr Teach again! Well, what about your father? Very handsome and very good, I guess.' She laughed.

'Wrong again! Oh, perhaps he was handsome. In a military sort of way. Iron-grey hair, well-kept grey moustache. He needed that moustache to cover up the weakness of his mouth, but the lines at the corners gave it away.' Rupert said now, with unusual vehemence: 'What a swine!'

'That's more like it. But what's all this grey stuff? He was old?'

'He left my wonderful mother when I was five. Just after the war. I didn't see him again till I was seventeen. He was old then.'

'You were five – just after the war. You must be more than forty-nine . . . like you said you were.' She laughed. 'Actually, I knew that already. When I looked at your passport I saw you were fifty-one.'

His eyes glittered. 'What a thorough little lady!' But then he smiled: 'As a matter of fact, I've always felt there's something fearfully boring about reaching fifty. When I left England, I decided to stick in the forties for a year or two.'

'Okay. Why not? Go on about your father. Why did he leave your mother . . . so good, so beautiful?' Then she laughed. 'You look great when you're angry. Most people turn red and ugly. You just get a little paler, and those bright eyes of yours flash like lightning. Why did he leave her?'

'For another woman. A German. He married her. He gave up his career in the army, and went to farm in Kenya. When my mother died, I went out there. He insisted. He made it a condition of paying for me to go to Oxford. I spent nearly a year there.'

'With him and his lady? What was *she* like?'

'Ilse? She was extraordinary.' After he had said this, he relaxed. He rested his chin on his hand, with a reminiscent look. Then he said, 'She initiated me.'

'Introduced you to fucking, you mean?'

'Yes. How elegantly you put it! After she found out I'd been watching her and my father.'

'Watching them doing it?'

'I suppose you could say that. But she was responsible for most of the doing. He was pretty passive.'

'And you were the young voyeur?'

'The young voyeur – now that *is* elegant! Yes, I was just that – the young voyeur. And Ilse saw me. He didn't – he was lying with his eyes closed, groaning.'

'In ecstasy?'

'I suppose you could call it that. He was a masochist.'

'And she was a sadist.'

'A professional one, actually.' He paused. Then he said, 'She'd been a guard in a concentration camp. At Belsen. He protected her, hid her, got her out of Germany and later to Kenya.'

For a moment Disa said nothing, and then, 'She *told* you that.'

'No, I found a photograph and some documents. A record he'd written of the whole history. It was in a drawer in his desk. I discovered it after he died. She didn't know about it.'

'He died? While you were staying there?'

'Yes, he caught Ilse and me. *In flagrante delicto*. Evidently *he* wasn't a voyeur – he had a massive coronary, and died at once.'

'Wow!' she said. 'That's quite a story.'

'So I've impressed you at last.'

'Perhaps . . . a bit. But what happened then – after he died?'

'I told you I found those things. It was lucky I did. She inherited everything, and she'd never have given me the money for Oxford. It was quite a shock, finding them. I felt quite strange. But then I pulled myself together – enough to use them.' He laughed.

Now Disa laughed, too: 'That's my boy!'

He said, 'I've often wondered why he kept those things. Whether he was afraid of her and wanted to have something in reserve he could use against her. Or whether he just liked the stuff. Perhaps he took it out and looked at it from time to time. Perhaps it turned him on.'

'Did it turn *you* on?'

He said, as if he hadn't heard the question, 'I got the money I needed, and went back to England. That was two months before I went up to Oxford.'

'Did you take that stuff about her with you?'

He said, 'No. I handed it over in exchange for the money.'

'What happened to her?'

'Ilse? Heaven knows! As you can imagine, we didn't keep in touch. She probably went on running the farm. I just took what was in the bank.'

'I'm surprised she didn't try to get rid of you. Such a tough lady!'

'She might well have. But when I found the stuff, I deposited it at a lawyer's office in the nearby town, with instructions that if anything happened to me, they should open it. I didn't tell her I'd found it till I'd done that.'

'You were certainly clued up! And only seventeen!'

'Eighteen. My birthday was a week before he died. She baked a cake. It was called an *igelkuchen*. That means a hedgehog cake. It had almonds stuck all over it. And he opened a bottle of champagne.'

'A real family occasion!'

'Yes.' Now they both laughed.

She broke the silence that followed. 'Was she as good as me?'

'Ilse? As *good*?'

'In the sack'.

He said, 'I was young. It was different.'

'You'll be saying *you* were innocent next. You certainly developed fast. Voyeur, fucker of your father's mistress, black-

80

mailer.' Then she said, 'I'm surprised you let that Vee blackmail you.'

He poured the last of the Bianchetto into his glass. 'What else could I do?'

She laughed 'Did you ever think of killing her?'

'I must admit it crossed my mind.' He smiled. Then he said, 'But I don't kill people. Anyway, I'm a practical fellow. It wouldn't have achieved anything. I told you I believed her when she said she'd left the tape with a friend.' He paused. 'My son, perhaps, though I didn't have any idea of that when I saw her.' He paused again. 'But I must admit that, when I realized, in the dreary little café where we met, that she'd won, I felt . . . well, almost possessed – yes, that's the only word. I stood up, and as I left this dog started barking and pulling on its lead. It was strange.' He laughed. 'Lucy once told me that, when she was a child, some maid of theirs said that when dogs barked for no reason it was because the Evil One was passing by.'

'The Evil One!' Disa exclaimed. 'Wow! So you think you were possessed by the Devil?'

He laughed. 'No, of course not. It just crossed my mind. I don't believe in that sort of thing.'

'So why are you so keen on that picture of yours: *The Evil Angel*?'

He corrected her: '*The Good and Evil Angels*.'

'I told you – the good one's silly. It doesn't count.'

'Anyway, I like that picture for aesthetic reasons.'

'Aesthetic!' Again her tone was mocking.

'Do you prefer the word artistic? Anyway I certainly don't like it because I believe in the Devil.' He laughed. 'As I told you, I'm a practical fellow.'

'So, instead of dealing with this Vee, you left the country?'

'Yes. I packed up. I stored my things. I sold my car. I closed my bank account and made other financial arrangements.'

'And then – don't say it! – "He travelled". You travelled till you met me.'

'Till I met you. Till you kidnapped me, and carried me off to your opulent lair.'

'That's right.' She laughed. Then she said, 'But why did you travel?'

He said, 'Oh, just another of those whims of mine, you know. I felt I needed a change.'

'Hmm. It seems weird to me.' She was silent. Then she said, 'Was it that sweet innocent Lucy who cried at that Elvira movie? Come on – surely you can tell me that?'

After a moment, he shrugged and said, 'Yes, it was. Though I can't think why you should be interested.'

'Oh, but I am. I'm interested in all sorts of things. I'm interested in that tape. It must be quite something. And now you have to tell me all about it.'

He smiled. 'You're wrong. I don't have to. I'm tired of talking. In fact, my dear Miss Dis, I'm going to leave the tape to your fertile imagination. I'm sure you can brew up something far more *amusing* than anything I could tell you.'

Glittering blue eyes encountered cloudy brown. It was she who, smiling, looked away. 'I see,' she said. Then, 'Okay, Mr Cagey, you win.'

His laugh held a note of triumph. 'Winner takes all,' he said. This time he turned her over on her face. With arms out-stretched, she twined her fingers round the wooden coils of the bedhead. Her eyes were narrowed now: there was only a glimpse of their opacity; her lips were almost closed: there was a mere glint of teeth.

PART TWO

ONE

'I was wrong,' James said. 'When you rang last month to tell me that you were going to take the job in London, I thought I couldn't be happier. But now you're here, it's better . . . far, far better, darling Vee.'

'I feel the same.' She squeezed his hand. 'Oh, it's all so exciting . . . and yet it's sort of peaceful, too, now everything's sorted out – except the apartment, of course. And I'm sure we'll settle that tomorrow.'

Once she had decided, in the middle of June, to take the job running Greg Marshall's London office, Vee had moved into action with habitual verve. By the end of the month she had leased her Hollywood apartment, and shipped her rugs, pictures, stereo and other personal things to storage in England until she found a London flat. With Greg's help, she had obtained a temporary work permit.

'Three months – to organize the new set-up,' she had told James on the telephone.

'Only three months!' he had exclaimed.

'Oh, I'm sure it can be fixed once I'm in London. Otherwise I wouldn't have leased my apartment.' She laughed. 'My Higher Power will organize it.'

'Or *we* could organize it – we could get married.'

'You're so sweet.'

'I'm persistent.'

She laughed. 'Yes, but sweet, too.' Then she said, 'I start work in August. But I thought I'd come a bit early, and spend some time in Suffolk. Will that be okay?'

'Okay?' he said. 'It'll be marvellous.'

Now, at the end of July, she had been there two weeks. This morning she and James were sitting on the lawn on a rug laid

85

down at Sarah's insistence – 'The grass may *seem* dry, but I'm sure it's damp' – surrounded by estate agents' print-outs of flats to let in North London; this was the area with which – apart from the West End – Vee was most familiar. A blackbird perched on a branch of the apple tree that grew in the middle of the lawn; bees hummed round the flower-beds that edged the path, and a white butterfly hovered over a clump of catmint.

'I just love butterflies,' Vee said. 'They're so delicate and airy.'

'Yes.' James sighed. 'But Mum remembers when they were all sorts of different colours. Red admirals and tortoiseshells and painted ladies. Now you hardly ever see any but the white ones. Destroying the hedgerows plus so-called "pesticides" have killed off almost all the others.'

'That's so sad,' Vee said. 'All the same, the white ones are pretty.'

'Mmm. You really think you'll find a flat *tomorrow*?'

She nodded vigorously. 'Sure – I feel it in my bones. With your assistance, of course. You've got to like the place, too – you're going to see a lot of it.'

'Yes, I am, aren't I?' He smiled.

'Oh James, I love the way you smile.'

'Then I'll smile a lot! In fact, I'll wear a permanent grin.' He produced an inanely wide one, and they both laughed. Then, looking down at the print-out in his hand, he said, 'All these places seem terribly expensive.'

'Yes, London's a really expensive city.' But her shrug was carefree. 'Of course Hampstead's prohibitive. Pity! It would have been nice to be near Lucy. Islington's not *quite* as expensive, and I rather like it – as long as I don't run into Chris Deyntree.'

He said, 'No, I can imagine you wouldn't want to do that.'

'I bet she still hates me. I felt sorry for her – but she's an awful woman.' Vee sighed. Then she said, 'I rather go for the description of this place in Noel Road. First floor – we call that the second floor, in the States, of course – and overlooking the canal. That sounds fun. Two bedrooms – so Sarah could come up and stay. A couple of minutes' walk from the Angel tube – "Angel"! That's such a great name for a subway station. And the Camden antique market just round the corner, to stroll through on Saturday morning. Yes, I feel Noel Road is the one . . . though of course we'll look at other places, too. And after we've fixed something up, we'll have our celebration . . . and come back here quite early next morning so that poor old Mansfield's not alone too long. Are you sure he'll be all right?'

'Of course he will. He's quite safe in the garden, with the gate shut. And he's got his kennel. Admittedly he usually sleeps on Mum's bed and only goes in there when we're out and it's raining. But it's quite cosy.'

'Poor Mansfield! I wouldn't like to sleep in a kennel.'

'Well, you won't ever have to, I promise.' Vee giggled, and James went on, 'Really he'll be all right. Though I must say he's been a bit restless lately. And all that barking last night – he doesn't usually bark like that.'

'Bizarre! Perhaps he senses we're going away,' Vee said, but James laughed.

Sarah was coming with them, despite initial demurs. While Vee and James were flat-hunting, she was going to shop and visit the National Gallery. In the evening, despite further demurs, in which James participated, Vee had persuaded them to be her guests at dinner and for the night at a hotel. 'An hotel!' Sarah had exclaimed. 'I haven't stayed at an hotel for years. Terribly extravagant.'

'I've told you before that you guys' – Sarah smiled as she always did when Vee addressed her and James in this manner – 'are going to have to check out my lifestyle. And we're celebrating my new job. Where shall it be – the Mayfair?' But she had yielded to their cries of outrage: 'Well, then, the Halcyon?' They did not know it. 'Or where?'

After a moment, Sarah had said tentatively, 'How about the Basil? Of course that's expensive, too, but not quite so outrageous.' She added, 'We used to stay there when I was a child.'

'The Basil Street Hotel? That's one of Lucy's mother's haunts. I hope we don't run into *her*.'

'Oh, well, of course we can go somewhere else.'

'No – what nonsense! She hardly ever comes up to London nowadays. Poor Lucy – it quite upsets her that her mother never wants to see little Edward. The Basil it shall be!' Immediately, Vee had gone to the telephone and booked two rooms, a double and a single.

'They won't mind?' Sarah asked her afterwards in a slightly anxious tone. 'You and James sharing a room, I mean.'

Vee's expression, for a moment, was puzzled. Then she said, 'Oh, because we're not married? Dear Sarah, of course they won't. Things have changed – even at the Basil Street Hotel.'

Now, on the lawn, gathering up the print-outs, Vee said to James, 'Just as soon as I'm settled, I'm going to tackle Lucy.'

'Tackle her?' He smiled. 'That sounds quite aggressive.'

'Oh, I won't be aggressive. But I'll tell her about you and me. And I'll make her accept it. She'll have to, when she realizes how important you are to me. And, once she meets you, I know she'll like you.' Vee paused. 'Of course, how much you look like *him* may be a bit of a shock at first.'

'Not nearly as handsome,' James said. Although his tone was light, his face took on its remote look.

'I'm sorry. I know you hate talking about him. But anyhow I think you're far more handsome than he is.'

James smiled, though faintly. 'You're biased.'

'No I'm not. I don't like that sulky mouth of his or those eyes that people say are so amazing – I think they're weird. And he's got a kind of jaded look. Your face is so sensitive. It's so *fine*.'

James laughed. 'Oh, yes, I'm a very fine fellow! A very fine fellow indeed!'

Vee laughed too, but then she said, 'I *mean* it.' She half rose, and he followed her example, but, kneeling on the rug facing each other, they paused to kiss. They were interrupted by whines and barks. Mansfield was scratching at the fence that separated the back of the garden from a small patch of woodland. Then he gave three loud barks.

'Mansfield!' But James had to repeat the call, before Mansfield came to join them.

Stroking his fringe, Vee said 'Mansfield, what's the matter?' He gave a small whimper, but then wagged his tail. She said, 'I really think he knows we're going away.'

James said, '*I* think there's a fox or some other animal prowling about.'

'It couldn't get in and attack him?'

'No – Vee darling, it's quite obvious you aren't a country girl.' James put his arm round her shoulder and they moved towards the cottage, Mansfield lagging behind.

He barked once that night, but when Sarah, woken from a deep sleep, reproached him, he curled up again at her feet and was silent thereafter. In the morning, he was delighted to receive his midday dinner at breakfast time. Sarah left biscuits and a large bowl of water by his kennel. When, carrying light overnight luggage, they left, and James had closed the gate, Mansfield stood on the path with his tail between his legs.

'He looks so reproachful,' Sarah said.

'Yes,' Vee agreed. 'It's a shame we have to leave him behind.'

'Mansfield in London!' exclaimed James. 'What a nightmare for everyone concerned!' He started the car.

Vee's instinct was proved correct: she and James looked at three flats in Islington; the one in Noel Road was the most attractive and convenient. Its furnishings were modern and impersonal but Vee said, 'Better no taste than bad taste, I guess. Anyhow, when I've got my bits and pieces in, it'll be just fine.'

They looked down from the back window of the sitting room, and she said, 'A *canal*! That's so romantic!'

'Apart from those municipal rubbish-bins.'

She laughed. 'Oh well – better than litter!'

Vee had signed the lease by mid-afternoon. They met Sarah for tea at the Basil. She was amazed by how little it had changed. 'There's a bar now, but otherwise it's just the same. The same oriental vases. Even the stone Buddha's still here.' Sarah ran a hand over its smooth dark head. 'I used to do this as a child,' she said, and then, 'Even the people look the same. What one used to call ladies and gentlemen.' When James frowned at this, Sarah only laughed.

After tea, they went to their rooms: Sarah to rest and Vee and James to make love. The muted roar of the Knightsbridge traffic brought a pleasing sense of London, vast and vibrant, just beyond the dim cool bedrooms of the calm hotel.

There had been much discussion in the car that morning of where they should have dinner. Vee had suggested various elegant restaurants when Sarah said suddenly, 'Oh, couldn't we have curry? I hardly ever do, and I so adore it. Ever since I first tasted it at Oxford in a rather scruffy place called the Taj Mahal. I've bought a book on Indian cookery, but I haven't really got round to it yet.'

'Curry!' Vee exclaimed. 'That's what Lucy and I always have. We both love it. How about you, James?'

'Oh yes,' he said.

Curry was agreed on. However, Vee was determined that this meal should be something out of the ordinary. Firmly rejecting the flock-wallpapered places that she and Lucy frequented, she took them to the Bombay Brasserie. But, as they got out of the taxi, a shadow crossed her face. 'What's the matter?' James murmured.

'We just passed that café, where I met *him*.'

'And his flat was just near here, wasn't it?'

'What are you two whispering about?' Sarah asked.

'Oh nothing,' Vee said. A moment later, they were inside the restaurant with its fantastic domed spaces and deliciously subtle food.

'Well, I'm completely converted, 'James said halfway through the meal.

'Converted?' said Vee.

'Yes, I wasn't quite such a fan of Indian food as you two – until now.'

'But why didn't you say so?'

He shrugged. 'I said "until now". This food is simply marvellous.'

Vee said, 'Your trouble, James, is that you're too unselfish.' When she added, 'It has to stop,' they all burst out laughing.

At breakfast next morning in the hotel, James had his customary muesli and Sarah a croissant, but Vee ate a full English breakfast. 'A big dinner always makes me hungry next morning,' she announced.

Conversation was cheerful on the journey home. 'I'm dying to see Mansfield,' Vee said just before they entered the village. Then she said to Sarah, 'I'm afraid I'm a bit possessive about your dog. I guess it's because I chose him for you, with James, when he was just a pup.'

'The nicest present I've ever had,' Sarah said, and then, 'I'm delighted you're so fond of him.' She added, 'I can't imagine anyone not being.'

'The gate's open,' James said, as they reached the cottage.

'Oh!' Sarah exclaimed.

Mansfield did not come hurrying to meet them, as he always did when he heard the car. As soon as it stopped, Sarah and Vee, followed by James, jumped out and hurried up the path. 'Mansfield! Mansfield!' they shouted loudly; the only reply was the monotonous call of a cuckoo in the woodland.

James said, 'Who could have opened the gate? Everyone in the village knows Mansfield – and how much he dislikes callers.'

Sarah and Vee went round to the back of the house, still calling, 'Mansfield, Mansfield.' But his half-full water bowl and his plate, on which lay a single biscuit, stood beside his empty kennel.

James unlocked the front door and went into the small, silent house; there was the faint smell of damp which closed-up country cottages always exude. He turned, and saw the elderly farmer from the pink-washed farmhouse across the green, coming towards the gate. James went down the path to meet him. 'Good morning, Mr Pole.'

'Morning. I saw your car come back and came to tell you there's been a nasty accident. Your dog strayed, and must have been run over. Then they flung his little body in the ditch. These drivers today – they don't care what they do! My man, Ted, saw it there, in the lane just outside the village, when he was on his way to work early this morning. He recognized him – but only just – all mashed up and covered with blood. Poor little dog. It's a shame . . .' Seeing James's stricken look, Mr Pole came to a halt.

But James said nothing. Sarah's and Vee's voices could be heard from the back garden, still calling Mansfield's name.

After a moment, Mr Pole went on in a softer tone, 'I wouldn't think you'd want your mother to see him. Like I said, he's not a pleasant sight. I told Ted to fetch him to the farm and he's put him in a box in the barn. I don't know what you'd like to do about it.'

'Thank you, Mr Pole, you've been very kind,' James said. Then, 'I'll come and deal with it a little later.'

'Right you are, then. You know, I heard him barking and barking over here quite late last night – my old collie started barking too. Then, quite sudden, he stopped. I suppose that must have been when he got out.'

'But *how*?' James said. 'I know I fastened the gate when we left.'

'Perhaps he burrowed out somewhere.'

'No – the gate was open when we got back.'

'Well, that is a funny thing. He must have slipped the catch somehow. Little dogs are clever. I once had a fox-terrier—' Here, however, Mr Pole broke off, for Sarah and Vee were coming round the house. 'Best be off now,' he said, and then, 'So I'll be seeing you later?'

'Yes, yes. I'll come over.'

Raising his hand in a greeting to Sarah, Mr Pole turned and crossed the road to the green. Seeing James's face, Vee and Sarah said, in unison, 'What's wrong?'

He turned to face them. He was very pale. He said, 'It's Mansfield. He got out and was run over.' Then he said, 'It was quick . . . instant – a fast car in the lane.'

Vee's face flushed. She gave a great gulp and started to sob. Tears rose slowly in Sarah's eyes, then overflowed. Both of them came to James. He put his arms around them, murmuring, 'Dear, dear Mum, darling Vee.' Over their heads, which rested on his chest, his white, strained face was turned towards the gate.

Sarah's voice was muffled: 'I shouldn't have left him. He's never been alone all night before. Oh, *how*?'

James said, 'You mustn't reproach yourself, Mum. It's my fault. I can't have fastened the gate properly. I'm sorry, so sorry.'

'Oh, but surely—' Vee began.

He interrupted: 'No, I can't have.' His arms still round their shoulders, he started to move towards the open front door. 'Let's go inside,' he said, 'and sit down.' When they reached the door, he stood aside. They released him, and he stood back for them to go in ahead, but then, with gentle hands, shepherded them into the little sitting room on the left, and to the small Victorian sofa on which he sat them down, side by side. Vee put her arm round Sarah. They were both still crying.

James said, 'I'm going to make some tea. Then I'll go over to the farm. Mansfield's body's there. I'll bring him back here, and dig a grave for him in the lavender bed. We'll make it nice.'

'Oh James,' Vee said, then, with a gulp, 'I can get the tea.'

'No,' James said. 'You stay here with Mum. I'll do it.' He looked round the room, so tidy and tranquil, then went through the hall into the dining room, where he paused for a moment, his hand resting on the big oak table.

The kitchen was on the right, but he did not go into it. Stooping to avoid the overhead beam, he went slowly up the narrow stairs, slowly along the passage to his room. Inside, he looked round, paused a moment, then went over to the book-shelves, which completely covered one wall.

On the second shelf from the top were the twenty dark-blue volumes of the complete *Oxford English Dictionary*. He raised his right hand to Volume 10 (MOUL–OVUM). His fingers hesitated for a moment – they were trembling slightly – before he pulled it down. Holding the book in the crook of his left arm, and tilting his head back, he looked into the space behind. After this, he closed his eyes tightly for just an instant. When he opened them, he felt in the space, and behind the two neigh-bouring volumes, with his right hand – it was shaking now – to make certain. No, there was nothing there.

Automatically he put the book back in its place. Then, tightly closing his eyes again, he grasped his head between both hands. His whole body trembled. He stood like this for several moments before he straightened his shoulders, lowered his arms and clenched his fists. Last of all, he opened his eyes.

He blinked twice. Then he went downstairs and straight to the kitchen where he made tea in three mugs, with tea bags, though Sarah always made it in a teapot with proper tea, and used cups and saucers. He added milk to all three mugs, and sugar to Sarah's, took the tray into the sitting room, and put it down on the table in front of the sofa.

Vee and Sarah were no longer crying, though their eyes were reddened and their faces tear-stained.

'James darling, you look terrible,' Sarah said, and then, 'Please, please don't blame yourself for this awful accident.'

Vee said, 'Oh James, you're so pale.'

'I'll be all right,' he said. 'Mum, that's yours – it's got sugar in it. I'll drink mine' – he picked the mug up with both hands – 'and then go over to the farm.'

'I'll come with you,' Vee said.

'No!' His voice was loud. He lowered it to add, 'No, I'd rather go alone.'

Vee said, 'You sound strange.'

'Well, it's been a shock,' he said, with an attempt at a shrug. He drank the tea quickly, wincing a little at its heat.

When he put his mug down, Vee stood up. She said, 'I'll just come to the front door with you,' and followed him into the hall.

At the door she said, 'Are you sure you don't want me with you?'

'No,' he said. 'Really not.' He took her hand and kissed it.

'Oh James,' she said, 'you're trying to spare me, aren't you? To spare me pain.'

'Yes,' he said, and then, 'That's what I want to do.'

She put her arms round him. 'Oh, my dear one,' she said. 'You feel so tense.'

'Just a bit. I'll be better when this is over.'

'You're very brave.'

'I wish I were,' he said, and gently detached himself from her embrace.

'I think you are.' She stood by the door, watching him go down the path, cross the road, and start to trudge across the green. Tears had come into her eyes again. One brimmed over; she wiped it away with her hand, and went back into the sitting room.

Sarah, still sitting on the sofa, said, 'I've often wondered whether, if something awful happened, I'd want to drink again. Well, I find I don't.'

Vee, standing beside her, put a hand on her shoulder. 'That's good – really good.' Vee's look was affectionate, as was Sarah's when she glanced up at her.

Sarah said, 'Yes. All the same, I'm glad I've got my meeting tonight.'

'Would you like me to come with you? You know I like AA meetings.' But Vee's tone was hesitant.

'No, no,' Sarah said. 'You must stay with poor James. He looks terrible.'

'Yes, he does. I think he feels guilty about not fastening the gate properly. That's so odd . . . he's such a careful person.'

'Yes,' Sarah said, and then repeated, 'He looks terrible.' She went on, 'I never thought he loved Mansfield as much as I did, but he must have. James doesn't always show his feelings. Oh, poor darling Mansfield!'

'Yes, he was so sweet.' Again, they began to cry.

When James reached the farm, Mr Pole was in the yard, his collie dog at his heels. James followed him to the barn. Just inside the door was an oblong cardboard box with a sack over it. Gesturing to it, Mr Pole said, 'That's where he is.'

'Thank you,' James said. He took off the sack and dropped it on the ground. Two of the cardboard flaps of the box were folded in. Now the third rose in the air because the fourth was missing. A fly buzzed, and the collie whimpered.

'Take the sack with you. Wouldn't look inside if I was you. Just bury him in the box with the sack over it, I would.'

'I feel I must have a look,' James said, and then, 'You wouldn't happen to have any sellotape, would you? So that I can seal the box before I take it home.'

'Sticky tape? Wife's got some. I'll go and fetch it.'

'Thank you,' James said again, as Mr Pole set off across the yard to the farmhouse, snapping his fingers at his collie, which, tail between its legs, had shown signs of lingering, but came to heel at once.

James opened the box. He breathed in, then clenched his teeth. Mr Pole's description of Mansfield had been accurate. The farmworker, Ted, must have recognised him by his head, which was undamaged, as were his two front legs, now rigid. Beneath his fringe was a glimpse of filmed eyes. The car had mangled the middle and back of his body. James's teeth remained clenched. His pallor was extreme, and he breathed heavily as he bent down to look more closely at where, under the jaw, a deep gash had left a patch of fur matted with blood.

Several flies were buzzing round the box now. Clumsily James closed the cardboard flaps, and held them pressed down. Mr Pole, without his dog now, came back across the yard, holding a large roll of thick brown sellotape and a pair of kitchen scissors. Glancing at James, he spoke kindly: 'Here, boy, let me give you a hand with that.'

James held the flaps down while Mr Pole closed the top of the box with strips of tape. When it was firmly sealed, they both stood up.

'I'll take you round in the car,' Mr Pole offered.

'No, no. Thank you very much. It's just across the green. He wasn't heavy.' But a look of surprise appeared on James's face as he heaved up the box.

'Sure I can't drive you?'

'Yes, really – quite sure. It was just a little heavier than I expected.'

'Mmm,' Mr Pole said. 'Dead weight, they call it. Carcasses always seem to weigh more.'

'Carcasses,' James murmured. Then he said 'Well, thank you for everything, Mr Pole. You've been very kind.'

'No, no – least I could do. Poor little fellow – it's a shame!'

Carrying his burden in his arms, James started to cross the yard. Mrs Pole, at the kitchen window, raised a hand, and James nodded back.

Vee came to meet him. 'Oh James, you're quite green.'

'I'm all right.'

They walked in silence to the cottage gate. Then she asked, 'Did you look at him?'

'Yes, yes. It must have been as quick as anything.' He carried the box over to the back fence. 'I thought we'd bury him here. Under the lavender. I'll dig the grave now.'

'Oh, do have a little rest first. You look beat. Sarah's resting. I persuaded her to come upstairs and lie down.'

He said, 'I'd rather get it done.' Then he said, 'Though I could do with a drink. A shot of brandy. But of course there isn't any.' Although Sarah felt no temptation to drink, she preferred not to keep spirits in the house, though there was beer in the refrigerator, and wine for guests, and recently she had been using wine in her cookery. He said, 'Perhaps I'll have a beer.'

96

'No, please.' Vee looked at her watch. 'It's only a quarter of one. I'll go in the car and get some brandy from the "gentleman grocer", as Sarah calls him.'

Sarah, in her drunken days, had quarrelled with this village character, a retired army officer who stocked unlikely delicacies, as well as daily necessities, in his picturesque shop. Early in her recovery, however, she had apologized to him, and now frequently called on him for ingredients for exotic recipes.

'It's sweet of you, Vee. But don't bother.'

'I *want* to. Give me your keys.'

He handed them over. When she had gone, he stood quite still on the lawn. Only when he heard the car returning did he start from his deep abstraction, and hurry to fetch a spade.

Vee joined him on the lawn, triumphantly waving a bottle, which he examined. 'Martell Cordon Argent – good heavens, how extravagant!'

She said, 'He told me it was the best, and that's what you deserve – the very best!'

'Oh Vee, you're so sweet, so good.'

She laughed. 'I must buy brandy more often.' But then she said, 'James, what's the matter? Don't look so agonized.'

'I want to protect you.'

'*Protect* me? I don't need protection.' Her tone was almost indignant, but then it changed completely: 'Well, you *have* protected me – and Sarah – in all this business with Mansfield. You have – and it's been wonderful of you. Now I'll get a beer for me, and make your drink – how would you like it?'

'Neat,' he said.

'Okay, I'll bring a glass. I think you're right about digging the grave right away. Hopefully, it'll all be done with by the time Sarah comes down. But first we'll sit on the grass and have our drinks, and you can have just a few minutes' rest. You're too hard on yourself.' Then she said, 'It's you that needs protection!'

Off she hurried. But he murmured aloud, as she went into the house, 'No it isn't. It's you.' He ran the back of his hand over his forehead: 'But how, how, how?'

TWO

The relationship between Chris and Belinda could have been interpreted in terms of that between kindly master and faithful dog: Chris's pats and patronage were reciprocated with a humble and uncritical devotion, for Chris's acceptance of her thrilled Belinda. She admired everything Chris was and did: her style – her amazing thinness, her ultra-fashionable clothes, her cool manner, the certainty of her right-wing, quintessentially 1980s, views – and, of course, her well-known success in publishing.

Belinda loved to visit Chris's Victorian villa in Islington, with its elegant, austere modern decor – even when, most efficiently, centrally heated, the house, like its owner, made a cool impression – but she never dropped in. There had been an occasion, two summers ago, when she had rushed there in response to an urgent summons; this mission had been un-successful and Chris had never properly explained it to her. Only once had she presumed to suggest coming round: when she told Chris how much she wanted her to meet Keith, and had been rewarded by a dinner invitation.

It was to lunch on Saturday that Chris asked her now. Belinda accepted eagerly, cancelling a visit to her mother with an excuse about having to go to a meeting.

'A meeting!' Barbara exclaimed. Her own life was full of meetings – political, feminist and gay rights – but she had never known her daughter to attend one.

'At my office,' Belinda said in an irritable tone. 'There's an urgent campaign we have to work on this Saturday.'

'I hope you get paid overtime,' Barbara said.

'I'm not a trade unionist, working to rule.'

Barbara drew in her breath, then evidently decided not to

reply to this, for there was a moment's silence before she said, 'Gran looks forward to seeing you so much, and she's not very well. You know her heart isn't strong, and her blood pressure's been up this week.'

After another moment's silence, Belinda said, 'No wonder she's got a heart problem. She's terribly overweight.'

'Runs in the family,' Barbara said with a laugh.

But Belinda's tone, when she replied, was indignant: 'That's nonsense. It's just a matter of what you eat.' Indeed, she herself succeeded in keeping her weight down; her addiction to Mars bars was almost entirely under control; when yielded to – as it had been, briefly, after her parting from Keith – she punished herself savagely with days of total starvation. Now she said, 'I'll come soon. I'll call you and come round – as long as you don't cook a lot of fattening stuff for me.'

'All right, I won't – I promise.' Barbara laughed, but half-heartedly. 'So you'll come soon?'

'Yes, yes. But I must rush now. Bye.'

'Bye darling,' Barbara said, but as she put down the receiver she gave a sigh that was almost a sob.

'Oh, it's so lovely here, so peaceful,' Belinda said when she was seated on one of Chris's two big white sofas, sipping a glass of Chris's favourite Chardonnay.

'Your own flat's quite quiet, isn't it?' Chris had only once visited Belinda's two-room, top-floor flat in a long narrow street of late-Victorian terrace houses. Chris had been kind about the flat – furnished in a sparse imitation of her own – but had not revisited it. It was Belinda who came to Chris; in fact, they both preferred this.

'Yes,' Belinda said now. 'My flat's quiet, but this place is so spacious. It's got such a wonderful calm atmosphere.'

Chris's smile was brilliant. Probably no comment could have pleased her more than this tribute to the way her personality had triumphed over the events that had taken place here, in this very room, three years ago. Now she said, 'Thanks, Belinda. You're always so appreciative. It's quite a tonic.'

Belinda's face lit up; she even blushed, like a schoolgirl, praised by the idolized captain of hockey, and like that schoolgirl she exclaimed, 'Oh Chris!' She added, 'I'm sure everyone appreciates *you*.'

'Well, not *quite* everyone. *Some* people hate me. What about that awful magazine that called me "Queen of Crap"?'

'Nothing but jealousy! Trying to put down someone who's successful. You publish books that people want to read. I bet the person who wrote that is a failed author.'

Chris smiled. 'You could be right – a so-called intellectual.'

'Exactly! Left-wing and all bitter and twisted. Writing about down-and-outs – who wants to read about *them*?'

'Victims!' Chris's tone indicated that this was a term of extreme contempt. Then she said, 'Now our darling Maggie's gone, I can't help wondering if things will go to pieces. All this talk about "caring" that suddenly seems to have surfaced.'

'Mmm.' Belinda nodded. 'I've noticed.' Both she and Chris had been shocked and dismayed by the ousting, at the end of the previous year, of Margaret Thatcher, the Prime Minister who had once stated, 'Compassion is a word which has no place in my vocabulary.'

'All this talk about unemployment – anyone who really wants a job can get one.' Chris spoke with complete assurance. 'And homelessness – no one *has* to sleep in a cardboard box on the streets of London.'

'No.' Belinda shook her head vigorously. 'If they truly can't find jobs here, they should go back where they came from.'

United in their social perceptions, Chris and Belinda simultaneously raised their glasses of Chardonnay. Then Chris looked at her watch: 'I suppose we should have lunch soon. I got some smoked salmon – I know you like that.'

'Oh Chris, you do spoil me.' Belinda added, 'It's amazing that something so delicious should have so few calories.'

'You've lost weight lately.' Chris spoke with automatic approval, unaware or unconcerned that this weight loss made Belinda's large head look too big for her body.

'Yes.' Belinda smiled. But after a moment the smile was replaced by a look of dejection; she seemed to sag a little on the sofa. She said, 'I put off lunch with my mother and *her* to come today. I said I had to work.'

Chris was the only person to whom Belinda had ever

mentioned Barbara's relationship with Michel Porter and her feelings about it. Debbie knew that her friend's mother lived with someone Belinda disliked, but believed this Michel to be a man. Chris's initial shock and then her cool sympathy were balm to Belinda's wound. Now Chris said, 'One would think she'd have the grace to go out occasionally, and let you see your mother alone.'

'No such luck!' The sound Belinda made was half grunt, half laugh. 'They see themselves as a married couple, and me going round to family lunch. Some family!' She gave the grunting laugh again. Then she sighed and said, 'I suppose I'll have to go soon. My old grandmother's been ill and wants to see me.'

Belinda's grandmother lived on the ground floor of the house in which Barbara and Michel occupied the upstairs flat. Now Chris said, 'You hardly ever mention your grandmother. Are you fond of her?'

The movement Belinda made could have been a shrug or a small shiver. 'Oh, I don't know. She's sort of old and fat and . . . well, foreign. When I was a child I used to hate the way her flat smelled of cooking.' Belinda's nostrils twitched; perhaps this was at a recollection of those smells: chicken soup, chopped liver, gefulte fish. She blinked: perhaps to banish a vision of the faded photographs of her grandmother's parents and siblings, all murdered in the Buchenwald concentration camp. Now she said, 'Oh, I suppose she's all right. She dotes on me – can't think why!'

'Why not?' Chris said, then added, 'You shouldn't run yourself down, Belinda. It's a bad habit. People tend to take you at your own valuation, you know.'

'Mmm.' Belinda sighed deeply, then said, with a strained brightness, 'Perhaps I don't think I'm so great, really.'

'But that's silly,' Chris said. 'You're doing so awfully well in your career. And you dress well. And you're slim and . . .' There was hardly a pause before she added, 'attractive.'

'Attractive!' Belinda spoke the word with hungry yearning. 'Do you really think so, Chris?' But she did not wait for an answer. She hurried on. 'I don't. Oh, why didn't I take after my parents? Daddy – so wonderful-looking, even if he's not a nice person – and my mother was really beautiful before she let herself go. And me – you know, Chris, I think I take after my grandmother. So short – and with this horrible big nose.'

'Really, Belinda, that's absurd. You shouldn't think of yourself as short – you're petite. Lots of men like small women – it makes them feel *protective*.' The scorn with which Chris often spoke of men was evident in this last observation. 'As for your nose, it's not *that* big.' After a moment Chris added, 'At one time, I remember, you were thinking of having a little op. What the Americans call a nose job. Well, *I* don't think it's necessary, but if you've got such a *thing* about it – why not?'

'Yes, I was saving up for it. But then . . .' Belinda hesitated.

'Then?' Chris raised her elegant eyebrows.

There was a pause before Belinda rushed into speech. 'Well, I met Keith and we . . . liked each other and – funnily enough – he even seemed to like the way I look. So I forgot about the nose job, though' – she gave an abrupt laugh – 'I spent a fortune on clothes. He said he loved the way I always looked so smart.' Now Belinda fell silent, looking down into her – now empty – wineglass.

Chris refilled the glass, and her own. After putting down the bottle, she briefly touched Belinda's arm. 'Belinda,' she said, in a softer tone than usual, 'what actually happened . . . with Keith? When you brought him round here, you seemed so happy together. You looked really pretty that evening,' she added.

Belinda said, 'Oh, I don't want to talk about it.' She added, with a gallant attempt at sophistication, 'Too boring,' but tears rose in her eyes.

'Oh Belinda, do tell me. It'll do you good to talk about it. And you know you can trust me.' When Belinda remained silent, she asked, 'Was it to do with . . . sex?' She spoke the word gingerly.

Although a tear had brimmed over onto Belinda's cheek – she dashed it away with the back of her hand – she smiled. 'That's just what my friend Debbie asked me,' she said, and then, 'No, it wasn't that.'

'You told Debbie about it?'

'No – just that it's all over.' More tears fell onto Belinda's cheeks, perhaps at the irrevocable sound of these words. She dragged her fingers down over her face, saying, 'I'm sorry to be so stupid.'

'Nonsense. Everyone cries sometimes. Do tell me about it, Belinda.'

'Oh well, but . . . oh well, why not? It was at work one day. I was in my office, and Keith came in. The boss, Mr Gordon – he founded the whole business – had been really awful to Keith about something that wasn't Keith's fault at all, and he just wouldn't listen to any explanations. He fired him – told him to collect three months' salary and leave right away. And then Keith said to me, "That bloody Jew! I bet his name's no more Gordon than mine is – probably something filthy like Rabinovitch. My father always said you could never trust a bloody Jew, and he was right. If you ask me, Hitler had the right idea – gas the lot of them!"' Now Belinda gave a huge sob, and then was silent.

'Oh dear,' Chris said inadequately, and then, 'What did *you* say?'

'I didn't say anything. I was sort of struck dumb. And at that moment the copy chief came in and said, "Ready, Belinda? The client's due any minute, and the presentation's all set up in the little conference room." So I said to Keith, "I have to go now" – and I did have to, of course. But all through the meeting I had to struggle to concentrate. I kept remembering "Gas the lot of them!" So *horrible*! So absolutely horrible . . .' Belinda's voice trailed off.

Chris said, 'He was angry. People say things they don't mean when they're angry. And after all, he had been fired. Unjustifiably too, you say.' Then she asked, 'Did he *know* you're . . . half Jewish?'

Belinda fiddled with the stem of her wineglass. Her tears had dried. 'No, as a matter of fact. I don't talk about it all that much. And I never took him to meet my mother – you know, because of Michel and—' She broke off. Then she said, 'Actually I told him my parents were dead.'

'Belinda – you didn't!'

'Well, Daddy might as well be dead, as far as I'm concerned. Heaven knows where he is. You said he'd walked out on that girl he was engaged to, and that your father told you she'd had a baby up in Yorkshire.'

'Yes, that's right.' Chris's tone and expression were impassive.

'And my mother – the whole set-up would have shocked him so. And my grandmother . . .' Belinda paused. 'I've always felt she was, well, sort of yucky.' Then she said, 'Korn – what a name!' She gave the grunting laugh again. 'Not as bad as Rabinovich, I suppose!' She paused again. 'I remember, when I was still a child being furious with my mother for changing back to Korn from Deyntree.'

Chris's nod was one of complete understanding; after all, she herself had not reverted to Puttock after her divorce, but had retained the name Deyntree.

Belinda said, 'She asked me why I minded. I remember I said Korn was "corny". But . . .'

Chris broke the silence: 'So you told Keith.'

'No, I didn't. We were meant to go out that evening, but I said I didn't feel well. And next day, when he rang up, I told him I'd met someone else. He didn't believe me. He thought I'd broken with him because he'd been fired. He was terribly upset. When he got another job, he rang up to tell me. But I stuck to my story. The real reason never entered his mind.' She repeated, '"Hitler had the right idea – gas the lot of them!"'

'He was angry,' Chris said again. 'And after all, he didn't know about you.'

'That's not the point.' Belinda had never before spoken sharply to Chris, who slightly raised her eyebrows. Belinda went on, 'The point is – Hitler *did* gas all my grandmother's family. Her mother and father, her brothers and sisters. She was the only one who survived, because she'd married my grandfather and come to England.'

'How perfectly awful!' After a moment Chris added, 'You never told me that.'

'No, I don't talk about it. I've never told Debbie.' She added, 'Or about being Jewish.'

'Partly Jewish,' Chris said.

Belinda said, 'Jewishness descends in the female line.'

Chris said, '*I* never think of you as Jewish at all.' The glance Belinda gave her was an odd one, and she hurried on: 'Not that it would make any difference.'

105

Now Belinda gave a violent shake of her head, and said, 'Oh Chris, I really thought I was . . . well, in love with him.'

'Well, perhaps you were "in love", whatever that is. And he certainly seemed to me to be keen on you. Don't you think if you met, if you brought it all out into the open, you'd find he didn't really mean it?'

But Belinda shook her head. 'No, Chris. It's over.'

'Poor Belinda,' Chris said, and then, after a moment, in a livelier tone, 'About that nose-job thing – well, I've been thinking: if you want to have it done, I'd give it to you, as a present – I'd really like to.'

'Oh Chris! That's sweet of you. But I couldn't.'

'Why not? It would be a pleasure.'

'You're so generous, so kind – but I couldn't . . . really.' Belinda's expression was one of profound unease.

'I can afford it – and we'd get a really good man, I promise – the best.'

'It's not that.'

Chris shrugged. 'Well, at least think about it. Will you?'

'Okay,' Belinda said. 'And thanks . . . really.'

'I'll bring it up again. But now' – Chris looked at her watch – 'we must have some lunch. Why, it's nearly two o'clock, and I'm longing for a little nibble.'

At lunch they talked of work and office politics. Chris's approach to the latter – which could have been concisely summarized as 'Charm the bosses, and to hell with the rest' – had so far served her well, particularly as her nose for successful novels had always been so acute. However, a rival editor in her office – Chris thought of all her colleagues as rivals – had recently been causing her trouble.

Some time ago, at one of the weekly editorial meetings, this woman had advanced the claims of a novel called *A Country Story* which Chris described as a 'wishy-washy tale of housewives in a village.' Chris had been withering about its lack of glamour, of career and sex interest, and the genteel poverty of the characters. 'Nothing *happens*,' she had concluded, 'and, for Heaven's sake, the hero – if you can call him that – is a *clergyman*!' There had been some laughter at this, but Chris's 'rival' had stuck to her opinion, affirming that the book was about 'real people'. 'Ordinary people, you mean,' Chris said, 'and who wants to read about *them*?' However it had been agreed that the novel should be purchased for a modest advance. Later at the same meeting, when *Being the Best*, favoured by Chris – the story of a ruthless woman's advance, through sex and scheming, to business victory, and marriage to a handsome tycoon – was discussed, Chris had triumphed, though her 'rival' had called it 'stale' and not worth the six-figure advance demanded by the agent.

Now both books had been published, and not only were the sales of *Being the Best* disappointing, but *A Country Story* had become a runaway bestseller. 'I just can't understand it,' Chris confided to Belinda with a frown.

'A flash in the pan,' Belinda said. 'After all, the oddest books do become bestsellers from time to time, don't they?'

'That's true,' Chris said, but she was still frowning as she added, 'It doesn't necessarily indicate a *trend*.'

'No, of course not,' Belinda said, and added, 'I'd love to read *Being the Best*.'

Chris smiled. 'I'll lend it to you. It's in the bookcase upstairs. And I'll lend you that dreary *Country Story*, too, if you like.'

'Oh Chris, would you really? I'd love to read them – though, of course I'm no judge.' Belinda was once more the adoring schoolgirl.

Later, at the front door, when Belinda had put the two books in her bag, she looked up and said, 'Chris?'

'Yes?' Eyebrows characteristically raised, Chris smiled.

'You remember that time ages ago when you asked me to come round, and I rushed over in a taxi, and that woman was here, and you wanted me to help you get something from her, but she was obviously some kind of self-defence expert, and she got away?'

Chris's only answer to this long question was an expressionless 'Mmm'.

'At the time, you said she'd taken this thing of yours and was trying to blackmail you. That was all you'd say, and I haven't liked to ask, but I have wondered so much – did it turn out all right?'

Opening the front door, Chris said, 'Yes thanks, Belinda. Perfectly all right.'

Belinda said, 'Oh, I'm so glad.' A moment passed before she added, 'Well, thanks again for the lovely lunch.'

'See you soon. Bye, Belinda.'

'Bye.' When Belinda reached the gate, she turned to wave, but the black front door was already closed. Behind it, Chris, in the hall, had clenched her fists and started to mutter. 'That treacherous fucking Yankee bitch! I'd love to kill him, and I'd like to kill her too.'

However, killing those she hated was not actually on Chris's agenda. Over a year ago she had, after prolonged deliberation, hired the private detective whom she had used at the time of her divorce, to make enquiries into what had happened to them. When he had confirmed – to her delight – that one was already dead, and the second had disappeared, and had told her that the 'Yankee bitch' was living in Los Angeles, Chris had discontinued the investigation, and begun to establish that narcissistic calm which now made her unclench her fists, shake her head as if emerging from a trance and – after double-locking the front door and fastening its chain – go downstairs to clear up the remains of lunch and stack the dishwasher.

THREE

Now, in July, it was very hot, though not inside the villa. Once or twice, Rupert had swum from the stony beach. 'But that awful dog's barking gets on my nerves,' he said.

'Awful dog indeed! Poor old Karl! I must say he certainly hasn't taken to you. But he really loves *me*.'

Indeed, at Disa's approach, Karl's barks and the rattling of his chain would stop. Rupert shuddered when she patted and stroked the dog, which nuzzled up to her, whimpering with pleasure.

Disa, whose feet were soft, sensitive, meticulously cared for, did not appreciate the stony beach. She always swam in the pool in the gym, a low echoing room, edged with exercise machines.

Quite apart from the heat, Kameni, with its dense pines and high cliffs, was not a place for walking. There was only the short road to the beach, to Marios and Sophia's cottage, to Karl. So Rupert joined Disa in the pool, and used the exercise machines, though with less dedication than she did. He pedalled and stretched, but never lifted weights: 'I'm sure it's bad for one's heart,' he said.

She studied him. 'Perhaps you're right . . . at your age.' Then she said, 'I don't use the weights that much myself – I don't want to get to look like Mr World. There was this guy here once – I've never seen such muscles.' Then she said, 'But guys like that are really only keen on their own bodies.'

He laughed. 'I wouldn't have thought that would suit you.'

'Too right! I didn't keep him here for long.'

Recently, Disa had often used the telephone, always closing the door when she did so. She and Rupert were in the pool one Sunday when it rang, and she sprang, dripping, up the little steps to answer it. A few minutes later, she returned at a run, with the widest of all her smiles, and made a perfect dive into the deep end of the pool. She came up beside Rupert, her beaming face beaded with water, her blonde-brown hair snaky and darkened. She seized him by the shoulders and ducked him under. He came up spluttering and gasping. 'Don't *do* that—'

She cut him off: 'My guys have got it!'

He stared. 'Got what?'

'Why, your tape.'

'My tape?' He had turned pale in an instant.

'Why are you looking like that? I thought you'd be pleased. It's a *surprise*.' Now she frowned.

'A surprise!' he exclaimed. Then he said, 'But where? How?'

'It was easy. That Suffolk place where you said your ex-wife and son live. Why, she was in the phone book. There aren't a lot of Deyntrees about, you know. They cased the joint for a long time. Then that Vee came to stay. They all three went away for a night, and that was when my guys searched the place.'

'And it was there? I can't believe it.'

'Yeah – it was there. They said it wasn't hard to find – behind some books. They did a great job, they said. No one would ever guess they'd been there. They had to kill some little dog that was barking and trying to bite them – but they made it look as if he'd been run over. Isn't it great? 'Then she added, with a flicker of her eyes, 'They said it was hot stuff.'

He looked appalled. 'They watched it?'

'Well, of course they did. They had to see if it was the right one. Why, it could have been Elvira Whatshername.' Disa laughed. 'Don't worry! It didn't shock those guys – they've seen everything.'

He was recovering his colour. 'And you believe you can trust them?'

'Trust them? Of course I can. They're my pals.' She laughed. 'Besides, they're being well paid for their trouble. Anyhow, what's to trust? It's just a movie.' Then she said, 'Pity about the dog, but I don't expect that bothers *you*.'

'Absolutely not,' he said. He smiled now. His white-blond hair – darkened, like Disa's, by the water – clung round his handsome face, and his eyes glittered and sparkled.

'Fuck, you're good-looking,' she said, and then, in an almost plaintive tone, 'Don't you like my surprise?'

Now he laughed. 'Oh, I do, Miss Dis. The more I think about it, the more I like it.' He paused, then he raised his arms, fingers stretched and pointing upwards, and exclaimed, 'Free at last!'

'Free?' she said in a flat cold tone, 'How do you mean – free?'

Hearing the tone, seeing her frown, he put his hand on her smooth shoulder. 'Why,' he said, 'free of that bitch, Vee, of course.'

Now she smiled. 'Yeah, just imagine how she'll feel when they find out.' She paused. 'Why, she'll probably imagine that you'll be back hot on the trail of her girlfriend.' She paused again. 'Innocent little Lucy.' Then she said, 'I'd rather like to meet that Lucy.' When he said nothing, she added, 'Perhaps you could arrange it.'

'Arrange it?' he said, and then, 'Oh, I don't think so.'

'You don't? And why not?'

Hearing the cold tone again, seeing the frown, he stroked the shoulder on which his hand still rested, but she shook it off with an impatient gesture. He said, 'I'm quite certain, after the way I left her, that Lucy would never want to see me again.'

'Oh I don't know. That famous charm of yours – and after all you are "the father of her child", like they say in cheapo romances.' Now Disa smiled, but coldly.

He produced a laugh. 'Why, she might sue me for child support.'

Now Disa's smile was different. She said, 'I hadn't thought of that.' Then she added, 'But let's go to London anyhow.'

'To London? You and I?'

'Mmm. "You and I." You and me. Just for a bit. That's where the tape is.'

Up to his chest in the water, he now gave a little shiver. He said, 'I'm getting cold,' but then stood perfectly still.

She ignored this. She said, 'Yes, why don't we? Apart from the tape, I think a change could be good for both of us.' She laughed. 'If you get sued for child support, we'll come back here – pronto. And I'll pick up some new videos – apart from yours of course. We're running out of the stuff you go for.'

He said lightly, 'And I could buy some books.'

'Books – oh yes, to read when we get back here.'

'That's right,' he said. 'I've exhausted Suetonius.'

'And you don't much care for my library.'

'I wouldn't mind a little more variety.'

'Oh yes, I'm all for variety.' Then she said, 'I thought we might have guests in the fall.'

'In the fall?'

'Yeah. The autumn.'

'Oh yes. Of course. If you like.' Then he said, 'Though can custom stale *your* infinite variety?' He added, 'That's from Shakespeare. He was talking about Cleopatra. Another fascinating lady.'

'Oh yes – Cleopatra.' She laughed. 'Cleopatra's grip.'

'That's right – she resembled you in all sorts of ways.' He added, 'Antony gave up the world for her. All for love, and the world well lost.' He shivered again. 'I'm really getting cold.'

'Love!' she said, but she was smiling. Then she said, 'You're right. This pool is a bit chilly. I must turn up the thermostat when we get back from London.'

He said, 'When shall we leave?'

'Oh, in a day or two. I must start packing.'

'You'll take a lot of luggage?'

She laughed. 'It's a habit of mine.'

'And I travel so light, with my single suitcase and my picture.'

'Your picture? You aren't going to bring *that*, are you?'

'I take it everywhere.'

'But we'll be back in a couple of weeks.' Her strange eyes met his.

'Yes, of course.' He paused. Then, after a moment, he shrugged and said, 'All right. I'll leave it here.'

The melancholy of Oxford at this time of year – undergraduates absent on vacation, daytime armies of tourists with loud guides occupying the town centre, the colleges let to conferences, the heat grey and humid, with frequent drizzling rain – seemed to penetrate even into the Larches' large comfortable house in quiet prosperous North Oxford.

Here, by day, Francis fiddled with a textual difficulty in Petronius, a Latin author whose combination of refinement of style with a vivid savage evocation of the homosexual under-world of Nero's Rome had led to his *Satyricon* becoming the subject of Francis's lifelong academic study. For twenty-five years, his work on this first realistic novel in European literature had been a joy; nowadays he approached the frag-mentary text more as if it were a puzzle than a passion.

The summer days were long and slow, the light summer evenings longer and slower. Mrs Larch became slightly tetchy when her son's recreational visits to London were too frequent, and also when, at home, he was not disposed to conversation.

This evening, after their nightcap, they had gone to bed at ten. But Francis was still reading at midnight when the telephone rang – downstairs, for the Larches had never felt the need of upstairs extensions.

Francis jumped out of bed and hurried downstairs. He was panting when he picked up the receiver, and, before he could speak, a voice at the other end of the line said his name. He gasped. Then he exclaimed, 'Rupert!'

'Yes, Francis, it's me – it is I,' Rupert said. 'But what's this "Rupert" business? You always call me Rupe.' Then he said, 'You know I always telephone you on Sunday evening.'

'Always!' Francis exclaimed. 'Really you're quite monstrous. How *dare* you say such a thing when I haven't heard a word from you for nearly two years? Where have you been?'

'Francis, I can't go into all that now.' Rupert spoke more softly than usual. 'I'm abroad. It's the middle of the night. We mustn't talk too long. Let's just say "He travelled", as Flaubert put it in *L'Education Sentimentale*.'

'*L'Education Sentimentale* indeed!' Now Francis's tone was fiercely indignant. 'How can you be so frivolous after all the misery you caused when you disappeared like that?'

'Oh Francis, my dear Francis!' Rupert now spoke gently as well as softly. 'I wasn't being frivolous – really I wasn't – though I admit I was approaching the subject in a rather roundabout way. In that passage Flaubert goes on to talk about "the bitterness of interrupted friendships" – and I have missed you . . . bitterly. Oh, I really have. I promise you that.'

Francis was silent for a moment. Then he said, 'Well, I've

missed you too. Of course I have. But I'm not thinking of myself. I'm thinking of poor Lucy.'

'You've seen her? You've kept in touch? I thought you might have. How is she? Did she have the baby? Oh, tell me absolutely everything. Is she all right?'

'"All right"? I suppose she's "all right", if you mean alive and in good health. And she had the baby – you're the father of a one-year-old son now, Rupert.'

'There's that "Rupert" again! It sounds so forced and artificial. Even if you're furious with me – as I can hear you are – please call me Rupe, as you always have. But go on about Lucy.'

'Well . . . Rupe, when the baby was nearly due, she went back to Rivendale, to that terrible mother of hers. The baby was born there and they stayed there for a time, but now Lucy's back at her old job and she and Edward are living with those Dumbles she stayed with before. Mrs Dumble looks after him while Lucy's at work. I really get the impression that her mother made life at Rivendale quite impossible, though all Lucy said was that she was "difficult". Lucy's so incredibly loyal.' Here Francis came to a halt.

'Yes – darling Lucy! So sweet and so loyal. But she must hate me. Even she – so loyal and charitable – must hate me after what happened.' There was a silence. Rupert broke it: 'Francis, she does hate me – doesn't she?'

After another moment's silence, Francis said, 'Well . . . no. It's preposterous, but as a matter of fact she doesn't.' Again he halted.

'She *doesn't*?' Francis, can she possibly still love me? You have to tell me? Oh . . . come on now, old friend.'

'Well . . . yes. She does.'

'I can't believe it. She's a saint . . . no, she's an angel. But how *can* she?'

Francis said, 'I told you it was preposterous. She's got this ridiculous idea . . .' He broke off.

'What idea? Francis, what's holding you back? Tell me – please!'

'Oh well, when I saw her, after you'd gone, I happened to mention that I thought that, in the past, you'd done little jobs

114

for the government abroad, minor intelligence work. And Lucy seized on it – just as a drowning person will clutch at anything within reach. Then she blew it up out of all proportion. She decided that you'd had to vanish on some dangerous patriotic mission so secret that you couldn't even mention it to her.'

'You can't be serious?' Rupert gave an involuntary, incredulous laugh.

'Oh yes – it's perfectly true. But the important thing is that *she's* serious – absolutely serious. She thinks you're a hero – and she's been waiting for the hero's return. Though recently, since the Gulf War, I think she's begun to be afraid you were dead.'

'The Gulf War?'

'Yes, she wondered if you might be a victim of Saddam Hussein and his torturers – just as her ancestor was a victim of that dreadful Topcliffe in Elizabethan times. Something like that, anyway.'

'It's astonishing.' Rupert paused. Then he said, 'It's wonderful.'

'Wonderful?'

'Yes, of course it is. Lucy believes in me. She loves me. And she's in London. As I shall be in just a few days' time. Francis, aren't you the least little bit pleased that I'll be back?'

'Well, of course I am.' After an instant's hesitation, Francis hurried on: 'But it sounds as if you've decided to take up again with Lucy, after discarding her so cruelly – yes, I'm afraid "cruelly" is the only word – and break her heart again, no doubt, in the not too distant future.'

'Break her heart, Francis? I don't want to break darling Lucy's heart. I love her. I want to make her happy. I want to marry her.'

'Love her, indeed! Marry her and make her happy! You were going to do that two years ago – and then you left her alone and miserable and pregnant with your child.'

'Is she fond of it?' Rupert asked.

'Fond of *it*? I presume you're asking if she loves little Edward. She adores him. He's everything to her.'

'Well, now she'll have me as well.'

'Oh, Rupe! Really! And you still haven't told me where you've been.'

Rupert said, 'Francis, I'll tell you everything when I see you. In just a few days, as I said. Meanwhile – you won't say anything about this call to Lucy, will you? I want to explain things to her myself – I'm sure you can understand that. So – promise.'

After a moment Francis said 'Well, all right. I promise. But—'

'I'll be in touch in a few days. I must go now.' Rupert rang off.

Putting down the receiver, Francis sighed. He frowned, but then he smiled. Frowning and smiling, he slowly climbed the stairs. He was in the upstairs passage when, from her bedroom, his mother called his name, and he went into her room. The bedside light was on. As Francis came in, she said, 'Who on earth was that?' She looked at her watch. 'What a time to ring up!'

Francis said, 'It was Rupe, Mother.'

'Well!' she said. 'So he's turned up again? Didn't I always say he would? So – where on earth has he been?'

Francis laughed. 'Mother, Mother, what a lot of questions! He's abroad at the moment, but he'll be back here in a few days, and then he'll tell me what he's been doing.' After a moment he added, 'He says he wants to marry Lucy.'

'So he's got tired of whatever woman he ran off with.' Mrs Larch smiled.

'Really, mother! We don't know that he "ran off" with anyone.' Then he said, 'I always knew he loved Lucy. And of course she's never stopped loving him. Dear good Lucy! If possible, she deserves some happiness at last.'

'"If possible!" That's a big "if" where that scamp's concerned. Well, *nous verrons* – we shall see!' Then she said, 'It's quite extraordinary how you romanticize that poor misguided girl.' She added, 'I suppose that scamp will soon manage to have her eating out of his hand again.'

Francis sighed. 'Oh, Mother, why must you always believe the worst of people?'

Mrs Larch sighed. 'Experience, my dear boy. "The dirty nurse, Experience", as Lord Tennyson put it.' She sighed again more deeply.

Francis's sympathy was always aroused by hints of his mother's unhappiness in her marriage to the father he could not remember. 'Poor Mother,' he said, and his expression softened. Then he said, 'Oh, I really am so pleased he's coming back.'

Now Mrs Larch's smile was wholly benevolent. 'Of course you are, and I'm sure he must have missed you, too. I've always known how fond of you he is.'

'Yes . . . I think he is.'

'Of course he is! Kiss me goodnight now – and then off to beddy-byes!'

'Yes, Mother.' Obeying these instructions, he seemed as at ease as she was with their tone: that of an indulgent mother addressing a small child.

FOUR

On this hot August afternoon, Lucy was in her office. Although the Venetian blind was closed against the bright light, the window of the small businesslike room was open, and London traffic was loud outside. Cars and motorbikes were active in the foreground; in the background was the continuous steady roar of buses and taxis in nearby Oxford Street. Lucy, tapping at her computer – the name of a large company which, as a result of her efforts, had become a potential donor to Feed the Children was on the screen in front of her – paused to run a hand over her hair. Then, frowning, she started to type an outline of the next move in her negotiations. Completely absorbed, she started when her telephone buzzed. She picked up the receiver, and the receptionist said, 'There's a gentleman to see you.'

'Oh?' Lucy said, and then, 'But, Susie, I haven't any appointments this afternoon.'

'I know.' Susie broke off, and said, 'Please wait a moment' to the visitor. Then she said to Lucy, 'I'm so sorry. He's just barged through. He says he knows the way to your office.'

'Oh, really!' Lucy exclaimed.

'He didn't even give his name.' Susie's tone was indignant.

'But – oh!' Lucy, receiver still in hand, stood up, as her door opened, and a man paused in the doorway for a moment, then came in.

'Lucy! Lucy, my darling.'

The colour left her face. She swayed, put out her hands to clutch the edge of the desk, then became aware of the receiver in her hand, of Susie's voice on the line. 'It's all right, Susie,' she managed to say, though her voice trembled. Her hand shook as she replaced the receiver. Now, still standing, she gripped the rim of the desk with both hands, staring at the man who faced her, who now pushed the door shut, and came towards her.

'Darling Lucy, I've given you a shock. I shouldn't have done it, but I couldn't wait.'

'Rupert.' As he came round the side of her desk, she let go of it, almost fell towards him. Then, arms enfolding her, he was kissing her hair.

Her face was pressed against his chest. Now she turned it away, her cheek resting on his shoulder, and said, 'You couldn't wait, you said just now, but you've waited so long. And so have I.'

He said, 'I know,' and then, 'Lucy, you have to trust me.'

She raised her eyes – she was still very pale – to look into his face. Immediately he kissed her mouth. For a moment Lucy held back; then with passion she returned the kiss, closing her eyes, giving herself to it entirely.

When eventually she drew back – her face was flushed now – he murmured, 'Can you trust me, darling Lucy?'

Now for the first time she looked full into his eyes: usually so bright, they were blurred by tears. 'Oh Rupert, you're crying. I've never seen you cry before.'

'I never used to cry. But I've cried quite often since we parted. Do you despise me for that?'

'*Despise* you? Oh, Rupert. No, of course I don't. I've cried too.'

Wiping his eyes, he smiled for the first time: 'But a strong man in tears is meant to be a terrible thing.'

Very faintly she smiled too. 'Oh, Rupert.' But then her smile faded, and she said, 'You have to tell me. To tell me why.'

'Of course I will. I'll tell you all I can.'

'All you can?'

'Yes, I'll explain that. But you must try to trust me again.'

She said, 'I never really stopped.' At that moment her telephone rang.

'Let it ring,' he said.

'No, I can't possibly. Susie will think you've murdered me or something. You're a complete stranger to her. She's only been here a year.'

'Murdered you indeed! My angel!' He let go of her, and she answered the telephone's fourth ring.

'I just wondered if you were all right,' Susie said.

'Oh yes, I'm fine, thank you, Susie. Absolutely fine.' Lucy rang off. She laughed, and said to Rupert, 'You see!'

'So she did suspect I was a murderer? How very unflattering.'

'Oh, probably not a *murderer* – no one could possibly imagine that. But you did come barging in, as she put it.' The telephone rang again. Rupert groaned.

This time it was an outside call, to arrange an appointment. When it ended, and Lucy rang off, Rupert said, 'Can't we go out?'

'Out?' Lucy looked at her watch. 'It's only half past three.'

'You're as conscientious as ever, I see. But surely this is a unique occasion? Couldn't we go to the park – just for half an hour or so – and talk in peace under the trees?' He added, 'I've got an appointment I simply can't break this evening, unfortunately.'

'Oh! This evening!' For a moment she looked crestfallen, but then she said, 'All right – we'll go to the park for a little. Susie can take messages.'

Hand in hand, but not speaking, they hurried through the crowds of tourists in Oxford Street, crossed when the lights halted the noisy flow of traffic at Marble Arch. At last they were in Hyde Park. '*Rus in urbe*!' Rupert exclaimed, as they stepped onto the grass.

Lucy laughed. 'I hardly know a word of Latin, but I know what *that* means – country in the town. Bernard's always saying it about Hampstead. Though of course that's not proper country – and nor is this.' She looked down at the worn grass and then up at the dusty leaves of the trees – both, even so early in August, slightly yellowed. Then she said, 'Don't you want to hear about our child? About Edward?'

'Of course I do.' Then he said, 'I'm so glad you called him after your father. I've always thought he sounded such a marvellous person.'

Her smile in response to this was radiant. She said, 'Edward's beautiful. He's got your eyes. I think he's going to look just like you.'

'I'd rather he looked like you. Oh, darling Lucy, I want to

hear everything about you.' Then he said, 'As soon as I arrived today, I rang up Francis to find out if he knew where you were and he told me you were back at Feed the Children and staying with the Dumbles.' He added, 'I rang Francis instead of Rivers because I was terrified' – he smiled – 'that your mother would answer the telephone.'

'I can understand that.' Lucy's face was shadowed. 'She hates you more than ever now. That's one reason why I came back to London.'

'And *you* never hated me? Never at all?'

'No.' Then she said, 'I had faith in you.'

'That was amazing . . . wonderful. Yet actually you were right to believe in me.' They had reached an empty bench and they sat down, still hand in hand. He went on, 'I had to leave on important work. For our country. Can you understand that?'

'Oh yes.' Then she said, 'My family's always been patriotic – even when we were persecuted for our religion.' She went on, 'I guessed right away, at the very beginning, from something Francis said about your having done intelligence work in the past.'

'Dear old Francis!'

'Yes, he's so fond of you. I like him very much, but what I like best of all about him is that he's your friend.' She paused. Then she said, 'And there was no way you could let me know you had to go – not a word, not a message? Nothing for me to hold onto while you were away?'

He raised her hand, turned it over and gently kissed the palm. She shivered. Then he clasped her hand between both of his. 'Darling Lucy,' he said, 'just before I had to leave, something else happened.' He paused.

'Something else?'

'Yes. Something that stopped me getting in touch with you. Something that might have hurt you . . . upset you. And I couldn't bear that. So I'd rather not tell you about it unless I have to.'

'Hurt me? Upset me?' She looked bewildered.

'Yes. Something to do with my past – with old bygone days. And with a betrayal. I may have to tell you about it soon. I don't know. But I don't want anything to cloud this wonderful reunion. Lucy, you've trusted me so far – against all the odds. Will you trust me now about this one other thing?'

'But—' She broke off. 'All right then.' She smiled. 'Now you're back, trusting you should be easy. When you were away, sometimes it was hard.'

'Oh darling Lucy, it must have been.'

'When I was up at Rivers, pregnant, and then with my baby, Mummy was so hateful. I felt so isolated – I don't know how I would have managed without Vee's visits and calls. She was wonderful.'

'Ah yes, Vee. Your friend in Los Angeles.'

'Not any more! She's just moved to London.' Lucy's smile was happy.

'To *London*?'

'Yes. Why, what's the matter? You look absolutely staggered.'

'No . . . no.' Then he smiled and said. 'I was just surprised. I thought she was such a big deal in the world of so-called music over there.'

Lucy laughed. 'She's still in that world. But she's moved from touring to the management side. Running some big American manager's London office. She only started this week. She's just rented a flat in Islington – somewhere called Noel Road, which has a view over the old canal. It sounds lovely. I'm going to see it in the next few days. You must come too.'

'Noel Road,' Rupert said. He frowned. 'Why does that sound familiar? Oh yes, I remember – there was a murder there. The playwright, Joe Orton, was murdered by his boyfriend, who then committed suicide.'

'How horrible!' Lucy exclaimed. 'We mustn't tell Vee about that. She's so pleased with the place. And, do you know, I think at last she's having a really happy relationship. I'm sure that's part of why she moved to England.'

'Who's the lucky man?' Rupert's tone was light.

'I haven't met him yet. She's been very secretive about him – perhaps because I never liked anyone she was involved with before. But I know he's English and I think his name's Jim.'

'Jim,' Rupert said. 'A good plain name!' After a moment he added, 'Vee didn't like me.'

Lucy hesitated. Then she said, 'That's been the only cloud on our friendship. But she's so loyal to me. You can't really blame her for being angry when you disappeared.'

He said, 'She disliked me before that.'

'Oh, not seriously, I'm sure. Anyway now you've simply got to be friends. I'm friends with Francis – and you must be friends with Vee.'

He said, 'Darling, when are we going to get married?'

'As soon as possible. And when are you coming to see your son?'

'Also as soon as possible. I'm sorry it can't be this evening. Some loose ends I've got to tie up in connection with the work I've been doing. There are a few other things I'll have to do in the next few days. Oh, and though I'll telephone you all the time, I can't be reached on the telephone at the moment.'

'Mysterious!' she said, but with a smile.

'Mmm. So, as Romeo said to Juliet, we must say farewell until tomorrow.'

'Quoting again – oh Rupert, I love everything about you! So . . . why not come round to the Dumbles' tomorrow after I finish work, and meet Edward?' She paused, then said, 'Afterwards perhaps, for old times' sake, we might have dinner at the Firenze – Mag will babysit, I'm sure.' Lucy's laugh was joyful as she added, 'Perhaps all those characters you invented will be there. Al Dente, the Mafia man, and Sir Percy Flage and his wife Camou. Oh Rupert, it's so wonderful to be able to laugh again.' She looked at her watch. 'I really must get back to work now.'

As they stood up, he said, 'Yes. What a marvellous evening to look forward to. Oh, Lucy!'

'Don't come with me,' she said. 'I must rush.' Standing under the big tree, they embraced. 'Oh, I'm so happy,' she said.

'And so am I.' But, as soon as she had gone, a look of frowning perturbation settled on his face.

FIVE

Today was Vee's fourth day at work. It was nearly seven by the time she got back to Noel Road. She looked tired; all the same she ran up the front steps, between the delicate spiked railings, glancing upwards at the two tall sash windows on the first floor, fronted by tiny, merely decorative, wrought-iron balconies. Having unlocked the Georgian front door, with its pretty fanlight, she hurried through the little hall and up the stairs to open, this time with two keys, the door of her flat.

Inside, she gave a happy glance round the large, beautifully proportioned living room. Over the weekend she and James had arranged her books – ranging from Raymond Carver's short stories to the complete works of Beatrix Potter – and her stereo and large collection of compact discs. They had laid her Amerindian rugs and hung her Mexican pictures. Along the top of the hired television set, above a video recorder on a plain white trolley, prowled a painted – bright-orange and white-spotted, startlingly vivid – modern Mexican carving of a jaguar. Yet, in the Georgian room, these foreign objects looked curiously at ease, and had set Vee's personal imprint on the impersonal furnishings.

She went straight to the kitchen, where she activated her coffee machine, and then through into her bedroom, where she pushed up the sash window, put her head out, and leant her elbows on the sill to enjoy the evening view of the towpath: a linked couple, a purposeful runner, a boy with his dog. Vee was smiling, but then her smile faded.

She stiffened. Now her eyes were fixed on a man who was strolling along the towpath, swinging two green Hatchards carriers of books and looking up at the rear windows of the houses in Noel Road. She saw his white-blond hair, his handsome face, his startling eyes roaming the windows. Then he saw her, and halted.

Surely the stillness of these two would check every nearby movement, their silence deaden every sound, their stare close every other eye? But the runner speeded up; the dog, chasing a stick, barked; the couple ogled. Rupert smiled, and, swinging his green bags, strolled on.

He was out of sight in a few moments. As Vee stepped back into the room, the telephone rang. She almost stumbled as she hurried to pick up the receiver.

'Vee?' Lucy's voice said into her silence.

'Lucy . . .'

'You sound out of breath. Have you just got in?' Not waiting for an answer, Lucy went on, 'Oh Vee, Vee, I've got such wonderful news. Oh Vee – he's back. Yes, Rupert's back at last.'

Vee, gripping the receiver, said nothing.

'Vee – are you there?'

After a moment, Vee said, 'Yes . . . I'm here.'

'You're surprised. But, oh Vee, you can't be half as surprised as I was. Surprised and happy – oh, so, so happy. I can still hardly believe it. But it's all just as I thought, just as I told you. He *had* to leave – and now we're going to get married just as soon as possible. Oh, you can be bridesmaid just as we planned. Edward's too small to be a page, I'm afraid – wouldn't that idea shock Mummy? I haven't told *her* yet. I'll ring her later this evening – I'm rather dreading it. You're the first person to hear – except Mag and Bernard, of course. Mag was upset at first, but I told her I'd *kill* her' – here Lucy laughed – 'if she wasn't nice to him, and she's really being very good . . . though she's still a bit doubtful, I think. Of course, Bernard never takes much notice of what's going on in people's lives. Vee – *say* something! Though I suppose' – Lucy laughed again – 'I haven't given you much chance yet. Vee?'

All the time Lucy was talking, Vee had worn the same dazed expression. Now she said again, 'I'm here.'

'Vee, don't sound so flat. I know it's a surprise to you. But I want you to be pleased. You *must* be – for me. I know you didn't really take to Rupert at first. And of course, when he disappeared, you were angry, being such a faithful friend and not believing what I always knew was true – that he had to go, that it was his duty. You didn't ever believe that, did you?'

'No,' Vee said. 'No, I never did. And I don't—' But she broke off. 'Lucy,' she said, 'dear, dear Lucy, I have to see you. Will you see me?'

Lucy laughed. 'See you? Of course I'll see you – any time. Come round now.'

'No,' Vee said. 'No. Not this evening. But tomorrow – and not at the Dumbles'. Couldn't you come round here – please?' She added, 'Why, you haven't even seen my flat.'

'No, I haven't, and I really want to. Rupert and I are going to the Firenze.' She laughed. 'A rendezvous with Colonel Al Dente and Sir Percy Flage.' Then she said, 'I'd ask you to come too, if it wasn't our first dinner together again. But we could come round for a drink first.'

'No!' Vee exclaimed violently. She softened her voice to repeat 'No.' Then she said, 'I simply have to see you alone.'

'Why, what's the matter?'

'Oh, *please, Lucy!*'

'Well . . . all right. I'll dash in at about half past seven – if it's so very urgent.' Lucy paused for a moment. When Vee said nothing, she said, 'Half past seven – but with one proviso: that you don't say horrible things about Rupert. I promise you it won't do any good.'

After a moment, Vee replied, 'I won't say anything.'

'All right then. I'll see you tomorrow. I must rush now – Edward's crying. Bye.'

'Oh!' The drawn-out sound Vee made, as she rang off, was half a sigh and half a moan. But then, immediately, she picked up the receiver and dialled. The telephone rang for a long time before Sarah answered.

'Hello, Sarah.'

'Why hullo, Vee. I'm sorry I took so long. I was working in the garden. How nice to hear you. How are you?'

'I'm all right. How are you?'

'I'm fine.'

'Could I speak to James?'

'Of course. He's in his room, working on his book, though I

don't know that it's going very well – he still seems awfully depressed. It's a shame.'

'Yes,' was all Vee said. There was a pause.

'I'll get him, and go back to my gardening.' In a moment Sarah's voice could be heard calling, 'James! James – it's Vee.'

A few seconds later, James's voice said quietly, 'Hullo, Vee darling.'

'Oh James, James, it's so terrible.' Words poured from her: 'He's back. I saw him from my window, smiling at me like a devil, and then Lucy called me. To say he's back with her. How can he be? And he's told her what she believed all along – that he was on this patriotic mission. How dare he? It's incredible. She says they're going to get married. But of course we can't let it happen. Oh James, I'm going to have to show her the tape. I hate the thought, but I'm going to have to do it. Could you possibly bring it up to London tomorrow? Lucy's coming round here, before she meets *him* for dinner . . . but of course she won't do that after she's seen it. I asked her round here. It's best if we watch it quite alone. But you'll bring it, won't you?'

The silence that followed was total and extraordinarily prolonged. At last Vee said, 'Oh James, you're doubtful – aren't you? But surely it's the only thing to do?'

He said, 'The tape's gone.'

'*Gone*? *Gone*? What do you mean, "gone"? How can it be?' Her voice trembled.

'It's gone. It's been stolen.'

'How? When?' Her voice rose: 'You were keeping it safe.'

'Of course I thought it was safe. It was in my room, behind one particular volume in that whole wall of books.'

'In your room? I thought you'd have put it in a bank or somewhere like that.'

'Oh Vee, be reasonable. How could I ever have imagined that he'd track it down here, break in, leaving no trace, find it and take it away?' He paused. 'Mansfield was the only clue.'

'Mansfield?'

'Yes – I knew I'd closed the gate and fastened the catch properly. I always do – and I can actually remember doing it that morning. When we got back and I saw that it was open, I felt a sort of ominous chill. And then, when Mr Pole told me they'd found Mansfield's body – run over and thrown into a ditch – I knew. Why would anyone have opened the gate? Everyone in the village knows that Mansfield would have rushed at them and tried to bite them. Anyway, country people never leave gates open. No, I knew someone had killed him on purpose – to silence him and get rid of him. They left the gate open to make it look as if he'd run away, and then drove over his body to make it seem he'd been run over. I knew it in my bones and when I went over to the farm I examined his body before I brought it back here. There was this deep gash in his throat. No car could have caused that.'

'Oh, poor sweet Mansfield!' Vee exclaimed.

'Yes, poor loyal Mansfield. It was horrible, hateful. But, oh Vee, I can't tell you what a feeling of dread I had from the moment we got back. You remember how, before I went to fetch Mansfield's body, I made tea for you and Mum? Well, first, I went upstairs to my room, to the bookcase, and I took out the book I'd put the tape behind, and it wasn't there. What a moment! I'd guessed it wouldn't be there, I'd felt almost certain. But then I knew.'

'Why didn't you *tell* me?' There was passion and indignation in Vee's voice.

'Perhaps I should have, but I wanted to protect you. I knew what horror you felt for that tape – you've really only recovered from that quite recently. I couldn't bear the thought of your going through all that again.'

'Well, I'm going through it now. If you'd told me, I could have done something.'

'But, darling Vee, what *could* you have done?'

'I would have known that he'd come back, that it must have been him that stole the tape and killed poor Mansfield. I would have guessed that he'd go to Lucy. I could have told her in advance about the tape and that he'd be sure to turn up now he'd got it. Then, when he suddenly reappeared, even Lucy couldn't have believed it was a coincidence.'

'Yes, you could have done that – but would you? Would you really have guessed he'd go back to her after all this time? You would have had to tell her about me, and about all the concealment and lies of the past two years. You would have had to tell her how you kept the tape from her – and from the police. Would you have done that?'

'Yes. Yes, I would. She would have understood that I did it to protect her.'

'Perhaps we both ought to stop trying to protect people. You wanted to protect her. I wanted to protect you. You feel indignant – perhaps she would too. I think your Lucy may be tougher than you think. From what you've told me about the Rivens, they're a pretty tough bunch – prepared to face death rather than sacrifice their convictions. The Riven who was hanged after the Pilgrimage of Grace. The Riven who was so horribly tortured and executed under Elizabeth. And all those other Rivens who endured centuries of discrimination and exclusion – oh, they were tough all right. What about Lucy herself? Even when he abandoned her, she went ahead and built a life for herself and her child. And she has her faith that never wavers.'

'Yes, her faith . . . and she had faith in him. In that monster. I never imagined she'd have that. I was wrong . . . wrong all the way. As soon as I'd seen the tape, I should have shown it to her. I was going to, although she's so innocent – till I heard she was pregnant with his child. Then I couldn't face her with the horror . . . the horror of it.' Vee gave one gulping sob. Then she said, 'But I was wrong.'

'*We* were wrong, darling Vee. *We* were wrong. I watched the tape with you. We took that decision together – and yes, I think now it was the wrong one. Just as I was wrong not to tell you when the tape was stolen. Vee, I'm so sorry.'

'Oh, James!' Then she said, 'But you've been through such hell, haven't you? After it happened, when I was still at the cottage, you weren't able to work at all, were you?'

'Nor since,' he said.

'Even when we were fixing up my flat, you were so quiet . . . and you looked so tense and strained. I thought it was because of Mansfield, but it was because you were trying to bear my burdens, wasn't it?'

'Something like that.' Again he said, 'I'm so sorry.'

'Oh darling James – no, don't be. Like we've just been saying, we've both been wrong. What you've just done isn't half as bad

as what we did two years ago . . . actually what *I* did mostly –
blackmailing that devil and letting him escape just so as to
protect Lucy. And now it turns out I didn't even succeed in that,
just as you didn't succeed in protecting me for more than a
week or two.' She said again, 'Oh darling James.'

'Sweetest Vee – oh, you're so generous-hearted. How much I
love you.'

'And I love you. Oh James, as a matter of fact, I've never
loved you so much as I do right this minute.' Vee paused; then
she said, '"The serenity to accept the things we cannot change"
– well, we can't change those things we did. We have to accept
that.' She paused again. 'But that isn't all – it would be pretty
negative if it was. Next comes "the courage to change the things
we can". James, that's what we need now.'

'But darling, what *can* we change?'

'Well, when I was over here in the spring, I remember telling
you how I interpreted all this at that time. I'd decided the whole
situation about having let him escape was something I couldn't
do anything about, so I had to accept it – I decided that was
"the wisdom to know the difference" between the things I
could and couldn't change. Maybe it was true at that time – but
everything's different now he's back. We *must* stop Lucy
marrying him.'

'But how?'

'When she comes to see me tomorrow, I'm going to tell her
the whole story. I'm going to tell her about the tape and tell her
the real reason why he vanished and tell her how he managed to
come back.'

'But will she believe you?'

'I'm her best friend. We've always loved and trusted each
other.'

'But she loves him – apparently she trusts him too – and don't
you think the way she loves him is bound to triumph? If Lucy
told you something terrible about me, would you believe her?'

Vee was silent. Then she said, 'It would have to depend on
the evidence. Just as it would if you told me something terrible
about her.'

'Darling Vee, you see! You talk about evidence – but you
haven't got any now the tape's gone. And she loves him blindly.

That's quite clear from the way she cooked up and swallowed all that patriotic nonsense. Besides, you haven't even been able to tell her about me, because you've been so worried about her reaction.'

'I was going to.'

'But you haven't yet. Are you going to mention it when you tell her about the tape?'

'I'll have to work that out.'

'Yes, you will. Darling Vee, do you really think you should rush into this so quickly? Do you really think it shows "the wisdom to know the difference"?'

'Oh James, you're so intelligent, and I guess some of the things you say make sense. But I have to do this. James, Lucy said they were going to get married "just as soon as possible" – those were her very words. No, I have to take the chance. My mind's made up.'

James sighed. 'And I suppose nothing I can say will change it.' Then he said, 'But couldn't I be with you when she comes? Really, you know, you're going to have to tell her about me – about how we took the tape together. And I could back you up, support everything you say. I'm a witness. I saw the tape too.'

But Vee said, 'No, no. I think I will have to tell her about you, but how could I talk to her about all those terrible things on the tape with you there? No, it's impossible. Really it is.'

He sighed again. 'Well anyway, I intend to come to London tomorrow. *My* mind's made up about that. You say she's coming at half past seven. Well I'll wait till eight – in a pub or somewhere – and then I'll come round.'

'Say she's still there?'

'Then that'll mean she believed you. It won't matter.'

'Make it half past. I'll need more time alone with her.'

'All right, half past. You do want me to come, don't you? Don't you think you may need me?'

Vee started to cry. Then, between sobs, she said, 'Yes, yes, I'll need you. I need you now. It was so horrible seeing him. I know he was looking for me – I suppose Lucy told him where I live. I felt such dread.'

'I'll drive up tonight. Right away.'

But she said, 'No. Please don't do that. I have to rest. I have to try to get some sleep. I have to go to work tomorrow. I'll get through it somehow. My work's different from yours. I've only just started the job – I just can't take a day off. I've got a list a mile long of things I have to do.'

'You're so brave, my darling. Tomorrow, then. I love you.'

'Tomorrow. And I love you too, darling James.'

Unlike Chris, Vee had no alarm system and no metal blinds. But, as soon as she had rung off, she double-locked the door. Then, in spite of the heat, and of their inaccessibility, she shut and fastened all the windows. She drew the curtains closely. When she went to bed, it was with her mobile phone beside her, and she lay, sweating and sleepless, until almost dawn.

SIX

When they had arrived at the Park Lane Hilton the night before and had been ushered to their suite, Rupert had wandered through it: the huge sitting room, overlooking Park Lane, the two bedrooms and bathrooms. He said, 'I've never stayed at a Hilton before.'

Seeing his expression, hearing his tone, she had raised her eyebrows. 'And you don't think much of it?'

He shrugged. 'A little bland, perhaps.'

She said, 'I suppose you'd have preferred one of those quaint old stuffy places – Claridges or that Savoy dump. They make me kind of claustrophobic. I feel watched. This place isn't like that.'

'You like its impersonality?'

'Yes, I guess that's it.'

'Anyway, it's very comfortable.' He smiled. 'Don't imagine I'm complaining.'

Her turbid eyes narrowed. 'I guess I wouldn't have expected you to.'

He smiled. 'No indeed. Let's have a drink.' He glanced towards the mini-bar near the window.

She said, 'I know you don't like that stuff. Nor do I. We'll order up some good champagne.' Then she added, 'I think you'll find the wine list's okay, even if this is only a Hilton.'

'Don't be like that, Miss Dis. Everything's simply splendid – and I'm quite sure the wine list will be too.'

She smiled. When she had rung room service, she said, 'An early night don't you think? I've got a busy day tomorrow. And by evening, of course, I'll have the famous tape.'

Tonight they had arranged to meet in the suite at eight. Rupert had taken a taxi from Islington and by a quarter to was

135

at the hotel. Disa had not yet arrived. In the sitting room, he went straight to the telephone by the sofa, sat down and dialled Oxford.

'Francis!'

'Rupe!'

'Can you, by any chance, come up to town tomorrow?'

'Rupe! Of course I can.'

'Good. Where shall we meet? A pub?' There was a sound at the door. 'Quick – I'm in a hurry.'

'There's that one opposite the British Museum.'

'Right. One o'clock. Goodbye.' As Disa came in, followed by a page loaded with parcels, he put down the receiver and stood up. He said, 'What a lot of shopping!' and then, as the page, lavishly tipped, departed, 'You've got it?'

'Yes.' With a smile, she gestured to her large handbag.

'Ah.'

She said, 'You were making a call when I came in?'

He paused, then said, 'That's right. To my old friend, Francis.'

'Oh, Cosmopolitan Clara?'

He laughed. 'Yes.'

'Will you be seeing him?'

After a moment he said, 'Yes. For lunch tomorrow.'

'I wouldn't mind meeting that guy.'

'He's changed a lot since his Cosmopolitan Clara days.'

'But you said he's still amusing. Does he still go in for rough trade?'

'I expect so. But I really think you'd find him a bit donnish.'

'Schoolmasterish, like you? Full of weird information?'

'That sort of thing.'

She said, 'Can't I come too? Tomorrow?'

He said, 'Well . . . not tomorrow, if you don't mind. We haven't seen each other for so long. We've got a lot to catch up with. It would bore you stiff. And probably masses of "stuff", as you call it.'

'I don't mind that. After all, I put up with you.' She said, 'I'd like to meet him.'

'Well you shall. Another time.'

Her eyes narrowed. But then she said, 'Okay. Another time. I won't forget. And what did you do with yourself today?'

'Oh. Nothing much. Wandered around. Bought some books.' He gestured to the Hatchards carriers on the sofa beside him.

'Books? Anything that would amuse me?'

He laughed. 'Absolutely not.'

'What a way to spend your first day in London after all this time!' Then she said, 'You didn't get in touch with Miss Innocence by any chance?'

'Miss Innocence?'

'You know who I mean.'

'Lucy, I suppose.' Then he said, 'Of course not. She'd never want to see me again – I told you.'

'Yes, you did, didn't you? Well, why don't we have something to eat and drink? And then we'll watch the tape.'

They watched it as they had watched videos on the island: in Disa's bedroom, with glasses of wine. When he had put on the tape, Rupert sat down on the edge of the bed but Disa pulled him down to lie beside her.

When James and Vee had watched the tape two years before, they had sat side by side on a sofa, in silence, each gripped by a horror too great to share. Now Disa nestled close to Rupert at the first glimpse of the bound, gagged, blindfolded, naked woman. 'That's Chris?' she asked. Eyes fixed on the screen, he nodded. But, during the variations of rape and abuse that followed, Disa, gazing enthralled, did not speak again.

The perpetrators were always partly clad: she – lean and brown – never took off her black boots, stockings and suspender belt, nor he his blue polo-necked sweater. Sometimes, when both of them were active with their bodies and their implements, the camera was stationary; at other times – when only one of them was busy on the screen – it shifted about; once – when the sound on the tape was the woman's laugh at what the man was doing – it jumped. No words were spoken: apart from that one shrill laugh, there were only grunts, gasps and panting breath. Muffled by her gag, the victim's groans were scarcely audible.

After the last shot – the woman still bound, gagged, blindfolded, and now apparently unconscious – when the screen went blank, Disa said, 'Wow!' and put out a caressing hand. But Rupert leapt from the bed. He stopped the cassette, and turned off the television.

Disa laughed. 'What's your hurry? Come right back here.'

He did so and, back beside her, laughed too. He was relaxed now: 'I said it would amuse you – my best experience ever with two women.'

She said, 'It's certainly quite something. And your partner – quite a gal!' Then she said, 'But, afterwards, didn't Chris go to the police?'

'Chris? Not a chance! She could never have described what we did to her to anyone . . . let alone to a bunch of coppers. Anyway, she didn't know who we were. She let my friend in – she'd never seen her before. Meanwhile I'd come in through the back window. I came up from behind and put the pad over her face and then I blindfolded her.'

Disa said, 'She might have recognized your smell.'

'Oh no – I'd drenched myself in a particularly pungent aftershave.'

'Ingenious! But tell me about . . . *her*.'

Now he smiled. He said, 'Her name's . . . Jeanne Duval.'

'French?'

'No – Cape Coloured. I met her in South Africa years and years ago. In those days sex between people of different races was illegal. That added a spice to the thing – a touch of danger. Like you, I've always enjoyed that.' He leant his head back, reached for his glass and took a sip of wine. He said, 'You can see she wasn't beautiful,' he said, 'but rather a fascinating face, and a wonderful body. Her father was some kind of Calvinist clergyman – always ranting about hell-fire. He used to beat her. She was sure he got a thrill out of it, though he said he did it to drive the Devil out.' Rupert laughed. 'He certainly didn't succeed. When I met her she was quite ignorant sexually, but I soon changed that – with her enthusiastic cooperation.' He paused, then he said slowly, 'I invented her. She was my creation.' He paused again, then continued in a lighter tone, 'Barbara – she was my second wife – caught me in bed with her one day. I must say she behaved impeccably. She could have made things very awkward for me, with the racial aspect of the situation, but she was the embodiment of Political Correctness – though of course that absurd phrase didn't exist in those days. Anyway, she just left me and went back to England with our daughter. She even let me divorce her for desertion.'

'She must have been a real dummy.'

'Yes, very stupid – and very boring, especially about the evils of apartheid. But I must admit that she was amazingly beautiful – though last time I saw her she'd really let herself go. Fat and dowdy and living in bliss with some butch lady lawyer. After she left me, D–Duval and I carried on for a long time, but then I got a feeling we were being watched. Anyway, I was tired of my job. So I went back to England.'

'Leaving another abandoned lady to mourn for you?'

Rupert was staring at the ceiling now. 'I don't know that Jeanne Duval *mourned* for me exactly. She was obsessed by me. She worked for years with that amazing body of hers to get the money to follow me to England. In the end, some rich stupid man paid her fare. He planned to set her up in a flat for his private enjoyment: she knew how to gratify all sorts of men by then, especially those with special tastes.'

'Like I do?'

'I doubt if anyone's quite your sexual equal. Anyway, what did become rather tiresome was her obsession with me. Oh, it was exciting at first. When she arrived in England, I'd been married to Chris for what seemed like a thousand years, though, actually, it was ten.'

'Ten! That sounds almost as bad as a thousand!'

He laughed. 'But quite good when it came to the divorce settlement. Because we'd been married so long, she had to split her assets with me. Anyway, Jeanne Duval put an end to the marriage. There was a telephone call. Chris answered, and a woman asked for me. Chris said, "Who's speaking?" and she answered, "Who the fuck are you?" Then Chris said she was my wife. I was in the room and I could hear a lot of shouting and swearing at the other end of the line, so I took the receiver from Chris. And it was . . . Jeanne Duval. I was astonished. And, I must admit, delighted. My life was really very tedious at that time. Oh, I had women, of course. But none of them were as good – or should I say bad? – as Jeanne. I went straight out to meet her that evening, and we . . . began again. But she was terribly jealous of Chris.' He laughed. 'She used to send her nasty little parcels.'

'Parcels?'

'Of shit. And, another time, a bag of blood. And I'm quite sure she once tried to push her under a bus. Rather a pity she didn't succeed, really. Then I would have inherited everything.'

They both laughed. 'And when did you have your bit of fun with the camcorder?' Disa asked.

'Oh, that was much later, after the divorce. As soon as Jeanne Duval and I got together again, we found a little flat for her. She ditched the man who'd brought her to England. She said she wanted to be independent, so she went on doing a bit of business on the side. Those special tastes, you know.' He laughed again. 'She'd do the most astonishing things with her clients. She was always telling me she was more an actress than anything else, and I suppose it was true, in a way. She had this fantastic collection of outfits and equipment in a huge cupboard that we fitted with a two-way mirror. Sometimes I used to sit inside and watch the happenings in her bedroom. When they were particularly interesting, I used to film them with the camcorder.'

'What a gag! Yes – quite a gal.'

'Oh yes. She was.' He sighed. 'If only she hadn't had her sentimental side. All those things she did with her clients – yet she wouldn't allow actual penetration to anyone but me. As I said, she was obsessed. Do you know, I think she wanted me to *marry* her. Can you imagine anything so preposterous? But she had this dreadful statuette of a bridal couple in her room, and once she said it made her think of her and me. Of course I burst out laughing. I could see she didn't like that. She changed the subject, but I really believe she had marriage in mind. And I think she hated Chris so much because I'd *married* her. That was probably why she was so keen on making that little visit. Afterwards she used to want me to watch this tape with her over and over again. I got almost bored with it in the end – though I must admit I enjoyed it again just now. The thing is . . . I'd become really rather bored with *her*. And yet I kept on seeing her.' He sighed. 'Well, actually, I couldn't stop. She was so amazingly keen to please me – and so very good at it. If only she hadn't had this sentimental thing . . .'

'But you got rid of her in the end?'

'Got rid of her?'

'Mmm. I suppose it was when you met Miss Innocence that you . . . ditched her?'

He said, 'Yes, that's right.' Then he added, 'She went back to South Africa.'

'Back to South Africa! How convenient for you! But I'm sorry. After seeing her in action, I really would have loved to meet her. That's impossible, I suppose?'

'Oh yes, I'm afraid we've lost touch completely.'

'You must have.' Disa laughed. Then she laughed again.

'Why are you laughing like that?'

'Can't you guess? Oh, come on!' She sighed. 'I think it's time to see the rest of that tape now.'

After a moment he said, 'What do you mean?'

'Oh come on,' she said again. 'No need to look so shocked. I know what's there. My guys told me. Did you think they'd turn it off where you did? Not a chance. They're *thorough*. Well – get going.'

Pale, expressionless, he did as she told him. For several minutes, the screen remained blank. He was standing by the bed when a new picture of the woman who had been so active in the rape of Chris appeared on the screen. She was not active now.

She lay on a bed. The camera approached slowly; the only sound was the deep breathing of whoever held it. The woman lay still – her eyes were shut – as the camera came closer. Now her head filled the whole screen. Her dark face was blanched and calm. The picture started to jiggle but she did not move. Her calm face, her closed eyes, were drifted with feathers like a fall of snow.

After a moment Disa said, 'You can see she's dead.'

The screen was blank again. He said, '*Can* I turn it off now?'

'Oh, sure – now there are no more tidbits!' Then she said, 'You told me long ago you didn't kill people.'

'I don't.'

'Oh, come on. I'm quite sure you killed her.' Again she pulled him down on the bed beside her.

'What nonsense!'

'Don't be like that! Can't you see I think it's great – your very own snuff movie? Can't you see it turns me on?' She took his head between her hands, made him look into her face. She said, low, 'I love it.'

He closed his eyes against her but then slowly opened them. Her look possessed him. His face took on the same melting, almost swooning, aspect. He murmured, 'Yes, I killed her.'

'Did she . . . struggle?' Disa's voice was almost a whisper.

'No, she was unconscious. I'd hit her. Then I put the pillow over her face. When I took it away, it had broken. She looked so peaceful with those feathers on her face. I left them there when I filmed her.'

'Oh, that's so cool – that you filmed her.'

'Cool? I didn't feel cool when I took that camcorder from the cupboard. Somehow, I felt compelled to do it. She'd been playing this tape of Chris, and I knew there was space at the end, so I used it to film her. That gave me a sort of . . . extra *frisson*.' Then he said, 'I had to have her again afterwards.' He added, 'She was still warm, but she felt so different from usual. Usually, her body seemed to radiate heat. And of course she lay so quiet. That was unusual too.' He gave a small soft laugh.

Disa said, 'That was what you remembered. Wasn't it? Wasn't it? That time on Kameni when you put the pillow over my face.' She lay back now and closed her eyes. 'Say yes. Oh, say yes,'

'Yes, that was what I remembered.' This time it was slowly that he took a pillow from behind him. Her eyes opened, then closed again, but her lips were parted as though for a lover's kiss when the pillow came down. Under it and under him, she lay absolutely still.

He gave a deep groan. But, as he opened his eyes, consciousness returned to them. For a second he hesitated; then he raised the pillow. She was gasping; she was in the throes.

When her breath returned, it came with a sigh that could have been regretful or relieved; his sigh, as he slid off her, was an exact replication.

There was a silence. She broke it. Her voice was slightly

husky as she said, with a gesture to his wineglass, 'Give me a sip of that.'

He handed the glass to her. She sipped, grimaced, handed it back. 'It's gone flat.'

He took a gulp, laughed, said, 'Yes, quite, quite flat.'

She said, 'We're so alike.'

'You think so?'

'Of course.' Then she said, 'Did you plan to kill her . . . or did you just get carried away? You must have been angry to knock her out like that.'

He said, 'I told you how tiresome she'd been getting.' After a moment he added, 'But "carried away" isn't a bad description.'

She said, 'Why didn't you tell me all this long ago? I told you about my daughter.'

He hesitated. 'You're always saying I'm cagey. Anyway I didn't know you so well then.'

'And I didn't know you.' A moment passed. Then she said, 'Perhaps you didn't think you could trust me.'

'Trust you? Perhaps I didn't.'

'But *now* you do.'

He said, 'Of course. But what about your "guys"?'

She laughed, 'Oh, you don't have to worry about that. This is all in the day's work to them. Why should they be interested in Jeanne Duval?'

He smiled. 'Why indeed?'

'Anyhow, they're my pals.' Then she asked. 'Did that Vee know who Jeanne Duval was?'

He said, 'I can't imagine how she could have.'

'But she must have realized the woman was dead. Why didn't she take the tape to the cops – being so self-righteous and all?'

He said, 'Lucy was pregnant by me. I'm sure Vee realized she would have been shattered if she'd known . . . all those things . . . about the father of her child.'

'The father of her child! It's just like some lousy old movie. And you've used that word "shattered" before – sounds as if she's made of glass. Anyhow, she could have had an abortion.'

'Oh, never in this world! Lucy's a Catholic through and through. You don't know her.'

She said, 'It's a pity you can't introduce us.'

'Mmm.' Then he said, 'I could do with a glass of red wine. And the Hilton – unlike your lair – does have half bottles. Incidentally, the wine list's excellent. You were quite right.'

She smiled. 'I'm always right.'

SEVEN

Next morning, Disa slept late. Rupert, awake much earlier, ordered and ate a kipper, drank several cups of coffee, looked through his new books, but did not read. He was restless. Often he stood up and paced the suite, pausing by windows to look down on Hyde Park, where, yesterday, at the other end of Park Lane, he had walked with Lucy.

He was still wearing the white towelling bathrobe provided by the hotel when Disa left – late – for a hair appointment at twelve.

'What time's your date with Cosmopolitan Clara?' she asked.

'Oh, one o'clock.'

'Where are you meeting? I could give you a lift in the limo.'

Rupert laughed. 'No thanks. That car's just like a hearse. We're meeting at a pub quite near here.'

'Tell him I'm looking forward to meeting him.'

'Yes, I will.'

'I'm going to do some shopping this afternoon. So we'll meet up after that and go someplace amusing tonight.'

He said, 'I'm afraid I've got an engagement this evening.'

'An engagement? Tonight?' She frowned.

'Mmm. Business.'

'Business? What business?'

'My stockbroker.' He added, 'We're having dinner. He's an old friend.'

'Another old friend! And I'm not invited?' She looked sullen now.

'My dear Miss Dis, I promise it wouldn't amuse you.' He added, 'I'll be free tomorrow.'

'Oh, okay then.' But, leaving, she still wore her sullen look.

As soon as she had gone, he headed for her bedroom. The

145

night before, when he went to his own room, the video cassette had been lying on top of the television, but it was not there now. He started a search, opening the drawers of the dressing table where he found only cosmetics and heaps of Disa's pure-silk underclothes. He went to the big walk-in closet, and gave a grunt of irritation at the rows of hanging clothes, the stacks of luggage. A knock on the door of the suite made him start. He closed the closet door and hurried through into the sitting room. 'Yes?'

The door was opened by a maid with a trolley stacked with fresh towels and sheets. Behind her was another maid with cleaning equipment. 'Would you like us to come back later, sir?'

'Yes – in another ten minutes.'

He went back into the bedroom, to the closet again. He tried the fastening of a small crocodile case on top of the pile of luggage. It was locked. He ran a hand over his hair. Then he looked at his watch, gave an exasperated shrug, and went to his room to dress.

A taxi took him to the Museum Tavern. Here, two years ago, James and Vee had met for the first time. Now Rupert's eyes searched the crowded, smoky room, picked out Francis standing by the bar. All the tables were occupied.

Francis started as Rupert put a hand on his shoulder. He turned. 'Oh, Rupe.' His face flushed with pleasure.

'Francis!' Rupert too looked pleased as he grasped Francis's hand. But then he said, 'What a frightful crush! We certainly can't talk in comfort here.'

'No, everyone's taking a break from the Library. You were in such a hurry that I mentioned the first place that came to mind.'

Rupert laughed. 'You can tell they're academics – that earnest, rather dowdy look.'

'I hope that doesn't include me.'

'But of course not,' Rupert said. In fact, Francis looked by no means out of place in this studious crowd. 'Why don't you finish that pint of bitter and we'll move on? Unless you're hungry?'

'No, I'm not hungry – Mother always insists on my eating what she calls a proper breakfast.'

'And I had a nostalgic kipper this morning, though usually I never eat breakfast.'

'Hence that boyish figure.'

'Boyish? Francis, you're so good for my ego. Well, why don't we go across to the Museum and have a look at the mummies? I used to be rather fond of them.'

'No accounting for tastes. I've never really cared for the Egyptians. But by all means.'

As they crossed the road, Francis said, 'Yes Rupe, you look as handsome as ever but perhaps a trifle . . . tired today.'

'Well, life's been a trifle tiring lately. I'll tell you all about it.'

'I certainly hope so.'

They were mounting the steps to the portico. 'Francis, don't sound so severe. You'll put me off. And I've forgotten the way to the mummies.'

'They're on the upper floor.'

They went through the bookshop and a long gallery of Egyptian sculpture. Francis said, 'Rupe – have you seen Lucy?'

'Yes, and all's well.'

'Really?'

'Yes. We're going to get married as soon as possible.'

'Congratulations. But Rupe – where have you been?'

'Well, it's a long story.'

'It's been a long time.' Francis panted a little as they went up the West stairs.

'You're out of condition, old boy.' Rupert laughed.

'I don't think I've ever been in it.' Francis laughed too but, as they entered the mummy galleries, stopped abruptly. In its open case, each mummy, human-shaped, was yet incalculably far from human. The representation on the accompanying tomb cover – however rigid its stare and hieratic its pose – was far more vital than the thing beside it that swelled and dented its pale wrappings.

Francis shivered. 'Well, here we are – in the kingdom of the dead. I suppose the garish colours on the walls are meant to create an Egyptian atmosphere. But these mummies were meant to be sealed away in dark caverns in the rocks. That's where they belong.'

Rupert laughed. 'With all those *objects*. Jewellery and furniture and all that *food*. The Egyptians were so optimistic.'

'Materialistic, *I'd* say.' Francis paused. 'Well, Rupe?' he said. 'I'm listening.'

'Who's that unpleasant dog-headed person? I don't care for him.'

'That's Anubis, god of the dead. "Lord of the Mummy Wrappings", they sometimes called him. Well, Rupe?'

Rupert sighed. 'Well, Francis . . .' He paused. 'You remember how I used to talk to you about "Jeanne Duval"?'

'How could I forget? Mother thought you'd gone off with her – but I never believed that. Actually I came to feel that, after you met Lucy, Jeanne Duval might have become, well, almost an encumbrance to you, just as Baudelaire's Jeanne became to him.'

'Francis, you're so perceptive. You were absolutely right. She had become a burden to me – a perpetual anxiety. You know how you kept advising me to tell Lucy about her?'

'Yes. In the circumstances, I felt it was the only thing for you to do.' Francis gave Rupert a questioning look. 'I even wondered if Jeanne Duval was responsible for that awful thing that happened to Lucy – her lovely plait being cut off in the Underground.'

'And you were right – yet again! It was Jeanne Duval – she'd found out about our engagement. When I discovered that, I decided I must tell Lucy everything.' Rupert paused. 'But then something else happened. That last time we talked, do you remember me telling you how that awful American friend of Lucy's – that woman called Vee – had insisted that I meet her next day at some café? And I asked you not to mention it to anyone except your mother – I know you tell your mother everything.'

'Yes, I remember your saying that – and I said "*Almost* everything," and we both laughed. And then we said goodbye, and I never heard from you again. Well, anyway, I never did speak of it to anyone but Mother, though, after you'd gone, I did think of mentioning it to Lucy. But Mother agreed with me that my first loyalty was to you.' Then he said, 'After all, you are my best and oldest friend.'

'Just as you're mine, Francis. I'm so lucky to be involved with such loyal people – Lucy . . . and you. Anyway, I met that awful Vee – and she blackmailed me.'

'*Blackmailed* you?'

'That's right. Can you believe it? All the time she was here that summer, this unspeakable woman was digging into my past, trying to find something – anything – that would discredit me in Lucy's eyes. Well, she succeeded. She broke into my flat and stole a tape – a video cassette – of me and Jeanne Duval.'

'What? I can't believe it.'

'Yes it's true. While I was away, she broke in, went through all my things, and found this tape – and stole it.'

'A video tape of you and Jeanne Duval, you say? What was on it?'

'Well, Francis, I know you're well aware that – till I met Lucy – I'd always had quite an active sex life.'

Francis's laugh was spontaneous. 'Rather an understatement, Rupe, surely?'

'Well, exactly. And especially with Jeanne Duval. In a long relationship with someone so . . . inventive as Jeanne, one tends to become . . . a trifle experimental. We tried out – well . . . rather unusual positions, and so on. Let's say it wasn't precisely *missionary*.'

Now they both laughed. Francis said, 'I can imagine – or perhaps I can't.'

'Anyway, one evening, just for fun, we set up a camcorder and filmed our activities. Another little experiment – however, it was one we didn't repeat. Actually, when I watched the film I felt a teeny bit embarrassed.'

'Did you indeed?' Again they laughed.

'Yes. But I kept the tape. I should have destroyed it but it never occurred to me that anyone else would get hold of it – and threaten to use it against me.'

'Which is what Lucy's friend Vee did? I see. That's really quite abominable. You know, what you should have done was go to the police – they're quite sympathetic when it comes to blackmail.' He added, 'Even – occasionally – to homosexuals nowadays.'

'Perhaps I should have done that. I wasn't thinking clearly at the time. I was so horrified at even the idea of Lucy – my darling, innocent Lucy – seeing that cassette that . . . well, frankly, Francis, I panicked. When Vee told me that, if I didn't vanish completely from Lucy's life, she'd show it to her, that was what I did – I vanished.'

'My poor Rupe! But why didn't you tell me? We could have talked it over. Together we might have thought of some solution.'

'Yes, but, as I just said, I panicked. Actually, you know, it was worse than that. I think I had a sort of breakdown. When I left England, I holed up in a little hotel in France. I stayed there for weeks, just brooding and staring at my picture.'

'Your picture?'

'Yes, my Blake, you know. *The Good and Evil Angels*. I took it with me. That picture has always meant so much to me. And even more after I met Lucy. I've always thought of her as the Good Angel in my life – don't laugh, Francis.'

'I'm not laughing,' Francis said. He added, with indignation, 'This terrible Vee certainly sounds like your Evil Angel.' Then he said, 'And it took you all this time to decide to come back?'

'Yes. It's a strange thing. I was so lonely, so unhappy. I wandered round Europe, looking at pictures, going round museums, in a sort of trance. And then suddenly, only just recently, I got back my courage. One thing helped me. I learnt that Jeanne Duval had gone back to South Africa. I suppose – after I disappeared so completely – she finally decided to start a new life without me. That was when, although I felt certain Lucy must have come to hate and despise me, I realized I must try to get her back.'

'But what about the tape?'

'Ah, the tape! Well . . . I decided that I'd go to Lucy and confess my past affair with Jeanne Duval. And I'd tell her that, once, when we were together, she'd set up a camera and filmed us without my knowledge. Then I'd reveal what Vee did – burglary and blackmail – from no motive but sheer, irrational hatred of me. And then I'd beg Lucy not to watch the tape – make her realize how much it would upset us both for her to see me making love to another woman. Francis, you know how fine Lucy is, how pure and fastidious – wasn't I right to believe she'd agree?'

'Of course, you were – if only you'd realized it two years ago!

Well, better late than never. But poor Lucy! I know how fond she was of Vee. Wasn't she horrified when you told her?'

Rupert was silent. Then he said, 'Well, Francis, actually I haven't told her . . . yet.'

'Haven't told her?'

Rupert said, 'Just look at that cat-mummy. Now that really is charming. It's better to have the body tucked away in a basket – isn't it? – than in those wrappings.'

'Rupe! Stick to the point.'

'Francis, you're just like the Grand Inquisitor! Well, you see, I thought, at our first meeting, it would be too upsetting for Lucy to hear all that. After my long absence – without a word, without a sign.' Then he said, 'It was you who gave me the answer, Francis.'

'I did?'

'Yes. On the telephone. When you told me how Lucy believed I'd been on this noble mission – I thought it would be such a shame to disillusion her. So, when we met, I said that what she believed was true. Later, I'll explain that Vee made her shocking move just before I got . . . called away.'

'Oh Rupe, I think you should have told Lucy the simple truth.'

'But the truth isn't simple. I don't want to talk to Lucy about panic and breakdown. You know how brave she is – how she values courage.'

'I'm sure she'd realize what courage it takes to tell the truth.'

'Oh, Francis. Perhaps it is wrong of me to want her to believe I'm a hero . . . but is it so wrong – when it makes her so happy?'

Francis was silent.

Rupert said, 'Francis. I love her.'

'Yes, I believe that,' Francis said slowly. He was examining a mummy cover. The head area was occupied by a Roman painting of a handsome youth, crowned with a laurel wreath. Under the portrait was a heavy gold Egyptian necklace, and, below that, a Greek inscription. On the lower part of the cover, Anubis, with dangling phallus and dog's head, presided over a body on a table.

'Admiring that pretty fellow in the portrait?' Rupert asked with a little laugh.

Francis's smile was faint. 'No, I was thinking what a weird hotchpotch the whole thing is. Egyptian, Roman – even Greek.'

'What does the Greek inscription mean?'

'"Artemidorus – your soul be well". That's the gist of it.'

Rupert said, 'Mine wouldn't be well with that awful dog-god hanging around.'

Francis said, 'Mmm, Ancient Egypt is a bit creepy.' Then he frowned. His tone gained intensity as he went on, 'But, you know, I've really come to detest Roman painting much more. It's so slick and shallow. So vulgar – well, just look at Pompeii!'

'Slick, shallow, vulgar – you make the poor old Romans sound just like bloody Yanks.'

Francis said, 'Yes, in a way. But Americans are sentimental – and nicer, too.'

'Nicer!'

Francis said, 'I can see you've been influenced by the activities of that dreadful Vee.'

'Perhaps.'

Francis said, 'At times, I really feel I hate the Romans.'

'But what about your beloved Petronius?'

'I'm sick of the Satyricon, too. All that empty, decadent sex.'

'Francis, Francis! What's come over you?'

Francis paused. 'Sometimes nowadays I feel trapped by things that no longer interest me. Yes, trapped by Petronius for instance – how I wish I'd concentrated on Greek instead of Latin when I was young – and . . . I feel trapped by aspects of my own life, too. Oh Rupe!' Suddenly Francis was speaking with passionate conviction: 'You're so fortunate. It's love that counts.'

Rupert said, 'Yes, that's true.' And then, 'Oh Francis, dear old friend, I really have had rather a tough time these last two years. Won't you forgive this small weakness of mine about . . . well, slightly misleading Lucy? Her love for me's so perfect, I don't want to cast any shadow on it.'

'Oh well . . .' Now Francis's smile was warm. Then he said, 'Anyway, who am I to forgive?' He laughed. 'You're mistaking me for Jessop the Jesuit.'

'Which reminds me. I've decided I'm going to be received into Lucy's Church. I shall renounce the Devil and all his works and pomps.'

'That's at Baptism. Surely they don't require you to be baptized *again*?'

'No, you're right. Nowadays I just confess and make my First Communion. There isn't a special ceremony as there used to be with conditional baptism and recantation of errors.'

'I should hope not.'

'I think it's rather sad.' Rupert sighed. 'I'd love to recant my errors – *and* renounce the Devil and all his works and pomps.' He laughed. 'It sounds so dramatic, doesn't it'

Francis said, 'Rupe, sometimes you're too frivolous.'

'Francis, I'm not frivolous about Lucy. You must believe that.'

'I do. But you're being frivolous about what matters to her most of all: her faith.' Then he said, 'I know Lucy wouldn't want you to convert insincerely.'

'It's because her faith means so much to her, that I want to share it with her.'

'But—'

'Stop worrying. Everything's going to be all right. Stop being so "heavy", as those Yanks say, and start to think about dancing at our wedding. But not in drag, I'm afraid – remember Cosmopolitan Clara? Francis, I want you to be my best man. You will, won't you?'

'Yes, Rupe, I will.' Then Francis laughed and added, 'And not in drag, I promise. And now let's go and have a quick look at the stolen marbles to refresh us after these gloomy mummies.'

'The Elgin Marbles? Byron thought we should never have taken them from the Parthenon. But wouldn't they have fallen to bits if we hadn't? The Greeks weren't bothered about preserving them.'

'Well, they are now. And we should give them back. They belong in Athens.' Then Francis said, 'It's one of my criteria for judging if a person is truly civilized – believing we should give back the Marbles.'

Rupert laughed. 'Goodness! I haven't felt strongly either way until now. But I suppose I'd better join you and Byron. And what *other* criteria have you – for being truly civilized?'

'Oh well . . . opposition to the death penalty, of course.'

'Really? But think of the sheer awfulness of life imprisonment.'

'You're looking at it from the murderer's angle.'

'I am?' Rupert laughed. His eyes sparkled.

Francis shook his head, and went on, 'I'm looking at it from the point of view of society. I think killing – legal or otherwise – utterly degrades those who do it. A modern country that murders its criminals in retribution is barbarous.'

'America, for instance?'

'In that respect.'

'Splendid! Down with the Yanks! Well, here we are.'

From the temple to Athena, goddess of wisdom, had been brought sculptures of gods, men and horses. Yet such definitions seemed ambiguous. Watery draperies were all that distinguished naked river god from naked man. A centaur's gaze was human but its hoof ground down a Lapith's thigh.

Now Francis was gazing at the procession to the holy festival. 'Horses and riders – all are one,' he murmured. Then he said, 'Greek art . . . renews me. It gives me courage.'

'It does?' Rupert sighed. Then he laughed. 'Well then, you shouldn't be so keen to send it back to Athens.'

Now it was Francis who sighed. With a quick glance at him, Rupert said, 'I'm sorry. It just doesn't mean the same to me. Too heroic, perhaps. As you so often say, perhaps I *am* incurably frivolous.'

'I hope not.' Francis said, but then – evidently unable to resist Rupert's smile, Rupert's sparkling eyes – he smiled. 'Oh Rupe!'

Disa tired of her shopping early. By four that afternoon she was back in the suite at the Hilton. She took a shower and changed. Then, in the sitting room, she sat down on the sofa and started, in a desultory fashion, to look through Rupert's books, grimacing impatiently at their titles, wincing, when she opened them, from lines of poetry or solid blocks of print. However, she smiled at the title of a life of Joe Orton, *Prick Up Your Ears*, and at the picture on its cover. The playwright sat in a deckchair, legs spread wide; he wore only white, bulging briefs. His body was bronzed by the Moroccan sun. Forty days' indulgence in bought Moroccan boys had given him an appearance of smug insolence: one reason why his lover would bludgeon him to death six weeks later.

Disa's next pause was at a paperback translation of a recent life of Baudelaire, her attention captured either by the poet's strange face – so ravaged, yet so curiously calm – or by the quotation from a review that accompanied it: 'The 46 years of his life have all the demonic ingredients of some modern thriller of Satanism and debauch.'

She opened the book, flipped through its densely printed pages, came to a glossy inset of illustrations. Here, eyebrows raised, she studied other portraits of the poet. Then another face, another name, caught her eye. She stopped, peered, gazed, then turned to the index. Half an hour later, she made a telephone call.

EIGHT

It was twenty to eight and, during the past half hour, Vee had glanced at her watch every minute or two. These time checks were not the only signs of her nervousness. Since her return to the flat, she had drunk three cups of coffee, and she had put no music on the stereo. She wandered round the living room, where she unnecessarily straightened cushions and several times adjusted the position of the jaguar on the television set. Now she went through into the bedroom, where her beloved Hopper print of a gas station on a lonely road hung above the bed. She crossed to the window, and glanced down at the canal and the evening strollers on the towpath. Until yesterday evening, this had been a pleasing sight, but now she shivered and turned away. At that moment the doorbell rang.

The admission buzzer of Vee's flat was out of order: a situation she had not yet bothered to rectify since the journey down from the first floor was so short. Now she opened her door and ran down the single flight of stairs to the hall. Here she paused for an instant – clenching her fists and straightening her back – before she opened the front door. On the top step, facing her, stood Rupert Deyntree.

At the sight of him, Vee took a step back; her eyes were fixed on his handsome face and brilliant eyes. A deep flush rose on her face, then drained away, leaving an unusual pallor.

For a moment, neither of them moved or spoke: it was as if Vee's horror and Rupert's hate had been captured in a dreadful film-still. Then, with a faint cold smile, Rupert said, 'Can I come inside? Lucy sent me.'

There was a moment when Vee's body swayed forward and she raised a hand as if to push the door shut. But then she

157

straightened and pressed her arms stiffly against her sides. 'Sent you?' she said.

'Yes. She didn't want to see you after what I told her about you.'

'About me?' Vee said, and then, 'Lucy knows you've come here?'

He laughed. 'Yes. So you've no need to be frightened,'

'Frightened?' She said, and then, louder, 'I'm not frightened of you.'

He laughed again. 'Then why don't you let me in?'

'Come in, then.' She spoke defiantly, then stood back for him to enter. He pushed the door shut behind him. She waited for him to go up the stairs ahead of her, lagging slightly behind him, her fists clenched tightly at her sides. He went through the open door into the living room; following him, she did not close the door. Looking round, he glanced at the open door with raised eyebrows.

'Nice little flat,' he said. Then, 'There was a murder in one of these houses. Perhaps it was this one. The playwright Joe Orton's lover battered him to death with a hammer. When the police found them, there was blood everywhere. Orton's brains were splattered on the walls and ceiling. The lover had killed himself with pills afterwards. He was naked and covered with Orton's blood.' Rupert flung himself down on the sofa, crossing his legs, clasping his hands behind his neck.

Vee stood facing him. She said, 'Your murder wasn't so messy and unfortunately you didn't commit suicide afterwards.'

'My murder?'

'Yes. Your murder of Dink November at that awful house in Finsbury Park.'

At the name, his face changed. He blinked once. He took his hands from behind his head, and sat upright on the sofa.

Long ago, in the café near his flat, his face had darkened like this, and then paled, and his eyes had glittered. Vee said now, 'When I met you at that café, I'd only seen the first part of the tape – the terrible things you and Dink November did to Chris.'

Again he blinked.

Vee went on: 'I didn't see the end of the tape till later. But when I saw it, and found out all about Dink's death, you'd vanished and poor Lucy was pregnant with your child. I wanted to protect her. I was wrong. I should have shown it to her anyway – and then to the police.'

'And now it's too late,' he said, and then, 'Oh what a busy little digger you've been. Just like the wolf in *The White Devil* – "the wolf that's foe to men", the wolf that scrabbles with its nails and digs up corpses.' Now he smiled, and leant back on the sofa again. 'I always seem to find an appropriate quotation.' He went on, 'And now, of course, in spite of all your digging and scrabbling, you've got no evidence at all. But do tell me – did you visit *all* my ex-wives? Did you visit Chris?'

'Yes, I did. I showed her the tape of what you did to her.'

'Oh really? That must have been quite an occasion. But I'm sure you didn't enlist *her* cooperation. I'm sure *she* wasn't prepared to go to the police.'

When Vee was silent, he smiled. 'No. I thought not. I know my Chris.'

She burst out, 'Whatever lies you told to Lucy, you can't keep me from her for ever.'

'I don't have to keep you from her. She won't see you.'

'I'll make her see me.'

'Even if you do succeed in that, she'll believe *me*. Whatever you tell her. When she said you wanted to see her alone this evening, I knew what you were going to do, and I . . . preempted you.'

After a moment, Vee said, 'I suppose you'd say you love her.'

'Of course I love her.' Now his tone was calm. 'And I'm going to marry her.'

'You say you love her. How can you want her to marry you? A rapist, a liar, a murderer.'

Suddenly he stood up. He said, 'Be careful. Oh, you're safe now, but if you go on interfering with me, you little Yankee whore, you may not be immune indefinitely.'

'Don't threaten *me*.'

'Threaten—' He made what seemed an involuntary movement towards her. He said, 'There are things I could do to you now that you'd never be able to prove.' He smiled.

It was at that moment that the doorbell rang. Both started.

Then Vee ran from the room and down the stairs. She opened the front door, then stared, astonished at the figure on the steps. 'Lucy!'

Lucy too was pale: a scattering of golden freckles on her skin stood out. She said, 'I had to come. At first I thought I couldn't, but that was cowardly. I can't let Rupert bear my burdens alone. He's still here, isn't he?'

'He's here. Oh, but Lucy I'm so glad you've come, Lucy!' Vee held out her arms, but Lucy shrank away.

'Don't touch me.' Lucy went up the stairs ahead of Vee, increasing her pace when she saw Rupert standing in the doorway of the flat, looking as astonished as Vee had done. 'Oh Rupert.' Lucy took his hand. She said again, 'I had to come.'

'You shouldn't have. It's too painful for you. Someone you thought was your friend—'

'I *am* Lucy's friend.' Vee spoke loudly.

Inside the flat Lucy let go of Rupert's hand. She turned to Vee. Tossing back her hair she said 'No, Vee – you aren't my friend! I've known that ever since I said to Rupert that I was coming here this evening, and he told me all those dreadful things.'

'Dreadful things?' said Vee.

'Yes, dreadful things. How, from when you very first met him, you'd been plotting against him – yes, I'm afraid plotting is the only word. Plotting with Rupert's son, whose mother brought him up to hate his father. She's a terrible woman. I've known that ever since she rang me up, blind drunk, when Rupert was away just after we got engaged. I should have told Rupert about that, but I didn't want to upset him. And I should have told him how his son spoke to me on the telephone and begged me to meet him, and I agreed because I felt sorry for him about his mother.'

'Darling, you're too good, too sweet,' Rupert murmured.

Now Lucy took his hand again. She continued to hold it while she spoke: 'I should have told him how I didn't feel it was loyal to meet his son, who hated him so much, while he was away – anyway I was too upset after that awful thing that happened to my hair. So I sent you to tell him I couldn't come.

160

Oh, Vee – and you never told me, all this time, that you'd gone on seeing him. Perhaps you're still seeing him – are you, Vee?'

After a moment Vee said, 'Yes, I'm seeing James.'

'You're probably having one of your . . . affairs with him.'

Vee said, 'It's not an "affair" – we love each other.'

'And you never told me, your best friend, anything about it? That's the same as *lying*. Oh Vee, I can't *believe* this . . . or perhaps I can – after all the other things Rupert's told me that you've done. Of course, you were influenced by this *James*' – Lucy stressed the name in a disgusted tone – 'but how could you have *plotted* with him like you did? How could you have tried to blackmail Rupert? Blackmail him over that Cape Coloured woman he'd befriended under apartheid and then saw again when she first came to England.'

Vee said, 'So he's told you about Dink November?' Then she said, 'Did he tell you how he murdered her?'

Lucy made a small sound, and Rupert grasped her hand more tightly. Now both of them stood facing Vee. '*Murdered*!' Rupert exclaimed. 'You're suggesting I *murdered* her? You must be mad. Why, I didn't even know she was dead. This is the first I've heard of it. You say she's been murdered?'

'You know that better than anyone.'

Turning to Lucy, he ignored this. 'Oh, poor Dink,' he said softly. 'I'm so very sorry to hear this. She was such a sweet girl when I first knew her in South Africa. Before she turned to prostitution – oh, that made me so very sad. Such an awful life – and such a dangerous one. As this proves.' He sighed deeply. 'Those poor women come into contact with such awful men.' He said again, 'I'm so very sorry.'

'Oh darling Rupert, I'm sure you are.' Fiercely Lucy turned to Vee. 'Rupert told me all about this woman. He didn't mention her name – why should he? But he told me how they defied the apartheid laws and . . . came together when he found out his second wife was a lesbian.'

'Barbara didn't know she was a lesbian in those days.'

He turned to Lucy, 'You see – she's been visiting all my former wives, lapping up their malicious stories about me.' Now he looked boldly straight at Vee. 'I expect you've met Chris as well.'

161

'You know I have.'

Lucy rushed on: 'I know everything about Rupert, and everything I need to know about his wives. And I know all about this . . . Dink November. How she drifted into prostitution when she came to England, and Rupert tried to help her to get out of that life and take a decent job, and how he kept on seeing her until he realized it was absolutely hopeless. And I know that you found out about her, and thought the worst, of course – that he was still involved with her after he met me. I know how, just before he had to leave England on his mission, you tried to blackmail him into breaking off our engagement. Rupert thinks you've always believed that was why he left the country – is that true, Vee?'

'He left because I said I'd show you a video tape.'

Lucy said, 'I know about the tape, too.'

Vee stared at her.

'Yes Vee. And I'm shocked – I'm shocked by *you*. Of course, it's a shocking story, too. That this Dink, when they were still involved, could have got a man to film them without Rupert's knowledge, when they were . . . making love. When he found out about it, of course he was horrified. That was what finally made him realize that she was, well . . . almost beyond redemption. And of course he took the tape away from her. And then you and this *James* inveigled your way into getting his spare key that *I'd* told you about – I remember it clearly – and you stole it. You used it in your filthy blackmail. How could you imagine Rupert wouldn't have told me all about it, if he'd been here? And how could you imagine I would have watched it?'

'So you think he would have told you all about a tape of him committing rape and murder?'

'Just listen to her!' Rupert said to Lucy. 'Listen to what she's capable of inventing. Lucy, I know it would be worse than distasteful, but perhaps you ought to watch that tape, just to prove it isn't what she says.'

'Proof – I don't need proof!' Lucy exclaimed to Rupert. 'Proof of what you say, when I've always believed in you. When I've always known, ever since you disappeared, why you had to go away.'

Vee was angry now. 'Oh Lucy – how can you be so stupid, so gullible?'

Lucy's voice trembled. 'You're right. I *am* stupid and gullible. To have trusted you. To have believed you were my friend.'

Rupert said, 'Tell her to show it to us – this tape. Probably she's got it here. Darling, let's get this over once and for all. Tell her to put it on that video recorder.'

'Oh Lucy, Lucy' – Vee's tone was desperate – 'he knows I can't show you the tape and all its horrors. He knows because *he* stole it.'

'I stole it? Oh really?' Now Rupert's tone was coolly sarcastic. 'When did I steal it, and from where?'

'You know where you stole it. From your first wife Sarah's cottage last month. And you killed her darling dog.'

Rupert laughed. 'I'm not particularly fond of dogs, but I hardly make a practice of *killing* them. I've never been to my first wife's cottage – I don't even know where it is. And, as for last month, I had to stop in Europe on my way back from the Middle East. My passport can prove it – why, I only came back to England two days ago. I'll show you, Lucy. I want to. As a matter of fact, I've got my passport on me.' He fished in his pocket, and pulled the passport out. 'Look! See the date I left Greece. Oh Lucy darling, please look.'

'I don't need to,' she said, but he touched her shoulder, and she looked down at the page. 'Yes, it's quite clear,' she said. 'Absolutely clear.'

That was when the doorbell rang, startlingly loud. None of them moved or spoke for a moment. Then Rupert said, 'Aren't you going to answer it?' Releasing Lucy's hand, he stood up and went over to the tall sash window. Looking down at the front steps, he said, 'Lucy, I think her co-conspirator has arrived. I suppose they planned to gloat over what they imagined would be their success in poisoning your mind against me.'

Lucy stood up. 'Rupert, please let's go. I can't face anything more.' Now she was crying. Tears flowed down her cheeks, as she turned to Vee: 'How could you? How could you? I shall never understand.'

'Lucy, I'm telling you the truth.' Now Vee, too, was crying. 'Lucy, I love you.' She took a step towards Lucy, but Lucy drew back, and Rupert came quickly from the window to put his arm around her.

'*Love* me? *Love* me?' Lucy gave a sob. 'How can you expect me to believe that?'

Rupert spoke quietly: 'Perhaps it's true. But oh, what a strange perverted thing that love must be.'

At his words, and at a look of dawning horror on Lucy's face, Vee raised her right arm and flung herself towards Rupert, but Lucy leapt forward from his embrace to stand between them: 'No!' The doorbell rang again, was pressed urgently, twice, then three times, and Vee lowered her hand.

Rupert put his arm around Lucy again, 'My darling,' he murmured. 'My poor, poor darling.' He guided her towards the door. Now, slowly, Vee followed them onto the landing. As Rupert gently propelled Lucy towards the top of the stairs, he turned his head and looked at Vee. He smiled; his eyes dazzled, and Vee cried out, 'Oh, God!' Gripping the banister, she stood still, her other hand raised to her forehead. Then she followed them down the stairs.

Rupert opened the front door. James, on the top step, pressing the bell again, took a step down. Then, as Rupert guided Lucy forward, James moved backwards down to the pavement, drawing in his breath, then releasing it in one word: 'You!'

'My misguided son!' Rupert's tone was regretful. 'If only . . .'

James flinched. 'James, oh James,' Vee called out from the hall, and he looked up into her stricken face. Pushing past Rupert, with a shudder and a stare, James bounded straight up the steps to Vee.

Now James knew the whole story. After she told it, Vee had cried. Now her tears were over, but they had been succeeded by an absolute despondency.

'There's nothing we can do,' she said. 'Nothing at all.'

He said, 'I never thought I'd hear those words from *you*, my darling.'

'I never thought I'd say them.' She made a sound and movement that were half sigh, half shiver. 'But I've never felt absolutely hopeless before. Hopeless and helpless.'

James said, 'Just what *he* wanted you to feel.'

'Yes, I guess so. He's so clever – and so evil. He's what the word evil really means. No one – no one in the world – could be more evil than he is.'

James was silent for a moment. Then he said, 'Something so strange happened to me there, by the door, when I saw him. I recognized him at once. I seemed to know him. Darling, have you ever heard of a Döppelganger?'

'A Döppelganger?'

'Yes. It's the ghost of a living person. When I saw him, when he spoke to me, I seemed to see my own ghost, and it was terrible. As if everything horrible I've ever thought or known or imagined was concentrated there in him, in his presence, in his *being*. Darling, after we'd first seen the tape, when we were walking near the cottage, I quoted something to you.

> *'Like one, that on a lonesome road*
> *Doth walk in fear and dread . . .*
> *Because he knows a frightful fiend*
> *Doth close behind him tread.'*

She was staring at him. 'Yes, I thought it was horrible.'

'You said so. And then I told you that of course there was no fiend. I wonder if I believed myself – I don't now. Oh, it's not exactly a fiend – it's my, Döppelganger, my living ghost that treads close behind me. And that Döppelganger is my father.'

Vee gave a nervous little laugh. 'James, don't try to frighten me any more than I'm frightened already.'

'Darling Vee, I'm not trying to frighten you. There's only one thing to do with a ghost, living or dead, and that's to exorcize it.'

'*Exorcize* it?'

'Oh, I don't mean with bell, book and candle. We have to defy it. We have to destroy its power. We have to defeat it, or we'll never be free of it.'

'Defeat it? Oh James – but how?'

'We have to *act* – oh, I know that sounds funny coming from me.'

165

'I'm not laughing. Far from it. If only I could think of anything to do.'

James said, 'I think you should telephone Chris Deyntree.'

'*Chris?*' Now Vee sounded incredulous. 'After all that happened? After I cheated her into talking to me by giving her a blank cassette instead of the real one? Oh no.'

'She doesn't know he's got the tape back. She doesn't know that now he can live happily ever after with Lucy Riven.'

'Happily ever after! Oh, my poor Lucy! Sooner or later she's bound to find out what he's like.'

'Well,' James said, 'we're going to make sure it's sooner rather than later. And surely, in the present circumstances, Chris will want that too. How she must hate him!'

'I'm sure she hates me, too.'

'But not as much as she hates him.'

'No, she can't hate me that much . . . Well, I guess I could try.' Now Vee frowned: 'You know when he showed Lucy his passport? That was weird. I wonder if he got someone to help him.'

James shrugged. 'Who knows? And meanwhile I'm going to get in touch with Francis Larch.'

'Francis Larch? You know him?'

James smiled. 'I can't exactly say that. But he's my god-father.'

'Really?'

'Yes. Somewhere at home, there's a silver christening cup he presented me with. He was always my father's best friend – still is, you say, according to Lucy.'

'So how could *he* help us?'

'Well, Mum always said he was a nice man. But of course, after a divorce, you know how things go. They lost touch completely – he being so close to my father.'

'Lucy says he's really nice, too. They got to know each other quite well, and kept in touch while your father was away. If he is nice – I can't say I've got a lot of trust in Lucy's judgement right now, but Sarah liked him too – he can't know what's been going on.'

'That's just what I'm going to find out.'

After a moment she said, 'Oh James, it's quite amazing –

you're giving me hope. Really, I was in despair. Oh, my poor Lucy! She despises me – she thinks heaven knows what about me. And she's always been my dearest friend.'

'She will be again.'

'I hope so.' Vee sighed. 'Are we going to make those calls right away?'

'I'm going to track down Francis in Oxford. I'm going to telephone and ask if I can come and see him tomorrow. I'll get his number now from Directory Enquiries. But I think you should leave Chris till tomorrow. Darling, you look completely exhausted.'

Vee sighed. 'Yes I'm beat.'

'And you need some food.'

'I'm not hungry.'

'Yes you are. You just think you aren't. We both need a drink and something to eat.'

'Perhaps you're right.' She sighed again. 'I suppose we could find a take-out.'

'You and your "take-outs"! Isn't there anything to eat in the flat.'

'A few eggs . . . some bread.'

'Butter?'

'Yes.'

'Thank goodness you aren't one of the low-fat-spread brigade.'

She made a face: 'It tastes so vile.'

'And I'm convinced it's full of vile ingredients. We'll have scrambled eggs on toast. Can you make that?'

She laughed. 'You turkey! Of course I can.'

'"Turkey"! – I love that. Well, go ahead while I get in touch with Francis. We'll eat and then we'll sleep. "Tomorrow to fresh woods and pastures new".'

'I thought that was "fresh fields".'

'So do a lot of other people – but I'm a lecturer in English.'

Laughing, she went into the kitchen, and he picked up the telephone.

Back in Oxford in time for dinner, Francis had exclaimed, 'Mother, Mother, what a lot of questions! Yes, he's back. He's in London. He's been abroad all this time.' He paused. Then he said, 'He really had to go.'

'*Had* to? That sounds fishy.'

'No – not really.' Francis paused. Then he said, 'Actually, not at all.'

Mrs Larch said, 'You'll be telling me next that he actually *was* on some secret mission, just as that poor deluded girl believed.'

Francis paused. Then he said, 'They say truth is stranger than fiction.'

'You mean she was right? I can't believe it. And *what* precisely was the nature of this secret mission?'

With some satisfaction, Francis said, 'Oh, of course he couldn't discuss that . . . even with me.'

Mrs Larch raised her eyebrows. 'I see.' Then she said, 'And meanwhile, what has happened to the mysterious Jeanne Duval?'

'Oh, she's gone. She left the country – she's back in South Africa.'

'How fortunate! So are he and his Lucy already blissfully reunited?'

Francis said, 'Yes, they are. And they're going to be married very soon. And I'm to be best man at the wedding.'

She smiled. 'I should hope so.' Then she asked, 'And am I to be invited?'

'Oh, I'm sure you will be.'

'I should hope so,' she said again, and then, 'I still think there's something fishy about that mission. You haven't considered the possibility that he's leading *you* by the nose?'

Francis's smile was almost smug. 'No, Mother, I haven't.'

'He's such a scamp.' She shrugged. Then she said, 'I'm feeling just a little chilly – please fetch my black cardigan from upstairs. It's on a chair in my room.'

'Yes, Mother.' Like an obedient child, Francis hastened to carry out these instructions, but, in the passage he gave a sudden little skip and giggle, also childish: those of a child keeping a secret from the grown-ups.

They were just finishing dinner when the telephone rang, and Francis hurried to his study to answer it.

'Well, what a surprise!' Francis said to his mother on his return. 'Just imagine who that was! It was Rupe's boy, James. Do you remember – he's my godson? Though I'd really almost forgotten that – it must be nearly thirty years ago.'

'How extraordinary!' Mrs Larch said. 'What on earth did *he* want?'

'I've really no idea – except that he wants to see me. He said he had to talk to me – he's coming here tomorrow morning.'

'How extraordinary!' Mrs Larch repeated. 'He didn't say what it was about?'

'No, not a word. It's really very odd after all this time.'

'*Very* odd!' Her large face was alive with curiosity. Then she frowned. 'Perhaps he wants to borrow money?'

'Do you think so? I certainly haven't been very forthcoming as a godfather. I suppose that might be it. He said he wanted to see me alone.'

'Really? Then I must make myself scarce, I suppose.' She added, 'You can tell me all about it afterwards.'

'Yes, of course.'

'He's probably in some scrape – a scamp just like his father!'

'I did lend Rupe some money once – but he paid it back in a month or two.'

'Yes, I remember – I was quite surprised.'

'*I* wasn't. Despite all the vicissitudes of his career, Rupe has never let me down. I'm sure *he* doesn't know anything about this – and I can't ask him: I haven't got his telephone number. Though I suppose I could get in touch with him through Lucy. But I think I'll wait until after this interview. "By our first strange and fatal interview",' he murmured.

'Ah yes, Donne!' Mrs Larch was an admirer of the metaphysical poets. Then she added, with a laugh, 'Strange, but I hope not *fatal*!'

Francis laughed too. 'No, indeed!'

'My guess is that it's money he wants.'

'Rupe would be furious, but I suppose I could let him have a hundred pounds – accumulated birthday tips, you know.'

'*More* than generous. Shall I let him in?'

'No, I'd better. You can watch from your observation post at the drawing-room window.'

'Observation post, indeed! You make me sound like a spy.'
Again they both laughed. Then she said, 'I wonder if he looks
like his father. Oh well, *nous verrons* – we shall see.'

Just as James had done his best to cheer Vee, so Rupert strove
to console Lucy.

After James had closed the door, Lucy came to a sudden halt
on the pavement, and gave way to a further burst of sobbing.
Rupert, with his arms around her, kissed her hair and patted
her shoulders: 'Lucy, Lucy, my sweet angel.'

'I can't bear it. All this horror . . . about Vee,' she said,
between her gulping sobs.

'We must comfort each other. Oh, I can't bear to see you
suffer.'

It was in response to this that she stifled her sobs and let him
wipe her eyes. 'I'm sorry,' she said. 'I couldn't help crying.'

'Of course you couldn't. Darling, where shall we go?' he
asked as, his arm still round her shoulder, they went along Noel
Road in the direction of Upper Street.

'Oh, not to the Firenze – or any other restaurant. I couldn't
face it. I think I'd better go back to Hampstead. I'm exhausted.'

He said, 'I wish we could go to this place where I'm staying –
but, as I told you, I can't even give you the telephone number
because it's connected with the work I've been doing.'

'Sort of what they call a "safe house"?' she said.

'That sort of thing. Ridiculous, isn't it? Sounds so melodra-
matic. But I'll be out of there . . . oh, any time now. Just a few
loose ends to tie up. Then I'll move to a hotel while we find a
place of our own.'

'A place of our own!' For the first time, there was something
other than misery in her voice. 'What a lot there is to do. A flat.
Furniture.' Then she said, with a faint smile, 'We'll hang up
your famous picture, *The Good and Evil Angels*.'

After a moment, he said, 'No, that was stolen.'

'Oh no! I know how much you loved it.'

'Yes, I did. I was sad to lose it.' Then he said, 'But I've put
that behind me.' He added, 'Anyway, I've got my own good
angel now.'

'Your own good angel? Do you mean me? Oh no, you

mustn't say that. Not seriously. Angels are guardian spirits.' Then she said, 'I must try to put Vee behind me, as you've put your picture. And try to think about our marriage – and living in a place of our own. You and me and Edward. Though I don't know what I'll do when I haven't got Mag to look after him.'

'Couldn't you put him in a nursery school?'

'Oh no – he's far too young. Of course I couldn't. Perhaps I'll have to give up work for a little.'

'Why not?'

'Well, money for one thing.'

'I've got enough. Anyway, couldn't your mother help out a bit?'

'Oh, I'd die if I had to ask her.'

He smiled. 'Then don't, on any account!'

At this she too smiled faintly. They had reached Upper Street. 'We'll get a taxi here,' he said, and then, 'Oh, how I wish we could spend the night together. I long for you so.'

'Oh – and I long for you. But, this time, I don't want to sin. I don't want to spoil things. This time, everything's going to be perfect. This time we're going to wait until we're married, just like we should have last time – though of course then I wouldn't have had darling Edward.' She was silent for a moment. Then she said, 'God has been so kind to me.' She squeezed his hand. But then she sighed. 'Oh, I can't help feeling so terribly sad about Vee.'

'Darling, don't start crying again, please. Look, there's a taxi.'

'Yes.'

He hailed it, and gave the Dumbles' address to the driver. He got in beside her, and held her tightly. When they were nearly there, he said, 'I'm going to ring up Father Jessop tomorrow. I want to be received into the Church immediately.'

She said, 'Oh Rupert, are you quite sure?' And then, 'You know you don't have to.'

'I want to. I'll be received just as soon as possible. I've been thinking about it all the time I was away. I'll confess all my sins and take Communion, and soon we'll have our nuptial mass. I want to share everything with you.'

'But that's not your main reason?' Her voice was anxious.

'You know it isn't.'

They reached the house in the quiet, countrified street. Telling the taxi to wait for him, he saw her to the door, kissed her in the rustic porch, waited while she let herself in, returned her farewell wave. Then he went back to the taxi. 'Park Lane Hilton,' he told the driver with a smile.

NINE

When Rupert returned to the suite at the Hilton, Disa was sitting on the sofa. She looked at her watch. 'Half past nine! Your business took a long time.'

He said, 'Oh, after I finished it, I went to the National Gallery.'

'You've been in that joint all this time?'

He laughed. 'No – it closes at six.'

'Oh yes?'

He said, 'Afterwards I dropped into Jules Bar in Jermyn Street. It's an old haunt of mine.'

'Yeah, I know it. It's not bad. You should have called me. I'd have joined you there.'

'Good idea – I should have.' When she said nothing, he added, 'But I thought you'd probably be out.'

'Out? No I was here waiting for my guy to come home. Aren't you touched?' Her laugh was mocking.

He laughed too. 'Oh yes, deeply touched!' Then he said, 'I'm sorry if you've been bored.'

'Bored?' Her eyes flickered. She said, 'I'm never bored.'

He laughed. 'That's good. Bertrand Russell says that at least half the sins of mankind are caused by the fear of boredom.'

'Is that so? Who's this Russell – a pal of yours?'

'No, a dead philosopher.'

'Oh.' Then she said, 'Have you fixed up our date with Cosmopolitan Clara?'

After a moment's hesitation, he said, 'Oh, I'm afraid he can't make it. He's off to France on holiday tomorrow.'

'Is that so?' Then she said, 'Have you eaten?'

'No,' he said, and then, 'I wouldn't mind a sandwich.'

'A sandwich? I thought we might go out. And there's this club I've heard of.'

'Well, I'm a bit tired this evening.' Then he said, 'Oh, by the way, Disa, where's the tape?'

'The tape? It's in my room. In the drawer of the bedside table. Want to watch it again?' But he was already on his way to her bedroom. She followed him. She stood in the doorway as he opened the drawer, and took out the tape and examined it. She raised her eyebrows as he slipped it into the video recorder, switched on, and turned to fast-forward. She came to stand beside him as Chris's agonies spun past; the blank stretch of tape was only a brief pause. Now Dink's dead feather-strewn face zoomed close, was held for an instant outside time, was sucked into darkness and then swallowed by it.

Taking out the cassette, he said, 'Just checking.' Holding it, he came past her into the sitting room. She followed. 'Disa – I'm off.'

'Off?' Her voice was higher in pitch than usual.

'Yes. And so many thanks, my dear Miss Dis. I can honestly say that knowing you has been a unique experience. Absolutely fascinating, in fact – and I'm truly grateful for all you've done for me. Do give my regards to Kameni.'

She turned away from him: only a glimpse of eyes and teeth, then just the smooth beige fall of her hair.

He took a step towards her, then halted. 'Disa?' After a moment he asked, 'Aren't you going to say anything?'

Now she swung round, her face expressionless. 'What do you expect me to say – "This is so sudden"?' Out came her two-note laugh, louder than usual. 'Surely you know by now that nothing surprises *me*.'

'That's my Disa!'

'*Your* Disa?' She laughed again. 'I'm no one's Disa – just my own.'

'That's what I meant. I've always admired your detachment.' Then he said, 'I'm going to pack now. It won't take me long.'

When the beautiful maiden Medusa coupled with the sea god in the goddess Athena's temple, the angry goddess changed her to a gorgon whose stare turned all beholders to stone. Perhaps it was fortunate that Rupert, cassette in hand, did not look round as he left the room.

A moment or two passed. Disa shook her head, just as she did when emerging from a plunge in her swimming pool. Then she went into her bedroom, to the telephone.

She was on the sofa, swinging one elegant foot, when he came back with his packed suitcase and his two carriers of books. He said, 'As you know, I travel light, so I won't bother with a porter.'

She faced him, smiling. 'So that's it?'

'Well, yes. I know you really feel the same. Fun's fun, but there comes a time when the kissing has to stop.'

'Kissing?' she said. 'We haven't done all that much kissing.'

He laughed too. 'No.' Then he said, 'And a clinch now would be a bit of a cliché for us, wouldn't it?'

'Oh, I guess so.'

'So I'll just say goodbye.' He crossed the room, and put down the suitcase to open the door into the corridor. Then he turned. He said, 'Well, you've got my picture as a memento. *The Good and Evil Angels.*'

'I could always get it back to you.'

He hesitated, but then he said, 'No, no. Don't bother. You keep it – I'm only sorry you don't like it more.'

'I don't mind some of it. Perhaps I could just cut it in half.' She laughed.

He winced. Then he said, 'It's quite valuable, you know.'

She laughed and said, 'You know I don't care a fuck about that.'

'No, you're above money – lucky you! That's why I don't insult you by offering to pay the bill here. So . . . farewell, Miss Dis.' He raised his hand in salute. She, smiling, did the same. The door closed behind him.

Out in the passage, he drew in then let out a great draught of breath before he set off for the lift. Outside the Hilton, he took a taxi to a small but comfortable hotel in a street leading north off Piccadilly.

As soon as he was alone in his room he started his attack on the cassette. He split off the top, but could not pull apart the lower casing; he jammed it in a drawer, and wrenched at it till he cracked the tough plastic.

Now he was able to start dragging out the tape: the black shiny streamer could have decorated a devil's Christmas tree. It was long, but at last, in bunched twisted loops, it all dangled from his hand.

He took the tape into the bathroom and soaked it in the washbasin, squeezing it between his fingers. Then he returned to the bedroom where he tipped the books out of one of the carriers and fumbled in his case until he found a pair of nail scissors. With scissors and carrier, he went back to the bathroom, where he chopped the drenched tape in the basin into fragments. He wrung out the sodden mess, and dumped it in the carrier.

Back in the bedroom he collected broken bits of plastic and shoved them in with the tape. He screwed the top of the carrier into a knot and dropped it in the waste-paper basket. Then he went downstairs to the bar and ordered a half bottle of vintage champagne. He smiled at the barman. 'I'm celebrating,' he said.

PART THREE

ONE

'You must be James,' Francis said as he opened the front door. Then he added, 'You're very like your father.'

'So people say. And you're Mr Larch.'

'Oh, call me Francis, please. After all, as I'm sure you know, your father's my best friend.' Francis spoke in the firm tone of one stating an irrefutable fact. Then he said, 'Do come into my study and tell me what this is about.'

In the study, he said, glancing at the drinks tray and then at his watch, 'Eleven o'clock – a teeny bit early, but do have a glass of sherry. I'm going to.'

'Thanks.'

Francis gestured James to the chair facing his desk, poured out the sherry, gave James a glass, and moved to the seat behind the desk. 'Well, godson, greetings!' he said, raising his glass.

'Yes,' James said, raising his own, with a not quite steady hand.

'The tutorial position,' Francis said, 'as my mother often remarks when she occupies that chair you're sitting in.' He smiled. 'My undergraduates sit there. You were at university?'

'Yes, at Cambridge.'

'Ah – the other place. And now?'

'I lecture in English – at Norwich, you know.'

'Oh, really. How very interesting.'

'I want to talk about my father,' James said.

Francis said, 'Oh, really?' There was a pause. 'Have you seen him recently?'

'Yesterday, as a matter of fact.'

'*Really*? So did I. He didn't mention he was going to see you! But how splendid! A reconciliation – after all these years?'

'Far from it!'

'I see.' Then Francis said again, 'As you know, he's my best friend.'

'Yes, yes, I know. But my mother says you're a nice person. And so does Lucy Riven.'

'You know Lucy?'

'Not really. Oh please, couldn't I just tell you . . . this whole thing? And then you can say whatever you like.'

'Very well. But I must warn you I didn't care for your remark a moment ago when I said that Rupe's my best friend. You said *but* people think I'm a nice person. I regard those two statements as perfectly compatible – leaving aside of course the question of my "niceness".'

'Oh, *please*!'

'Go ahead then.'

James said, 'There was a tape—'

'Ah, a tape. I see. Your father told me about the tape you're referring to, I think. It was stolen by a repellent American woman called Vee, who used it to blackmail him.'

'Vee's not repellent. She's wonderful. She's Lucy's best friend.'

'You consider it friendly to blackmail the man Lucy loves with evidence of an old affair?'

'An old affair! So that's what he said to you. That's what he said to Lucy.'

'Oh, so he's told her now?' Francis added, 'That was brave of him.'

'Brave! He told her a pack of lies. How, just before he left the country on this so-called patriotic mission of his – did you really believe in that? – Vee telephoned him and told him she'd show Lucy this tape if he didn't break off the engagement. Anyway, Vee didn't steal the tape alone – I helped her.'

'*You* did? How perfectly disgusting! Really I don't think there's any point in our continuing this conversation. In fact, I think you should leave this house immediately.' Francis rose from his chair.

'*Please*!' James said again, and then, 'You said I could tell you the whole story. Just let me do that. Then I'll go at once.'

Either these words or the passionate desperation with which James uttered them made Francis sit down again. He shrugged and said, 'Well?'

'Of course he didn't tell you or Lucy what was actually on this tape of Dink November – do you know about Dink, the Cape Coloured woman he met in South Africa?'

'Oh yes, I know about her. I didn't know her name – Rupe and I always referred to her as Jeanne Duval . . . after Baudelaire's dark mistress, you know. But of course I was perfectly aware that wasn't her real name. Anyway, what has that got to do with the fact that they made a tape of their . . . sexual activities.'

'Oh? My father told Lucy the tape was made without his knowledge.'

'Well, that was obviously out of consideration for Lucy. Anyway, this woman's back in South Africa now, and the whole business can – and should – be forgotten.'

'Back in South Africa? She's been dead for two years – murdered. I've got a copy of the report from the local paper. Here it is.' James took the photocopy from his pocket, and handed it across the table to Francis, who, after an instant's hesitation, took it: his hand trembled. When he had read the brief item, James went on, 'There wasn't much coverage – just another prostitute, you know, killed by one of her clients. Except that the "client" happened to be my father.'

'Oh, *really* – how dare you come to me with such a preposterous story?'

'He taped it. Her murdered body is on the tape. The same tape as the terrible things he and this Dink did to Chris.'

Francis drained his glass of sherry. 'Chris?'

Francis sat in silence, absolutely still now, as James told him of the rape of Chris. He grew paler. The lines on his face showed in sharper relief. James described Vee's meeting with Rupert in the café, and her later discovery of the second episode on the tape; he described his and Vee's long night of debate, leading to their final decision not to go to the police. 'We were wrong,' he said. 'We see that now, but Lucy was pregnant with his child, and Vee wanted to protect her – Vee really loves Lucy. So I hid the tape behind Volume Ten of the *OED* in my bookcase, down in Suffolk. I thought it would be safe there. I thought the whole thing was over. I thought he'd gone for ever.'

181

Francis had bowed his head. With one finger he was tracing circles on the surface of his desk. He said, very low, 'Go on.'

Now James described the killing of Mansfield and the theft of the tape, followed by Rupert's almost immediate reappearance; he told Francis about the previous day's confrontation at Vee's flat. When he had finished, he said, 'We must stop him. We have to do everything we can to stop him marrying Lucy. That was why I decided to telephone you.'

Francis looked up. He said, 'And what did you think I could do?'

'Vee and I thought perhaps you might talk to Lucy. We thought she might believe you.'

'And why did you think that?'

James said, 'Because she knows you're his best friend.'

'I see.' Francis looked down at his desk again. Then he said, 'You'll have to let me think about all this. You must give me time.'

'Time!' James said. 'But they'll be getting married soon.'

'I shall know when,' Francis said, and halted. 'I'm meant to be best man.' Then he said, 'I really must have time to think.'

James said, 'And when you've thought?'

Francis said nothing.

James said, 'Will you just let me know what you decide? I'll give you my telephone number.' He repeated, 'Please!'

After a moment Francis said, 'You can give me the number.'

James gave him both his Suffolk number and Vee's London one. Francis's hand trembled as he wrote them down. Then he said, 'I'd like you to go now.'

'Right. Yes.' James stood up. 'I can see myself out.'

'Yes, would you?'

'Of course.' But when he reached the study door, he turned. 'You do believe me?'

After a moment Francis said, 'If I had totally and utterly disbelieved you, I wouldn't have taken your telephone number.'

'No. I see. Goodbye then.'

Francis did not answer. As soon as the study door closed behind James, he rushed to it and locked it. Back in his chair, he rested his head on the desk, and began to weep. When, a few minutes later, his mother turned the handle and then said his name, he cleared his throat and then called loudly, 'Wait a minute, Mother.' But nearly ten minutes passed before he unlocked the door and opened it.

At the sound, his mother emerged at once from the drawing room. 'Francis! I've been so worried. I saw that young man let himself out – he's certainly very like Rupert – and then your door was locked. I wondered what on earth had happened.' She studied him keenly. 'You're flushed. You look upset.'

Francis said, 'It's nothing, Mother.'

'You're sure? What did he want?'

'Oh, well . . . it was unpleasant.' Francis paused. 'You were quite right. It was about money. He wanted to borrow . . . quite a large sum.'

'What cheek! I hope you said no.'

'Oh, of course I did. Why, I hardly know him.'

She said, 'I wonder what Rupert will have to say about this.'

Francis said nothing for a moment. Then he said, 'Please don't mention it if he rings up – just leave it to me. Now, how about a glass of sherry before lunch? I had one with that young man, but I must say I rather feel like another.'

'What a good idea!' She followed him into the study, saying, 'Yes, it must have been most unpleasant for you.'

Apart from familiarizing herself with her new job, Vee had other problems to overcome at her office. There was a certain passive, not quite sullen, resistance on the part of surviving staff members to the dismissal of their former boss and his replacement by a foreign woman. In addition there was what she had described to James as the 'laid-back' English attitude to work when compared with the 'gung-ho' American approach.

James had laughed. 'Remember your Serenity prayer,' he had said.

'I try to. But there are things I have to change.'

'And things you have to accept, too, perhaps?'

She had sighed, but then said, 'I guess so,' and today, while James was in Oxford, she exerted herself, in the intervals between continual international calls, to achieve this balance.

It was nearly eight by the time she reached home that

evening, but she ran quickly up the stairs to her flat, where James was waiting. 'Well?' she said.

'What a greeting.'

She laughed. 'I'm sorry.' They embraced. Then she repeated, 'Well?'

'I told him everything.' James paused. Then he said, 'He believed me. I'm sure he did.'

'He did? Great! So what's he going to do?'

James said, 'I gave him this number and the one in Suffolk. I think he'll telephone me.'

'Telephone you? What's that going to achieve?'

'Calm down, darling. He was stunned. It was like Dorian Gray . . . he almost aged before my eyes. When I arrived he kept saying that my father – "Rupe", he calls him – was his best friend, and I'm sure it's true. He looked absolutely overwhelmed. He said he had to have time to think. When he has, I believe he'll telephone . . . quite soon.'

'Quite soon! They could be married by then, if they got a special licence.'

'He'll know when they're to be married. He said he was to be best man. Poor old Francis. I felt really sorry for him. He looked absolutely stricken.'

Vee sighed. Then she said, 'Do you still think I should telephone Chris – even though she hates me? Even though she said she'd never let anyone see the tape.'

'But now there *is* no tape. Yes, I think you should telephone her. We can't put all our eggs in one basket. After all, my father is Francis's best friend. We can't be certain what he'll do. He could manage to convince himself that I told him a pack of lies. So just try Chris. To see how she feels about him living happily ever after with Lucy.' Then he said, 'I'm sorry to suggest it when you look so exhausted.'

'That's okay.'

When she picked up the receiver, James said, 'My dauntless lady.'

She blew him a kiss with her left hand as she dialled Chris's number, and was answered, on the third ring, with Chris's customary silence.

'Is that Chris Deyntree?'

184

A moment passed. Then Chris said, 'Who *is* that?'

'It's Vee Westwood.'

'I thought I recognized your voice – you little bi—' Chris did not finish the word 'bitch'; now she substituted 'horror'.

'Hey, easy does it. Listen, I'm sorry about that business with the cassette. When I gave you a blank one in exchange for your talking to me. I had to do it.'

'You're *sorry*. You *had* to do it.' The tone in which Chris repeated Vee's words was withering.

'Listen, I have to see you.'

'You have to see me.' This time Chris imitated Vee's American intonation.

'Yes, I do. Listen – Rupert's got the tape back.'

'How could he have? I don't believe you.' Chris's voice was momentarily low and breathless.

'He stole it – or had it stolen – from where I'd hidden it.'

'This is quite incredible.'

'It's true. And I want you to help me—'

'Help you? I wouldn't help you if you were drowning.' Chris's laugh was shrill.

'I believe you. But Chris, there was something else on that tape as well as what happened to you. Further on, after a blank track – I only found it later. There was the dead body of Dink November. Chris, he killed her.'

There was a silence. Then Chris said, 'Oh, is that so? You told me she was dead, and then I found out she'd been murdered – I was very glad to hear it. But I didn't know he killed her. Well, that's the best thing I've heard about him yet. Congratulations, Rupert old boy! You're the nastiest bastard in the world – but you've got one achievement to your credit.'

Vee said nothing for a moment. Then she said, 'Perhaps I can kind of understand that – after what she did to you. But wouldn't you like to help to bring him to justice?'

'Bring him to justice? *Ms* Westwood, you've really got a nerve. You lie to me and cheat me. Then, through what's obviously an incredible piece of bungling, you allow Rupert to get back that tape. Now you're asking me to help you "bring him to justice". How exactly are you proposing to do that?'

'I'm not quite sure. But now that you don't have to show

185

them the tape, I thought you might confirm its existence to the
the police . . . you wouldn't have to go into any details.'

'You're insane.' Chris's voice rose as she said this, but then
she lowered it: 'Quite insane. Didn't I tell you all along that I
had absolutely no intention of involving the police? Now, after
two years, do you really expect me to change my mind in order
to "bring him to justice" for getting rid of that disgusting
whore?'

'I hoped you might . . .'

'Well, you hoped in vain. And if you dare to try and involve
me, I warn you I shall deny all knowledge of that tape. I shall
tell the police you're obviously mad to have invented such a
thing.'

'I see.' There was a moment's pause. Then Vee said,
'Rupert's back in England. He's going to marry Lucy.'

'Marry Lucy Riven? But that's impossible.' Now Chris was
unable to control the fluctuations of her voice. 'Are you
telling me that, after you showed her that tape, that Riven
religious fanatic is going to *marry* him? I simply don't believe
it!'

Vee said, 'I never showed it to her. I told Rupert I would if he
didn't break off the engagement – and it worked . . . until now.
Until he stole the tape. You see, I couldn't bear to show it to her
. . . unless I absolutely had to. She was pregnant with his child.
I'm her friend. Or I was until yesterday, when I tried to tell her
about the tape. Now she hates me.'

This time Chris's silence was a long one, but at last she broke
it: 'Her friend! All that *sisterhood* people like you go in for . . .
all that *caring*! What a friend you turned out to be! Let me put it
rather crudely – all you've done is dump your friend Lucy in the
shit.'

'Oh, you're cruel!' Vee exclaimed. 'Chris, you're so cruel. But
you're right, though I'm sure you don't care what happens to
Lucy!'

'Too true – self-righteous little do-gooder!'

'She isn't!'

'Riven of Rivendale!'

Vee paused. Then she said, 'Yes – Riven of Rivendale' You
should think about that, Chris. How she'll inherit that estate –

and *he* will. Think of Rupert, Chris. Enjoying the life of a country gentleman. Lord of the manor, you could say. Married to Lucy Riven of Rivendale and living happily ever after.'

Chris drew in her breath, and Vee went on: 'He loves her in a way – I really believe he does. She *is* going to make him happy ever after. Think about that, Chris. *Really* think about it.' Then she said, 'I'm going to give you my telephone number. If you do decide to do anything about this, call me.'

Chris said nothing. Vee gave the number slowly, and then repeated it. A moment or two passed. Then there was a click. She put down the receiver.

'Well?' said James.

'She hung up on me.' Vee shivered. 'Wow, she really gave me the creeps. So icy cold, but so full of malice and hate.'

'So she'll do nothing.' He sighed, then smiled. 'What was all that business about Riven of Rivendale?'

'She said it first. Then, when I went on about it, and talked about him living like you said, happily ever after, she went dead quiet. Perhaps it kind of got through to her.' Then Vee shrugged. 'But I expect you're right. Probably she won't do a thing.'

'So we're left with Francis. The waiting game. But now let's eat. You're having a pernicious influence on me – I bought a takeaway. I'll heat it up.'

She laughed, but her tone was only partly joky when she said, 'Oh James, what would I do without you?'

He laughed. 'I can't imagine. And first thing tomorrow, darling Vee, we're going down to Suffolk for the weekend. You need a break.'

'But—'

'We both need a break. I mean it. We'll think better – and do better – if we have one. And anyway Francis has the Suffolk number.'

'Yes.' Then Vee said, 'It would be wonderful to get away. I'm beginning to hate this apartment.'

'There you are – you aren't seeing clearly. It's a very nice flat, as we both agreed. And you'll think so again just as soon as things get better.'

187

'If they get better.'
'They must. So tomorrow to fresh . . . what?'
'Woods,' she said, and then, 'I love you, James.'

TWO

In Willesden that Saturday it was with dragging steps that Belinda followed Barbara – the sway of her plump hips perceptible even in the loose, flowing dress she wore – downstairs and into old Mrs Korn's flat.

As they went in, Belinda's nostrils contracted at the familiar and distasteful smell: the stuffiness caused by her grandmother's fear of draughts from open windows, the mustiness of old furnishings and, as so often, the sweetish odour of chicken soup with what Belinda called noodles but her grandmother called 'lockschen', or with dumplings, which her grandmother called 'kreplach'.

In what she always referred to as the lounge, though Belinda – reacting in Deyntree mode – had long ago instructed her that only hotels had lounges, Mrs Korn sat by the window in her rose-velvet-upholstered armchair. Although, for years, she had spent most of her time in this chair, looking out of the window by day and at television in the evening, she adamantly refused to stay in bed except when she felt too ill to get up: only lazy 'schlemiels' spent the day in bed.

The room was crowded – this in itself was not to Belinda's taste – with heavy and elaborate furniture and with what Belinda once described to her mother as '*objets* but certainly not *objets d'art*'; Barbara had shaken her head: 'Oh Belinda, you mustn't be so unkind.' Mrs Korn's family photographs, in silver frames, were arrayed on top of a piano that no one in Belinda's experience had ever played.

'Belinda, my schnooky!' Belinda winced involuntarily at the Yiddish endearment, but her grandmother was holding out her plump arms for an embrace. Belinda slowly approached. Although Mrs Korn was fat, her yellowish skin hung in loose folds, and her face, which had a mauve tinge, looked haggard; she smelt of powder and cupboards.

'And how's my little grandchild?'

'I'm fine,' Belinda said.

'But you're too thin. You don't eat. You're fading away.'

Barbara came to Belinda's rescue: 'Oh Momma, that's a bit of an exaggeration. Anyway, stop kvetching. It's the fashion.'

'The fashion! I remember when *you* were in the fashion – oy vey! That modelling – your father always said it would come to no good! You were skin and bone.'

'Not any more!' Barbara's laugh was hearty.

'And a good thing too. You must keep up your strength.'

'I'm strong as a horse, Momma. I'll go and fetch your soup.'

'Belinda, come and sit by me. You're quite a stranger. You must have a lot to tell me.'

Belinda glanced after her mother's retreating figure. Close to her grandmother's armchair was a carved chair of dark wood, its imitation-tapestry seat and back depicting wreaths and bunches of flowers. Belinda perched on its twin, which was slightly further away.

'So . . . tell me.' Mrs Korn's expression was hungry.

'Well, I'm very busy – especially since my promotion at work.'

'Work – I don't want to hear about your work! Have you *met* someone? That's what I want to know.'

Belinda parried the question. 'Met someone? I meet lots of people.'

'You know what I mean. A boy. A nice Jewish boy.'

Barbara, returning with a tray holding a bowl of steaming soup and two matzos on a plate, heard this, and intervened: 'Momma, don't embarrass her. She's shy.'

'Shy of her own bubba!' But Mrs Korn's eyes were on the tray now, and her hungry look was transferred to it.

Barbara put the tray on the small table next to her mother's armchair. She pulled up the chair Belinda had avoided and prepared to help her mother eat: Mrs Korn's hands had become shaky since her heart attack.

Belinda stood up, and wandered over to the piano. She examined a family group: her grandmother's bearded, serious

THE LAIR

father and small mother, their son and their three daughters; the whole family had dark eyes and large noses. Next to this picture was a portrait of Belinda's grandfather, as a young man: Barbara had inherited her neat regular features from him. 'Your father was very handsome – very English-looking,' Belinda had once said to her mother. 'Well, he *was* English,' Barbara had replied with one of her rare sharp glances.

'I think you look quite like I did as a girl,' Mrs Korn said now, licking her lips after a spoonful of soup.

Belinda half turned. 'I wish I'd inherited your lovely eyes,' she said.

'What's wrong with your eyes?' Mrs Korn said, but she smiled with pleasure, and so did Barbara, as they both looked up at Belinda. Then Barbara frowned: she, though not her mother, had observed that a single large tear was rolling down Belinda's cheek. Belinda turned back to the photographs, brushing at her face.

When she and her mother were upstairs again in Barbara's and Michel's flat, Barbara said, 'Darling, I saw you were crying downstairs. What's the matter?'

Michel was out, at a women's-group meeting, though due back at any moment. If she had been present, Belinda would almost certainly have denied that she had been crying. Now, sitting at the kitchen table while Barbara assembled the lunch – for once, from Belinda's point of view, impeccable: cold chicken and salad – she responded to her mother's look of concern with a little wail. '*Oh* . . . it's so sad, so awful.' She started to cry again.

'Darling – *what* is?' Barbara bounded round the table, put her arms round Belinda's shoulders and hugged her, pressing her lips against her daughter's hair.

For an instant, Belinda stiffened, but then she slackened again. Between sobs, she said, 'All of them being murdered like that – Gran's family. Her father, her mother, her brother, her sisters. All of them except Gran.'

'Darling Belinda!' Barbara's tone held astonishment as well as warmth: this was a subject of which Belinda never spoke, and when others referred to it she always remained silent. 'Yes, it's the most terrible thing in the world.' There were tears in her

191

own eyes. Now she added, 'But we must never forget it. Never!'

There was a silence. Then, 'No, never.' Belinda's murmur was hardly audible, but she groped for her mother's hand and squeezed it.

'Well, what a touching scene!'

They both looked up at the woman standing in the doorway, her right elbow propped against its frame, her left hand resting on a lean hip.

'Michel!' Barbara exclaimed – for once, her voice did not express its usual enthusiastic welcome – while Belinda, breaking from her mother's embrace, immediately sat bolt upright in her chair.

Asked which of the two disliked the other more – Belinda or Michel – most people would have plumped for Belinda. Her unchanging aversion to her mother's lover was obvious in her frequent rudeness, but also evident in her stance, her voice, the sullen glances angled to evade eye contact. Michel, on the other hand, usually adopted an attitude of humorous, if deprecatory, forbearance in her dealings with Belinda; yet her body language could have been interpreted as conveying, though more obliquely, an equally hostile message. There were the little backward jerks of the head, eyes closed and face expressionless, when Belinda expressed her – invariably unacceptable – views, the apparently casual pats and squeezes of proprietary affection for Barbara, always most frequent in Belinda's presence. Above all, there was an exaggeration of her usual macho quality: a flaunting of that particular sexuality from which Belinda recoiled.

Now, all Barbara said was, 'We were talking.' Although so inveterately – and unjustifiably – optimistic about the relationship between her daughter and her lover, something made her hold back from bringing her recent moment of rare intimacy with Belinda under Michel's scrutiny.

'Anything interesting?' Michel's tone was detached, yet it gave the impression that she was provoked by Barbara's unaccustomed reserve.

It was Belinda, with a stony glance at her mother – now moving, with an almost furtive air, to the other side of the table – who answered: 'No. Nothing. Nothing at all.'

Michel, with a shrug, moved from her pose in the doorway to join Barbara on the other side of the table, examining the food laid out. 'Mmm. Looks good.' She put an arm round Barbara's waist. Then she said, 'Been downstairs?'

'Yes.' Barbara added, 'We had a nice little visit. Momma was so pleased to see Belinda.'

Michel said, 'I'm sure she was. Did she recognize her after all this time?' She followed this question with a jolly laugh.

'Oh, ha ha. Very funny!' Belinda's expression was sullen.

Michel picked up a piece of chicken breast in her fingers. As she raised it to her lips, Barbara said, 'Naughty!' and gave her hand a little slap. Then she said, 'I thought we'd eat in the living room today. Let's take all this stuff through.'

When Michel and Barbara were alone, they ate in the kitchen. Now Michel, savouring her titbit of chicken with sensuous relish, said, 'Very posh! But of course we have a visitor.'

Barbara said, 'Nonsense! I just thought it would be nice to eat in there for a change. Belinda's not a visitor. This is her home.'

Michel said, 'She doesn't spend much time in it. Anyway, *I* thought her home was over in her flat in yuppie land.'

Belinda said, 'You do that word "yuppie" to death, Michel. It's awfully boring – and out of date, too.' She had flushed, as she did when anything reminded her that Michel had lent her the deposit on her flat.

Michel laughed again. 'Find me one that suits you better, and I promise to give it up.'

Barbara said, 'Do stop teasing Belinda, darling.' Now they carried the food through into the front room, where Barbara had laid the table; it was spread with an Indian cloth; she had even put a vase of roses from the garden in the middle.

'Very posh,' Michel repeated.

'Just *civilized*,' Belinda said, and then, to Barbara, 'It looks nice, Mum.'

Barbara smiled. Michel did not. They began to eat: Barbara rapidly and voraciously, Michel with a more measured enjoyment; Belinda's approach, even to acceptable food, was always gingerly.

There was a silence, which Michel broke: 'One would think

that chicken was going to explode, the way you prod at it,' she said to Belinda.

Belinda put down her fork. 'Why don't you just shut up, Michel?' She turned to her mother. 'Can you wonder that I hardly ever come here when I have to put up with this bitching old cow?'

'You're mixing your metaphors.' Michel laughed, not looking or sounding in the least upset by Belinda's words.

Barbara, however, looked horrified. 'Oh Belinda!' she exclaimed.

'Oh Belinda! Oh Belinda!' Belinda's mimicry of her mother was scathing. Then she said, 'I hate spending time here. It's horrible!'

'Rather be at the office?' asked Michel. 'Working on an *advertising* campaign?' Her tone expressed all her disdain for Belinda's occupation.

'*Much* rather!' Belinda said. 'I *love* my work. And, as a matter of fact, I think it's very important.' She glanced at her mother, saw Barbara's look of pitying disbelief, and suddenly changed tack. 'So does Chris.'

'Chris?' Barbara said in a puzzled tone, and then, 'You mean Chris *Deyntree* – as she still calls herself? Where on earth did you bump into her?'

'I didn't "bump into her",' Belinda said. 'I often see her. She's a marvellous person, and she's been marvellous to me.' She glanced from her mother's face, hurt and surprised, to Michel's: Michel's head was tilted back, her eyes were closed; there was the very faintest trace of a smile on her lips. 'Chris is really sweet to me,' Belinda went on. 'She doesn't nag and criticize. She *understands* me!'

Michel opened her eyes. Still with the faint smile she said, '"Misunderstood!" Don't you feel you're a bit too old for that line?'

Michel did not notice Barbara's frown. Nor did Belinda, who said, 'I hate you, Michel. Yes, I really hate you. I always have. You ruined everything for me. All my childhood.' She spoke in a low voice; the effect was more impressive than if she had screamed or shouted. Now she turned to her mother. 'And you – you're worse. After all, you are my *mother*. My father may have been divorced a lot, and now apparently he's disappeared – just vanished off the face of the earth – and left that girl he was engaged to with his baby. But I don't think he's as bad as you are, living . . . like you do. Living with this horrible *woman*.'

Barbara looked stunned. Michel's expression was unchanged, though perhaps her little smile might now have been interpreted as one of triumph.

Belinda stood up. 'I'm going,' she said. She picked up her bag. She did not even glance at Barbara before she hurried from the room. Her feet clattered on the stairs; then the front door slammed.

'Belinda!' Barbara exclaimed, but not loudly. She leapt up and to the window. Belinda was almost running down the street, her footsteps loud in its suburban silence.

Michel came over and put an arm round her. She said, 'I told you so.'

This cliché – always a contender for the role of 'most enraging' – was certainly ill-chosen now. Barbara shook off the encircling arm, stepped back, and confronting her lover with an angry look – her eyes flickered like an alarm signal – said, 'Told me *what*?'

'Darling, cool down. I've always told you she couldn't accept our relationship – or me – and you've never believed me. Now she's proved it!'

Michel's rational tone did not calm Barbara. 'That's not true. She was upset today. By the way you treated her. You were perfectly awful to her.'

'Oh, really?' Now Michel's voice held a note of sarcasm. 'And just how was I *perfectly awful*?'

'Oh, stop interrogating me like a fucking lawyer.'

Michel laughed. 'Well, after all, I *am* a lawyer.'

'Well, I wish you'd keep your legal manner for the office.'

'I see. But you still haven't told me in what way I was *perfectly awful* to your darling daughter.'

'Oh, you know quite well what I'm talking about. You were baiting her – those everlasting remarks about yuppies.'

'You've often agreed with me that she shows all the characteristics of the archetypal yuppie.'

'Have I? Anyway I don't harp on it like you do. Even I find it monotonous, so what must she feel? And saying this isn't her home – how could you?'

'I merely pointed out that she hardly ever comes here.'

'Well, no wonder – you're so horrible when she does. Everything was perfect today. She was so nice to Momma. And then – up here afterwards – we were really communicating. That "touching scene", as you called it so nastily. And then you came and ruined everything.'

'Ah, the serpent arrived in your little Garden of Eden?' The tone in which Michel spoke these words was apt: hissing and poisonous.

Barbara evidently thought so, for she said, 'I couldn't have put it better myself.'

'Well, I do apologize for intruding on your little idyll. I always hate to be *persona non grata*. And I definitely feel that way now, so I think I'll take myself off.'

However, after she had said this, Michel stood still. Perhaps long experience suggested to her that Barbara, always the initiator of instant reconciliations after brief squabbles, would make some gesture or utter some word of protest. If so, she was mistaken. Barbara turned away and went back to the table. Standing by it, she mechanically picked up a chicken drumstick, and began to nibble at it.

'That's right!' Michel said. 'Fatten yourself up! Not that it's really necessary.' As she strode towards the door, Barbara hurled the drumstick at her. It hit her shoulder, and fell to the floor.

Now it was Michel who clattered on the stairs and slammed the front door. Barbara sat down at the table. She reached towards another piece of chicken, but then withdrew her hand. She rested her elbows on the table, her head between her hands. Outside, Michel started the car with a savage crash of gears.

Last time Michel had set off from Willesden to the house in Tolland Road, she had whistled her favourite aria from *Don Giovanni*. Today she drove in silence, with a frown. The frequent smooth changes of gear that characterized her normal driving style were replaced by vicious jerks, and when she reached her destination the brakes shrieked as she drew up.

Michel's last visit to 63 Tolland Road, nearly two years ago, had been for an assignation with Trish Pringle, a social worker who lived on the top floor. On that occasion, Trish's – somewhat *passé* – girlishness had suddenly seemed cloying; this had combined with a belated impulse of loyalty to Barbara, and Michel had retreated, exerting ingenuity and charm to do so without greatly offending Trish. It was from the stairs, as she left, that Michel had believed she recognized Barbara's former husband, Rupert Deyntree, coming out of the ground-floor flat, which, Trish had told her, was occupied by Dink November, a 'terrible creature' and perhaps 'some kind of prostitute'.

When she had returned home that day, Michel had felt – despite the blameless outcome of her call at Tolland Road – no desire to discuss it with Barbara, so she had said nothing of her glimpse of Rupert. However, when Vee Westwood had visited them in Willesden, seeking information about her friend Lucy's fiancé's past, Michel had made a confidential telephone call to her next day. Perhaps her motive had been a sense of female solidarity: sisterly concern for a woman in Lucy's plight, sisterly desire to assist Vee in her quest; perhaps it was detestation of 'Rupert the wrecker'; probably it was a mixture of the two.

First she had told Vee that she 'could have sworn' it was Rupert she had seen. Then – being a lawyer – she had temporized. However, with some reluctance, she had given Vee the Tolland Road address. When, a few weeks later, Vee telephoned her to say that Lucy's engagement was 'off', and also told her that Dink had been murdered, Michel had expressed satisfaction at the first item, and disgust at the second: 'These men who visit prostitutes are quite vile.' There, as far as she was concerned, the matter had rested.

Nonetheless, during the very long period that had now passed since she had last visited the house, Michel had often gone out of her way to drive past it. Sometimes she had slowed down; several times she had halted, with the engine running; twice she had stopped the car, but then quickly started it again and driven off. When she returned home on these occasions, Barbara remarked on her abstracted air, but Michel passed it off with a laugh or referred to some problem connected with her work.

Today she drove the car straight into the large bleak cement yard. She parked, switched off the engine, got out of the car and locked the door. Then she headed for the steep unrailed front steps, topped with the two urns in which Trish grew the geraniums that, despite her attentions to them, never flourished.

Michel flinched as she passed the filthy ground-floor bay window, and again by the unmarked ground-floor bell. She jabbed the top bell, labelled P. Pringle, with her forefinger, and then, a moment later, jabbed again.

Now there was a click and Trish's muffled voice asked, 'Who's there?'

'It's Michel – Michel Porter,'

'Oh!' Trish's exclamation was followed by a pause.

'Come on, Trish! Let me in.' Michel's tone was peremptory.

'Oh!' But a moment later, Trish pressed the buzzer; the door clicked and Michel pushed it open. By the time it had closed, Michel was striding up the stairs.

Trish was standing in her doorway on the top floor when Michel, not at all out of breath, arrived there. 'Michel! This *is* a surprise.'

Michel took hold of her shoulders, and propelled her back into the flat, shoving the door shut with her foot, back into the flowery living room, past the shelf of china cats, to the Laura Ashley sofa onto which she pushed her down. None of this was violent, but it was very forceful. However, Trish seemed to have no objection: as soon as they reached the sofa she became entirely limp.

Rustling garments were disarrayed rather than discarded. Decisive movements from one participant met passivity and soft sighs, a final small gasp, from the other. The frowning, seeking look on Michel's face gave way to one of triumph, almost immediately succeeded by dissatisfaction; Trish's closed eyes slowly opened, and she smiled: 'Ah!'

'Nice?' Now Michel smiled, raising her eyebrows.

'Oh yes . . . So you came back to me?' Trish closed her eyes again as she said this, and did not see Michel's little grimace.

'Mmm.'

'Just like *Gone with the Wind*,' Trish said in a dreamy tone.

'*Gone with the Wind*?' Again Michel raised her eyebrows.

'Yes – though not that horrible *man*, of course. But, you know . . . when she's carried to bed.'

'Ah! Though I didn't exactly carry you. Or to bed.'

'It felt like that.' Trish raised her head, and pursed her mouth for a kiss.

Michel leant down and touched Trish's lips with her own, which were firmly closed. Then she shifted to an upright position on the sofa; as she did so, she brushed the back of her hand over her mouth. 'Do you think we could have a drink?' she asked.

'A drink? Why yes, of course.' Rearranging the loose flowered smock she was wearing, Trish too sat up. 'What would you like? Beer? Wine?'

'Do you have any brandy?'

'Brandy? No, I'm afraid not. I never drink spirits. But I think there's some whisky someone gave me . . . ages ago.'

'That's all right. It keeps.'

'What?' Trish looked puzzled.

'I was joking. I'd love a whisky.'

Trish stood up. 'Right. How do you like it? I'm afraid I haven't got any soda water. But there's some Perrier.'

'No, I think I'll have it on its own.'

'Neat? You *are* a one!' Trish's tone was roguish rather than disapproving.

When she had left the room, Michel stood up, straightening her shoulders. She paced across to the window, looked down at her car parked in the desert of cement; she swung round to survey the dainty room with an expression of distaste, then turned back to the window, fidgeting with the edge of a flowered curtain.

It was several minutes before Trish returned, with tidy hair and light make-up, and smelling strongly of floral cologne. She carried a tray on which were a half-full glass of white wine, a tumbler and an unopened bottle of whisky. 'I thought I'd let you pour your own,' she said, putting the tray on the coffee table by the sofa, and then sitting down.

'Thanks.' Still standing, Michel opened the bottle, and poured herself a hefty slug. Holding the glass she moved towards one of the two armchairs, but Trish patted the seat of the sofa and, after an instant's hesitation, Michel came to sit beside her, raising her glass. 'Cheers,' she said loudly.

'Cheers,' Trish murmured, and, when Michel downed a swig of whisky, she took a sip of wine. Then she said, 'It's been so long.'

'Yes. A long time,' Michel said.

'So much has happened since I last saw you. Did you hear that that awful woman downstairs was murdered?' Evidently taking Michel's silence to express surprise, Trish went on, 'I can understand your not having heard – it wasn't in any of the proper papers.'

'As opposed to the improper ones?'

Trish responded to this with a peal of girlish laughter. 'That's right! Though I don't think there was much, even in them. It turned out she was a prostitute – just as I suspected. Apparently her flat was full of awful things – a two-way mirror in the cupboard and whips and goodness knows what. So sordid! And they never found out who did it. Of course the police questioned me – and that flautist downstairs – though naturally they realized at once that I'd know nothing about that dreadful woman's activities. They just wanted to know if I'd *seen* anyone suspicious.' Trish paused, then hurried on: 'I do wish someone would move in downstairs. It looks so depressing. That filthy window's even worse than the November woman's awful vulgar blind – at least that was *clean*. Really I must get out of this place, you know. But the rent's so low, and my flat *is* nice, isn't it?

Michel nodded.

Trish paused again, then she said, on an interrogatory note, 'Michel?'

'Yes.'

'You remember last time you came here?'

'Of course I do,' Michel said heartily.

'Well, you remember when you were leaving, someone was coming out of her flat – that fair man? He often came to see her. And you said you thought you recognized him?'

'Yes.' Michel put down her glass. 'But then I said I was mistaken.'

'Yes. But the thing is – he was here the night she was murdered.'

'*What*?' As if unaware of what she was doing – Trish raised her eyebrows – Michel poured herself another large measure of whisky.

'Yes. I saw him arrive, from the window. He was there for a long time. And when he left he was carrying a whole load of stuff round the corner – he never parked his car in front. You know – I think it really must have been him that killed her.'

Michel drained the contents of her glass. Perhaps this was why her face flushed; it paled again immediately, as she said, 'But what did the police say?'

In a very low voice, Trish said, 'I didn't tell them.'

'Didn't tell them? Why not?' Years of legal training and practice lay behind the sharp tone in which Michel spoke.

Trish bowed her head. 'I know it was wrong of me not to.'

'But why on earth—'

Trish broke in, 'I didn't want to get involved. Identification parades and looking at photographs and all that. And, after all, she was a prostitute. And anyway' – now a note of defiance was in her voice – 'she was such a horrible woman. Absolutely horrible! I can't describe what awful things she said to me.'

Michel said, 'So you felt she deserved to be murdered?'

'Oh no, not exactly, but . . .' Then Trish repeated obstinately, 'I didn't want to get involved.'

In the silence that followed, Michel tilted her head back and stared ahead. She rested her hands on her knees, the upper part of her body swaying slightly, backwards and forwards. Her whole appearance expressed extreme agitation.

Trish said, 'I should have telephoned you.'

'What?'

'Please don't snap at me. I should have telephoned you to ask your advice. But . . . oh, I don't know – I was a bit embarrassed. Michel?'

'Yes?'

'*Did* you recognize him – that man?'

It was after only a fractional hesitation that Michel said, 'No. No – I told you at the time.'

'But who did you *think* he was? At first.'

'Oh, what does *that* matter? Someone I met ages ago. He married a woman I used to know. I only saw him a few times.'

Trish said, 'He was quite different from most of the types who used to visit her.' She made a grimace of distaste. 'The man you saw here, I mean. Rather handsome, really.'

'Oh yes? Of course I only caught a glimpse of him. Down in that dark hall.'

'Actually, I was quite surprised that someone who looked like that could be involved with *her*. Men!' She grimaced again.

'You say he came here often?'

'Oh yes. Ever since I've been here – she was already living here when I moved in.'

'Hmm.' Now, abruptly, Michel stood up. 'I must go.'

'So soon?'

'Yes, I really must be off.'

Trish said, 'You must think I'm an awfully *silly* girl.' Her stress on the word 'silly' was indulgent.

'*Silly?*' Michel's tone conveyed that the word was wholly irrelevant.

'Well, you're shocked, aren't you? That I didn't tell the police.'

Michel said, 'Well, I must say, it does seem rather . . . irresponsible. And you in one of the caring professions, too! Ask not for whom the bell tolls, and all that, you know. Letting a murderer go free. I mean, you could have identified him, couldn't you? Having seen him so often.'

'Yes. Yes I could.' Trish drooped on the sofa like a tired daffodil. She said, 'I suppose you think I should go to the police now.'

'*Now?* After nearly two years? That *would* seem *very* odd. How could you possibly explain it?'

'Yes, that's true.' There was relief in Trish's tone. She added, 'Anyway, who knows who or where he is?' She paused. 'Of course, if you *had* recognized him, it would have been different.'

'Yes. Possibly. I really must go.'

Trish stood up. She said, 'Are you still with your partner – the woman you told me about who's older than you?'

'Oh, did I say that? There's only a few years' difference. Yes, we're still . . . married.'

'Oh. I see. Happily married, I hope?' This was the first time kittenish Trish had shown her claws.

'Oh yes. Very happily.' Michel's tone was airy, but for a moment she looked boyishly ill at ease. 'Well, thanks for the drink.' Then she added, with some recovery of grace, 'And, of course, for the great pleasure of your company.'

But Trish refused to be charmed. 'Goodbye then. Can you see yourself out?'

'Yes, of course. Bye.' Michel backed a step or two, then, with a gesture of farewell, hurried to the door.

It was target day for Michel. However, she was unaware, as she left the room, of the cushion Trish hurled after her.

Back in Willesden, she climbed the stairs with such a slow heavy tread that Barbara came to look over the rail at the top: 'Oh, it's you,' she said, and turned away.

'Barbara, darling!' Michel increased her pace. 'Barbara, my love.' She reached the top of the stairs, and followed Barbara's retreating back into the living room. Catching up, she put a hand on her shoulder. 'Barbara, I'm so sorry. Really I am.'

Barbara turned to face her. 'You were so *nasty*,' she said. 'To Belinda and then to me.'

'Yes, I know I was. I'm truly sorry. Please forgive me.'

Barbara said, 'I've been trying to telephone Belinda, but all I get is that damned answering machine. I left a message.'

'She'll ring back.'

'I wonder if she will. After all those things she said. And you were so awful to her.'

'I'm sure she will.' After a moment, Michel added, 'She's jealous of me.'

'Oh, that's nonsense.'

'No, it isn't, darling. You don't realize how lovable you are. People want to keep you to themselves.'

Barbara's face softened at this, but she repeated, 'Nonsense!' Then she added, 'Surely you can't love someone who's so *fat*!'

'Oh darling, I didn't *mean* that. I only said it because I was angry.' She added, 'You know I love your voluptuous figure.'

'Really?'

'Really.' Then she said, 'Who wants "a rag and a bone and a hank of hair"?'

'What on earth's that from?' Barbara asked, then added, 'I hope you're not going to start quoting all the time, like Rupert.'

'Like Rupert?' Michel gave a small shudder. 'I certainly hope I'm not like *him* in any way. It was Kipling, actually.'

'Kipling! That imperialist beast! Worse and worse!' They both laughed; then they embraced. When they drew apart, Barbara said, 'Where on earth have you been? You absolutely reek of whisky.'

'Oh, I drove around for a bit, and then I stopped at a pub and had a drink and brooded on my sorrows.'

'Your sorrows indeed!' But Barbara's laugh was affectionate. Then she said, 'It's my poor old Belinda I really feel sorry for. She's so confused. Enjoying that pointless job and admiring that dreadful Chris, too. Oh dear! I'd never imagined she was seeing her.'

Michel said, 'I've often told you – Belinda's cagey.'

'Well, perhaps you're right. She may even be in love with some nice young man. But I doubt it – she's so gloomy.' Barbara repeated, 'Oh dear!' then continued, 'And she's usually so difficult when she comes round here, and she's got no proper father at all.' Now Barbara paused. 'Of course I know she didn't mean it when she said I was worse than Rupert, but it really hurt me at the time.'

'Of course she didn't mean it. Of course it hurt you. No one could be worse than Rupert.'

'No, probably not. Imagine deserting that Lucy he was engaged to, when she was having a baby!'

'Yes – Belinda said he'd *vanished off the face of the earth*.'

'Goodness, you do make it sound sombre! The woman's probably far better off without him – just as Belinda is . . . I think I'll give her another ring now.'

'Darling, you must do whatever you think best.' Michel gave a deep sigh.

'Oh, you *do* look down in the mouth. Cheer up, darling – I've forgiven you,' Barbara said as she went to the telephone.

Belinda lay, fully dressed, on her bed, under the duvet. As soon as she reached home she had dialled Chris's number, but when Chris answered had instantly put down the receiver. Then she had gone out to the corner newsagent and bought three Mars bars. Their scrumpled wrappings were now strewn around her. After her aborted call to Chris, she had turned on the answering machine: although she listened to her mother's messages, she made no attempt to return her calls.

THREE

It was on Saturday morning at ten o'clock, when his mother went out shopping, that Francis telephoned the Dumbles' number. Mag answered, a little breathless: 'Hullo.'

'Hullo. I wonder if I could speak to Lucy Riven.'

'Lucy – oh yes, hang on a moment.' But two or three minutes passed before Lucy came to the telephone.

'Lucy Riven here.'

'Ah! Ah Lucy, it's Francis.'

'Francis! How nice! How are you?'

'In good health,' he said. 'And you?'

'Oh, so well and so happy. Isn't it wonderful that Rupert's back? He told me you'd met . . . and that you're going to be best man at our wedding. I'm so pleased. You got my letter, didn't you? Thanking you for that wonderful cheque for Edward? I'm starting a savings account for him with it.'

'Yes I got it, and thank you. Lucy, do you know how I can get hold of Rupert? He didn't give me a telephone number.'

'Oh, he rang me early this morning – he's got a number now. I'll give it to you. He's moved into a little hotel, just off Piccadilly. Terribly extravagant when he could stay here.' Lucy lowered her voice: 'But he's always found Mag a bit overpowering.' Then she said, 'You'd better hurry if you want to catch him. We're just leaving here to meet him at Farm Street. He's being received today.'

'Today?'

'Yes, into the Church. The Catholic Church.' Lucy laughed. 'Sorry, I mean the *Roman* Catholic Church, of course. We chose a Saturday because Farm Street will be so nice and quiet. Mag's daughter Perpetua's staying with Edward, so just Mag and Bernard are coming – and then we're having lunch here.

But oh, we should have asked you, too. I really wish you were coming. Francis, are you there?'

'Yes, yes. I'm here.'

There was a pause. Then Lucy said again, 'Oh Francis, I'm so happy. Do be happy for me too about Rupert's conversion. You see, I'm absolutely sure now that it's sincere. Francis?'

'Yes, Lucy.'

After a moment she said, 'We must meet very soon – but I have to rush now. I'll just give you Rupert's number.'

As soon as they rang off he dialled the number she had given him, and asked for Mr Deyntree. But Rupert had gone out.

The Church of the Immaculate Conception in Farm Street, headquarters of the Jesuits, was by no means Lucy's favourite London church. Although it did not have the distasteful associations for her of the ornate Brompton Oratory in Knightsbridge, which her mother always attended on visits to London, its position in the heart of Mayfair – a few minutes' walk from Claridges and the Connaught – tended to attract a congregation that was not to Lucy's taste. Nor was she instinctively drawn to the suave urbanity of 'Jessop the Jesuit' with his reputation for converting illustrious – and usually upper-class – intellectuals. In addition, he was a friend of her mother's, though now a less close one than before the ecclesiastical proceedings he had initiated had resulted – to Teresa's disgust – in a pronouncement that Rupert's three previous civil marriages were invalid.

Today, however, it was with a joyous smile that Lucy returned his greeting in the doorway of the church, though her smile faded when he asked her, looking round the tiny gathering, if her mother was not going to be present. Sadly she shook her head.

'So she's not reconciled?' he asked.

'Oh no, I'm afraid not. Far from it.' For Teresa's response on the telephone to the news of Rupert's return had been glacial.

'We must trust in God's grace. And I'll see what *I* can do. Perhaps it's time for me to visit her again at Rivendale.'

'Oh, I wish you would!' Lucy's tone was eager, and Father Jessop patted her hand. At that moment a taxi drew up; and

Rupert emerged from it, wearing a dark-grey suit and a blue-and-white-striped shirt.

Lucy hurried to meet him: 'Darling how smart you look!'

'Well,' he said, 'this is a very important occasion. And you look quite lovely in that charming dress.'

She squeezed his hand. In this pale-blue silk dress – no one would have guessed she had acquired it from an Oxfam shop – she did indeed look lovely. Her fair shoulder-length hair shimmered. Her face, its seriousness always relieved by the classical curve of her mouth – Rupert called it her 'archaic smile' – was today illuminated by her happiness.

Now the Dumbles greeted Rupert. Bernard, too, was wearing a suit, though it had the dishevelled look that all clothes instantly acquired on his bulky figure. Mag, in a floral garment, wore a black lace veil: a custom she had never discontinued, though it was many years now since Catholic women had been required, as enjoined by St Paul, to cover their heads in church.

Inside, light filtered dimly through the great stained-glass window over the altar; the sanctuary lamp glowed red in the empty church. Lucy, crossing herself with holy water, looked round at the statues of familiar saints, then up at the ceiling on which stars gleamed in a deep-blue sky. From her expression it appeared that – today, at least – Farm Street was a beloved place. She and the Dumbles knelt waiting while Rupert and Father Jessop went into the confessional.

The place was so quiet and peaceful that a sound made Lucy turn her head. A man had entered the church and was sitting, head bowed, in a back pew. The curve of Lucy's mouth widened slightly: she occasionally remarked how much she liked the way people dropped into Catholic churches for casual prayer; it was a practice of her own.

When, after several minutes, Rupert came out of the confessional, he gave Lucy a brilliant smile. Then he knelt to say the penance that had been allotted to him by the priest.

Father Jessop and Bernard, who was to serve the mass, went to the vestry. When Rupert had finished his brief penance, he, Lucy and Mag made their way to the Ignatius chapel, where the service was to be held. Soon Father Jessop, in his vestments, followed by Bernard in a surplice, entered the chapel, and began the Mass.

'I must put all my fervour in executing zealously and exactly what I am ordered. I must consider myself as a corpse which has neither intelligence nor will . . . be like a statue which lets itself be stripped and never opposes resistence.' So wrote the Spanish saint and founder of the Society of Jesus, Ignatius Loyola of his relationship to God and his religious Superiors. Now, at Farm Street, more than four hundred years later, his statue stood at the entrance to the chapel named after him.

In Mozart's *Don Giovanni*, a statue comes to life, and grasps the Don's hand in an icy, killing grip. Here, Ignatius's statue received no divine command when Rupert participated in the Mass. It did not stir as, absolved of the sins he had confessed, he spoke the responses, recited the Creed, bowed when bread and wine were changed into Body and Blood. Stony it stayed as, kneeling at the altar rail, he took the sacred wafer in his mouth.

The mass ended. Soon the little party emerged into the dazzle of the bright day; a few moments later, the lone figure in the back pew also departed. Now the church was empty, silent again, its statues for ever still under its starry ceiling.

Gradually, during that weekend, the peace of the Suffolk cottage and the enjoyment of Sarah's good meals exerted a soothing influence on James and Vee. But after Sunday lunch, when they were sitting on the lawn, Sarah remarked with a laugh, 'Really, you know, you two are very lazy this weekend. You haven't been for a single walk. How about one now? In fact, I'll join you.'

James said, 'No, Mum. Vee's had such an exhausting week. She just wants to rest. But why don't you go?'

'By myself? Somehow it's not the same without Mansfield.' Now Sarah glanced towards the bed of lavender where Mansfield was buried.

'Oh Sarah, I'm so sorry,' Vee said, looking dejected. 'But I'm really beat.'

'You work too hard,' Sarah said. 'They don't even leave you in peace at the weekend. Why, they've rung you at least five times on that contraption of yours.'

'You're just like James. You're both against my poor old mobile phone.' Vee laughed. Then she added, 'But it's part of my life. Just like in my last job. Always on call.'

'It seems such an intrusion,' Sarah said. Then she added, 'But a lot of people used to feel that about the ordinary telephone when I was young.'

'Life without a telephone – I can't imagine it,' Vee said.

'Nor can I really – now I'm in AA. Anyway, I shall work off my energy in some weeding.'

'I could help with that,' Vee offered. 'Of course you'd have to tell me which the weeds are.'

Jame and Sarah both laughed. Sarah said, 'No, you relax. Weeding's just as tiring as walking. And I'd hate you to pull up all my favourite plants.'

When she had gone round to the back garden, James sighed. 'I'd love a walk.'

'Me too! You should have given Francis my mobile-phone number as well as this one and the one at the flat.'

'Yes. I didn't think. I wish he'd ring.'

'Me, too!' Vee said. 'But we'd better not call him. We'd better wait to hear from him. *If* we hear from him.'

'I think we will. If we don't, I'll ring him.'

'You will? When?'

He said, 'Tomorrow, perhaps.'

Vee said, 'Say he rings when we're on our way up to London?'

'So early in the morning? Surely not?'

'Anyway, we'll have to chance it. And he may ring this evening.'

'Yes.'

However, the telephone rang only once that evening, at ten o'clock, just as they were going upstairs to bed.

James sprang to answer it, but the caller was a sobbing woman, asking for Sarah.

'That woman sounded as if she was drunk,' James said as he and Vee went up the stairs, and Sarah settled down to talk in a low, soothing voice.

'She probably was. They call it Twelfth Step work in AA. Helping alcoholics who are still suffering to get sober.'

'Suffering?'

'Oh yes.' Vee sighed. 'When I think of my mother . . .'

'Mmm. Mum, too. But isn't it unsettling for alcoholics who are getting better to have to deal with drunk people?'

'Oh no. It's one of the things that help them to stay sober.'

'Mysterious.'

Vee sighed again. 'Yes, life is full of mysteries.'

He said, 'Too full!'

It was at eleven that evening, after his mother had gone to bed, that Francis reached Rupert at his hotel.

'Hullo,' Rupert sounded drowsy.

'It's Francis.'

'Francis – you woke me up. Lucy told me you'd telephoned. I should have rung you back. I meant to this evening, but I fell asleep. Lots of religion, you know. Renouncing the devil yesterday. Church again today. Awfully exhausting.' Rupert yawned.

Francis said, 'I want to see you.'

'Yes, we must meet again soon. With Lucy perhaps. A reunion.' Rupert yawned again.

'No, I must see you alone. I thought of tomorrow.'

'Tomorrow! Goodness! What importunity! And how mysterious! Well . . . all right. Why don't you have lunch with me? A decent lunch – tell your mother to cut back on that "proper breakfast" she always gives you. Why don't we go to the Firenze – that place in Kensington where I first introduced you to Lucy? One o'clock?'

'All right.'

'See you then,' said Rupert. 'Splendid!' But when he fell asleep again, it was with a frown on his face.

FOUR

Vee and James left the cottage at six next morning, to avoid the rush-hour traffic. James was to spend the day in Vee's flat, working, or as he said, trying to work, on his book, while he waited for a call from Francis.

But he could not work. He wandered round the flat, looking down from the bedroom window on the canal. He took books from the shelves. He tried out two of Vee's compact discs, but found neither to his taste. He even turned on the television, but quickly rejected the vapidity of the daytime programmes.

It was just before one when he suddenly clenched his fists. He went to the telephone and dialled Francis's number.

Mrs Larch answered, repeating the number.

'Could I speak to Francis Larch?'

'I'm afraid he's not in. Who's speaking?'

'Er . . . James Deyntree.'

'Oh!' Mrs Larch exclaimed. Her tone was indignant as she went on, 'Well, I know he certainly doesn't want to speak to *you.*'

After a moment James managed to say, 'He doesn't?'

'No, he does *not*. He told me all about your little visit last week. And he quite definitely doesn't want to be pestered by you again.'

'But—' James said.

'Please have the decency to leave him alone.' Mrs Larch rang off.

It was lunchtime at the Firenze: chairs of blond wood and pale-green tablecloths; the walls white, and even whiter the starched table napkins and the jackets of the hovering waiters. Near the door a table of variegated antipasti: olives, dark and light, paper-thin pink prosciutto, glistening anchovies garnishing a salad of raw mushrooms, tunny mayonnaise encased in bright-red peppers, snowy slices of sheep's-milk cheese. Opposite, among the creamy pleasures of the sweet trolley, a glass bowl of deep-green figs, shiny with syrup, stood out in dark relief. Everything – food, decor, sparkling wineglasses and gleaming plates – asserted a quintessentially Italian consecration to display.

Now, at five to one, as Francis stood by the door, peering round the restaurant, the head waiter approached him with no great appearance of enthusiasm: in old grey trousers and light tweed jacket, white shirt and nondescript tie, he was hardly an example of *bella figura*. However, when he mentioned the name Deyntree, the waiter's demeanour changed immediately – 'Ah, Mr Deyntree! He has not yet arrived!' – and Francis was ushered, with beaming smile and expansive gestures, to a table under a window overlooking a tiny courtyard of green plants surrounding a small splashing fountain.

The wine waiter approached immediately. 'Something to drink, sir?'

'Yes.' Francis hesitated, and then said, 'A Dry Martini, please.'

'With gin, sir?'

Again Francis hesitated before he said, 'Oh yes, with gin.' Then, perhaps recollecting the smart dissipation of his Cosmopolitan Clara days, he added, 'Four parts gin to one part vermouth.'

The drink – it was lavish, in a larger glass than the tiny Dry-Martini glasses of his youth – came quickly, and he drank it fast. A quarter of an hour passed, and by the time Rupert arrived, greeted warmly by the head waiter, Francis had ordered a second. He drained it as Rupert, in his charcoal trousers and dark-blue silk polo-neck, approached the table.

'Francis! I'm sorry I'm late – I've been looking at dreadful flats, and I need a drink.' He sat down and raised a finger to the hovering wine waiter. 'What are you drinking?' he added, with a glance at Francis's empty glass.

'Oh, I had a Dry Martini. I'll wait for the wine.' Francis was slightly flushed. 'They're quite strong.'

'Dry Martini with gin? That's not like you, Francis. Or have you changed your ways during my absence? I thought you never drank spirits. I hardly ever do myself – all this health rubbish must have got through to me. But let's be evil this once – you'll have to join me. I insist. Waiter, two Dry Martinis.' The waiter departed, and Rupert went on, 'You're very silent, Francis. I'm quite devoured with curiosity about this urgent meeting. But, come to think of it, I've hardly given you a chance to utter.' Smiling, Rupert put his hands on the edge of the green-clothed table, and leant forward with an expectant look.

Now, however, another waiter arrived, with two large red-bound menus. Rupert said, 'Oh, let's get this ordering business over, so that we can talk. What would you like to eat?'

Francis was not studying the menu. He said, 'Oh . . . pasta.'

'Pasta, indeed! What kind? Spaghetti, lasagne, tagliatelle, fettucini, cannelloni?'

Faced by this choice, Francis said, 'Oh, perhaps not pasta. I'll have . . . saltimbocca.'

'Nothing first?'

'No, no.'

'I don't usually either, at lunch. One saltimbocca, one fettucini alla marinara. And a green salad. Right, Francis?'

'Yes, fine.'

'No vegetables? Some spinach?'

Francis shook his head.

The waiter was now replaced by the wine waiter with their Martinis. 'And some wine,' Rupert said. 'White, I think – that's all right with your veal, Francis. Yes – a bottle of the white Corvino.' As the wine waiter left, Rupert said, 'Peace at last!' He raised his glass: 'Francis – your health!'

They both drank, and Francis's flush deepened.

Rupert laughed. 'You're very red in the face. You see – gin at lunchtime! I'll be purple myself any moment.'

But Francis was not smiling. He took a gulp of his Martini, leant forward, and said, 'Rupert!'

'So it's "Rupert" again—' But, seeing Francis's intense, agonized expression, Rupert broke off. 'Francis, what on earth's the matter?'

'Oh, Rupert!' Francis spoke loudly; it was almost a cry.

215

The tables in the crowded restaurant were close together, and a man at a neighbouring table looked up and then murmured something to his woman companion. 'Steady, Francis,' Rupert said, low. And then, in the same low tone, 'What is it?'

Francis finished his Martini. He said, his voice quietened now by the influence of Rupert's, 'Your son came to see me on Friday.'

'My son?' Rupert blinked as the waiter arrived with their food, put their plates in front of them and a bowl of green salad on the table. They were both silent until he had gone. Then Rupert said, 'I'm sorry to hear that. He's very nasty – or perhaps a bit mad. Constant indoctrination by Sarah, you know.' Then he said, 'I suppose he told you about his involvement with the dreadful Vee. I forgot to mention it last time we met. I had so much to tell you.'

'*He* told me everything.' Francis gave a wild glance at the wine waiter who now brought their bottle of Corvino, opened it and poured a little into Rupert's glass. Rupert tasted it, nodded, and the waiter filled both their glasses, then put the bottle in a bucket on a stand at Rupert's side.

As he left, Rupert said, 'I'm sure he told you a tissue of lies. Just like the ones his frightful girlfriend told Lucy. We all had a most unpleasant encounter. Of course, Lucy didn't believe a word they said.'

Francis drank some wine. He said, 'Rupert, *I* believed it. I believed it all.'

Rupert blinked again. Then his dark-blue, slate-tinged eyes widened. 'Oh, Francis,' he said. 'How could you?'

Francis said, 'Everything fitted. It was like a jigsaw. Dink November, alias Jeanne Duval . . . so conveniently returned to South Africa, according to you. But, you see, I read a newspaper cutting about her murder. Oh, Rupert, your explanation of your sudden departure was hard to believe . . . but I trusted you.'

'And you should trust me now, Francis.' Rupert spoke earnestly, his eyes fixed on Francis's face.

'After that murder, Rupert . . . that murder?'

'Well, yes . . . Dink was murdered. But not by me, Francis. Not by me. I should have told you she was dead, but I didn't want to complicate things. Believe me. Are you going to believe some hate-crazed youth instead of your best and oldest friend?'

'He wasn't crazed. Yes, he was young – he looked like you as a young man. And he was earnest and unhappy and desperately serious.' Francis drained his glass. Rupert, who had drunk only half his Martini and hardly touched his wine, started mechanically to fork up his fettucini. Francis did not eat. Now he went on: 'And when he told me about that tape—'

'*I* told you about the tape, Francis.'

'Oh, you told me about *a* tape, but not the real one. When he described it, he found it so painful to talk about – he could hardly bear it. Those terrible things you did to Chris – oh, Rupert – and you *photographed* them, and you *photographed* that wretched woman's dead body.'

'There is no such tape, Francis. He was lying.'

'No, he wasn't. I could tell. He'd *seen* it.' Francis's voice rose again on these last words.

'Please keep your voice down, Francis. You know, I can hardly credit that you'd believe this of me.' There was a chill in Rupert's tone.

'But I do, I do. Oh, I've agonized over it so much. The last few days have been hell . . . pure hell.'

Now Rupert's tone softened: 'I can imagine. Poor Francis, my poor old friend – to have been bamboozled into accepting all this.'

'I tell you I wasn't boozled . . . bamboozled. Rupert, I *know* it's true. Oh, I've always been so very, very fond of you, ever since Oxford – why, I quite loved you then – and Mother has always been so fond of you—'

'You've told *her* about this?' Rupert's tone was incredulous.

'Oh no, no, no. How could I? I didn't even tell her why James came. I let her think it was to borrow money. Even today I didn't tell her I was meeting you. I said I was going to the library. I didn't want her to start chattering about your wedding . . . and so on. Oh, Rupert it was so difficult to decide what to do.'

Rupert raised another forkful of fettucini to his lips. Then he said, 'You decided the right thing – to talk it all over with me. I can explain—'

Francis cut him off. 'No you can't. I know you can't. I've made my decision.'

Rupert raised his eyebrows. 'Your decision?'

'Yes. Oh, Rupe – if you don't break off with Lucy right away, I'll tell her everything.'

Rupert stared at him. He took a sip of wine. Then he said, 'Suddenly I have a sense of déjà vu. Francis, don't tell me you're trying to blackmail me like that dreadful woman, Vee.'

Francis swayed slightly in his chair. 'Blackmail? Perhaps it's blackmail. I suppose it is. Oh, I'm not asking you to leave the country or anything. I'd never dream of betraying you to the police. Not that I could anyway – I'd have nothing to tell them except hearsay. Rupert, I know that all this means the end of our friendship. Because of what I know about you and because of what I'm going to do. But, Rupert, you can't marry that sweet innocent girl – it's . . . impermissible.'

'I see. Yes, this is blackmail. Just like Vee's. But she had a tape – as I told you. Anyway, Lucy would never believe you. She loves me.'

'Oh, I know she loves you. But I also know she'd believe me. Of course I'd tell her all the discrepancies in your stories – and how you admitted to me that the patriotic mission never existed. But it wouldn't be anything I said that would make her believe me. Oh, no, no, no.' Francis shook his head. 'She'd believe me because she knows I'm your best friend. She's always felt it – always *known* it.'

Rupert was pale now. 'Francis, you couldn't do that. Francis, I love her. Whatever I've done in the past is over and done with. I'm going to make her happy – I promise.'

'Happy? By deceiving her? You've lied to her so much – and gratuitously, too. What about this false, cynical conversion to Rome?'

'You know that was a formality.'

'But not a formality to Lucy. Her religion is the most important thing in her life. I wonder what you confessed on Saturday when you made that first Confession of yours. Did you tell Father Jessop you were a rapist and a murderer?'

Francis had spoken quietly, but Rupert glanced round. The buzz of voices in the restaurant had increased in volume; no one was paying them any attention. 'Now, Francis, really!' he said, and then, 'How could I confess something that never happened?'

'Oh, Rupert, it's no use. I've made up my mind.'

'So you're setting out to destroy that sweet innocent girl, as you call her? And it's true, of course – she is sweet and innocent.'

'Lucy won't be destroyed. She has her faith – and she has her child.'

'My child, too, Francis.'

'Oh Rupert, don't try to persuade me of your paternal feelings.'

'I feel differently about this one,' Rupert said. 'It's Lucy's. Oh, Francis, I'm appealing to you. I love her. I need her. She's my good angel.'

'It's no use.'

'Not after all our years of friendship?'

'No, Rupert.' But tears welled up in Francis's eyes.

A waiter approached the table, glancing enquiringly at Francis's untouched plate. Rupert waved him away. Then he sat back in his chair, his marvellous eyes fixed on Francis's flushed, tortured face. Now a tear rolled down Francis's cheek. There was a silence.

Rupert spoke. 'All right. I agree. I'll break it off.' He raised his hands to his face and covered his eyes for a moment. He gave a small shudder.

'You will?'

Rupert lowered his hands. He nodded. Now Francis saw that his eyes, too, were blurred with tears.

'Oh, Rupe.' With an impulsive movement, Francis leant forward. Then he said, 'I'm sorry.'

'I'm sorry too. I'm in such pain about Lucy. But there's something else. Francis . . .'

'Yes?'

'Must I lose you, too?'

Francis brushed ineffectively at his eyes with his napkin.

Rupert went on: 'Give me a chance, please. I'll tell you everything that happened. The whole truth. I've nothing to lose now. But I can't do that here. Please, dear old Francis, let's go somewhere quiet where we can be alone. Anyway, I might break down . . . very embarrassing! How about that flat of yours?'

'My flat?'

'Yes. We can talk in peace there. I'll tell you the whole sad story. I will, Francis. Yes, I truly will. You're the only person who'll ever know the real truth. Then, if you want, we can . . . "shake hands for ever".'

'"Shake hands for ever, cancel all our vows",' Francis murmured. He looked into Rupert's eyes. Then he said, 'When we were at Oxford I once told someone I felt one could drown in your eyes.'

'And what did he say?' Rupert smiled.

'He said I was very sentimental. You'll tell me everything?'

'Everything.'

'All right then.'

Rupert's raised hand brought a prompt response. 'The bill, please.' Seeing the waiter's surprised glance at Francis's face and untouched plate, he added, 'Quickly. My friend's had some bad news. Please order us a taxi.'

The bill came and was paid, with a generous tip for the now smiling waiter. As they stood up, Francis swayed a little, but then he straightened his shoulders and picked his way carefully to the door.

The head waiter was standing by it. Francis swayed again, and Rupert said with a smile, 'Your Martinis are too strong.'

'Ah Mr Deyntree!' Then he murmured, 'The gentleman had three.'

'Good heavens! Then you're not to blame.' Smiles and farewells were exchanged before the head waiter, with a glance through the door, announced the arrival of the taxi. As they got into it, Rupert glanced around. A woman was walking a poodle. Two men were talking in a car on the other side of the road. Now one of them started up his engine. Nothing else disturbed the peace of the quiet Kensington street.

In Vee's flat the telephone rang at two. James answered it:

'Yes?'

'It's me,' Vee said. 'No news?'

'Worse than no news – bad news!' said James. 'Francis won't help.' Then he added, 'And I was so sure he believed me.'

'So what did he say?'

'I didn't speak to him. I spoke to his mother. She said he wasn't in. Then she asked me who I was. When I told her, she sounded really annoyed and said he didn't want me to pester him again.'

'You believed her?'

'Why on earth should she lie to me?'

'I can't think. Do you suppose he told her everything? About the tape, for instance? Lucy said they're very close, but his mom must be an old lady. It's hard to imagine.'

'Yes, it is.' James sighed. Then he said, 'Perhaps he gave her an edited version.'

'Mmm. Anyhow, I guess he chickened out. All those years of friendship won – and to hell with Lucy! Or perhaps he didn't believe you after all.'

'I was so convinced he did. Oh well, it's nice to hear your voice. I didn't want to disturb you at work.'

'Disturb me! I'm finding it so hard to concentrate today. Luckily there's a slight lull – things aren't quite as hectic as usual.' She paused. Then she said, 'I've been thinking . . . that perhaps we need an outside opinion. A legal mind. Do you know, I think I'm going to ring Michel Porter. After all it was her seeing Rupert in Dink's building that put us on Dink's trail in the first place.'

'But she said she wouldn't be prepared to swear it was him.'

'Not in court. But she was pretty certain. Anyway, she doesn't know the full story.'

'Well, good luck.'

As soon as she and James had rung off, Vee rang Michel. 'It's Vee Westwood,' she said when she was put through. 'Remember me?'

After a moment, Michel said, 'Oh, yes.'

'You don't sound too pleased to hear from me.'

Michel said, 'It's not that. I'm astonished.' Then she said, 'Lately I've been worrying a lot about the things we discussed.'

'After all this time?'

'There's been a new development.'

'Really? And I've got a lot to tell you, too.'
'Could we meet after work?'
'Yes. Can you come to my office?'
'Sure. Give me the address again.'

FIVE

It was eight o'clock when Vee came home. 'Hi there,' she said, putting her bag and mobile phone down on a chair by the door.

'Hullo, darling.' After they had embraced, he asked, 'Any news?'

'Oh, yes. So much! I saw Michel. I told her the whole story. About the tape and everything that happened. She was really shocked, you know. Not just by the tape – but that we hadn't gone to the police with it in the first place. They would have compared the pictures of Dink on it with the photographs they'd taken of her body. Oh James, she made me feel so guilty. But then she told me about this woman who lives upstairs in that awful house and let her know just the other day that she actually *saw* Rupert there on the night of the murder.'

'What?'

'Yes. Oh, she didn't know who he was, but she said he often came there. And she saw him there that night, taking away stuff from Dink's flat.'

'So this woman gave the police a description of him at the time?'

'No, she didn't.'

'Why not?'

'Well, apparently she absolutely hated Dink – and she didn't want to get involved.'

'I see.'

'Anyway, Michel says she'll do what she can. She's going to call me later this evening.'

'Mmm. I'd thought we might go out to eat. But I know you'll want to wait for Michel's call. So I'll go and fetch some "take-out" again. There's a Greek place, isn't there, just up the road? Could you manage a kebab?'

'You bet – and a glass of red wine. Will you get a bottle from the off-licence?'

'Definitely. But first I'm going to try Francis one more time. It probably won't do any good, but I'd like to speak to him, rather than that dragon of a mother.'

However, when James had dialled the Oxford number, he made a little grimace at Vee for it was Mrs Larch who answered.

'Yes?' She sounded breathless.

James sighed. 'Hullo. I'd like to speak to Mr Larch.'

'Why – is that by any chance *James Deyntree* again?'

'Yes.' Then he said, 'I really need to speak to him – just for a moment.'

Mrs Larch's voice rose: 'He's out.'

James said, 'Still?'

'How dare you question me? He's out – out to you at any time. Please get off the line – I'm expecting a call. And do not – I repeat *do not* – telephone again.' She slammed down the receiver.

'Phew!' James said, replacing his own receiver. '*What* a dragon! He's obviously primed her. She said he was out to me at any time. Too ashamed to speak to me, I suppose.'

'He must be . . . if he believed you.'

'I felt so sure he did – at the time. But perhaps afterwards he managed to convince himself that I was lying.' James sighed. 'And Chris was a vain hope. Such an unpleasant person – though of course I'm sorry about what happened to her.' He ran a hand across his eyes as if to blot out a sudden hideous vision. He said, 'It was awful, talking about the tape to Francis. It brought it all back.' Then he added, 'And he looked so shocked and horrified.'

'Well, obviously the shock and horror didn't last.' Now she sighed. 'We really have to forget about Francis and Chris. We just have to wait to hear from Michel. But now – I could eat a horse.'

'Sorry.' He smiled. 'You'll have to make do with a kebab.'

*   *   *

224

'You're late, my love,' Barbara said. 'But it doesn't matter. I made a stew. In the slow cooker. I opened a bottle of plonk. There's a bit in the stew but we'll drink the rest, shall we?'

'Mmm,' Michel said, and then, 'Barbara, we must talk.'

'Had a bad day? You do look a bit low. Well, let's talk while we eat. I'm sure you're hungry – I certainly am.' Barbara headed for the kitchen, and Michel followed her and sat down at the kitchen table. 'Pour us a glass of wine,' Barbara said, taking the casserole from its metal container, and placing it on the table, between the bread board and a bowl of salad.

Michel filled their glasses. Barbara raised hers and said, 'Cheers!' adding, as often before, 'I love saying that – Rupert always told me it was vulgar.'

Michel took a gulp of wine from her glass. Then she gave a sort of groan, and started on the story of her visits to Tolland Road and then of her meeting that evening with Vee. She spoke falteringly, in contrast to her usual brisk delivery, and Barbara – also unusually – did not touch the food on her plate.

When Michel finished speaking, Barbara said, 'Oh Michel, how *could* you!' After a moment she added, 'I've always so treasured our fidelity. Apparently you haven't.'

'Oh I have, darling.' Michel put a hand on Barbara's, but Barbara jerked hers back as if it had been stung. Michel said, 'It was only once. I told you nothing happened the first time. Because I thought of you.'

'But you went there . . . with the intention. And you lied to me. And then you went back. Obviously you've been brooding on that awful woman for years.'

'That isn't true – I promise. It was after that scene with Belinda. I was angry. I had to . . . let off steam!'

'Well, I've never heard it called *that* before. I've heard it called fucking or making love' – after the last two words Barbara gave a little gasp of pain – 'but I've never heard it called *letting off steam*. Anyway, I'm the one who should be angry about Belinda – and I am. You've estranged me from my daughter – she won't even talk to me on the phone. And now you tell me you've betrayed me, with some perfectly awful woman. How many others have there been?'

'None, darling. None.' Michel took another gulp of wine.

'How can I believe you? Anyway, apart from all this, whatever happened to your integrity? As a lawyer. As a woman. What about that poor, wretched creature he killed.'

'I didn't actually know that till I talked to Vee today.'

'Now there's what I call a true Sister, a loyal friend – Vee. How very, very different from you.'

'Oh Barbara!'

'Oh Barbara, indeed! Oh Michel! Anyway, since Saturday, you've known it was Rupert who killed that poor woman – haven't you?'

'I didn't *know*,' Michel said. Then she added, 'I didn't want to hurt you.'

'Well, you've hurt me now. And, apart from betraying me, you've betrayed everything we stand for. Go to her, to that Trish – what a bloody stupid name! – now, this minute. If you want food, you can eat later. I don't care whether you eat or not. Go there now.'

'She may not be in.'

'Well, wait till she *is* in. Don't come back here till you've seen her. I don't mind how late you are. For all I care, you can be late, even if she is in . . . if you feel the urge to *let off steam*.'

'Oh, how can you . . .'

'How could *you*? Go!'

Michel went, and Barbara wept tears of misery and rage. But, within considerably less than an hour, Michel's slow steps ascended the stairs and Barbara, still sitting at the kitchen table, violently wiped the tears from her face. When Michel appeared in the doorway, she said, 'Well?' and then, 'Did you see her?'

'I *saw* her,' Michel said. 'But it's absolutely hopeless. When I rang the bell, and told her who was there, she didn't press the buzzer to let me in. She came down – just to tell me to go away. I put my foot in the door – I really couldn't force my way in – and tried to talk to her. When I asked her – pleaded with her – to tell the police what she'd seen, she said she didn't know what I was talking about, that, as far as she was concerned, we'd never discussed that subject or any other. If the police came round, she said she'd stick absolutely to her original statement.

Then she slammed the door. Barbara, I promise you there's no way I could ever get her to change her mind.'

'So much for the great lover's powers of persuasion. Poor old Don Giovanni – that fucking aria you're always whistling. Well, what are you going to do now?'

'I don't know.'

'Well, you've got to do something. And you can give the subject the benefit of that great legal brain in Belinda's old room. Make up the bed there. I don't want you anywhere near me.'

'Oh, Barbara.'

'For God's sake stop bleating "Barbara" – you sound just like a bloody sheep. Now you'd better ring up Vee to inform her of your great success.'

Michel looked miserable and was silent.

'Putting it off, are you? I'm sure she'll want to know as soon as possible what you've done – or rather *not* done – to help her friend. Go on – ring her.'

So Michel went to the telephone and spoke to Vee. 'It's no use,' she told her. 'This woman absolutely refuses to speak to the police – let alone testify. I don't know what we do next. I'm going to try to think of something.' Michel's voice broke as she added, 'I promise.'

'Oh, you do sound down. I'm sorry. Well, thanks for trying.'

'I must go now.' Michel sounded on the edge of tears. But then she said, 'No, wait a moment, Barbara wants to speak to you.'

Barbara said, 'Hullo, Vee'

'Oh Barbara – hi!'

Barbara gave a heavy sigh. 'I heard about all this terrible business.' Then she said, 'Of course he can't be allowed to get away with it.'

Now Vee sighed. 'The problem is how to stop him. Perhaps Michel will come up with something when she's had time to think it over.'

Barbara's tone chilled. 'I doubt that. Now that this Trish person has turned out to be so utterly irresponsible. I believe she calls herself a social worker, but she obviously hasn't a social conscience.' Barbara paused. Then she said, 'No, I'm afraid

Michel appears totally devoid of inspiration. One wouldn't expect an experienced lawyer to be quite so clueless, would one?'

Vee said, 'Well, it is a difficult situation – no tape, no willing witness – and it all happened such a long time ago.' Then she said, 'You must realize, Barbara, that Michel had no idea the tape existed until I told her on Friday.' Suddenly Vee exclaimed, 'Oh, I've made so many mistakes!'

'Well, at least you've done your best to be a loyal friend. That's really something to be be proud of.' Barbara added, 'Loyalty! Such a wonderful quality – and so much rarer than I ever imagined.' Then she said, 'Chris is my daughter Belinda's friend. And also her heroine, apparently!' Barbara's sigh sounded heartfelt. 'She has always stood for everything I most dislike. Politically and in every other way.' Barbara paused. Then she said, 'Of course I was absolutely horrified when Michel told me about the terrible experience she went through. Yet I hear she's never been prepared to do a thing to save your friend Lucy from marrying that fiend.'

After a moment Vee said, 'No, Chris isn't prepared to do anything.'

Barbara said, 'Yet, after all, she is a woman. And apparently she's been . . . good to Belinda. Why don't we go to her – all we women – together? You, me, Michel – perhaps we could even get Sarah to come along, and try to persuade her to change her mind. Sisterhood *is* powerful, you know.' Her voice was eager.

Vee said, 'Barbara, I appreciate what you're saying. But quite frankly, Chris can't stand the sight of me. Sarah knows nothing about any of this, and I don't want her to – she's recovering from a serious illness. And anyway, well . . . well, let's just say I'm certain nothing we said would have any influence on Chris. I'm sure Michel would agree.'

'Michel!' Barbara exclaimed, but then she called out, 'Michel! Michel – don't you feel we should at least try to persuade Chris?' Then she said to Vee, 'No. She's shaking her head.' Now Barbara spoke passionately: 'We don't even share the same ideals any more.' She was silent for a moment before she said. 'Well, goodbye, Vee.'

'Goodbye, Barbara.' Vee rang off. Then she exclaimed to

James, 'Ideals! That's all I need to hear about at this stage.' There was bitterness in her tone, as she added, 'I've had too many myself. I idealized Lucy – and now I've begun to feel she's just a fool, blinded by passion. Passion for a fiend – that was what Barbara called him, and I guess it's a fair description. I can't imagine anyone exists who's as bad as he is. On the other hand, perhaps lots of people are. Perhaps I just haven't noticed . . . being an idealist! Look at Chris! Look at Dink November! Oh James, everything seems so hopeless.'

'You may feel that now. But, my darling Vee, don't let it make you feel like abandoning all the things you stand for. Vee, you've always told me how good Lucy is. I don't know her, but I know you – and I know *you're* good. Whatever Lucy is, your feeling for her is something pure and perfect. And that *can't* be wasted. It's there . . . it's on a kind of scale. On one side, there's all the horror that's summed up in him, in my Döppelganger, in what I felt when I saw that tape – and what I felt when I saw him. And on the other – there's that pure, perfect thing. And – whatever has happened, whatever's going to happen – that pure, perfect thing remains. And, Vee, you must keep faith with it.'

'Oh, James!' Tears in their eyes, they embraced and clung to each other, murmuring reassuring words. Later, after making love, they fell asleep under only a sheet; it was a hot night, but they lay close together. When the mobile phone rang, Vee woke with a dazed look, and it was in a dazed voice that she said, 'Hello?'

'Ms Westwood?'

'Is that Chris?' Surprise banished doziness. Now James, also woken, half sat up, leaning on one elbow.

Chris said, 'That's right,' and then, 'I'd rather like to know what's been going on since we last spoke.'

'You would? Well, we found someone who saw Rupert at Dink November's on the night of the murder. But she refuses to testify. Just like you – unless you've changed your mind. And your ex-husband's best friend, Francis Larch, has decided not to help us.'

'Francis Larch – that boring little queer – did you really expect him to help you?' Chris laughed. 'I always thought he had a crush on Rupert. Anyway, men – I suppose you'd have to call him a man – always stick together, don't they?' Not waiting for an answer to this question, she went on, 'Actually, I'm quite relieved about your witness.'

'Relieved!' Vee's tone was indignant. 'But I suppose that's what I should have expected from you. Anyhow, now that I've satisfied your curiosity – and *relieved* you – I think I'll say goodbye.'

'Keep cool, Ms Westwood – and do hang on a moment. I'm relieved because, as I've told you all along, I have absolutely no intention of getting involved with the police or describing anything I experienced to them. Nor have I any interest whatsoever in bringing the killer of Dink November "to justice" as you put it. As far as I'm concerned, she got exactly what she deserved. Ms Westwood, I've always been a believer in capital punishment. I'd love to see Rupert hanged for what he did to me . . . hanged for anything – even for killing Dink November. But unfortunately he can't be hanged at all. Stupid do-gooders – people like your friend Lucy, or so I should imagine from her high-minded job – have abolished the death penalty here. Well, that's *one* way your country's superior to this one.'

Vee broke in, 'One way it isn't, as far as I'm concerned.'

'Ah! Of course I suppose I should have guessed that from your busybody behaviour. All do-gooders are busybodies – it goes with the badges they wear. "Save the whale" and all that, you know.'

'I don't happen to wear—' But Vee broke off.

'I suppose you want to get Rupert locked up in one of those prisons they have nowadays that are just like luxury hotels. Well, thanks to your bungling, that's not an option. But certainly I want him punished.' Chris's laugh was chilling. 'Certainly I don't want him living "happily ever after". Or strutting around as "lord of the manor" at Rivendale. That's why, if you think it will do any good, I'm prepared to talk to your friend, Lucy Riven.'

'Talk to Lucy?'

'Yes. I'm prepared to see her and tell her what happened to me. Oh, not for *her* sake – please don't start calling *me* a bloody do-gooder.'

Vee opened her mouth – perhaps to deny any such intention – but then closed it again.

'No, not for *her*,' Chris repeated. Then she said, 'For *me*. I'd send him to hell, if I could. But the best I can do seems to be to try to foil him, thwart him, stop him getting what he wants. He does want Lucy Riven, doesn't he?'

'Oh yes, he wants her. I'm sure that was one reason why he killed Dink. Because she was persecuting Lucy. Because she cut off Lucy's beautiful hair. And he's gone on wanting Lucy for two years, plotting, planning till somehow he managed to track down that tape and steal it. But Chris, I don't think Lucy'd believe you. Why, she didn't believe me – and I've always been her best friend.'

'Well, I'm prepared to take the chance.'

'She'd probably refuse to see you.'

'Oh, I wouldn't make an appointment. I'd just turn up. At her office, perhaps. Then I could be sure *he* wouldn't be there. I could give a false name at the desk.'

'Well . . .' Vee paused. Then she said, 'Chris, can I come with you?'

'No, you can't. This is *my* plan, you know. I just rang to check things out. Is she still working at the same outfit – Save the Children, was it?'

'No, *Feed* the Children.' Vee visibly braced herself. When she spoke again, it was calmly: 'You know, I really do think I should come along with you. Oh, I'd wait outside, but if Lucy went into some kind of hysterics after you talked to her, it might be helpful if I was around. Of course, it's a bit difficult for me to get away – I'm running Greg Marshall's London office now.'

'You are?' Chris's tone conveyed that she was impressed by this connection with a famous impresario from the world of popular music.

'Yes. Of course I know you're very busy too, but I wonder if you could slip away from your office at about four tomorrow.'

'Tomorrow?'

'Yes, let's finalize this deal fast. Don't you usually find that's best?'

'Mmm. Four . . . four. I have a lunch appointment . . . but yes, I think I could manage that.'

'Right. We'll meet outside the building.' After giving the address, Vee said, 'Well, thanks a lot, Chris. See you. Bye.' This time, she managed to ring off before Chris did.

'Well,' she said to James, 'that happy-ever-after-at-Rivendale thing did get through to her. She hates him so much that, as you'll have gathered, she's going to see Lucy. And I'm going along.'

'I shall take you there,' he said.

Back at his hotel, Rupert soaked in a hot bath for a long time before he stood up, and turned on the cold shower, full blast. Afterwards he dried himself and dressed in fresh clothes. Then he rang room service. Today he did not order red wine. He ordered a bottle of whisky. When it came, and the waiter had gone, he drank half a tumbler neat. Then he rang the Dumbles' number and asked for Lucy, who had just come home from work.

'Darling,' he said. 'I've got a fearful headache. It must be the heat plus the awful day I've had with business things. Do you mind if we don't meet this evening? I really think I'd better go to bed with a couple of aspirin.'

'Oh, I'm so sorry. Would you like me to come round?'

'No darling. I'd be bad company. After a good night's sleep I'm sure I'll be fit as a fiddle.' He added, 'Though I can't think why fiddles are meant to be so specially fit. Can you?'

Lucy laughed. 'No, I haven't the faintest idea.'

'Then I'll see you tomorrow. How about lunch?'

'No, not lunch,' she said. 'I really must catch up on a few things at work. My secretary's away on holiday. Anyway, I've been a bit distracted lately.'

'Darling, you're so conscientious. Dinner, then?'

'Oh yes. Firenze?' she asked.

'No,' he said, and then, 'Why don't we eat somewhere in Hampstead? Nice and cool. I'll pick you up at about seven.'

'If you come a little early you can help me give Edward his bath.'

'Yes. Right.'

'I do hope you'll feel better. Sleep well.' Then she said, 'Pray to your guardian angel – that often works for me.'

'You're my guardian angel, darling.'

'No!'

'Now I've shocked you. I'm sorry. Remember I'm a very new Catholic, Lucy.'

'Oh . . . I know. *I'm* the one who should be sorry. I was silly.' Then she said, 'It's so wonderful that we can share everything now.'

'Yes, darling Lucy. Everything. Always.'

When they had rung off, he suddenly bowed his head, and covered his face with his hands.

He sat in this position for some time before he raised his head. He ran his fingers down from forehead to chin: the slow movement with which a blind man learns an alien face. Then he poured another whisky.

Two-thirds of the bottle and more than two hours had passed when he took an address book from his pocket, and looked up a number.

Ten minutes later he was walking up Piccadilly, carrying his second green Hatchards carrier. He was walking in the direction of the Hilton. However, that was not his destination: he turned off Piccadilly into the narrow street that leads to Shepherd Market. Halfway down he turned his head and looked behind him, perhaps thinking he heard a footfall, but he saw no one. He stuffed the carrier into a litter bin under a lamp post, and continued on his way.

In one of the narrow passages that edged the other side of the Market, he rang the top bell of three, each marked only with a woman's first name.

He paid when he arrived; an hour later, he added a substantial tip. Faintly smiling, he said, 'You know your job.'

She was sitting on the edge of the bed in her strange apparel, the tools of her trade around her. Now, quick to sense a client's change of mood, she laughed and said, 'And you're a glutton for punishment.'

'Mmm. For punishment,' he repeated. Then he said, 'And this is my farewell to arms.' Seeing her blank expression, he added, 'The war is over, and I'm going home.'

233

He was at the door when she said, 'Oh, you mean you won't be back.'

'That's it.'

But, when she heard his footsteps on the stairs, she murmured with a sneer, 'You'll come back – oh, yes! They always do.'

SIX

Vee and James came early, to find a place to park. They drove round till, at last, in a street behind Lucy's office building, a car drew away from a parking meter.

They had ten minutes to spare, and they sat holding hands till it was time for Vee to go. 'Oh, I'm so nervous,' she said, and then, 'Well, this is our last chance, I guess.'

'Mmm,' he said.

'And a pretty slim one.' Vee paused. 'If this doesn't work out, I guess we just have to leave Lucy to her fate.'

'Her fate,' he said, and then, 'I don't think we can do that.'

'But what else?'

'I've been thinking – we'll just have to go to the police.'

'The police?' she said. 'But, James, we haven't any evidence.'

'I think we should just tell them everything from the beginning. What would we have to gain by inventing it? I'm sure Michel would back us up and tell them about Trish.'

'But Trish would lie.'

He sighed. 'I feel as if we're tangled in some awful spider's web – we must break free!'

'And he's the spider?'

'Of course. Who else?'

Vee looked at her watch. 'I must go now.'

'Yes. I'll wait. As long as it takes.'

She kissed his cheek and got out of the car. 'Perhaps Chris won't turn up after all.'

'That's always a possibility.'

But, exactly at four, a taxi drew up outside Lucy's building, and Chris stepped out.

'Oh Chris, I'm so glad to see you.' Eagerly Vee came forward.

Chris, cool in green, merely raised her eyebrows.

'The office is on the third floor – it's at the end of a passage,' Vee said. 'I'll come up and wait for you by the elevator.'

'To pick up the pieces of Ms Riven?' Chris laughed.

Vee winced, but all she said was, 'Oh, Chris, don't be too tough.'

Chris smiled. 'It's a tough story.' As they got out of the lift, she said, 'What a shabby old building! But I suppose that impresses potential donors with the worthiness of the cause.'

Watching Chris recede down the dim passage, Vee started to tremble. Twice she paced the narrow hall in front of the lift, then looked up, startled to see Chris coming back towards her.

Chris was frowning. 'It's weird. The woman at the desk seems to be in a sort of panic. She said she didn't think Ms Riven was available. She was stuttering and stammering.'

Vee frowned. Then she said, 'I'm going to see what I can find out – they know me here.'

She hurried down the passage and pushed open the swing door into the small reception area. Susie, at the desk, exclaimed, 'Oh, Miss Westwood, I'm so relieved to see you. I haven't known what to do.'

'But what's happened?'

'Well, just after two, Lucy went rushing out. She'd just had a phone call, and she looked terribly upset. She didn't say where she was going or anything . . . not at all her usual self.'

'And she hasn't come back?'

'Oh yes, she has. About half an hour ago. But she just dashed past me and into her office. She's locked the door, and she doesn't answer her phone.'

Chris had followed Vee back into the reception area. Now, cucumber-cool, she said, 'Well, well! Do you think she's committed suicide?' Seeing their horrified expressions, she added, 'I was only joking.'

Witheringly, Vee said, 'Lucy would never commit suicide.'

Susie said, 'I didn't know what I should do. Lucy's secretary's on holiday. The director and his assistant are both out.'

Vee said, 'I'll see what I can do.'

When Vee reached Lucy's office, she automatically tried the handle of the locked door. Then she hesitated. She did not call out; perhaps she feared how Lucy would react to her voice. She hammered on the door. When there was no answer, she crouched down, her ear pressed against the keyhole. From inside came a steady, continuous murmur.

Vee stood up, and took several steps back along the landing. Then she ran at the door and hurled herself against it; the lock broke, and the door burst open. Vee, staggering to regain her balance, took a step inside. Lucy sat at her desk, looking down into her lap.

Certain monks of Mount Athos spend their lives repeating a single prayer for mercy. This was what Lucy was doing now: 'God have mercy on me. God have mercy on me.' She had not even glanced up when the door burst open. Still looking down, she went on saying her prayer.

'Lucy, Lucy.' Now Vee knelt beside her. 'Lucy, Lucy, what's happened to you?'

For hardly an instant, Lucy's lips stopped moving. Then again the monotonous murmur began.

Vee seized Lucy's head between her hands, tilted it up and sideways in an attempt to make Lucy's eyes meet hers.

'God have mercy on me.' Lucy's eyes seemed sightless or, now, to look past Vee to where Chris was standing in the doorway.

'God have mercy.' But now Lucy's speech faltered. 'God . . .'

When a taper is lit in the night, it is first only a wavering dot of brightness; pointing, this aspires; it becomes a flame that dispels the dark. As light grew in Lucy's eyes, Vee again called out her name, but Lucy was looking past Vee: her light shone on Chris.

'Oh, I'm so sorry. Oh, you poor woman!' Lucy's voice was soft with the same compassion that now slowly filled her eyes with tears.

Chris stared; then she flinched from what flowed towards her: from what her face showed she felt, recognized and, in an instant, rejected.

'Poor woman, indeed! Don't you dare pity *me*! Keep your pity for yourself.' Chris swung round. 'I'm leaving,' she said. She pushed past Susie, standing gaping behind her. Hands clenched at her sides, holding herself stiffly, she marched away.

Vee said to Susie, 'Lucy'll be all right now. I'll take care of her. Why don't you go back to your desk? The phone's ringing.'

'Oh right. Yes, I will.' Looking and sounding relieved, Susie departed.

A single tear lay on Lucy's cheek. Vee raised her hand and gently brushed it away. Then, still crouching beside her, she took Lucy's hand. It rested limply in hers. Lucy murmured, 'Oh – that poor, poor Chris.'

'To hell with Chris!' Vee exclaimed. Then she said slowly, 'You recognized her. So . . . you've seen the tape?'

Lucy gave a violent shudder. She nodded. Then the dazed look came back onto her face. She said, 'Oh Vee, please take me home now.'

'Yes. Yes, of course I will. There's a car outside. James will drive us.'

'James? Oh, please take me home.'

'Yes. We'll go now.' When Lucy did not move, Vee pulled her to her feet. She picked up Lucy's bag, and swung it, next to her own, over her shoulder. Then she guided Lucy along the passage.

At the desk, she said to Susie. 'Lucy's had a shock. There's no need to talk about this to anyone. Will you just say she felt ill and went home?'

'Yes. Yes, of course I will. You're sure she'll be all right?' Susie's glance at Lucy, standing blank-faced beside Vee, was anxious.

'Yes, yes. I'll ring up in the morning and let you know if she's not well enough to come in.'

The noise and dazzle of the outside world seemed to strike Lucy like a blow as they left the building. She flinched, then started to pray again: 'God have mercy on me.'

'It's all right,' Vee said. 'We haven't far to go.' But, as they made their way to the car, Lucy kept on with her muttered prayer.

They reached the car. Vee propelled Lucy into the back seat and got in beside her. Leaning forward, Vee said to James, 'She's seen the tape. God knows how or where. She's in shock. We must take her home to Hampstead.'

'Right.' James started the car. Then he said, 'And what happened to Chris?'

'She turned up,' Vee said, 'but let's forget about her now – for ever as far as I'm concerned.'

There had been an accident in the Euston Road, creating a traffic jam that lasted nearly half an hour. Now the rush hour had begun. As they waited, suddenly Lucy's murmuring stopped. Her head sank onto Vee's shoulder. A minute later she was asleep. Their progress through Marylebone and St John's Wood and up the Finchley Road and Fitzjohn's Avenue was slow.

All the way, Lucy slept and James and Vee, anxious not to wake her, sat in silence. At last they reached Hampstead. There was less traffic in the village and soon James, directed by Vee, drew up outside the Dumbles' house.

'Come inside with us,' Vee said to James. She was gently shaking Lucy's arm.

Lucy woke. When she saw Vee peering anxiously at her, she looked bewildered for a moment, but then her face turned pale, and she exclaimed, 'Oh!'

'We're home, Lucy. Let's go inside.'

'Home,' Lucy said and got out of the car. She and Vee, followed by James, went up the path. Mag Dumble, on the sitting room window seat, holding a struggling, bawling Edward, saw them and came to the door.

'Why, Vee,' she said, and then, 'My goodness, Lucy, Edward's been so difficult this afternoon.' She moved to put him in Lucy's arms. But Lucy walked straight past towards the stairs.

'Well!' Mag's exclamation was astonished, and Edward increased his roars as Vee followed Lucy up the stairs. 'And who are you?' Mag asked James.

Upstairs in her room, Lucy went straight to her bed and lay down on it, staring up at the ceiling. Vee pulled up a chair beside the bed and sat down.

'Lucy,' she said. 'You have to tell me what happened. You have to tell me now.' But Lucy went on staring at the ceiling.

Downstairs, in the rather dusty living room, the Sistine Madonna smiled above the fireplace, and Edward was fast asleep on the sofa.

When James introduced himself, Mag exclaimed, 'Oh,

Rupert's son – how very nice! I'd gathered that there was some kind of estrangement.' Then, seeing his expression, she said, 'Why, what's the matter? Is something wrong? I know Lucy's upset . . . but engaged girls are often so moody.'

After a moment, James said, 'I think she's just learnt something very bad about my father.'

'Really? Oh dear! Very bad? Do you mean the engagement will be off?'

'Yes, definitely off.'

Mag sighed. 'Oh dear! I always thought he was too . . . worldly, you know, for our dear Lucy. And of course . . . disappearing like that, well I was shocked, though Lucy said he had good reasons for it. But then, well, I changed my mind . . . and he was received on Saturday, you know, and made his first Confession and first Holy Communion.'

'What?'

'Oh yes – and dear Lucy was so happy.' Mag sighed again. Then she said, 'So will she break it off this evening?'

'This evening?'

'Yes, they're going out. They were going to dinner at some place in Hampstead . . . so much more pleasant than town in summer. Would you like some coffee?'

'Coffee? Yes, coffee. . . . Is he coming *here*?'

Mag looked at her watch. 'Yes – any time now. He's coming early. He was going to help Lucy give Edward his bath, but I suppose I'd better do that – when he wakes up. Oh dear, how awkward all this is. I wish Bernard were here but he was going straight from work to a meeting – Catholics in media, you know. Well, I'm glad Lucy's friend Vee's here to back her up if it's going to be difficult. Shall I go and make the coffee? Or there's some red wine, if you'd prefer that?'

'No, coffee will be fine.'

'You *do* look upset. Come along to the kitchen, and tell me all about it.'

Very slowly, James rose to his feet. At that moment, there was the unmistakable sound of a London taxi drawing up at the gate.

Mag went to the window. 'Oh yes, it's him.'

James had become very pale. He said, 'Don't let him in.'

'Oh, but surely that's up to Lucy. Anyway, we never lock the door in the daytime. Bernard and I believe in trust. He'll just walk in.'

The taxi drove off and now footsteps came up the path. 'Lock the door,' said James.

'Oh – *really*!' But all the same Mag moved into the hall. The front door opened just before she reached it.

'Mag! Good evening!' Rupert – smiling, eyes sparkling – stepped into the hall and pushed the door shut behind him.

Mag took a step back. 'Oh, Rupert . . . could you wait a minute? I must just speak to Lucy – she's rather . . . upset.'

'Upset?' The smile was gone. 'Where is she?'

'Up in her room. I'll just go and see . . .' Mag turned towards the stairs.

Rupert stepped forward again. Then he glanced into the sitting room where James was standing, motionless and pale.

'You!' Rupert exclaimed. Then he was across the hall and taking the stairs, two at a time, in loping strides.

Vee was still sitting by Lucy's bed, and Lucy's eyes were still fixed on the ceiling. Now suddenly she looked towards the door. When she saw Rupert in the doorway, she screamed. Her scream was piercing, shrill: a sound of total horror, followed by a total hush. Then Rupert cried out, 'Lucy!'

Vee was on her feet advancing towards him. 'Get out!'

He ignored her. 'Lucy!' But Lucy, shrinking back against the bedhead, was trembling. Then, with her shaking hand, she made the sign of the cross.

Vee advanced further: 'Get out. She knows now. The tape!' She was incoherent. 'This afternoon.'

He rallied: 'Tape – what tape? Lucy darling, what *is* this? What has this vile creature been telling you?'

'*Telling her*!' Vee exclaimed. 'Oh no, she's seen it now. She's seen it.'

Rupert stood still. Dark against his pallor, the slate tinge of his eyes quite overwhelmed the blue. He made a movement towards Vee. Then, behind him, James's voice called out, 'Go – you devil!'

Rupert turned. James stood at the top of the stairs. Rupert took a step towards him, then halted. Father and son now resembled each other only in their pallor: James transformed by courage, Rupert broken by defeat: he flinched; he seemed to shrink and crumble. He looked away, gave a last glance – it was despairing – at Lucy, stricken in the room behind him. Then down the stairs he went, lurching, stumbling – past Mag, transfixed in the hall by Lucy's scream – to fumble with the door handle, then stagger into the fading, softening brightness of the summer evening.

Vee had come to the bedroom door. As Rupert lurched down the stairs, she turned back to Lucy.

Lucy was no longer shrinking against the bedhead. She was sitting up. Now she spoke: 'Oh Vee, I'm so sorry that I doubted you.'

'Dear Lucy – please, please.' Now Vee turned to James, who, pale and gripping the banister, was standing at the top of the stairs. 'Dear James.' He came towards her and they embraced. Then she said, 'I'm so sorry – but will you wait downstairs for me? I have to talk to Lucy.'

'Of course,' he said.

'James, you're so good. So wonderful.' She went back into the bedroom.

Lucy said again, 'Vee, I'm so sorry.'

'Lucy, you mustn't worry about that.' She came back to the chair by the bed, sat down and took Lucy's hand. She said, 'It's all over.'

'Over?' Lucy shuddered, but she returned the squeeze Vee gave her hand.

'Yes. But now you have to tell me what happened.'

Lucy shook her head. 'No, I can't,' she said. 'I can't.'

'You must.'

Lucy shook her head again. Then she started to speak. She said, 'I never understood about hell before. I did then. I ran. People stared at me. They all looked like devils – I thought one man was Topcliffe. It was madness, and I kept on running. I bumped into a woman. She shouted at me, but I just kept running till I got back to my office. Susie must have thought I was crazy when I rushed past her. Then I locked the door and sat down, and then . . . well, I went away. I didn't hear

242

anything. I didn't see anything. I went to God. And then, when you took hold of my face, I started to come back. I didn't want to – but I knew I had to because God was letting go of me – and I saw . . . I saw Chris. Oh, Vee.' Lucy began to cry, and Vee, beside her, stroked her hair and murmured again and again, 'Oh, Lucy!'

After a few minutes, Lucy wiped her eyes. Then she made a move to get up. 'Oh how could I have just walked past Edward like that. And he was crying. I must go to him now.'

'Wait just a little. Listen – he's stopped crying.' Then Vee said gently, 'You don't have to describe the tape to me. I've seen it. But you have to tell me what happened this afternoon. Before you ran. I had James to help me. You've got me. You have to get rid of it.'

After a moment Lucy said, 'To . . . exorcise it.'

'Yes – that's right.'

So Lucy told her.

SEVEN

Rupert had reached the end of the crescent. There he halted. Sweating, panting, deadly pale, he gazed wildly round at trees heavy with leaves, gardens dense with shrubs and flowers. As if this summer scene were reeling round him he put a hand to his head and swayed.

The long black car drew up beside him. The chauffeur got out and came round to open the rear door. From inside, she said, 'Come on. Get in.'

The impassive chauffeur waited. Rupert sank into the car. The chauffeur closed the door, and returned to the front seat.

The interior of the air-conditioned limousine with its darkened windows was cool and dim; Disa sat at ease in this cool dimness: cream tinged with coffee, except for her rusted eyes. She said, 'I knew you'd need me.'

'*Need* you?' His voice had an unaccustomed huskiness and his eyes a dull hopeless look.

'Yes, need me.' She laughed her two-note laugh. 'But at this moment, I'd say you need a drink even more.'

The limousine contained predictable trappings: a cut-glass vase holding a salmon, scentless rose, a little bar packed with expensive drinks. Disa half filled a small heavy tumbler with brandy. She held out the glass to him. After an instant's hesitation, he took it and drank its contents down. He gave a little gasp. Then he said, 'I suppose you followed me here. But how did you find me?' He leant back against the leather-smelling upholstery, and closed his eyes as the car, almost silently, slid along. Then he said, 'I can't understand it. I can't understand anything.' He paused. 'I suppose she made a copy. But why did she hold onto it till now?'

Disa, watching him, now raised her eyebrows. 'She?'

'That fearful Vee. My Evil Angel. She showed Lucy the tape. Oh, my poor Lucy.'

Again Disa raised her eyebrows. Now she was faintly smiling. 'I see.'

He opened his eyes, dulled and weary. The car was driving down East Heath Road. 'Lucy screamed when she saw me,' he said.

'She did?' Disa's tone was conversational, held a mild curiosity.

He gave her a glance tinged with animosity. 'I realize I can't expect sympathy from you.' A silence fell. He closed his eyes. When he opened them again, they were driving through Gospel Oak, and he said, 'Where are we going?'

'On a farewell drive.' Then she said, 'I'm tired of London.'

'I see. So you're returning to your lair?'

'Yes, to Kameni.' Then she said, 'And what are your plans?'

'My plans?' He paused. 'I have no plans.'

'Ah!' she said. But Rupert, turning away from her, had made a sound very like a stifled sob. Then he closed his eyes again.

They drove through Tufnell Park. When, rubbing a hand across his eyes, he sat up, they were crossing the Holloway Road. Peering out of the window through the dark glass, he frowned. The car gathered speed. Then, as it made a smooth turn, he stiffened. After a few moments it slowed down.

Seen through these dark windows, the sun's late rays brought no brightness to the looming church, or to the builder's yard with its high wire fence behind which some large dog now made a sound between a bark and a howl. They brought no brightness to 63 Tolland Road. Stark and desolate, with its dust-clotted bay window, it reared from its grey desert of cement.

He stared. She spoke: 'A pilgrimage to the home of Dink November? Oh, yes I know her real name now. I realized you hadn't given it to me when I picked up that book of yours about that weird French poet and his woman.' She paused. Then she said, 'I didn't like you lying to me about that. You see, I'd believed we had this . . . rapport.'

'Rapport!' he said. A sudden gust of wind blew dust against

the car window. A ginger cat, back flattened, sped across the cement. Again the dog emitted a single barking howl

'That's right. Anyway, I was curious. A South African prostitute . . . smothered in North London two years ago. It wasn't difficult for me to find out about the case.'

He stared at the bleak house with as bleak a look. Then he said, 'But why should you want to?'

She tapped on the glass and smoothly, quietly, the car backed round the corner, turned again the way it had come. Then she gave her two-note laugh. 'I wonder!' Then she added, 'And did it never occur to you that I'd make a copy of that tape?'

'*You* – a copy?' He was staring at her. Then he said slowly, 'Do you by any chance imagine that that tape would convict me of killing Dink November? Frankly, I'd advise you to consult a lawyer. I'm convinced that tape wouldn't convict me of anything.'

'Oh no – I don't need to talk with an attorney. You see, I happen to believe you're right.'

The car had reached Highbury Corner. Now it circled the roundabout and turned into Upper Street. He said, 'I should have realized you'd want to add that tape to your collection.'

'Add it to my collection? So now you think that's why I copied it?'

After a moment, he said, 'Why else?'

She said, 'Did you really think you could ditch me?'

'*Ditch* you?'

She said, 'That's right.' She laughed again. Now she said, 'No one ditches Miss Dis?'

Upper Street, Islington, with its evening cafés, its bookshops and happy strollers, presented a pleasing contrast to the district they had visited earlier. But Disa's and Rupert's eyes were fixed on each other. He said, 'So?'

She said, 'And most especially no one ditches me for that stupid little cunt I met today.'

As he stared at her, points of light in his eyes gave them something resembling, yet different from, their usual sparkle.

She said, 'It was easy to track her down – I'll tell you all about that later. I called her at her office this afternoon. I said, "I'm speaking for Rupert Deyntree. He needs you urgently.

Right away." "What?" she goes, and I go, "It's very important. You have to come to the Park Lane Hilton." "The Park Lane Hilton?" says little Miss Lucy, and I say, "Yes, he needs you now. At once. Come to the reception desk." Then I ring off. And in a bit, I go downstairs to the desk, and wait till she comes running like a crazy thing. And I step forward and say, "You must be Lucy."

'Well, then she starts all these questions, "Is he ill?" and stuff. Then I say she must come upstairs with me, and I'll explain everything. So she comes up to the suite. I had it all set up – the video in front of the settee. She starts, "Where is he? Where is he?" Then I just said, "Sit down." And she did. So I pressed the buttons, and sat down next to her.

'I didn't do much talking. When it started, I said, "Look, there's your darling Rupert." And I told her the other two were Dink and Chris. And I said how you and Dink had made the tape yourselves. She sat there quite rigid all the time. She certainly was pale – as pale as you are now. Then, when the party ended on the screen, she started shaking, and she tried to get up, but I told her she must be patient, and she stayed. When the picture came on, I said, "There's that Dink again. But now she's dead – you can tell, can't you? Rupert killed her, you see, and now he's filming her. He's excited. Why, the camcorder's shaking almost as much as you are, Lucy – and you can hear his breathing, can't you? Heavy, like on a dirty phone call."

'When I switched it off, I said, "Well, all good things come to an end. But it's a pity the film stopped there. The next part would have been quite a tidbit. He fucked her after she was dead – that's what he told me. Oh, he's told me a lot of things while he's been staying with me the last few months. Some true – and some not so true. He told me that you'd refuse ever to see him again after he disappeared like that, but I see he managed to get round you somehow. He's kind of plausible, isn't he? But I wonder if he told you why he he left. Did he tell you it was because your friend Vee stole this tape and told him she'd show it to you if he didn't? Did he tell you how I got it back for him . . . and *set him free*?"'

Now Disa laughed. Then she said, 'I laughed then, too.' You should have seen that horror-movie look on her face. So I said,

"Lucy, Lucy, don't look so scared. I won't do you any harm. In fact I'm really pleased to meet you, and you should be pleased to meet me. Doesn't it interest you to meet the other woman in Rupert's life? He's needed another woman who understands his little ways ever since he got rid of Dink. But I'm not possessive. I'm always willing to share – in fact I love it. Why don't you come and stay for a while with Rupert and me? The three of us could have such great times together. So how about it? Hmm?" And I gave a big smile, and put my hands on her tits. Wow, did she jump! She leapt up and just tore out of the room. I don't know how you ever fell for such a frigid little—' But here Disa broke off. She said, 'Hey, don't look at me like that. Surely you're not planning on *another* murder?'

His face, his eyes, the hand clenched round his empty glass gave ample grounds for such a question. But then he glanced at the chauffeur beyond the glass partition. He gave a single shudder. Then he said, 'Stop the car.'

'Yeah. Soon. You don't want to get out here, do you?'

The car had passed the Angel, Islington, and turned off the Pentonville Road into the maze of streets that led to the Euston Road.

'Yes here,' he said. 'Anywhere. To get away from you. Bitch, whore – I've been tired of you so long.'

'Tired of me!' Something moved in her turbid eyes. Her voice rose as she said, 'No one gets tired of *me*.'

'You're wrong, you know.' Possibly her raised voice, her furious look – evidence that his words had assailed her, perhaps more unequivocally than any physical attack – were what made his eyes brighten, as the circus tiger's do when it sees the chance to take its hated trainer unaware. He smiled now for the first time. 'Of course I'm tired of you. Your cruelty, your stupidity, your vulgarity. You were so right just now. Yes – I ditched you.'

She looked away, but when she turned back she was smiling. She was what most people would have called 'herself' again. She said, 'Just tell me what you saw in her. In little Lucy.'

He said, 'That's something you'd never understand.'

'Oh, I can make a good guess. It turned you on that she was so *good*, so *pure*, so *innocent*. Well, she's not so innocent now she's seen that tape.'

He said, 'I can't bear to think of her seeing it. But I don't believe it could ever touch her soul.'

'Her *soul*! And you say you don't believe in God.'

'I don't. But I believe in Lucy.'

Disa's laugh was harsh. She said, 'Well, I wasn't interested in touching her *soul*. Even my interest in touching her body was pretty mild.'

'Let me out or I'll kill you.'

'Oh no, I don't think so. I'd say your sense of self-preservation's too strong for that. Anyhow, you know I've always liked a spice of danger. And we're nearly there.'

'There?'

The car was in the Euston Road now. It turned left, past the classical caryatids ranged on the façade of the Friends' Meeting House. They were in Bloomsbury. Only a few moments later, the car drew up outside a small block of flats. 'Well,' she said, 'shall we pay a call? On Cosmopolitan Clara?'

Now the expression of horror on his face surpassed any it had worn before. She said, 'They haven't found him yet.'

Waxen now, with eyes sheer slate, he had sunk back in his seat. She said, 'After I found out about Jeanne Duval, I had you followed all the time. By two pals of mine. To that Lucy's place. To that church. One guy waited in the car. The other went inside and saw you go through that weird performance – you do the strangest things, Rupert! And yesterday they followed you to that Italian restaurant and then here! One of them went inside after you and listened outside the apartment. When you came out in that old raincoat, he phoned the guy in the car to follow you, while he went inside. The door wasn't locked. It was easy to open it with a plastic card. He said it was quite a scene. Blood and bone and bits of brain. And all that broken glass and wine. You must have hit him more than once with that bottle to break it against his skull.'

'So much blood,' Rupert muttered. His eyes were closed. 'Blood everywhere. Matted with hair on the bottle. Blood splashed even on that photograph of the Parthenon he had above his bookcase. Blood on my clothes.'

'So you put the raincoat on. May I ask if you left prints?'

'So much blood,' he muttered again, and then 'Oh no, no prints.'

She said, 'I thought not. Especially since you'd been so careful to make it look as if some rentboy he'd picked up had killed him. Emptying his billfold and leaving it beside the body. Oh, you thought the cops would be sure to believe that when they found him – and when they saw all those magazines and books he had.'

There was a silence. He still lay back, eyes closed. Then she said, 'But, hey now – you have to tell me why you did it. I thought you really liked that guy.'

Rupert opened his eyes. He said, '*Liked* him? He was my best friend.'

'So – why?'

'He was going to tell Lucy. About the tape.'

'He'd *seen* it?'

'No, my hateful son told him, and he believed it. He wanted me to break with Lucy or he said he'd tell her everything. I knew *he* could convince her.'

'What made you think that?'

'I *knew* it. Because she understood how fond of me he was. I begged him. I pleaded with him – in the restaurant, at the flat, too. But he was adamant. Even drunk and sobbing – he was determined to betray me . . . to betray our friendship. I felt such rage that he could do such a thing.' Rupert paused. Then he said, 'What . . . happened was his fault. Not mine.'

Now she laughed. 'You don't have to justify yourself to me.'

'It's true.' His voice was almost shrill.

She shrugged. Then she said, 'Lucy, Lucy – always Lucy! What a hang-up! And all for nothing now.' Then she said, 'You know, those pals of mine can tip off the cops so easily. And then they'll find the taxi driver who picked you up at the restaurant and the one who took you back to your hotel from just round the corner here. And there are those bloody clothes you dumped in that bin last night, with his raincoat . . .' She paused. 'My pal picked up those, you know.'

She tapped on the glass. The car started at once. He said, 'So you're going to turn me in.' And suddenly he gave a wild laugh. 'Well then – nothing to lose!' And out came his hands, reaching towards her throat. But she stretched out her hands too, pressing them against his chest. All her strength was in her eyes and in her hands, as she said, 'Wait.'

He hesitated. She said, 'There's an alternative. You can come back with me to Kameni.' She laughed. 'To my lair.'

He exclaimed, 'I'd rather die!' But he lowered his hands a fraction.

She smiled. 'Oh, if you don't come with me, you won't *die*. But you'd certainly spend the rest of your life in prison. You wouldn't like that would you, Rupert?'

He lowered his hands to his sides now. She said, 'Oh and, by the way, those pals of mine will hang on to the evidence. If anything should happen to me, you can be sure they'd use it.' Then she said, 'Well, make your decision.'

'My decision!' There was a long silence. The car had reached Cambridge Circus when he said, at last, 'All right. I'll come.'

'I knew you would. My baggage is in the trunk. We'll just pick up your stuff and be on our way to the airport.'

They had reached Piccadilly when she said, 'There's one thing that puzzles me. Last night, when you went to see that hooker – how did *that* gel with your pure love for Lucy?'

He was silent. Then he said, 'It was an expiation.'

'A what?'

'You wouldn't understand.'

'Oh, I wouldn't understand.' She laughed. 'Perhaps I'll look it up in the dictionary one day. Did she give you a good time?' She saw the hatred on his face. She smiled. She said, 'Remember, those witnesses can come forward any time.'

Just before they reached the hotel, she said, 'It's just like old times. Like the first time we met, when we fetched your gear from that small hotel. I remember you said, "I'm being kidnapped. How exciting!" Now it's the same.'

It was the same; it was different. Her smile stretched her lips so thin, so wide that there were only her bright teeth, and something seemed to twine and slither under the cloudy surface of her eyes. And his look was the beast's: doomed to its nightly round of tricks, the growl in its throat stifled when its trainer – feared, detested – cracks the whip.

PART FOUR

ONE

At nine o'clock on a Saturday morning early in September, Belinda Deyntree's doorbell rang. After a minute or two it rang again. A few moments later, Belinda answered her entry phone: 'Who's that?' she asked in a drowsy voice.

'It's Michel.' There was a silence. Then Michel said, 'Please let me in.'

Several seconds passed before Belinda pressed the buzzer, and Michel went up the stairs to the flat. Belinda opened the door, fastening a cotton dressing gown. 'I was asleep,' she said. 'You woke me.'

'Oh I'm sorry.'

Belinda said ungraciously, 'What do you want?' But she led the way into her living room. Its furnishings, though modelled on Chris's, had cost much less; the room looked plain rather than elegantly austere, rather resembling the appearance of its owner in comparison with that of her ideal.

'I've come to apologize,' Michel said. 'Can I sit down?'

'Oh? Apologize for what?' Belinda's tone was hostile, but she gestured to the two-seater white sofa, and Michel sat down.

'For the way I've treated you.'

Belinda, who had remained standing, shrugged. 'You don't like me. I don't like you. It's mutual.'

Michel fidgeted with a lock of her short, but becomingly cut, hair. Then she said, 'I've always been so jealous of you.'

'*You* – jealous of *me*? That's a laugh!' Belinda's voice was shrill with surprise and disbelief.

'No, it's true. I have. And with reason. Belinda, your mother loves you more than anything else in the world.'

'Oh, don't give me that!' Belinda's tone was angry now. She

255

paused. 'If she'd really loved me, she'd never have set up house with you.'

'Belinda,' Michel said, 'would you say that if I was a man? If your mother, after an unhappy marriage and a divorce, had "set up house", as you put it, with a *man*?'

Belinda's eyes had started to wander round the blank walls. She said nothing until Michel's repetition of the question 'Would you?' made her burst out, 'Well, at least that would have been *natural*.'

'Natural to you, perhaps – but not to her.' Now Michel's hands were tightly clasped in front of her.

'That's nonsense. After all, she got married, didn't she? She had me.'

'Yes – she's often told me that you made all the misery worthwhile. She *was* miserable, Belinda – and not just because your father was such a bastard.'

Belinda said, 'I don't believe that. If you hadn't come along and . . . changed her, she would have stayed perfectly normal.'

'No, Belinda! Long before she met me, when she was still married to your father, she realized that she wasn't what you call "normal".' Michel's voice had risen; she lowered it again to say, 'Ask her.'

'It's not a subject I care to discuss with her.'

'I can see that. And I think your mother made a mistake. You were too young, it was too sudden, when, after her father died, she came out into the open, and I moved into her room.'

Belinda said bitterly, 'She was ashamed to let her father know, but she didn't mind *me* knowing. Gay rights! Gay pride! Gay shit!'

'Belinda, I can't change your views on homosexuality – I'm not even going to try – though I must say I feel they're a bit old-fashioned.'

Belinda said sullenly, 'I think people should be free to do whatever they want in their sex lives.' Then she said passionately, 'But she's my mother!'

'Yes – and she loves you. Belinda, she wasn't ashamed to tell your grandfather. She thought he was too old to understand – she thought it would just hurt him and bewilder him, as it would your grandmother. But Barbara believed it would be different with you. She was sure you'd understand.'

'Well, she was wrong.'

'Yes, she was. She tried to be honest with you too soon. But, Belinda, you're twenty-four now. Don't you think you're old enough to appreciate her honesty? Barbara's the most honest person I've ever met. She hates deception and lies. And, Belinda, she's so unhappy. Ever since that row – I admit it was all my fault, all caused by my jealousy – she's been so angry with me. Because she loves you more than me, more than anyone. I promise you that's true. And she misses you – she misses you so much. Please come and see her.'

There was a silence. Then Belinda said, 'I suppose you came here because she's angry with you.'

'Belinda, I'm not using you. I didn't tell her I was coming – and I won't mention it to her . . . ever. I came because I love her. Because I want her to be happy – and she can't be happy without you.'

Belinda sighed. 'Well, I miss her too.' Then she said, 'Okay, I'll try to think about it all.' Then she said, 'D'you want coffee or something?'

Michel stood up. 'No thanks. I must get back now. Saturday chores to do, you know.'

'Well, goodbye then.'

'Goodbye, Belinda.' But Michel's descent of the stairs was slow. As she let herself out of the front door she gave a heavy sigh: perhaps at the prospect of Saturday chores, but more probably at that of the atmosphere – nowadays so sombre – awaiting her at home.

When Michel had gone, Belinda went into the kitchen, and made herself some coffee with skim milk and artificial sweeteners. But she left it till it was too cold to drink: no great loss; she preferred it with whole milk and two heaped spoons of sugar.

Belinda sat at the kitchen table, her elbows resting on it, her chin cupped in her hands. Finally she stood up, and prepared to do her own Saturday tasks. Today these included a face mask, a hair appointment and the purchase of a bunch of flowers.

*   *   *

Belinda rang Chris's bell at precisely ten past eight. She had been wandering around the neighbouring streets for a quarter of an hour in order to achieve this appropriate degree of lateness for the eight o'clock invitation. Chris had not said on the telephone whether other guests were expected; if they had been, it would have made no difference to Belinda's preparations for the occasion: her smart dress, her best shoes and bag, her careful make-up and French scent were a tribute to Chris's own impeccable standards.

'Belinda – how nice! And what lovely flowers!' Even though it was so fashionable, Chris, with her intense distaste for physical contact, had never adopted the custom of a kiss of greeting. Now, taking the bunch of white roses from Belinda's hand, she stepped back.

'And here are your books,' Belinda said, handing Chris a plastic carrier. '*Being the Best* and *A Country Story*. Sorry I kept them so long.'

'That's all right.' Chris put the carrier down on the hall table. 'And what did you think of them?' she asked.

'Oh, well. Of course, *Being the Best* is awfully good. But I kept getting this feeling I'd read it before, though I knew I hadn't. Odd, wasn't it?'

'Mmm.' Chris said. 'And *A Country Story*?'

'Well, that was odd, too. Oh, the people weren't glamorous – like in *Being the Best* – and I suppose nothing much really happened . . . but it sort of got a grip on me.'

'Oh, really?'

Evidently Belinda noticed that Chris's expression was far from enthusiastic, for she said quickly, 'Of course, as I told you before, I'm no judge of novels.'

'Oh, don't say that. A lot of people seem to agree with you. It's still selling. Perhaps I should employ you as a reader.' Chris's tone was cool, but then she shrugged. Now it was with a smile that she ushered Belinda into the drawing room. 'Surprise!' she said.

Belinda's face revealed that Chris had chosen the right word as Keith, wearing a dark suit and expensive tie, rose from one of the two huge white sofas that faced each other across the glass-topped coffee table with its neat line-up of modish magazines.

'Belinda, do sit down,' Chris said. Belinda hesitated for a moment before perching on the edge of the other sofa. Chris went on, 'Keith, do pour Belinda a drink while I put these charming flowers in water.' At times – this was one of them – Chris's voice had the would-be-royal graciousness heard in the manufactured accent of her idol, the former prime minister.

As Chris left the room for the downstairs kitchen, Keith obeyed her instructions. 'Belinda, what will you drink?' He went over to the glittering array on the drinks trolley. 'Are you still fond of Campari?'

'Yes, yes, Campari,' Belinda muttered. She was flushed. So was Keith, who now busied himself with vermouth, soda, ice and lemon. They were both silent till he came over with the pretty pink drink and placed it on the coffee table in front of her.

'Belinda . . .' He hesitated.

'Yes.'

'This was Chris's idea – but it's an awfully good one I think. She's explained everything to me.'

'Oh?' Then Belinda said, 'So you knew I'd be here tonight?'

'Yes, of course. I told you – Chris explained everything. I'm sorry I was so tactless. But how could I know? You should have told me. I would have understood – really I would. I wouldn't have minded.'

'Minded?'

'Yes.' Keith gave a nervous little laugh. 'It's what people are that counts. Not where they come from. I mean . . . my own background's not exactly high class – but I can't help that.'

'Like I can't help being Jewish, you mean?'

'Partly Jewish. But it's all right. Why don't we' – he was gaining assurance – 'forget about the whole thing and start again? Anyway, I was glad to hear you didn't drop me because I'd lost my job. You know how . . . fond of you I always was. And you of me too, weren't you, Blini?'

This pet name – 'sounds like a Russian pancake,' she had said with a happy laugh when he first used it – made her look up at him. She said, 'Oh yes, I was . . . very fond of you, Keith.'

'Well, then . . . and here's our good angel!' he added as Chris, carrying the roses in a square black vase, appeared in the doorway.

Belinda, however, took no notice of this last remark, or of Chris. She said, 'But I can't forget. I won't forget. You see Hitler did "gas the lot of them" – all my grandmother's family.'

'I didn't really *mean* that.'

'You said it. And always, every time you came near me, I know I'd remember it. Oh, I should have told you – that's where *I* was wrong. I'm ashamed. But actually I suppose I'm glad I didn't tell you. Because I might never have found out what you were like, if I had!'

'Oh really, Belinda!' Chris said. Having put the vase in the exact centre of the coffee table, she now stood beside Keith.

'Shut up, Chris. Anyway, how could you have brought me here, without telling me you were asking this filthy Nazi?'

Keith's flush had deepened. 'I'm no Nazi – I'm British through and through.'

'I didn't say you were a German. I said you were a Nazi – and you are. I suppose if you'd put my mother in a concentration camp, you'd have made her wear a pink triangle as well as a yellow star. Because she's a lesbian as well as being Jewish – Jewish through and through.'

Keith said, 'You told me she was dead.'

'Yes, I know I did. I behaved like a Nazi, too. That's worst of all. Oh, Keith – get out of here. Get away from me. I never want to see you again.' Belinda, face crimson, sat stiffly upright on the sofa.

'Well,' Keith said. 'I'm very sorry, Chris, but I'd really better be on my way, before I have to hear any more political speeches about Jews and lesbians.'

'Keith, I'm so sorry!' Chris followed him into the hall. As soon as they had left the room, Belinda began to cry. But she had brushed away her tears by the time, a minute or two later, Chris came back into the room.

'Oh Chris – how *could* you?'

Chris's tightened mouth was smaller than ever; so were her eyes, narrowed by rage. 'How could *you*, you mean? How *dare* you – in my own house – tell me to shut up, insult my guest?'

'Why did you do it?' With just such desperation a defeated pagan warrior might have questioned the idol he had long worshipped.

Chris looked her up and down. 'I was trying to help you. To give you another chance. After all, you aren't exactly every man's cup of tea, are you? Well, it's the last time I do any welfare work.'

'Welfare work! Chris, I thought we were friends.' Belinda stood up.

'Friends! Well, just look how you've repaid all my kindness. I've been sorry for you, with your dyke Jewess mother and your father who's a sexual pervert . . . and worse! Shall I tell you about your father, Belinda, tell you the things he's done? He's a rapist, Belinda, and a murderer. I'll tell you all about it.' But after these words and also at the look on Chris's face and the sound of her voice – both seemed close to madness – Belinda put her hands over her ears. She ran from the room into the hall and then out of the house.

Chris, left alone, fell victim to one of the fits of trembling that had attacked her in earlier days, after Rupert's assault. However, as always, she soon regained control, though not quite her normal appearance of calm. She frowned and her hands still trembled as she collected the three glasses – Belinda's untouched, the other two drinks unfinished – on a tray, to which after a moment she added the vase of roses. Then she put the tray down on the coffee table. She closed the heavy wooden shutters on the front window and fastened them with their iron bar. She went to the back of the room and pressed the button that brought a metal blind down outside the window that faced onto the garden. Then she went into the hall and locked the double mortice and the Yale on the front door, and fastened the chain. She went back into the drawing room to collect the tray and, after lowering the metal blind on the door at the back of the hall, went downstairs. There, she put the tray on the elegantly laid table in the dining section, and closed the blind behind the sliding doors to the garden. She took the tray through into the kitchen and put it on the breakfast counter while she closed the blind on the front window.

In the kitchen, the ingredients of the expensive ready-cooked meal were ready to be microwaved; she put them back in the refrigerator. Then she opened the garbage disposal unit, took the roses from the vase and dumped them in the sink. She tore their white petals with her fingers but, careful of thorns, cut up their stalks with kitchen scissors before she pushed them into the black hole of the disposal unit and switched it on. It roared, made a growl or two of protest, but then sucked the mess of flowers down.

Chris went upstairs again. In the hall, she switched on the alarm system for the two lower floors before she went up to her bedroom: to her bed and the beautifully word-processed novel – by an author whose last book had not quite reached the bestseller list – on her bedside table. In the dark rooms below, the little red sensors glowed, ready to trigger the alarm system at any intrusion on her aloneness.

The side door of the house in Willesden was still open – Barbara and Michel never bothered to lock it until they went to bed – when Belinda paid her taxi, hurried up the path and tried the handle. She ran upstairs and into the living room. Barbara, who was lying on the sofa, jumped to her feet; a large cat dropped from her lap with an angry miaow.

'Belinda!' Then seeing her daughter's miserable face, Barbara said, 'Darling – what's the matter?'

'Oh – Mum!'

Barbara opened her arms, and Belinda, in tears, flung herself, for the first time in many years, into her mother's ample, but now comforting, embrace. Soon they moved to the sofa, and gradually Belinda became able to recount the whole story of Keith, culminating in this evening's encounter, his departure, and Chris's parting words.

'Oh darling . . . I'm so sorry . . . Oh, you did the right thing . . . oh, he could never be for you . . . oh, of course you were upset . . . oh, that dreadful woman!' Barbara's comments provided a soothing accompaniment to Belinda's recital.

Then Belinda asked, 'What did she mean – saying my father was a sexual pervert, saying he was a rapist, saying he was a *murderer*? Oh, Mum, what could she have been going to tell me?'

Barbara hesitated. Then she said firmly, 'Oh, of course that was all complete nonsense. She was just trying to hurt you.'

'*Really?*'

After an instant's pause, Barbara said, 'Yes.'

Belinda sighed. Then she said, 'Oh, I'm so glad I came. Though I'm not sure I would have, if it hadn't been for Michel.'

'Michel?' For the first time there was a coolness in Barbara's tone.

'Yes. She came to see me this morning. She said she wasn't going to tell you. She didn't?'

'Why, no,' Barbara said, and then, 'What did she want?'

'Oh, she came to say how sorry she was that she hadn't been nicer to me, that she'd been jealous of me. But mostly she wanted to tell me how much you love me.'

'Oh, but surely, you could never have doubted *that*?'

At the utter incredulity of Barbara's tone, a smile slowly came onto Belinda's face. Then she shrugged, and said quickly, 'Could I stay here – just for tonight? In my old room.'

'Oh, darling, of course. For as long as you like.' But then Barbara paused. After a moment she said, 'Shall I go and make some cocoa?'

'Cocoa! Oh, how lovely!' Belinda exclaimed. Then she added, 'Well, just this once.'

'I'll go and make it. You stay here and rest.' As Barbara left the room, the cat jumped back onto the sofa. Rather reluctantly – for many years, cats, too, perhaps, had been seen as rivals – Belinda allowed it to subside on her lap.

Formerly, when Michel worked in the evening, she had done so at the table in the living room. Nowadays she used the room where she also slept: Belinda's former bedroom. She looked up with a startled expression as the door opened and Barbara came in, closing the door behind her.

'Michel, Belinda's here.'

'Oh, really? I didn't hear her arrive.'

'Poor darling – she's had an awful time.' Quickly, Barbara narrated the events Belinda had described to her.

'Dreadful!' Michel said, and then, 'Well, she was right to break with both those awful people.'

'That's what I said.' Barbara paused. Then she said, 'She was terribly upset when Chris started to tell her about Rupert.' Barbara paused again. Looking down, she said, 'I think perhaps you were right. Perhaps we should drop . . . all that, after all.'

Ever since Vee had telephoned to tell them of what had led up to Rupert's defeat – his banishment from Lucy's life – Barbara had urged Michel to follow it up: to find a way to bring him to justice. 'He can't be allowed to get away with it,' she had continually asserted. Again and again, Michel's arguments that there was no legal recourse – no tape, no witness – had been met with contemptuous rejection: 'You should *find* a way!' Barbara had insisted. Under pressure from Barbara, Michel had gone to the Hilton to attempt to discover the identity of the woman who had summoned Lucy to her ordeal. Michel had encountered just what she had expected: a blank refusal to divulge information about hotel guests. 'They'd have to talk to the police,' Barbara had declared, refusing to believe Michel's reiteration that there was no basis for a police enquiry. Perhaps this irrational obduracy expressed other emotions besides her desire for justice.

Now, at this sudden willingness to 'drop all that', Michel raised her eyebrows and drew in a breath. Then she said, 'Well, if you really think . . .'

'Yes, I do.' Barbara's tone was decisive, but her voice softened at her next words: 'It was good of you to go and see Belinda this morning.'

'Oh – she told you about that?'

'Yes, she said she probably wouldn't have come here now, if it hadn't been for you.' Barbara paused. 'Thank you.'

'That's all right.'

Barbara hurried on: 'She wants to stay here tonight. I'm just making her some cocoa. Could you make up the bed in here with some fresh sheets while I do it?'

'Yes, of course.' Then Michel said, 'But where shall I sleep?'

'Oh well . . . in our room, I suppose.' Barbara spoke briskly, but then she smiled. 'Like some cocoa?'

Michel smiled too. 'You know I can't stand it – but I'll have some coffee.'

'It'll keep you awake.' But, as Barbara left the room, they were both still smiling.

On the second day on which she heard nothing from her son, Mrs Larch had gone up to London. She did not contact the police – doubtless unwilling to involve them unnecessarily in Francis's private life – until, admitted by the caretaker, she found his body. Then it soon became obvious to the investigating officers, from her silent assent to their suspicions, that she shared their assessment of the crime.

Silence was her refuge during the fruitless investigations that followed and during the flurry of tabloid scandal that accompanied them. She spoke to no one of her grief. She refused admittance to all callers, except the police and a lawyer whom she instructed about the sale of her house and most of its contents. The rest she took with her to a small flat in a seaside town where she and Francis had spent his childhood summer holidays.

She took his work on the Satyricon of Petronius Arbiter with her, tried once to read it but, with a shudder of revulsion from its contents, put it away in a drawer where presumably it would remain until her death. This, since she saw no one and ate and slept hardly at all, probably lay, perhaps mercifully, not too far ahead.

TWO

'Poor old Francis,' James said, after they learnt from the papers of Francis's murder. 'I liked him, you know, when I met him.' He sighed. 'His kind of sex has always been very risky. There was some well-known author, a few years ago, who was killed in just that way, by a pick-up.'

'Did they catch the guy who did it?' Vee asked.

'No, I don't think they ever did.' He sighed again. 'London's so big, and there are so many of those boys. No jobs, and such tiny social security . . . if any. So they go on the game to get a bit of cash. And when they do, because they aren't gay by nature, they feel guilty . . . so they get angry. Sometimes their anger carries them away.'

'Mmm. Poor Francis. Lucy was terribly upset when she heard. She'd *really* liked him.' Vee paused. 'So I didn't tell her how you went to see him about Rupert, and he decided not to do anything.'

'Still protecting Lucy?'

Vee flushed. 'Well, there wouldn't have been any point in telling her, would there?'

James smiled. 'You're quite right – none at all.'

'Lucy actually said she was glad that Francis never learnt the truth about Rupert. She said Francis was so fond of him . . . and so loyal.'

'*Too* loyal – we felt!' Then James said, 'I wonder what *he* feels about Francis. That is, if he knows – wherever he's gone.'

Vee said, 'I guess neither of us can ever imagine what *he* feels about anything. I do wonder about that terrible mystery woman, though.' She sighed. 'But it seems she'll remain a mystery. They wouldn't tell Michel a thing about her at the

267

Hilton. She must have had some reason for showing Lucy the tape. Obviously she must be . . . involved with him.'

James said, 'Vee, we simply have to put this whole thing behind us. It's water under the bridge now. We must get on with our own lives.'

'Water under the bridge – such dark water, so muddy, so filthy!' Vee paused before she said, 'Yes, of course you're right.' Slowly her smile grew: 'Our own lives!'

Their own lives flowed on: clear, transparent, with an occasional small eddy when James railed too long against the greed and suffering of a privatized world or Vee's mobile phone rang too often.

He applied, after some hesitation, for a lectureship in London. Sarah – showing none of the fear that perhaps she felt at the prospect of his leaving home – encouraged him. Now he waited for the result; the forthcoming publication of his book would probably add to his chances. Its dedication – 'For my mother and for Vee' – delighted both recipients, though, when Vee finished the book, she was in tears: 'Oh, what a sad life!' The Suffolk shepherd boy, self-taught, had enjoyed a fickle patronage in Regency society. Then fashion had passed on; he had sunk into poverty and despair, and died, forgotten, in an asylum.

'Yes, a sad life,' James said. 'But such beautiful poems. That's what counts in the end.'

'It is?'

'Well, so it seems to a humble academic!' A shadow crossed his face. 'But we can't all create.'

'Oh, we can! Not poems perhaps. But happiness, friendship, love, and . . . children.'

'Darling Vee!'

She was succeeding in her work. The London office ran smoothly. Her colleagues had become her friends. She had managed to obtain a renewed work permit, telling James, 'One thing I won't marry you for is a passport!'

'One thing? What are the others?'

She was silent. Then she laughed. 'I have to be absolutely sure.'

'And when will that be?'

'Soon – I promise!'

'Well, I'll keep on reminding you of that.'

Vee gave the same answer – 'I have to be absolutely sure' – to Sarah and to Lucy when they questioned her. Now both maintained a tactful silence on the subject.

In the aftermath of the day of revelation, Lucy had asked Vee, 'Why didn't you tell me two years ago? Why didn't you show me that horror?'

'I was going to. And then you got pregnant by him. I thought you wouldn't be able to bear it.'

Lucy said, 'Even with my faith to sustain me?'

'I guess I didn't take enough account of that. And I guess I didn't take account of the Riven who was hanged after the Pilgrimage of Grace or the Blessed Hugh who was tortured and died that dreadful death.'

'Mmm. They would have helped me . . . when I turned to God.' Then Lucy's tone changed. She said, 'After everything else, I can understand why you didn't tell me about James. "The one true love".' She said, 'James was yours. Just as mine was Rupert.'

'Rupert!' Vee exclaimed. 'Oh, how can you say that – now that you know what he is.'

'But what he is doesn't alter what I felt. Oh, Vee, the day we went to Farm Street, I was so happy. At the Dumbles' afterwards, Mag found this old Polaroid camera someone had given her. There was one shot left in it. She wanted to photograph me and Rupert and Edward. But Rupert took the camera from her, and said 'No, I just want Lucy.' And he took my picture, and put it in his pocket. I was so sure he loved me, though I don't want to think about that. The point is – I loved him. It *was* love, Vee, true love. The one true love – I know I'll never have another.'

'Oh, how can you say that? Oh, Lucy, of course you will. I know it!'

'And I know I won't. Vee, it's once for me. Anyway . . . I'm not interested in the idea of that kind of love any more. You see, that afternoon when I . . . went to God, it was the most extraordinary experience of my life. I feel I have to . . . well follow it through.'

'Oh Lucy!' Vee's tone was one of utter horror. 'You're not going to become a nun?'

Lucy — a former Lucy, back again — burst out laughing. 'Become a nun? Oh Vee, you are ridiculous. You sound like one of those old novels in the library at Rivers. Of course I'm not going to become a nun. I'm a mother. I have my work.' She paused. 'I just want to spend more time well, waiting, becoming more open . . . to that experience of God's peace, God's infinite love.'

Just as James had looked confused, embarrassed when Vee first talked of the Serenity prayer, so Vee looked now. Then she said, 'If that's your way . . .' and then, 'Well, it's much better than loving Rupert.'

A silence followed. Then Lucy said, 'Sometimes his shadow falls on me.'

After a moment, Vee repeated, 'His shadow.' Then she said, 'I feel it like a chill.'

At different times, a chill fell on them all. Although the new puppy frisked on the lawn, Sarah, standing by Mansfield's grave, uttered a little moan. Barbara, perusing an article on battered women, suddenly stopped reading with a gasp. Belinda, assessing a sexy commercial, closed her eyes for an instant against the image on the screen. Michel, driving past the turning that led to Tolland Road, stopped whistling as though a cold finger had pressed her lips. For Chris, arming her house against the night, perhaps this chill – cause of a brief tremor – was mere reinforcement of an arctic, sealing permafrost.

In the heart of a dark night, Vee and James started awake simultaneously. The intense mutual impulse that now made them cling together would result, nine months later, in the birth of their daughter.

Lucy, of course, was already a mother. 'Darling Edward!' With boundless love, she smiled down into her child's small charming face. His brilliant blue eyes, tinged with slate, returned her gaze. 'Guardian angel,' she prayed, 'watch over him.'

THREE

In Disa's lair, Rupert sometimes stood on the terrace, watching the sun rise: fiery, fierce as a bull, it charged up from the horizon, then changed, in minutes, to a dazzling and more dangerous gold; the sea, briefly pink-tinged and pearly, became a day-long relentless blue. Sometimes Karl, roaming – Marios and Sophia, like Disa, still slept – barked up from the road, before disappearing among the pines.

In August, the morning heat of the terrace was soon unbearable; it was better to be inside the air-conditioned villa. Rupert would go indoors, by his own inclination or at Disa's call.

She had returned from London with two obsessions.

'Tired of me! You said you were tired of me. You didn't *mean* that, did you?' Sometimes she asked the question angrily, sometimes coldly, occasionally in a high, childish whine that, oddly, made him shiver.

Always he replied, 'No, of course not', or 'No, I never meant it', or 'No – oh, Disa, how could I be tired of *you*?' He would explain: '*I* was tired. So tired I didn't know what I was saying.'

'Yeah – you were tired!' And she added, 'I guess sometimes you still are.'

'Perhaps I am.' And at this he would produce a dazzling smile: dazzling but a little rueful for, nowadays, it sometimes required extreme stimulus – all her skills – to bring him to the climax it was essential to her vanity he should achieve.

Her other obsession had been Lucy, whom she constantly disparaged. Then, in her search of his luggage, she had discovered a snapshot in one of his pockets: Lucy joyful on the Dumbles' lawn. Eyes narrowed, Disa confronted him with it: 'Well – what's this?'

271

He had winced, reached out, then at once retracted his hand, turning the wince into a shrug: 'Oh, I forgot I had that.' He looked straight into her rusty eyes.

After a moment she said, 'Yeah? Well, perhaps you did. Anyway you'd better forget *her*. She's history. Gone for ever.'

'Yes,' he said, low.

Disa held out the photograph towards him: 'Spit on her, then.' He did not move. 'Well, come on.'

He looked down, moving dry lips, at the photograph. Then, suddenly, he snatched it from her, and tore it into tiny pieces. 'There!' he said. 'Does that satisfy you?'

But her face and eyes were motionless with rage: perhaps she – as perhaps he – had conceived further rituals to which Lucy's image might be subjected. 'Get away from me.' Her voice rose. 'Go on. Get out of the house.'

He obeyed. But first he went, for a moment, to his room, and fetched Lucy's braid: concealed in various places – though none could be called safe – since his return to the villa. He put it inside his shirt, and went out.

It was noon. Karl was chained; it was the sun that attacked Rupert, beating down on his head, and he took refuge in the pines. They grew so densely that there was hardly space to sit on the fallen, decaying pine needles. Half crouched between two trees, Rupert pushed aside thick layers of these needles, to reach the scorch-coloured soil at last. To Vee, he had spoken of the wolf that scrabbles with its nails to dig up corpses. Now, like that wolf, Rupert scrabbled in the dry earth, to dig a hole for Lucy's braid.

When it was done – his hands seemed coated, his nails clogged with rust – he pulled the frayed worn coil from inside his shirt. He kissed the dead hair for the last time, pressed it into the ground, spread the powdery soil over it. Then he covered it with pine needles: it was safe: no one would ever find it here. Rupert leant against a tree, shielding his eyes against rays of light that pierced the forest darkness, then lay, like the light from stained-glass windows, in uneven patches on the ground.

When he had left his room, his Blake picture had been in its usual place above the bed. On his return, he found it, mutilated, on his pillow.

The Good Angel was gone: only a fragment of pale arm –
behind the Evil Angel's outstretched fingers – had been left by
the hand that had ripped away a third of the picture. Alone –
blind and fettered – the Evil Angel hovered against the inferno
of his pointed flames.

'I can tear pictures, too, you see!' Disa stood behind him in
the doorway. When he turned and she saw his stricken face, she
said, 'Oh, come on!' Then she said, 'It was mine. You gave it to
me in London – remember?' As she left the room, she said,
'Anyhow, I always thought that other angel was silly.'

This action seemed, in some way, to purge her. Afterwards,
she no longer asked him if he was tired of her, no longer
constantly referred to Lucy. Now, in September, the barometer
showed a slightly lower temperature, but sometimes a dry dust-
laden wind – lashing the sea and the pine tops – made the
weather worse. Guests arrived.

Chet – blond and empty-eyed – had been a professional
football-player till a knee injury ended his career. Now he
attended on Elaine: probably twenty years older, possibly more;
it was difficult to assess her age. Elaine 'just loved' the heat.
When the wind was not blowing, she lay for hours, coated in
top-strength sun-block, on the terrace. Once, Rupert, coming to
summon her to lunch, had to address her several times before
she answered.

'I could have sworn she was asleep,' he said to Disa later, 'but
her eyes were open.'

Disa laughed. 'Oh, she can't shut them – she's had so many
facelifts. Elaine's crazy for surgery: tits, liposuction, upper arms
– she's done it all.' Disa laughed again. 'When she's not asleep,
out there on the terrace, she's probably doing exercises to
tighten her vaginal muscles.'

'Ah!' Then he laughed too. 'You know, Miss Dis, you'll
probably be just like Elaine one of these days.'

Her eyes narrowed. After a moment she said, 'You know,
I've been wondering if they'd enjoy it if I brought Karl up . . . to
"party", one evening.'

'Disa!' he said.

She laughed. She said, 'I can control him. I've done it before.'

'Disa!'

She was silent for a moment, but then she laughed again and shrugged. 'Okay – let's forget it.'

At meals Elaine was garrulous, talked of fashion shows and celebrities and, inevitably, of 'partying'. In the intervals, Disa liked Rupert to entertain them with his 'weird talk'. Elaine sometimes laughed drily at his jokes and references; Chet maintained his habitual, uncomprehending, white-toothed smile.

After dinner came – though Disa did not suggest Karl's participation – an assortment of diversions. Elaine was hungry for youth: for Chet and for Disa. Disa wanted everyone, with as many variations as possible. Rupert and Chet concentrated on the women. Elaine's body – imprinted, here and there, with its tiny scars – was as slim and almost as smooth as Disa's.

When they flagged, there were the tapes; there was *the* tape, shown proudly by Disa. After seeing it, Elaine regarded Rupert with a new interest, but Chet's smile conveyed a slight suggestion of unease.

Perhaps it was a relief to Rupert when the guests departed: taken to the mainland by Marios, in the yacht. But, when they were alone together, Disa's demands that he should amuse her were heavy; she expressed irritation when he read or sat in silence. 'Why do you keep your nose stuck in that dreary book?' she would ask, or 'Missing your old friend, Cosmopolitan Clara?' There was no answer to these questions.

In late October, Disa went away on a trip. When she had gone, he found that Karl was permanently off his chain. Attempts to communicate with Sophia – the ugly-faced and reputedly evil-eyed – were met with silence as she went about her cleaning. Rupert stayed indoors, heating frozen meals, drinking – perhaps sometimes rather too much – good wine. He read the books he had brought from London, except *Prick Up Your Ears*, which he had put away.

Jeanne Duval regarded him, with knowing, almond-shaped eyes, from Baudelaire's drawing. Donne speculated on 'Air and Angels'. In Byron's *Don Juan*, Rupert read the lines he had quoted in the letter he wrote to Lucy after their first meeting:

She looked as if she sat by Eden's door,
And grieved for those who would return no more.

She was a Catholic, too, sincere, austere,
As far as her own gentle heart allow'd . . .

She gazed upon a world she scarcely knew,
As seeking not to know it; silent, lone
As grows a flower, thus quietly she grew,
And kept her heart serene within its zone.
There was awe in the homage which she drew;
Her spirit seemed as seated on a throne
Apart from the surrounding world, and strong
In its own strength — most strange in one so young.

Disa travelled . . . she returned. He had given her a list of books to buy for him, but she said that she had lost it, though she had brought more pornography and also – for his delectation – a mass of paperback novels, many of them published by his ex-wife, Chris.

Now Rupert and Disa resumed their life: their long days and evenings. Possibly, late at night, alone in his room with its bare walls, Rupert remembered something he had said when he first knew her.

He had spoken of the infernal kingdom of Dis, of how at its entrance, to prevent the dead from escaping, the dog, Cerberus, stood always on guard. For, as he had explained, whoever entered that kingdom was never permitted to return.